Parisian NIGHTS

A NOVEL

LOUISE BAY

Published by Louise Bay 2015

ISBN: 978-1-910747-28-5

“The thunder drowns out what the lightning sees.”

Prince

the nights SERIES

Parisian Nights

Promised Nights

Indigo Nights

Each book in the series is stand alone, following a different couple.

chapter ONE

Haven

I loved my city but I didn't love the traffic. I was *never* late. And with a promotion to Deputy Editor of Rallegra, the UK's premier glossy weekly woman's magazine, on the horizon I needed to be on time to the Monday morning staff meeting. I was currently Features Editor but I'd been working hard to position myself for the next step. Just thinking about the possibility made my heart skip.

My eyes kept flicking to the clock as I stripped off my coat, checked my make-up in my compact and smoothed down my hair. I scanned the tops of the cubicles. No one seemed to be making their way to the conference room yet, thank goodness.

I picked up my pad, pen and drink, and took a deep breath, releasing the muscles clenched in my stomach.

I filled my lungs again as I opened the door. I was always first to this meeting and it meant that I always got to sit in the same place, but today someone unfamiliar had beaten me to it. Equally unsettling was my boss Robert, sitting at the head of the table. He was normally ten minutes late to everything.

"Oh sorry, I didn't mean to disturb you," I said as they turned toward me.

"No, come in. We were just catching up before the meeting. This is my good friend Harry who is going to join us. Harry, this is Haven, Features Editor. Prompt, as usual."

The stranger in my seat uncrossed his legs, stood up and held out his hand. "Very nice to meet you, Haven."

He was smooth and confident and the way his eyes locked on mine and crinkled at the corners made me think he assumed that everyone he introduced himself to was delighted to meet him. He was way too pleased with himself. But most of Robert's so-called "friends" were way too pleased with themselves. Robert came from money and was one of those people who had been to school with the whole world. Or at least he knew the brother or dated the sister of every person that was worth knowing.

His family owned some huge estate in Scotland and I imagined he didn't have to have a real job, but unlike most of his friends that he'd introduced me to, he worked hard and was good at what he did. He was everything I wasn't: from a good family, well connected and very wealthy. I wanted to resent him for it but he was so bloody charming I just couldn't. I was sure he'd had a little help from Daddy's cronies along the way, but I couldn't deny he was a talented editor and a great boss. No doubt Harry was one of those friends who dabbled in various "projects" which was code for spending time holidaying and partying.

I shook Harry's hand and managed a tight smile. "And you."

I set my things down on the table opposite Harry as the rest of the office began to file through the door. All eyes were on our interloper.

Robert continued to chat with Harry as everyone settled down. I kept my head down, focusing on the to-do list in front of me but I was concentrating on Robert and Harry's conversation. I was trying to work out who he was and what he was doing in this meeting, but they just seemed to be discussing mutual friends. No doubt they'd be comparing the size of their trust funds later. Did he have an accent? There was a trace of something mid-Atlantic in the way he spoke.

"Good morning," Robert said. "I hope everyone had enjoyable weekends, your hang-overs have passed and everyone is ready for a busy week. We'll go around the table in a minute, but I have a couple of pieces of good news that I want to share with you. First, Harry is going to take over for Brad and handle our photography until we find a replacement. He's very talented and a great friend of mine, so I'm sure you'll make him very welcome."

A small wave of tittering came from the other end of the table and Robert turned to Jenny. "But not too welcome."

"Don't worry," Marie said. "We'll help settle him in." The laughter started again. The guy was being picked over like fresh meat.

I rolled my eyes and locked gazes with Harry. Shit, no one was supposed to have seen that. My cheeks burned. Harry cocked his head at me and I smoothed my hair, checking it was still tightly captured in its bun. I refocused on my to-do list.

"And that leads me to my second piece of good news, which is that we got the Sandy Fox interview and it's going to be big."

People started clapping and my heart began thumping in my chest. I didn't do celebrity, but I wanted this and Robert knew it. It would be really high profile and whoever pulled it off would be well placed for any promotion. Robert hadn't told me we had managed to secure it, so perhaps he'd given it to Emily. She was our celebrity editor and Sandy Fox was as A-list as it got. I couldn't look at Emily for a clue, I couldn't bear to see her face if she knew she had it. She had made it clear after I joined Rallegra that we'd never be anything but competitors, and she had been true to her word. I caught myself chewing the inside of my cheek and reached for my Diet Coke as a distraction.

"It's going to be a huge feature. We have access to her on set for the new movie she's in. It's going to be shooting mainly at Pinewood Studios. She's keen we see the real her. She's also agreed that Harry goes along and takes some candids."

What? It's Harry's first fucking day and already he's on the story of the year? What kind of celebrity agrees to candids? Her representation must suck.

"The feature will run across a number of issues, so it's going to take a lot of work."

I want it, I want it, I want it.

The interview, if I managed to pull it off, would land me the promotion. My brother would be so proud and I hoped I would finally feel safe and established.

"We still have some wrinkles to iron out, but we hope

the first session will happen this week while she's still in rehearsals. Right, let's go round the table. Haven, what do you have on?"

"The piece on our Top Ten Speakeasies had turned out well and then today we're finishing up the first in our Summer Detox plan. I'm working up a proposal for a feature on dating that will run across a number of issues." I heard a number of people groan when I mentioned my plan. Robert didn't look impressed. Articles on how to meet your match weren't uncommon. "I've been looking at a number of agencies where your net worth has to be over a certain amount. Basically Match for Millionaires. I think it could be good."

"Okay. Well, I'll take a look at your proposal when it's done," Robert said. It had potential but I'd have to convince him.

The rest of the meeting seemed to pass in a blur. All I could focus on was what I was going to say to Robert to convince him to give me the Sandy Fox feature.

Finally, things wrapped up and I got up and gathered my notebook.

"Haven, can you stick around? I'd like a quick word," Robert said.

Shit, this was where he was going to tell me that he'd given the Fox piece to Emily. I always tried to prepare for bad news. I forced a tight smile and sat back down as everyone else filed out. Harry stayed seated too, and I watched him as he leaned back, put his hands behind his head and observed people leaving. As if he knew I was watching, he turned his head toward me and looked me in the eye.

His eyebrows lifted and his eyes widened like he was asking me if I was done looking at him. I got the feeling he was used to being looked at. I could imagine if I was one of *those* girls, I might be distracted by that strong jaw and those sparkling eyes. The difference was, I wasn't ogling him as I imagined most people would be. I wasn't interested in his long fingers that periodically swept through his dirty-blond hair or the way his shirt seemed to skim over his tight body. I simply wanted to figure him out.

I took a deep breath and refocused as the door closed. I resisted every instinct that told me I should make a last minute plea to Robert for this feature. I wasn't sure I would have been able to stop myself if Harry hadn't been there, I couldn't imagine Harry had ever been desperate for anything in his life. In that moment my pride overruled my ambition.

"Haven, I want you to work on the Fox piece with Harry."

Shit. The. Bed. I had not been expecting that. I wanted to jump up and hug Robert, but I restrained myself and checked my hair for stray strands, smoothing it into my bun.

I nodded. "That's great. Thank you. I hope Emily's not too disappointed." I meant it. Although Emily and I were competitors, I didn't wish her ill.

"She understands and she's completely supportive. I think you'll be the best . . . shall we say, fit, with Sandy."

What did that mean? Robert was looking at Harry, avoiding my unspoken question. I glanced at Harry but he was focused on Robert, nodding.

"Yes, these celebrity interviews are so much about the chemistry between the interviewer and interviewee, and from what we know of Sandy, we think you're more likely to get on with her. You know she's got quite the reputation," Robert said.

I nodded and the muscles in my stomach clenched. There was a lot riding on this.

"I understand. I've seen some of the research, but I'll immerse myself in it today. Do you need help making the final arrangements? Shall I speak to legal?" I offered.

"No, I'm almost there with everything. I need to ensure you're free Thursday and Friday anytime of the day or night so if we get the green light, you can get your ass over there."

Of course, I'd drop everything.

"And I want a de-brief after each meeting. We're not going to fuck this up. We don't want another Beckham incident."

I nodded resolutely and stood, leaving Robert and Harry. Robert was worried about the Sandy Fox interview if he mentioned the Beckham incident. No one ever dared speak of it. We hadn't had A-List celebrity co-operation for about a year after Emily ran a piece on his alleged extra-marital affairs alongside a week in the life article that he'd co-operated on.

I headed back to my desk, mulling over what Robert had said. My initial excitement was overtaken by a sense of confusion over what he had said about my fit with Sandy. What had he meant? I knew Robert thought I was a bit uptight, he was always telling me to relax. Maybe Sandy was the same?

Jake

"So Harry, you think Haven will work?" Robert asked. He called me Harry as everyone, other than those closest to me did. It was a nickname I'd acquired in college, and not the most creative one, given my last name was Harrison.

I shrugged. "I think so. It's hard to tell. She's blonde, which helps. I remember Sandy saying she thought blondes were tacky. But she's not as unattractive as I expected."

"But you wouldn't call her attractive. I mean she dresses like . . . I don't know what. She's not exactly beating them off with a stick."

It was true, Haven was dressed like she was going to a funeral, in a black turtleneck and gray skirt with thick black tights and flat shoes. Her blonde hair was pulled back into a severe bun and she wore the expression of someone ready for a fight. But she was undoubtedly attractive with delicate features and something curious behind her eyes, and Sandy didn't like anything overshadowing her.

I didn't know Sandy well, but I'd met her a few times at parties and we had a mutual friend, Gay Dave, who I went to college with. She'd tried to kiss me once. She'd been very drunk and trying to piss off her boyfriend. I'd pretended I hadn't noticed and she hadn't held it against me. I hadn't seen her much since her first album had been released and gone double platinum, but I'd dropped Dave a text to say that I'd be the photographer on the article for Rallegra if she signed up for the piece and she'd emailed me to say she was excited to see me again. She was a fun girl—as long as she was the center of everything. Haven seemed to be exactly the opposite, which I hoped would mean that Sandy wouldn't see her as a threat. I'd suggested to Robert that he use a male journalist for the interview if possible, or a woman who wasn't going to outshine Sandy. It was curious to me that he'd chosen Haven. She wouldn't have been my choice.

"Do you want to grab lunch today?" Robert asked.

"Actually, I have a thing with some investors. Later in the week?"

"Sure, you know where you're sitting, right? It's by the small meeting room, so if you need to make calls . . ."

"Thanks man, I appreciate it."

"Don't thank me, you know you're doing me a massive favor filling in like this. I should have made Brad work his notice, but he was such a pain in my arse."

"You never know, I might become a professional photographer at this rate," I said.

Robert laughed and I headed toward my newly allocated seat. Not that I would be in it a lot. I needed to check my email and then I'd head to my lunch. I wasn't planning to be in the office unless we were meeting to discuss a feature. I was sure Robert would have Brad replaced within a month or so, and I was happy to help him out while I finalize the funding on my next project.

I fired up my laptop and started working my way through emails. There was an overwhelming amount to do to get things off the ground. Unlike my last business, this required coordination of scientists and computer geeks, but it could lead to something really special. I hoped this Sandy thing didn't take up too much time.

My phone started to vibrate on the desk as Haven approached. "I'm sorry Haven, I have to get this. Can I come and find you?"

She nodded and headed off. I wasn't sure where she was sitting, but I'd find her.

"Hello, lovely girl," I greeted my sister.

"Hey, Jake. How's your first day going? Did you find what I left you?" Beth asked.

"You put something in my bag?" I reached under the flap and rooted around and pulled out a sandwich box. "You made me lunch?"

Beth laughed. "A snack really. A juice box, an apple and an energy bar."

"You'll make someone a lovely wife one day."

"If I was there, I'd hit you."

"If you were here, I wouldn't say it." I laughed. "Is everything okay?"

"Of course, it's fine. Stop fussing," she said.

"I'm not the one calling." As much as my sister accused me of being over protective, she was made the same way. "I'll be home early, though, and I can tell you all about it. Unless you've got plans?"

"Nothing other than a House of Cards marathon. I'll see you later. Try not to break any hearts before you get home."

"No promises."

"Loser." It was her typical sign off.

"Likewise," I replied.

I hung up and went to find Haven. I didn't have to search very hard. She was in the cubicle next to mine.

"Sorry about that, did you want to talk?" I asked.

She kept her eyes on the computer screen. "I don't want to interrupt any emergency you're having, so please, in your own time."

I couldn't help but grin. She had clearly overheard my telephone call and was being a little bitchy because she thought I was prioritising my personal life over work, which I was. Beth would always be top of my list. "My emergency's over, so if you want to talk, you know where I am."

She pressed her lips together and turned. She looked at me, narrowing her eyes and paused as if she was deciding whether or not to say what was on the tip of her tongue. "Okay, let's go into the small meeting room."

"Lead the way."

As she had done when she came into the earlier meeting, she set her pad, pen and drink on the table in front of her and smoothed down her hair before she started speaking. I wondered if she ever wore her hair down? Was it long? And did she always wear those turtlenecks?

"Are you American?" She asked. I hadn't expected that.

"Yes. From Chicago. But I went to college over here."

She put her hand up as if to stop me from revealing any more information. "So, as an American, you won't be offended if I speak frankly?"

Jesus, this girl. I wasn't sure whether I should laugh or shake her. She needed to loosen up. I shook my head. "Please, go ahead."

"I understand you're friends with Robert, like most of the rest of the world. And I get that this is no big deal for you, and that you're probably playing at photography until the next part of your trust fund pays out, but I need this job and I really want this feature to be a success. My job is important to me. I work hard and I'm good at what I do. I really can't have you mess this up for me."

"You think *I'm* going to mess this up for you?" I stared at her, not quite believing what was coming out of her mouth.

"I know men like you. You've probably never had a real job have you? You've done a series of so-called freelance jobs at friends of Daddy's companies. And that's fine. Good luck to you. I just need you to take *this* feature seriously. Please. I need you to turn up when you say you're going to. I need you to be available to discuss the article, not constantly on the phone to whichever poor girl you're shagging this week."

It wasn't the first time people had made assumptions about my background and character. I was used to it being an American living in London, and normally I didn't give a shit. For some reason, Haven's outburst got under my skin. "Wow, you're a bitch."

She opened her mouth and there was a split second of hesitation before she hit back. "So I've been told. You're a spoiled, entitled rich boy. We all have our crosses to bear. If you want to tell Robert that you didn't want this assignment, I'm sure we could find someone else."

I was pretty sure that there was no way Sandy would be doing this feature with Rallegra if I hadn't said I was going to be the photographer. But I wasn't about to tell Haven that. She'd find out soon enough, and I was going to enjoy the expression on her face when she did.

"Maybe you should tell Robert that you don't want the assignment if you think I'm going to be such a problem for you."

She blushed, and for a moment she seemed stumped. "Robert isn't going to bump me from this article. I'm really good at my job."

"Well, guess what, sweetheart, so am I." Frustrated, I pushed my hands through my hair and stood up to leave.

"Don't ever call me *sweetheart*. How dare you? And where are you going? I'm not finished."

"Well I am. If you decide you want to be polite and professional, I'll be around. But you're not my boss, not now and not ever. And if you were? I'd resign. Get your shit together." I really didn't need more drama in my life, especially from a job that I was doing as a favour to a friend. Anyone would think Haven was on the brink of curing cancer, not planning an interview with Sandy Fox.

chapter TWO

Haven

Bollocks. That wasn't how that was supposed to have gone. I was just so fucking angry that he'd waved me off while he took a call from his girlfriend. Who did he think he was? This was his first day at Rallegra. I wouldn't do that to a colleague, and I'd been here years. It might not be The Times but we had the highest weekly readership of any magazine in the UK. This was a great gig for him.

I hated people who didn't appreciate the charmed life that they had, particularly when it was handed to them on a plate. There must be a million people gagging for his job, but because of his connections he'd waltzed into it and therefore had no regard for it, or any of us that had worked our way up to get here. Life was just too easy for some people.

But at the same time, I hadn't set out to have an argument with him. I just couldn't hold my tongue. I should have been more patient. I had enough enemies in the office, I didn't need to make new ones.

I had to get some air. I grabbed my coat and purse and headed to the stairs. I was the only one that used them. I never took the lifts if I was on my own. Six floors up and down. That and running were the only two bits of exercise I did.

I bit back the tears of frustration that started to form. I seemed to have an amazing ability to sabotage anything good that happened to me. I didn't want him going to Robert to tell him I was a bitch, and that he wouldn't work with me. I couldn't lose this feature. I might be good at my job, but that wouldn't matter if I pissed off one of Robert's friends. Jesus, why couldn't I have sewn my mouth shut? I found it difficult when people brought their personal lives into the workplace, because I tried to keep my life inside and outside the office separate. I didn't understand why everyone didn't do the same.

Once I was outside, I called my brother—one of two people in my life I could rely on. He and my best friend Ash were *my people*. The ones who I let see all of me. They saw the good and the bad and loved me anyway. Luke was always on my side, and right then I needed to be the whole Haven and not focused, driven, work Haven. "Hey. Am I interrupting?" I asked.

"No, sweets, what's going on?" Luke replied.

"Oh, someone just called me a bitch."

"A bitch?" He wasn't asking me to confirm what I'd said. He was asking me if it was justified.

"Yeah. A bitch," I replied sheepishly.

"And? Were you?"

I took a deep breath and tears began to trickle from the corners of my eyes.

"Perhaps a little bit."

"You know people don't get to see your beautiful heart if you do that. What brought that on?" Luke always said exactly the right thing.

"I didn't want to be, it's just I found out I got the Sandy Fox interview and I want to do a really great job on it."

"That's amazing. Well done, you deserve it."

"I'm not sure I do. Anyway, Robert will probably give it to Emily now I've upset his friend. I just got stressed because if I do a good job, it will help my chances at the promotion I told you about. I want it to be perfect. I want it to be the best celebrity interview we've ever done. I have to work with a new photographer, and he's not taking it seriously. I lost my temper with him."

"Do you want me to kill him for you?"

I laughed and it broke through the self pity. "Yeah, come down and fight your little sister's battles for her."

Luke laughed with me. "I will though, if you want me to. Alternatively, you could apologize."

"You're right. But it's hard. I want him to care about this as much as I do."

"No one is going to care as much as you do about their job. You can't hold everyone to your high standards, or you're going to spend your whole life disappointed. So do what you've got to do and apologize."

I nodded, then realising he couldn't see me, gulped "Okay" into the receiver.

"Are you coming over next weekend? Emma's on call so she might not be around," he asked, changing the subject. Emma and Luke lived together, but as she was a doctor, she was gone a lot and we normally arranged to see each other when she was at work. It wasn't that I didn't like her, it was just that I wasn't sure anyone would be good enough for my brother. Anyone except maybe Ash, my best friend since I before I could talk. Ash, Luke and I had grown up together, and Emma didn't fit when it was the three of us.

"I told Ash she could come over. But we could both come to you. I know she'd love to see you if Emma's not around, probably because she can flirt outrageously with you."

Luke laughed again. "You're such a pain. Ash just likes to joke around and she's known me a long time. She's like another annoying little sister to me."

"Whatever. She's been in love with you since she was five and she first saw you naked in the paddling pool."

"Stop it, Haven. I'm hanging up."

I laughed and pressed cancel before he could hang up on me.

Speaking to Luke always improved my mood, it was good to be reminded that outside of work, I had people who knew and loved the whole me. I marched purposefully toward the coffee shop on the corner and returned to the office, a latte in each hand. Buying Harry a coffee might be a good start at an apology.

Thankfully he wasn't around when I got back, so I scribbled a note on a Post-It, apologizing if he thought I'd been a bitch, stuck it on one of the lattes and placed it on his desk quickly before he came back.

I heard him return, but I didn't glance up from my computer. I hoped I'd be forgiven. I'd over reacted and if we were going to be working together, I needed him not to hate me. My body clenched as I waited for him to say something.

He didn't react at all, just packed up his laptop, put on his coat and headed out of the office, taking his coffee, sans Post-It, with him. I guess he was a man who held a grudge. My stomach started churning. How was I going to make this right? I'd have to try a different tactic, but now I needed to be buried in work to take my mind off of it.

"Jenny," I said as she walked past my cubicle. "Can we go through the Sandy Fox research?"

"Sure," she said.

"Five minutes in the conference room?" I suggested.

She nodded curtly, clearly not happy to be working with me. I wasn't a tyrant. I sighed.

"Okay, this is exciting. You must be pleased all your work won't have gone to waste?" I asked Jenny as she sat opposite me. I wanted to try and motivate her. She could really help with the prep for this interview, and I knew she was a hard worker.

"Sure." She said tentatively.

Okay.

"So, do you want to run through the main parts, highlighting things you think might create a good angle? We'll go from there and identify areas that we can dig into during our time with her."

"Well, she's twenty-four. She's had three number one albums, sold twenty million records and was the youngest female Brit award winner when she won Best Female Artist for the first time."

This was all stuff I knew, but I didn't hurry her along as I usually would have done. Instead, I nodded encouragingly. Sometimes I felt like this job and I were oil and water. I didn't get the people, and they didn't get me.

"*Toxic Love* will be her first film, but she's a stage-school kid, so it's not like she's never acted before. People say she's pretty good," Jenny said. Her shoulders dropped and she sat back slightly. She was starting to relax.

"What about her personal life? She went out with that Justin Bieber wannabe for a while, didn't she?"

"From what I gather, that was all a publicity thing. They share the same manager."

"Oh, right. How bloody cynical is that?"

"That's show business," Jenny said as she smiled. I grinned back at her.

"I guess. Okay, what about other boyfriends? Drugs?"

"There were rumors going around about her and her manager. She seems very anti-drugs. She's spoken quite publically about it. I'd be surprised if there was anything there."

I sighed. "You think she has a thing for older men?" I asked.

"Perhaps. I can do a bit more digging if you like? Speak to some of her old friends from stage school?"

"Yes, that would be great. Good job Jenny. I think we're going to make a good team." I was relieved that she was going to be working with me. I needed someone good backing me up.

"So, we'll work together on this?" Jenny asked.

"Of course, unless you don't want to?"

She nodded, and grinned. "Yes! I really want to stay involved. I thought you'd kick me off the piece when you got it."

I smiled at her, but didn't respond. What could I say?

"I heard Harry is going to be involved too?"

I raised my eyebrows at her.

"Don't worry, he's hot, but not my type. Not enough of a loser."

I laughed at her confession.

"I heard he's not a proper photographer though," Jenny said. I liked that she was opening up to me, sharing information that she didn't strictly need to.

"What do you mean? Who said that?"

"Something Robert said to Emily. I think he's a keen amateur and is just passing time here. I'm not sure he needs to work. He's loaded apparently."

I bloody knew it. No wonder he didn't respond to my apology. A spoiled rich kid living off Daddy's money.

"I'll let you know as soon as I get the go ahead from Robert. I can't promise that I'm going to take you to the interviews, but if I get the opportunity I will."

"Okay, that would be awesome. I'm just happy to be involved, I wasn't expecting to get to meet her or anything."

Jake

"You've lost your first mover advantage, Jake."

"Hal, you and I both know that there's no such thing. Apple has made a business of letting everyone make their mistakes first and then swooping in and doing it better. That's exactly what I'm suggesting here. We're going to do renewable energy better. The initial results of the simulation are incredible."

This lunch meeting wasn't going as well as I'd expected. I'd made a lot of money for Hal in the past. Apparently that didn't count for much. If I'd known that our conversation was going to be this tricky, I would have chosen a different restaurant. The tables were close together and there seemed to be a million waiters buzzing around, filling our water glasses, bringing us bread, then drinks, then food. It was never ending.

"But renewable energy is such a long-term game." My gut twisted at his negativity and my mind started to race, thinking of ways I could break down the science so Hal really understood the potential here.

"Yeah, but it's a means of spreading your risk and saving the planet at the same time. I bet you don't get offers like that every day." I tried to sound calm and confident, but my palms were beginning to sweat. I should have started investigating getting funding elsewhere. I'd been complacent, assuming Hal was going to hand me a pile of cash.

"I don't care about saving the planet, and everyone who's met me knows that. I don't get offers like this because I don't want them."

I paused while the waiters interrupted again to clear our plates away. Shit. I could go to other investors, but it would be a long road. I thought Hal would come through for me. I thought he trusted me.

"We can always go down route two, which means selling out to a Shell or BP at year five. Take a look at the proposal.

I think you'll like it," I said. I'd done my homework on this technology. If my initial tests were right, we could become a real alternative energy source.

"You don't think the oil giants have this capability in house already?"

"I know they don't. They try it but ultimately they're crap at the entrepreneurial stuff, which is why they go around buying companies like Elemental Energy once it's proven. I know this industry, I've seen the results of the testing and I know it will work."

"And what are you putting in?" he asked, wiping his mouth with his napkin and placing it on the table. Was he about to leave? My heart started to race.

"I'm contributing thirty percent of the funding up to year five," I replied.

"Fifteen million?"

I nodded. Would that make a difference?

"You're committed, I'll give you that. I'll look at it, speak to some people and get my guys to crunch the numbers. No promises."

"Good. Thanks. I know you'll like it."

I felt like I'd been in the ring with Tyson when I put a slightly inebriated Hal into his car and started to walk home. I'd been working on this business plan for eighteen months since the sale of my first business, Energy Trade. But Energy Trade had been simple in comparison and hadn't required anything like this amount of start-up capital. We'd just needed phones, computers and office space to start operating. With Elemental Energy we would need lab research, computer expertise and a much longer lead time before we were making any money. I didn't want it to fall apart now. Energy Trade had made me money, but Elemental Energy, as well as being profitable, might actually do some good. It could be a legacy.

"I'm home," I shouted into the apartment as I closed the door.

"Hey," Beth replied. "How did it go?"

"It was exhausting, but I think I had a break through by the end. He's going to read the proposal."

"You look so tired. Why are you doing this to yourself? You don't have to work. Why not buy a yacht and become an international playboy?"

"Yeah, nice idea, but I don't think that's really me, do you? I really believe in this renewable energy thing. I know I can make it happen," I said

"Well at least get a decent place to live. This place is really starting to gross me out." My sister had lived with me since following me to England from Chicago. We'd both had our reasons to escape Chicago.

"I'm sentimental about the place, what can I tell you?" I was still in the apartment I rented while I was in college. I'd bought it, and my two roommates had moved out eventually, but I'd never had time to decorate it so there were nicer places to live, for sure. I didn't notice the stuff Beth hated. It was home and it was comfortable. I didn't want to become one of those guys who started making some money and then felt the need to let everyone know. The wealth didn't and wouldn't define me. I was my father's son however much I made.

"I'm going to start looking at new places for you."

I grinned at her. "You mean for you."

"Well for me too. But think how you can impress your dates if you bring them back to mews house in Mayfair or an apartment in Marylebone."

"A mews house in Mayfair? You're planning for me to drop a cool five million on a new house when I'm perfectly happy where I am?"

"Think of the women."

"Now, you're being offensive. You think I can't get girls without a big house?"

Beth laughed. "I admit, my logic is flawed a little there. You've never had an issue getting women. But how nice would it be to have somewhere new with more space and a nicer kitchen? And you could get a place without the rat problem or the damp problem or the seventies carpet problem."

"Okay. You can look, but I'm not committing to moving."

"Wooohooo!" Beth flung her arms around me.

Seeing her happy was worth every penny of the money I was sure I'd end up spending on a new place. She seemed to be getting better and better since she'd moved to London. Chicago hadn't been good for her, but in the last few years, she had blossomed. She was sober and about to graduate—neither of which I would have thought possible four years ago when she'd landed at Heathrow. Distance from our father and his new family had helped us both.

"You've not told me about Rallegra? How was it? How's Robert?" Beth asked.

"He's good. He says hello."

"Did you enjoy your first day?"

I shrugged. "I think I ran into some office politics. The girl I'm working on this Sandy article with doesn't seem to like me very much."

"You mean she didn't beg you to sleep with her within five minutes of meeting her."

"I mean she called me a spoiled, entitled rich boy."

Beth threw her head back and laughed. "Well she's right about the rich."

I shrugged. There wasn't much that got me ruffled, but apparently being accused of being spoiled, entitled and rich by Haven did. Maybe it was because it was partly true, and I'd never seen myself like that. I grew up a cop's kid. We lived in the south side of Chicago among the criminals that my father arrested. It hadn't been a privileged existence. I didn't feel money had changed who I was, and I hated when it altered how people saw me.

"Don't say that," I said, disturbed by the label.

"What? That you're rich? Why?"

"I don't know. It's not me."

"Jesus, most people would be shouting it from the rooftops. You should be proud of yourself. I know I am. What you did with Energy Trade was amazing. Stop being so shy about it."

"I've been lucky," I muttered. Beth was my greatest champion, but even her praise made me uncomfortable. My father was the same. My feet were firmly on the ground and that's where I was determined for them to stay.

"A little. Most of all you've worked hard, you've got a brilliant brain and you have some kind of chip in here," she said tapping her head. "It gives you great ideas and the ability to follow through with them. Jeez, and you say I beat myself up."

Beth always saw the best in people. I swear she'd find the good in a serial killer. "What are you cooking?"

"You're not so talented at subtly changing the subject though." She grinned at me.

"Whatever."

The following Monday, I was back at Rallegra.

"I saw your photographs in a gallery over the weekend. You kept that quiet," Robert said. It was good to catch up with him again. I'd not spent much time with any of my friends since I started Energy Trade.

"You did? The one in Chelsea?"

"You have your pictures in more than one? You dark horse."

"Just two. They don't sell very well, but for some reason the owners still like to have them." Photography helped me relax. I didn't do it to make money, and I certainly didn't tell my friends that they were in galleries. It was no big deal.

"From what I saw, they were selling just fine. You make me sick, you know that?"

I drew my eyebrows together. "Sick?"

"Yeah, you piss me off. The way you pick up a camera for fun and suddenly you've got galleries wanting to sell your work. You set up a company and the next thing you know, you're selling it for millions. And the women? You couldn't keep them away, even before you had money."

"Dude, right place, right time. What can I say?" He made it sound like I had the Midas touch, but I'd been lucky and I enjoyed what I did.

"I have no idea how you have any friends because you make all of us look bad. Oh, that's right, because on top of it all, you're a really good guy. Piss off, I'm sick of your handsome face."

I chuckled. "Okay, I'm out of here. I only came in to drop off your coffee, Mr. Bossman. I'll see you in five."

I wandered into the room we'd used for Monday's meeting and found Haven sitting in the spot where I sat last week.

"Good morning," I said, unsure of what sort of reaction I would get from her.

"Hi, Harry. How are you?"

Okay, she was making an effort. That was promising. "I'm all good thanks. You?"

I watched her. Her hair was still severe and she was still dressed as if she were in mourning, but the light bounced off her cheekbones in a way I hadn't noticed before. She would probably photograph really well. Her lips were naturally pouty—

"Harry?" She broke my internal train of thought and I realized I hadn't been listening to her while looking at her.

"Sorry, what?" I asked.

"We've been given the green light to go to the first day of Sandy's filming on Thursday. So it would be great if we could have a meeting—you, Jenny and me after this to agree on our approach?"

I nodded. "Oh, and thanks for the coffee."

"I'm really sorry I overreacted." She seemed worried and searched my face for a reaction. "I was stressed and I have a lot riding on this interview. I took it out on you. I hear you're really talented and I'm really excited to be working with you."

I started to laugh. I couldn't help it. She was a useless suck up, but I appreciated the effort. "Shall we call a truce?" I asked.

She quickly responded, "That would be great and I promise to keep my bitchy side medicated and unconscious in future."

"Oh, don't do that," I said, teasing her. "I can handle a little bitchy." It was true. I liked that she was obviously passionate about what she did. She just didn't manage to channel it in the right way.

Her eyes narrowed slightly and she cocked her head at me as people started to file in.

chapter THREE

Haven

Harry had been good to his word—he didn't seem to be holding any grudges and I was grateful.

"So, remember, let me do the talking. She's volatile and I don't want to upset her," I reminded Harry as we headed to the building that we'd been told to.

"You think *I'd* piss her off." He smirked at me.

Shit. I hadn't meant it like that. "No, not at all. I'm sure she will love you. Better than me, in any event. I just don't want to fuck this up."

"So you keep saying."

We showed our passes to the security guard and he let us through a door. "Follow signs for stage two," he grunted.

We went down a dark corridor, which led us into what looked like a huge airport hangar with lots of scaffolding and people bunched at one end. My belly was fluttering with the unfamiliar. I'd never been on a film set before, and I didn't know what to expect. I really hoped Sandy liked me. It would make interviewing her a lot easier.

"Come on," Harry said.

I'd stopped dead. I took a deep breath and headed toward the people. The set started to come into view. I couldn't quite make out what or where it was supposed to be. Was it an office or a call center? A squeal broke my concentration and I searched for the source and saw Sandy Fox with her hands thrown up in the air, staring in my direction.

"Oh my god!" she squealed again and started running toward me. She couldn't be that excited to see me. I turned to Harry, who wore a shit-eating grin and was holding his arms out, ready to catch her. *What the fuck?*

Sandy launched herself at Harry and he spun her around.

"Hey kiddo," he said as he hugged her and winked at me over her shoulder.

I should have fucking known.

"Harry, I'm so excited to see you. It's been too long," Sandy said as she clung to him.

It was like I was in a movie. Nothing was making sense. All I could do was roll my eyes at the pair of them.

When he finally put her down, she grabbed his hand.

"Kiddo, this is Haven. She's the journalist from Rallegra."

"Hey, Haven."

"Hi, Sandy, it's a pleasure to—"

"You know you're not allowed to call me kiddo anymore. You promised." Sandy pushed out her lips in an exaggerated pout. I rolled my eyes.

"Well, if you promise not to be a brat, I won't." He ruffled her hair. They seemed very familiar with each other.

"When have I ever been a brat?" she asked.

"Every time you drink?" Harry replied.

She threw her head back and laughed. I felt uncomfortable, like I was intruding on a private conversation. Should I give them some space to catch up? They were completely ignoring me. Where could I go?

"How's Dave?" Harry asked.

"He's dating some guy and neglecting me." She pouted again.

"I'm sure you have more than enough attention from your many admirers."

"None are as handsome as you, Harry," Sandy whined as she pulled on his hand, getting him to follow her across to the set.

"You'll go blind if you keep rolling your eyes like that," he whispered to me as he followed her. "Come on."

As we got nearer to the action, the director scooped Sandy up and we were ushered over to a couple of chairs at the edge of the cameras and lighting equipment.

"So you know her, huh?" I asked Harry, desperate to understand the extent of their relationship.

"A little." His eyes were fixed on the scene in front of him.

"I should have guessed. Go to school with her brother?"

"No." He wasn't going to make this easy for me.

"You haven't slept with her, have you?" I was almost certain that he had.

"Nope." Was he being deliberately obtuse? He was starting to irritate me.

"Why are you even working at this magazine? You clearly

don't need the money. Shouldn't you be interning at an investment bank or something?"

"I know you find it difficult, but will you just try not to be bitchy for thirty minutes? If you had any sense, you would be doubly nice to me now that you know I know Sandy."

Was he saying he could make things awkward if I didn't suck up to him? "You're blackmailing me?" I asked him.

He sighed. "Jesus, you're hard work."

"I'm the one trying to keep it professional. You clearly have a personal relationship with the subject of this article," I said. It's like I'd pressed a button I couldn't turn off. I'd slotted into giving him grief and I couldn't row back.

"You think consistently insulting me is professional?"

I didn't. I needed to stop. I had to unpress my bitch button. I couldn't work out what had started it. Did I resent his charmed life? The way everyone seemed to eat out of the palm of his hand? The way women began tittering around him. Check, check and check. I wasn't normally this bad. At least I didn't mean to be. The problem was that he seemed like a nice guy, and despite calling me on my shit, he didn't seem to hold it against me. I pushed back my stray hairs into my bun.

"I'm sorry if you thought—"

"Stop it with your half-assed apologies. There's nothing worse than the non-apology apology. Either apologize and mean it, or don't bother. Don't try and be clever and half apologize and think I won't notice—like on the Post-It. I'm not dumb. Say sorry and we can all move on, but don't dare say you're sorry *if I thought* you were a bitch. It's a cop out. You *were* a bitch."

I pushed my lips together. I'd always found apologizing hard until I discovered a way of apologizing without *actually* apologizing. No one had ever noticed before, or they never told me they had. Shit. Shit. Shit.

Harry uncrossed his too-long legs and stood, clearly wanting to make every inch between us count.

He was right. I was going to have to try to be nice to him. I couldn't have him turning Sandy against me, and I didn't want him not to like me.

"Okay. I'm sorry for being a bitch."

He slid his hands into his pockets and nodded.

I pulled out my laptop and started to take some notes. If I focused on the article, at least I would have less opportunity to be mean to Harry. I guess he couldn't help it if he came from a privileged background any more than I could help not coming from one. I would try and make more of an effort with him.

There was lots more to take in than I expected. I had thought I'd be tucked away in a dressing room, waiting for a break in filming, but being on set was fascinating. There seemed to be a lot of people not doing much but staring intently at Sandy and her co-stars as they ran through what seemed to be the same scene again and again and again. We were too far away to hear what they were saying, and no one had given us headphones. I checked to see if there was a free seat closer to the action.

"Do you think they would mind if we moved forward?" I asked Harry.

"I think if you were a little nicer to me, I'd ask Sandy to get them to move us forward, but as you're not, I think we should stay put."

I felt like I was being taught a lesson, like a schoolgirl who'd been caught talking in class. "Okay," I replied.

"Okay?" he asked.

"Yes, if you think we should stay here, then that's what we'll do."

"Okay," he said, giving nothing away.

"I am sorry. I don't mean to say those things. My lips get loose when you're around."

"Your lips get loose?" He turned to look at me and raised his eyebrows.

"You know, things just tumble out."

"I think you're a little crazy," he said as he turned back to the set.

I nodded and took a deep breath. "You're probably right. But there's a little crazy in everyone, isn't there?"

He chuckled. "In everyone worth knowing."

My cheeks heated. *Did he pay me a compliment?*

"I'll make you a deal," he continued.

"What kind of deal?"

"Something to focus your loose lips and to help me to pass the time."

That sounded interesting. I looked at him, as his eyes flitted across my face. He didn't elaborate when I didn't reply straight away, he just kept his eyes on me. "Okay, what's the deal?" I asked softly.

"I'll help you get what you need from Sandy, but in return, you have to answer any questions I ask you completely honestly."

"What sort of questions?" I asked. I was worried he was going to report things back to Robert.

He shrugged.

"Personal questions?" I asked.

"Maybe. Anything I want."

"This is just between us? I mean, you're not going to tell anyone what I say?" My heart had begun to beat rapidly. I was going to accept his deal.

"Of course," he said as if he thought I was ridiculous for thinking otherwise.

"Why?"

"That's the deal."

"Are you blackmailing me?"

"Call it what you like. I just want to pass the time, and you want to get access to Sandy. Accept, don't accept."

I was being pulled toward him with each word he spoke to me. What was he trying to do? Keep me quiet? Gain control? A warm sensation passed up my spine and I didn't know if it was fear or anticipation. Before I knew what I was saying I replied, "Deal."

Jake

I grinned but I kept facing forward so she wouldn't see. A sense of victory washed over me. Despite herself, Haven was fun. You could tell that there was a little more to her than most of the women I came across. She was clearly ambitious and driven, and I admired that about her. I liked that she wanted to do a good job on this article, however vacuous it might be. And she was funny, sometimes not intentionally, but that clueless part of her was kinda endearing.

There was no particular question I had in mind for her when I suggested our bargain. I wanted to see if she'd take the deal. I was surprised she had. She might lie, but something told me she wouldn't. Her pride would stop her. She liked rules and she'd stick to them. This might be fun, and it was better than being a victim of her loose lips.

"So, do you have a question?" she asked.

"Nope. Not at the moment. I'll let you know."

My mind was full of too much to think about. Hal had asked for some additional information about Elemental Energy, which I'd sent to him. He was asking smart questions, but I took satisfaction in the fact that I'd already asked them of myself. I had a couple of meetings this week with other investors, but I hoped I'd have an answer from Hal before then.

And then there was Beth. She seemed really happy at the moment. Her studies seemed to be going well. But I wanted her to have a circle of friends—a support system other than me. I couldn't be there all the time, and she needed to get out more.

Jesus, I was tense. I should get back into my running, or perhaps I'd call Millie. I wasn't sure I'd categorize Millie my girlfriend, but she was who I was dating at the moment and I needed a release.

"So, what can you tell me about Sandy?" Haven asked.

I sat back down next to her. "Nothing really. I don't know her that well."

"Seems to me you know her pretty well."

"She's just friendly. We have a mutual friend in common,

that's all. Anyway, isn't that why you're here? To get to know her?"

"Don't tell me her sister is your ex-girlfriend?" she asked.

"Why is it you think you have me all figured out? You keep making all these comments about me and who you think I am. I thought you were meant to be a journalist. Aren't you supposed to research, ask questions and look for evidence rather than jump to conclusions?"

"It was a question," she replied, trying not to sulk.

"It was a leading question, full of assumptions. For your information no, Gay Dave is our mutual friend, who I met in college. And before you ask, I've not fucked him either."

Haven started laughing, and I couldn't help but smile.

"So tell me, have I got it so wrong about you?" she asked.

"I have no idea who, in that twisted little head of yours, I'm supposed to be. All I know is that you haven't known me long enough to know anything about me."

"So tell me."

"I'm the one asking the questions." I wasn't about to start spilling my life story to her, but I liked that she'd asked.

"Not so far," she said.

"Patience is a virtue, haven't you heard?"

"I don't have any. Haven't *you* heard?" she asked me back.

"You don't have any virtues?" What did she mean?

She shrugged. "You'll hear them gossiping, if you haven't already."

"In case you haven't noticed, I haven't been in the office much."

"You'll see," she said.

"What? I'll see you being bitchy to everyone?"

She sighed. "I don't know. I don't think so. Anyway, there's not many people there that think I have any virtues."

"Does that bother you?" It sounded like it did.

"Is that an official question?" she asked.

I nodded.

She shrugged. "Sometimes." It seemed like it upset her, which I didn't understand. Why didn't she make more of an effort to be likeable if it bothered her?

"Harry! Get over here," Sandy screamed from across the set. She was waving and bouncing up and down next to some people huddled over a screen.

I made my way across to her and she clasped her arms around my waist. I hoped she was just being friendly.

"What do you think?" She pointed to the monitor and the scene that they'd been shooting was playing out. "I'm so nervous! I hope I'm not going to sink this ship."

"You're amazing, doll. A very talented lady," one of the men dressed in black said to her. She grinned up at me.

"I'm sure you're doing great," I reassured her. "Seems great."

I glanced back at Haven. She was watching. I held her gaze for longer than I meant to. That girl was going to be trouble for me.

"Do you have a break now? You, me and Haven could have coffee."

"Can't it just be you and me? I don't think she likes me."

"What do you mean? She's a total fan. She told me that she's really nervous about meeting you. She was playing your songs in the car on the drive up here. It's been driving me insane."

"She has?" She giggled.

I was going to hell.

"Sure. You'll really like her when you get to know her."

A special place in hell reserved only for the biggest liars.

Sandy didn't let go of me as we made our way back to Haven.

"Come on Haven, let's go and grab ourselves some coffee." I winked at her and was sure I saw a trace of pink in her cheeks.

"So, how is your first day going?" Haven asked Sandy as we found a table toward the back of the stage and coffees magically appeared in front of us. Haven pulled out a Diet Coke from her bag.

"Well, I have nothing to compare it to. I'm just trying to enjoy myself and leave it to all the talented cast and crew to make me look good."

"Is this the first film offer you've had?"

Jesus couldn't she have phrased that a little differently? Sandy could be prickly, Haven needed to tread lightly. I could see the pout start to form around Sandy's lips.

"She meant the first one you've had a chance to seriously consider. Now that you're established in your singing career."

Haven's eyes flicked to me, she looked slightly frightened and started to nod. "Yes, exactly. I mean, you must get tons of offers. What made you accept this one?"

Sandy relaxed her shoulders. "Well I adore the director. *Love Etcetera,* his film before this one, is one of my favorite films, and he told me when he read the script he couldn't see anyone but me in the role. He said he'd wait for my tour to be over to start filming. And the writer said he'd written the part just for me. Plus, I love the fact that I can spend some time in London. I know we have to film in Paris a little, but mostly we're here at Pinewood Studios so it's great. I can get to catch up with old friends like Harry."

She reached across and stroked my thigh. I was going to have to discourage her attentions without upsetting her.

Haven's eyes went to Sandy's hand and then up to my face.

chapter FOUR

Haven

I bet he had slept with her despite his denial. She was all over him like a disease, and she was gorgeous and tiny and had a permanent smile on her face. She couldn't keep her hands off him, and was offering it up to him on a plate. There was no way a guy would say no to her. He wasn't fighting her off, but there was nothing I could see that made me believe he wasn't encouraging her. Maybe he hid it well, or perhaps he just didn't have to.

"Sandy, we need you." One of the crewmembers interrupted our short conversation, leaving Harry and me on our own again.

"She seems friendly," I said. I started to roll my eyes and stopped myself. He was holding up his end of the deal. Sandy had been about to get pissed off about the question about it being her first film offer before he saved the day. I didn't want to alienate our star before I'd even begun.

"Do you always wear your hair scraped back like that?" he

asked as he stood up and headed back toward our allocated chairs. I could do nothing but follow him.

"Is that a question?" It sounded like a criticism. I glanced back at Sandy with her beautiful chestnut hair, blown out so perfectly. Surely she didn't look like that every day?

"If you don't understand whether or not I'm asking you a question, you might want to rethink your day job." Harry grinned, and I automatically smiled back at him.

"I meant, is it one of your questions that I have to answer?" I asked.

"You have to answer everything I ask."

I frowned at him. "I always wear it up for work."

"It's quite severe."

My stomach clenched. Had he compared me directly with Sandy?

"Okay, not a question," he said. "It's just . . . I think it would look better down."

I couldn't decide if I was insulted or intrigued that he had considered what I would look like with my hair down. I fought a smile that he'd thought about it at all.

When I didn't respond he started to speak again. "Tell me what I'm meant to have heard about you at work. You mentioned before about people talking about you."

I shifted in my seat and smoothed my hair back. Was he deliberately trying to make me feel uncomfortable? I shrugged.

"We have a deal," he said.

"I'm not sure why you'd want to torture me. Maybe it's a sport for people like you." He didn't respond. Shit, I'd managed to be bitchy to him again. I hoped if I answered, he'd overlook it. "People don't like me in the office. You must have realized. I'm not part of the gang. I'm not one of the cool girls who socialize and gossip together."

"One of the cool girls?" He turned and smiled, raising an eyebrow at me. My stomach tilted. Was he flirting?

"You know. The ones who everyone wants to be or is desperate to fuck." Saying the word fuck in front of him felt weird but it was on my tongue before I could stop it.

"We're not in high school," he said, still grinning. When he smiled, his whole face joined in, it wasn't contained to his mouth.

I caught myself staring at him and quickly looked away. "Have you not been paying attention? The class sizes might be bigger and we might get paid, but we're still in high school."

He chuckled and the corners of his eyes crinkled up. I bet he was an excellent kisser. *What? Stop it?* I was sure he had his pick of women and left the bodies scattered across the city like litter.

"What do your parents do?" he asked.

"I think I should be able to veto some of these questions."

"That wasn't the deal—"

His phone began to vibrate and he drew his eyebrows together. "I'm going to have to take this. Try not to get into trouble while I'm gone."

I rolled my eyes and went back to my laptop. What on earth was I going to write about? I had nothing so far other than Sandy wanted to dry hump Harry. That was why I didn't do celebrities. They were never quite as interesting as you imagined them to be. And they were always smaller than they seemed on screen. It was like the entertainment industry had a height restriction.

Harry seemed to have received good news from his phone call.

"Why are you in such a good mood? Did your girlfriend's chlamydia test come back negative?"

"Give it a fucking rest, Haven. Misery is not most people's default status."

"I'm not miserable."

"Okay, rude then," he said. I cringed inwardly but tried not to let it show.

"Sorry. Ask me a question." My tongue was particularly acerbic when I was around him. It was like I wanted to poke about a bit in that charming exterior and see how deep it went. Was I trying to goad him into losing his cool so I could see who he really was? I was thinking too much about Harry when I should be concentrating on Sandy.

"You can't keep doing that, being like that."

"Sorry. It was meant to be funny." I felt silly and embarrassed. I had wanted to make him laugh.

"By joking about my girlfriend's STDs?"

I shrugged. Luke would have laughed.

"We don't know each other well enough to be joking about chlamydia." He chuckled and shook his head.

I bit back a smile.

"So tell me about your parents," he said, going back to the question he'd asked before his phone call and the one I most dreaded from people.

"They're dead," I replied.

He burst out laughing and I found myself smiling at him.

"Jesus. You are dark. Seriously, though . . . "

"Seriously. They died," I said. Nobody had ever laughed when I'd told them about my parents—not that I told many people. I found that it was a reaction I preferred over what was normally pity.

"Shit." He went white. "I thought you were joking."

"I know. It's fine." I smiled at him. I didn't want him to feel uncomfortable.

"When did they die?"

"I was fifteen." Most people didn't ask follow up questions when I told them that they said they were sorry and then tried to change the subject. Harry didn't seem to be embarrassed at all.

"How did it happen? At the same time?"

"Yeah. They were in a car accident." A familiar pressure built across my temples and a sharp stab of pain hit me between my brows. I reached for my forehead, hoping my fingers would usher it away.

"I'm sorry," he said, like they all did.

I kept rubbing my forehead.

"Well, unless you were the drunk driver who ran into them, you have nothing to be sorry for." I didn't want people's pity, it made me feel weak and it was unacceptable for me to feel that way in front of strangers.

"Haven, I'm sorry for your loss. *Let me* be sorry for your loss."

I hated the bit straight after I told people. Everyone was uncomfortable. They didn't know what to say. I didn't know what to say. I wanted to disappear, I didn't want their sympathy or sorrow. It felt private, like I didn't want to share how I felt about my parents, the accident and their death. Those feelings were mine and I guarded them. People's reaction felt like a call for me to open up. That was why I hated telling people. I didn't mind people knowing, but I didn't like the time just after they knew.

Murmurings from the crew in front of us brought our attention back to our surroundings and Sandy came rushing over.

"Harry—I'm done for the day. Shall we go into town and get me drunk?" She giggled.

"I've just had a phone call that I have to deal with but another time? When are we back here?"

"Monday," I said. Drunk Sandy might be more interesting than sober Sandy. Couldn't Harry's phone call wait? Although, I wasn't sure she'd planned to have me tag along.

"Your mind is always on your work, Harry. You need to carve out some time for a little fun." She turned, winked at him over her shoulder and spun off.

"Well, there are no mixed signals there. I'm guessing she's a sure thing," I said.

Harry shrugged and we packed up our stuff and headed to the car.

"Do you like her?" I asked.

"You keep forgetting that I'm asking the questions." I hated that he dodged the question. I wanted to know whether he found her attractive. What was his type?

"So ask." I liked that he wanted to know things about me. That he was interested enough to keep this up. It was like our own private game, and somehow he made me feel safe, like I could answer truthfully and nothing bad would happen.

"What's your favorite food?"

I laughed. He was keeping things on safer ground. "Eggs," I replied.

"Really?"

"Yeah, love 'em." It was true. There was nothing nicer than an egg.

"Served any particular way?"

"I'm not fussy."

"Well, I know that's a lie," he said and grinned.

I poked him in the ribs, our eyes met and I quickly pulled my hand away. All of a sudden touching him didn't seem very appropriate. I'd forgotten myself. I'd thought I was with Luke or Ash.

"With eggs, I'm not fussy."

"What about time of year?" he asked.

"It seems very one sided and unfair that I can't ask any questions of you."

"That's the deal, and anyway, my favorite food is steak. Not very original, but true nonetheless."

He helped me load my bag into the back of the car and folded his too long legs into the passenger seat of my tiny car. Maybe he wasn't spoiled as I'd thought he was.

"I like the spring," I told him. "The pussy willow, the daffodils. The lengthening days and the promise of summer."

He nodded and smiled. "Me too."

Luke scooted Ash and I up his sofa so he could sit down. I loved it when it was the three of us together. We were in a bubble and nothing could touch us, nothing could hurt us. Even though my brother lived with his girlfriend, somehow their flat was very much his. There weren't many signs of Emma at all.

"So how's it going with that guy who called you a bitch?" Luke asked as he set down the popcorn in front of Ash and me.

My cheeks burned at the thought of Harry.

"Who called you a bitch?" Ash asked.

"A new person. Harry. But it's fine now. I think."

"A new guy?"

I nodded. "A photographer. Some Uni friend of Robert's. You know how Robert gives his friends jobs."

"Is he being an asshole, or were you being a bitch?" Ash asked.

"No, actually. I think I was being a bitch."

I caught Ash and Luke exchange a glance.

"Are you two flirting?" I asked, trying to throw the spotlight back on someone other than me.

"No we are not. When I make a play for your brother, he won't be able to resist me and we'll be wedding planning within weeks, so you'll be well aware."

"Ash," Luke said, a warning in his voice. I wasn't sure if he really didn't like her teasing him about their imaginary life as a couple, or whether he felt he should say something because he was living with Emma.

"Anyway, back to you. Is this new guy hot?"

I rolled my lips together. He was very definitely hot. And very definitely too hot for me to even consider him hot. "He's fine, if you're in to that kind of thing."

"Interesting," Ash said.

I glanced at Luke and he raised his eyebrows.

"What? I asked, raising my palms.

"Well, normally you make gagging sounds when I ask you if a guy is hot. Or you tell me that he smells like he hasn't washed since before Robbie left Take That, the first time. Or that he walks with a limp, or—"

"Okay, I get the picture, funny girl."

Luke was laughing. "It's true though, Haven. 'Fine' is the equivalent of you saying that you want to lick him all over."

"Well, I have no intention of licking him anywhere. You guys are gross," I said as I got up and headed over to the kitchen. "No kissing while I turn my back for five seconds to get more booze."

"Okay, we'll skip straight to the sex," Ash called after me.

Ash and Luke started to argue about which film to put on. I was still thinking about my tongue trailing down Harry's chest.

My phone vibrating interrupted my inappropriate thought and my mouth went dry when I saw it was a text from Harry. Shit. That was a coincidence.

H: Sorry, can't do Monday. Will have to rearrange or go without me.

What a fucker. Just when I thought he was a half-decent guy he went and pulled a stunt like that. I tossed my phone onto the table and Luke and Ash snapped their heads toward me.

"It's nothing. Someone at work being a wanker."

"Was it licky Harry?" Ash asked.

I threw a napkin at her. "You're gross."

"Come on Rapunzel, let down your golden hair and pour out the shots," Ash said.

The call of tequila. Something I could never resist.

"Can I play with it?" she asked as I started pouring out too-full shot glasses.

"You are a freak," I said. "Luke, you're never to marry this girl, do you hear me?"

"Have you both forgotten that I'm living with Emma?"

"She's just a phase," Ash and I said in unison and then collapsed into laughter. Emma was okay, but I honestly couldn't see him with her forever. She didn't laugh enough. She didn't make Luke laugh enough, and it always seemed to be him who was making all the compromises. I wanted my brother to be happy, and I wasn't sure he was.

"If you don't want me to play with it, perhaps you could have it cut and make a wig and I could have that?" Ash asked.

"You're not playing with my hair and I'm not having it cut, you weirdo."

"I'm not weird, you know I've always wanted your Rapunzel-like hair."

Jake

I was pretty sure Haven would be mad at me for cancelling the Monday trip to the studio, but there was nothing I could do. I couldn't miss this follow up meeting with Hal. Robert was fine with me setting my own hours, and Haven could go on her own. I didn't need to be there every time she went, although she hadn't exactly hit it off with Sandy. Or anyone, apparently.

"Are you okay? You're frowning," Beth said.

"Yeah, I've had to cancel on Haven on Monday because Hal wants me to meet with his corporate finance guy."

"Haven's the uptight one who's writing the story on Sandy?"

I nodded. "I think she'll struggle with Sandy on her own."

"You're a good man Jake."

"Hardly, I'm letting her down."

"Yeah, but at least you have the decency to feel bad about it." Beth laughed and I grinned at her.

"I'm not sure that counts, but thanks for your faith. I better get going or I'm going to be late for my date with Millie and I'll have another woman mad at me." I scanned the room for my keys and wallet.

"Well that's no bad thing as far as I'm concerned."

"Millie isn't as awful as you think. You just caught her on the spot."

"Whatever. I can smell a gold-digger when I see one." Beth was very protective of me.

"You think all women are after my money."

"That's because they are."

"Maybe it's my big dick," I said, grinning at my sister.

"You're gross. Get out."

"I'm going. Don't wait up." I leaned over the sofa and kissed her on the head. She swatted me away.

Sure enough, Millie texted me to check if I had left before I'd had a chance to get out of the building. When I arrived at her place, she opened the front door as soon as I knocked, like she was standing behind it, waiting.

"Hey, you look beautiful," I told her. She always looked good. We'd been dating about three months and I'd never seen her anything other than fully made up with a new outfit on or naked.

She smiled at me. "Thanks. I do try for you. So where are you taking me?"

"It's a surprise," I replied as I opened the car door for her.

I might be still living in the flat I was in when I was a student but I'd upgraded my car. I had two in fact. An Aston Martin DB9 for nights like this and then a run-around Golf.

As I rounded the hood to take the driver's side, I glanced back at her. She suited the car perfectly, like she was made for it. No one could deny she was beautiful, and she was good in bed. A surprisingly rare combination in a woman, I'd come to realise. She was the kind of girl that made other guys jealous—not that that was my intention, it was just a fact. But it came at a price. She liked the finer things in life, and there was no chance of us kicking back on the sofa on a Saturday night, or a long walk and lunch in a pub on Sunday. Millie was all about high-end glamour. She made me work for it, but I was okay with that. I liked to work for things that were worth it.

"Chiltern Firehouse sound okay?"

It was a good compromise. Relaxed enough that I could wear jeans but full of enough designer-clad celebrities to keep Millie happy.

The twitching at the corners of her mouth suggested that she was trying to hide a shit-eating grin.

"What would you like to drink?" I asked her as we arrived at the bar adjoining the restaurant.

"Something bubbly," she replied.

Of course. I ordered a beer and a glass of champagne. "So how have you kept yourself busy today?" I asked in an attempt to get her to stop so obviously scanning for celebrities.

"I went to the spa with Cissy, and then we went shopping." She smiled at me. "Underwear shopping," she whispered. "You deserve a reward for getting a table here."

Normally a comment like that from her would create a dozen mental pictures of Millie in various states of undress and a distinct stirring in my trousers. For some reason, I didn't feel anything.

"Come on, let's get seated if you're so keen," I said and guided her through to the restaurant, my hand on the bottom of her back.

The waiter led us to our table and handed us our menus. I wasn't sure what the fuss was about. It seemed like a hundred restaurants I'd been to before. I'd been given a token for some private members' club for after dinner, but I'd decided not to tell Millie about that yet.

"Was it what you expected?" I asked her, glancing round again.

"Yes, I mean, if it's good enough for Orlando Bloom and Victoria Beckham then it's good enough for me."

I smiled at her. I was glad she was pleased.

I turned my attention to the menu. I grinned when I noticed one of the starters was a soft poached egg. "What's your favorite food?"

She stared at me and her eyebrows knitted together. "What?"

"Your favorite food, what is it?"

"I've never thought about it. Caviar? Why? Have you arranged for us to have some?"

My heart sank and I shook my head. I wondered if she liked caviar or if she liked it because that was what she was supposed to like. I wondered if I really liked Millie, or if was I was dating her because she was the kind of woman I was supposed to date.

"Apparently there's a super-exclusive private members' club at the back that some customers get invited to join," she said.

"Really?" I feigned ignorance.

"Getting in there would mean I would give you free entry anywhere, if you get my meaning."

Was she offering me anal sex if I got her into a nightclub? My appetite died. I always understood our relationship was a transaction of sorts, but it had never been in such sharp focus for me.

"Another night," I said.

I signed the bill and felt relieved. I hadn't enjoyed the evening. Being with Millie had made me feel uncomfortable.

As we headed out, I caught her doing a final scan of the restaurant. "Disappointed you didn't see any celebrities?"

"Maybe a little," she said. "But it's a good excuse to come back. Now let's get back to mine so I can thank you properly."

We made our way toward the car and she reached for my hand. I didn't resist her.

"Jesus, are they wearing pajamas?" she asked me, pointing at two girls coming in our direction, huddled up in coats that didn't quite hide the pastel-colored leggings beneath. They were laughing like crazy people, then stopped suddenly beside my car as one of them finished what they were saying and then they both burst into another round of laughter. I couldn't help but smile at them, they were having their own private party.

"They're going to scratch your car," Millie warned.

Something about one of them seemed familiar. I stepped forward, trying to see better. "Haven?" I asked. The girl on the right looked like her, but I'd never seen Haven with her hair down, so perhaps I'd got it wrong.

"Haven?" I asked again, surer this time.

I was close enough to have both their attention, and it was most certainly Haven. Haven with her hair down. Haven far from sober. She stood stock-still and put her hand over her mouth.

"I thought that was you," I said when she didn't say anything. Her friend was shaking her shoulder.

We were a couple of feet apart. Millie had gone round to the passenger side of the car and I was on the sidewalk with Haven.

"Are you okay?" I asked.

Her friend answered for her. "Yes, thanks, handsome, we're just a little drunk, but it's alright because soon we'll be a lot drunk." She thrust a bottle of wine in the air.

Haven laughed again.

"It's licky," Haven said to her friend, not taking her eyes from me and pointing in my direction.

"It's what?" I asked. I didn't understand what she'd said.

"What? Oh!" Her friend squealed. "Do you guys work together?" she asked.

"I'm Harry. Yes I'm at Rallegra with Haven." I held out my hand and she shook it in an exaggerated greeting.

"This is Millie," I said, pointing across the roof of the car, trying to be polite. Millie grimaced.

Haven threw her head back and laughed. "Don't tell me that's your car."

"What?" I asked.

"You're such a fucking cliché, Harry."

I winced slightly. Most of the time I loved my car, but every now and then it felt like I shouldn't own it. Cars like that weren't meant to be owned by a cop's kid from Chicago. Haven's reaction was like salt in that particular wound.

"A hot cliché, though," her friend said.

They both started laughing again. I could count on the fingers of one hand how many times I'd seen Haven smile, let alone laugh. Drunk Haven seemed much more fun than uptight, work Haven. The laugh brought her to life and she became all the more beautiful.

"Bye, Millie," Haven shouted as she ran off down the road, her friend trailing behind as I watched.

"Baby, can you get me in this fucking car? I'm freezing," Millie said.

I unlocked the car. "Do you know those girls?"

I nodded and smiled. "I know the one with the long blonde hair."

"If that's what working does to you, I'm pleased I don't do it."

I cringed at her reaction. Despite all the effort that Millie had gone to tonight with her appearance, Haven in her pajamas, laughing with windswept hair trumped her hands down. The night was nearly over and so were we. I couldn't understand how we'd been dating for three months. We had nothing in common. I wouldn't tell her tonight, I'd wait until she was sober.

Seeing Millie and Haven together, right in front of me, my feelings or lack thereof for Millie became all the more pronounced. I realized I liked verbally sparring with Haven more than I liked having sex with Millie.

chapter FIVE

Haven

I had the god of all hangovers. I could tell without even opening my eyes. I turned over and came face to face with a snoring Ash. I pushed my palm against her face. "Get away from me if you're going to sleep."

Ash opened her eyes and grinned at me.

"You fucker. Were you trying to wake me up by fake-snoring?" I asked

"You fall for it every time, Rapunzel," she replied.

"You are evil. I can't believe how much we drank last night." I lay on my back, ready to dissect the night before, like we'd done a million times. And then it came back to me. "Oh. My. God." I sat bolt upright and my brain knocked against my skull. I grasped my head in an effort to soothe the pain. "Shit, we bumped into Harry last night!" My stomach churned and I wasn't sure if it was my half memory of seeing Harry or the twenty-nine bottles of wine that I had consumed last night.

"Yes we did." Ash giggled. "You referred to him as licky as I remember."

I slumped back down into the mattress. "Kill me now. I'm going to have to resign," I said. How embarrassing.

"Well, as long as you're not overreacting. That's the main thing."

I didn't think I was overreacting at all. Harry might have seen bitchy Haven, but that was professional compared to drunk, out of control Haven. "We were wearing our pajamas from what I remember. Of course I'll have to resign." Just as our working relationship had improved, now he was going to think I was such an idiot. I wanted him to see that I was good at my job, not some silly, drunk girl who wandered around London giggling in her pajamas. I covered my eyes with the palms of my hands.

"It was the only way you'd come with me to replenish the wine supplies," Ash said.

"What, if we went in our pajamas?"

She nodded.

"Oh god. What must he think of me?"

"Why do you care? I'm sure his girlfriend fucked his brains out last night, so he won't remember anything this morning. Don't worry about it."

My stomach flipped at the thought of him with Millie or whatever her name was. She was so beautiful it almost hurt to think about her. I thought women like her only existed in magazines. "I can't believe you're a medical professional, coming up with theories like that. I'm not sure that's how human biology works. She was a total glamazon, wasn't she?"

Ash laughed. "Yes, but probably crap in bed. Those model types always are. It's girls like you and me that have it going on in the bedroom."

"Is this the moment in time to point out the fact that you and I shared a bed last night, and that I'm wearing pajamas with flying pigs all over them?"

"Nope," Ash replied.

"Yeah, didn't think so."

Luke came into the room carrying a tray of tea.

"You are my hero," Ash said, beaming. "Promise me you won't stop making me tea when we're married. You've got to work to keep the magic alive."

Luke rolled his eyes. "In this fictitious scenario where we're married and I'm bringing you tea to cure your hangover, will you still share my sister's bed?"

"Absolutely. I'll still make you earn my physical affection. And I will demand that she sleeps over every Saturday night. Licky can come too, if he wants."

"Ash, that's gross. I don't want to hear any more about you and my brother."

I leaned over to the nightstand to retrieve my phone as Luke plonked himself at the end of the bed.

"Oh, my god," I said, reading a text from Harry.

Harry: I was right about you with your hair down. It looks good.

My belly twisted and I started to chew the inside of my mouth. I wasn't sure what to make of his comment. I was embarrassed to find that I hoped he was being genuine. I wanted him to think my hair looked nice down, but it hadn't—I'd had drunk girl in pajamas hair.

"What?" Ash asked.

"Nothing. My bank balance. Horrifying." I didn't want to

tell her and have her say she thought he was being sarcastic. If I kept it to myself, it could be real.

There were two texts after the first.

Harry: Can you let me know you got home safely?

Harry: Haven, seriously, let me know you're not in a ditch.

All three had been sent last night. Before or after he was having his brains fucked out, I wondered. I turned away from Luke and Ash, I didn't want them to see my grin spilling out as I replied. I liked that he was worried for me and that he was kind enough not to mention my pajamas. I quickly typed out a response.

Haven: Not in a ditch.

"I have to get in the shower. I feel like I slept with a tramp last night," I said, leaving Luke and Ash to their flirting.

I pulled my phone from my bag to text to Harry. He hadn't replied to my not in a ditch comment yesterday, but I hadn't expected him to. Now, I needed to be back in work mode.

Haven: I'll rearrange our next set visit. Can you let me know when you will next grace us with your presence?

I tried to immerse myself in the Sandy research, to get my head in the game, but I couldn't stop thinking about Harry's texts to me over the weekend and our conversations the previous week. I was like a teenager, playing it over and over in my head. It was embarrassing to admit, even to myself but I liked the attention. He was different. He didn't take my bullshit, but he cared enough to call me on it. Millie, from what I remember of her, was exactly who I would put with someone like him. Tall, beautiful, head to toe designer everything. I would have to run into him dressed in pajamas. How mortifying. And as if I didn't have enough to be embarrassed about, I'd actually called him "licky".

I kept checking my phone, but no reply. He was clearly doing something far more important than worrying about his day job. Or texting me.

It was gone seven when he finally texted back.

Harry: Sorry, busy day. I'm around Thursday and Friday if that works. Glad you're not in a ditch.

I grinned and set about making the arrangements for later in the week.

I arrived at the studios almost half an hour before Harry and I had agreed to meet in the parking lot. I hadn't wanted to leave the engine running, so I was gradually getting colder and colder in the car. I'd resorted to covering myself with a blanket that Luke made me keep on the back seat for emergencies. I'd closed my eyes for only a second when tapping on the window jolted me awake.

"Did you sleep here?" Harry asked through the glass.

What? I threw the blanket off me and got out of the car. Why did he always catch me in the most embarrassing situations?

"You looked comfortable. How long were you there?" he asked.

I shrugged.

"Am I late?" he asked.

"No. I'm just always early."

"So you can nap when you arrive?" He started laughing at me.

"Shut up," I snapped. "Where's your car?"

He thumped the roof of the car next to mine. Now it was my turn to laugh. "Did you rent the Aston Martin? Trying to impress your date? Did it get you laid?"

"Fuck off. It's at home. I have two."

I opened my mouth to call him spoiled, but he put his hand across my mouth. "I know, I'm a spoiled little rich boy. Don't be so predictable, Haven. Think of something new to say."

"Jesus, someone's touchy," I replied when he took his hand away.

"I just don't want to deal with your crap today." He was scowling at me. I must have misread his texts over the weekend. I'd tricked myself into thinking that maybe he liked me, that maybe he was flirting with me. I'd got it all wrong. I was mortified at my mistake. Better to be angry than hurt, I lashed out.

"My crap? *My* crap? I've said barely a word. You're the one who's giving *me* crap." I poked him in the chest and he grabbed my hand. I twisted my fingers to try and break away, but he held them firm.

"Stop, Haven," he said. He wasn't taking his eyes off me.

My heart was racing. "You're the one that started it this morning—"

"Stop," he said again, his gaze boring into me.

"Let go of me," I said, my anger dissipating as his eyes roamed my face, but I didn't struggle and he didn't let go.

There wasn't much space between us and he took a step toward me, closing any gap. Instinctively I moved back, but my ass hit his car. I had nowhere to go.

I tilted my head up, and his mouth crashed against mine, pressing into me. I couldn't quite process what was going on. He was kissing me and he felt good, warm. And he smelled like . . . sandalwood, heat and clean laundry. I relaxed back against his car and his hands cupped my face and he pressed his body against mine. I was trapped, deliciously so.

His tongue trailed across the seam of my lips. I gasped and he pushed through and against my tongue. He was surrounding me, overwhelming every sense I had. He was passionate and urgent as if he'd been saving all this up. I reached up and he moaned as I threaded my fingers through his dirty blond hair. He pulled back slightly and took my lower lip in his mouth and bit. It was my turn to moan. Christ, no man had ever bitten me before. And then his tongue was against mine again. I was melting under his touch, pliant and relaxed and burning hot.

Even through our coats, his hard-on pressed against me. Instinctively, I twisted my body under him. "Fuck," he whispered into my mouth as he pushed his hips against me. I wanted him. I really wanted him.

From somewhere I heard shouting, and I tensed beneath him. He pulled back slightly and rested his forehead against mine, looking at me and breathing heavily. He held my head between his hands, and I could still feel the warmth of him on my lips.

I placed my hands on his hard chest and gently pushed

him away. I scrubbed my hands up and down my face while he stood, bent over, his hands on his knees.

"Come on, we're going to be late," I said.

I collected my bag from the passenger seat, he grabbed his camera gear and we headed silently toward Stage Three.

Jake

I willed my hard-on under control. Thankfully it was winter and I had my coat on. When I'd seen her sleeping, she looked so peaceful. I realized that I kinda missed her and her smart mouth. And then when she started giving me shit about my car I remembered how infuriating she was, and somehow the only solution to it all had been to kiss her.

"We should go," she'd whispered breathily. "Someone might see."

My body had been pressed against hers and as I moved, the loss of her warmth against me was unexpectedly wrenching, as if unnatural. I wanted to stay there and kiss her, dive into her and explore her.

Walking to the studio, thehe smell of her lingered around me. She smelled sexy, if that was possible. She hadn't resisted, in fact she had kissed me back as if that was what we did all the time—kiss passionately in parking lots. It had been unexpected: the kiss, her response, my response. I liked that she gave into me, submitted to me as I touched her. Like somehow I'd found the key to taming her, discovered what she needed.

Now there was just silence between us as we walked toward the studio.

The security guard gave our passes a cursory glance and pointed at nowhere in particular. We followed the signs toward Stage Three.

Sandy's manager Phil, came scurrying toward us with his finger across his lips. He had nothing to worry about. We weren't speaking. This room seemed smaller, but probably because the set was bigger. It was like some kind of formal ballroom, there were loads of actors dressed in evening wear. The atmosphere seemed tense. Phil still had his fingers on his lips as he backed away from the two seats he had ushered us to. We took off our coats and unpacked our bags. I kept stealing glances at Haven, but she was strictly focused on firing up her laptop.

I took a few shots, but there was nothing much for me to do. I wasn't allowed to capture the images of the actors on set, so my busiest time was during breaks in filming.

I leaned into Haven. "You okay?" I whispered.

She nodded but didn't look at me.

"You sure?" I asked. Was this no big deal for her? Had she not felt what I had during that kiss? I was used to a different reaction from women than the one I was getting from her.

She turned toward me and raised her eyebrows and nodded again. She seemed completely unfazed by our encounter. Maybe it was guilt that was generating her response. She hadn't mentioned a boyfriend, but she might have one. Something deep in my belly exploded. I wasn't sure I liked that idea.

Haven was tapping away on her laptop. I couldn't

understand what she had to write about. I heard Sandy before I saw her. She came bouncing over.

"Harry!" she said, throwing her arms around my neck and pulling me into a hug. I turned to Haven, checking for her reaction. She shrugged. What was with her? I'd never seen her this relaxed before. Well, apart from dressed in pajamas in the street, drunk off her ass.

"Hi, Sandy," Haven said.

Sandy, her arms still around my neck, turned to Haven and said, "Hey. Nice to see you. Let's chat later."

"So, what's going on?" I asked. "Things seemed a little tense up there?"

"I think the director is going through the menopause," she replied. "He'll be fine now. Those last scenes went well, don't you think?"

How was I supposed to know? I just nodded.

"That's a beautiful dress," Haven said, smiling at Sandy.

"Thanks! They literally had to pour me into it, it's so tight," she said as her eyes darted to mine and her hands skirted her silhouette. I forced a smile as Phil came up behind her and pulled her away.

"See you later," she said, following Phil and leaving us behind.

I turned to Haven to find her smiling and waving at Sandy. She went back to her laptop.

A little later on, the mumbling from the crew increased and everyone seemed to relax a little. Sandy was still on stage with Bobby, the male lead. They were talking to the director and some other guy.

"What are you thinking about?" I asked Haven.

She turned to me and narrowed her eyes. "I'm trying to find an interesting angle to this piece. I'm worried about it. I haven't spent much time with her and I've got nothing to say. I think Jenny's wrong about Phil—there's no way Sandy's banging him."

"Right."

"I think I might ask if you and I can have lunch with her. It's just, she's so distracted around you," she said.

"I think that's how she is," I said.

"Distracted?"

I nodded. "I mean, I don't think it's personal toward me."

"I don't know. I think she's pretty available to you."

Was she trying to gauge whether I was interested in her? "Again, I don't think it's personal," I replied.

"Harry!" She opened her eyes and mouth wide in mock shock. "Are you saying our star is a slut?"

I laughed. "No, and don't quote me on that."

She smiled at me and went back to her laptop.

"So you weren't thinking about earlier?" I asked.

"Earlier?" she asked as if she was genuinely unclear what I meant.

"In the parking lot earlier," I said.

"Oh, you mean, am I worried about the chlamydia thing? Don't worry, I'll get tested and get antibiotics if I need to." She grinned at me.

"Haven?" She was funny, but it was killing me. I wanted to know what she was feeling. Her reaction, or lack thereof, to our kiss had been completely unexpected and it bothered me. I wanted her to tell me that she wanted it to happen again.

"What?" She sounded exasperated.

"Should we talk about it?"

"What, that you can't keep your hands off me? No, we should not talk about it."

I tried to think of a witty comeback but I couldn't. So I didn't say anything.

Haven managed to secure lunch in Sandy's trailer with her manager. Hopefully, it would give her the time with her that she needed.

"So, it's so exciting to be on a movie set," Haven said, smiling at Sandy. "Are you enjoying it?"

"Yes, I'm having such a great time. I've always enjoyed shooting music videos, but this is different but super-fun. But obviously it takes way longer." Sandy was in a good mood and I was pleased for Haven.

"Do you have a lot of creative input into your videos?" Haven asked.

"Sure, loads. The one for *Shout If It's Love*, I completely styled myself and I worked with the director on different ideas before we started shooting," she replied.

"Is it tough, not having the same control in a film?"

"No. I trust the director."

"You grew up singing and dancing. You're first public performance was at the age of three. Did you ever want to do anything other than what you're doing now?"

Sandy narrowed her eyes slightly, as if she was trying to process the question. "I can't remember there ever being a time when I didn't want to be famous, to perform, to sing. I love it. There's never a time when I don't feel incredibly lucky to have had my dreams come true, but I knew it was going to happen for me, like it was my destiny or something."

Haven smiled at Sandy and nodded.

Sandy turned to me. "And did you hear that we've got the date for Paris? You're coming to that Harry, right? Spring in Paris is so romantic."

"So, it's the first Tuesday in April, for three days, two nights" Phil explained. "You don't have to come for the whole shoot, or at all if you don't want to. It's to film the proposal scenes."

"It will be so fun, Harry! Promise you'll come," Sandy said, whining.

"This is the first I've heard of it." I looked at Haven and she shrugged. She clearly hadn't known about it either. "We'll have to check the schedules. I may be in the US. It depends on a few things."

"Please try." Sandy was pouting.

"We'd love to come, and we'll make every effort," Haven said. It seemed to placate Sandy, for the moment. "Paris is beautiful. You must have travelled all over the world. Do you have a favorite place?"

"Dubai, I think. The Atlantis Palm hotel is completely amazing. I loved it there, didn't I, Phil?"

Phil nodded. Of all the places she'd been to, she picked a hotel. She reminded me of Millie.

I got the feeling that it wasn't the answer that Haven had

been wanting, but she was pretty good at covering it up. Better than I'd expected her to be in any event.

"Do friends and family join you when you're touring?" she persisted.

"Of course. Phil here is like an uncle to me. And Patricia comes with me everywhere." Sandy replied. "I'm very lucky to have them."

"Patricia?"

"My assistant. You've met her, right?"

Haven shook her head.

"Phil, can you introduce Patricia to Haven?" She turned back to Haven. "She's lovely. We're so close, we're like sisters. I don't know what I'd do without her."

"It's good to have someone who has your back."

Phil excused himself to take a call and was soon ushering Sandy out of the trailer and back to the set. Of course, we followed.

"Holy crap," Haven said as we took our chairs in our designated spot. "I can't exactly write about what a lonely, vacuous existence she has, can I? This is Rallegra, not the fucking Times, but that's the bit I find fascinating. That's what I *want* to write about."

"Paris might help," I replied.

"I doubt it, I'm not sure Sandy's the problem. Robert might not even let us go," she mused.

chapter SIX

Haven

By some miracle I'd managed to pull it off. I'd played it cool, pretending I thought him kissing me was no big deal, when of course, I thought it was a huge deal. I'd done it more successfully than he had. He'd kept asking if I was okay and if I wanted to talk about it. I brushed it off, but wondered if his concern masked regret. As soon as he drove out of the car park at the end of the day, I collapsed onto the steering wheel. *What the fuck happened?* We were fighting, then kissing, and then he was moaning and panting and I was feeling things between my thighs that I'd only read about in books. *Shit.*

Why had he kissed me? To prove that he could? To demonstrate he could have everything he wanted? Did he want me?

And now it was the weekend and I was going to have to wait until Monday to see him again. A weekend he was probably spending with the glamazon, racing around London in his Aston Martin, tan and gorgeous, drinking champagne, and eating caviar.

I needed to bury the very thought of him. He wasn't my type. I didn't like men like him. I liked men who were ambitious and successful, kind and funny.

"So, you seem distracted," Ash said, jolting me from my thoughts.

"Do I? I'm thinking that I'm twenty-seven and single, yet I'm spending a second Saturday night in a row drunk with my best friend, at home, without the possibility of getting laid."

"I'll kiss you later if that makes you feel better," she offered.

"Let's see how you're looking after another bottle of wine."

"Anyway, we were at Luke's last weekend getting drunk, so it hasn't been two Saturday nights in a row drinking at home."

"Oh, that's okay then."

"How's the Sandy Fox article coming?"

"Terrible. Urgh." I slumped back onto the sofa. "There is just nothing interesting to say about her. Scratch that. The interesting stuff isn't very flattering, and of course, we're Rallegra, so we're not going to write a take-down piece about Sandy bloody Fox."

"If Vanity Fair couldn't stand up to Gwynnie . . ."

"Exactly. She's not a monster, don't get me wrong, but really, there's nothing much there and I want to be getting down and dirty. She spends the whole time flirting with Harry."

"Is that what the problem is? You don't like her flirting with licky? He is hot, from what I remember. I drank a lot of wine that night, so everyone looked good."

"Including his glamazon girlfriend," I said. "Anyway, why would I care if she flirted with him? I just wish that this wasn't the article that my future depended on. I asked her about her favorite place she'd visited and she told me it was the Palm hotel in Dubai. I mean, she must have travelled all over the world. How depressing."

"Maybe they have really good free toiletries."

"You're not helping."

"No, hear me out. Maybe she likes stealing things from hotel rooms. That's your story—Sandy Fox, superstar and thief of hotel amenities."

"Don't give up your day job," I said and swatted her

"Is licky up for a slice of Miss Fox?"

Despite Sandy being gorgeous and very available to Harry, I didn't think he was. "I don't think so."

"Perhaps it's serious with the glamazon."

"Maybe," I replied, and focused on my wine glass.

"Haven?"

"What?"

"What are you not telling me?" I didn't know if it was my lack of poker face or the fact Ash had known me twenty years that meant I could never keep a secret from her for very long.

"Harry kinda kissed me." My heart started thumping against my chest as I said it. Would she think he was ridiculously out of my league?

"He *kinda* kissed you? Are you not sure? Was it ambiguous? When did this happen?"

"I'm pretty sure he kissed me. On Friday. Outside the studio." Warmth spread over me as I remembered his breath on my skin, his tongue skimming across my lips.

"And you waited until now to tell me? So what happened? Was it a good kiss? Was it *just* a kiss? Was there groping? How did you leave it?"

"Do you want me to fill out a questionnaire?" I grinned at her.

"Come on! Tell me."

"It came out of no-where. And it was in the car park, of course it was just a kiss." But it hadn't felt like just a kiss. It had felt more important.

"Wow."

"Wow what?" Was she going to tell me I was an idiot for letting myself get into that situation?

"Wow, is it going to happen again? Do you want it to?"

My stomach tilted. I wasn't sure how to answer that question. My body was telling me I wanted it to happen again, I wanted it a lot. But my mind was telling me Harry spelled trouble. "I'm still processing. I don't really understand why it happened."

"You don't understand why people kiss each other?"

I narrowed my eyes at Ash. "You know what I mean."

"No, actually, I don't. He clearly likes you. I can't imagine he goes around kissing every girl he meets."

"I'm not so sure. He's used to getting what he wants. With that face and his money? I'm probably the first girl who didn't fall at his feet as soon as they saw his Aston Martin. Maybe I'm just a challenge."

"You're certainly that."

I threw a cushion at her.

"You didn't say whether or not you liked him," Ash said.

I shrugged. "Like I said, I'm still processing. I'm not supposed to like men like him." Harry seemed dangerous and out of my league. There was plenty of disappointment in life without encouraging it. "I'm not a glamazon like Millie."

"No, you're way more beautiful than Millie, you just don't show it off in the same way. Listen, you don't often get to the kissing stage with men. You must like him. I think you need to give him a chance. Don't write him off."

Ash was right, I didn't kiss many men. I certainly didn't feel the passion for other men that I'd felt for Harry in that moment but he had a girlfriend and so whatever I felt didn't matter.

I did a pretty good job of distracting myself all weekend, but I struggled to get to sleep on Sunday night. I couldn't wait to get to the office to see Harry. I wondered if he still wanted to talk about our kiss.

I tried not to seem too interested as people filed into the conference room for our Monday morning meeting. The last few meetings we'd sat opposite each other, but as I looked up from my to-do list, it was Emily who had taken the seat in front of me. I quickly scanned the faces of those around the rest of the table. No Harry. I hadn't brought my phone with me. Had he texted? Or emailed? I tried to think back to Friday. Had he said that he would see me today? Maybe he'd left and was never coming back? He was only filling in, after all. My heart began to race and I swept my hands across my hair, smoothing the stray hair back into my bun.

"So, Haven, I thought you could give us an update on the Sandy Fox piece. How's it developing?" Robert said.

Shit, that was the last thing I needed. I reached for my Diet Coke and took a swig. "It's going okay. We're getting a good amount of time with her and she's very friendly. I just need to find a good angle."

"This isn't the New York Times. You're not doing an expose," Emily said from across the table. My stomach clenched. Emily had once told me I acted like I was too good for Rallegra, but the opposite was true—I always felt like an imposter amongst the shiny, glamorous, upbeat staff. I never felt good enough. I guess that was part of the reason I wanted the promotion so badly. It would be evidence that I belonged.

"I think what Emily meant to say was, don't put too much pressure on yourself. Take lots of notes. I'm sure Paris will give you more insight."

I'd sent Robert an email about our invitation to Paris over the weekend. It sounded like he'd approved it. My stomach clenched at the thought. I'd not been to France since I was a student. Going to interview Sandy in Paris, with Harry . . . I had to force back a smile. It did sound romantic.

Robert didn't mention Harry, and neither did anyone else. Where was he? I couldn't wait to get back to my desk to check my messages.

When the meeting finally broke, I quickly went to retrieve my phone. Nothing. Bloody hell. We weren't due to be back on set until Thursday, but even so. I decided to text him.

Haven: Where are you?

I slung my phone into my skirt pocket and tried to keep myself busy. I had three articles to check. Two were from

Marie, and she'd never written anything for me before, so I wanted to take my time with them.

I rounded the corner back to my desk with a coffee in my hand. I glanced at the desk Harry was using, checking if he'd arrived late. He hadn't and I grinned as I remembered the non-apology apology latte I'd bought him on his first day. I caught the sound of Emily's voice in the meeting room, and slowed down when I heard my name.

"And now she's going to Paris? It's because she's ugly and dresses like she's five years old. Robert told me that Sandy didn't want anyone pretty interviewing her, so he had limited options and was forced to put her on it because I was too attractive."

What was I hearing? It sounded like she was talking about me but . . .

"She's lording it over us. She's off to Paris. Poor Harry, having to spend time with that thing."

My heart was thumping through my chest. I knew they didn't like me, but I'd never heard anything like this. It was so venomous and so unfair. I was frozen to the spot. My eyes began to water. I couldn't go back to my desk without running into poisonous Emily so I turned and headed out of the door and toward the back stairwell before anyone could see me cry. As soon as I was through the fire exit, I couldn't hold back any longer. I didn't have a tissue so I pulled the sleeves of my gray turtleneck down over my hands and held them under my eyes to catch the tears. There was nothing I could do to stop them from falling and taking my mascara with them.

What had I ever done to Emily? She'd never taken the time to get to know me. She'd decided I wasn't good enough, or that I thought I was too good. I wasn't sure which. Full body sobbing came next, I just gave into it and let it happen. No one could hear me, I was the only one that ever used the stairs. I stumbled down a few flights to get farther away from their poison. *Is it true what they were saying? Did I get the Sandy Fox interview because I'm ugly?* I was so sick of putting up with their sniping. I didn't get it right all the time, and my lips got loose, but did I deserve her being so nasty? Just because I didn't want to go out with them on a Friday night or waste half the day talking about the latest celebrity sighting didn't mean I was evil or didn't have feelings that could be hurt.

I dug into my pocket, retrieved my phone and dialed Ash's number.

"Hey," I said.

"What's the matter?" Ash asked immediately. I couldn't hide anything from her.

Instead of sympathy Ash started laughing when I told her what had happened.

"It's not funny."

"It's fucking hilarious. As if anyone could think you were ugly. She's just jealous."

"They're always taking the piss out of what I wear."

"Well that's because for some reason you dress like a boarding-school virgin while you're at work. But that's okay. That doesn't make you ugly, it makes you a conservative dresser. They're being ridiculous."

That started a fresh round of sobbing. I felt so sorry for myself and I was so sick of feeling like a leper. I just wanted to do a good job. I didn't understand what I'd done to deserve Emily's hatred. I was exhausted. Tired of trying so hard, working long hours, making everything as perfect as I could. It just didn't seem worth it. The downstairs fire door crashed open and I froze. My tears were on hold.

"Haven, are you still there?" Ash asked.

"Shhhh. There's someone here," I whispered.

"Where are you?"

"In the back stairwell. No one comes here—not normally."

"Who is it?"

I was stuck. I couldn't go back into the office because I was sure I looked like a raccoon that had just been run over. Footsteps began to clip the metal stairs. *Shit.*

I turned to face the wall with some vain hope that if I couldn't see whoever was coming, they wouldn't be able to see me. The footsteps got louder and then stopped.

"Haven?" asked a familiar voice behind me.

"I've got to go," I said to Ash and hung up.

"Hi, Harry." I turned around and kept my eyes fixed on the floor. At least when he'd caught me wearing pig pajamas I'd been drunk, so he hadn't been around when the embarrassment set in. Now, I got to feel it in real time.

"Haven? What—I—are you okay?"

I nodded and continued to stare at my shoes. My virginal boarding-school shoes. A shudder of sobs gathered in my belly and my tears started anew.

"Jesus, what's wrong? I hope this isn't because I missed the meeting this morning."

I pathetically attempted to punch him, but he grabbed my hand and pulled his arms around me, holding me to him.

Fuck, I was confused. Upset, but slightly happy at the same time. I wanted to laugh and cry. It was so good to have him here, close to me, comforting me.

"What's the matter with you?" he asked.

I shook my head. "Nothing." I gulped and I put my arms around his waist.

"It doesn't sound like nothing. It doesn't feel like nothing," he said, stroking my back.

We stood for ages, him rhythmically moving his hands up and down, my breath slowly returning to normal. A couple of times I tried to move away from him a little. He just pulled me tighter.

"Tell me what happened," he said again.

I shook my head into his chest. It felt good, too good. I could get used this. I twisted and he loosened his arm around me.

"I'm sorry, I didn't want anyone to see me like this."

"Don't apologize. Is there anything I can do? Want me to kick his butt?"

"What?" I looked at him. "No, it's not anything like that. It's work crap."

He didn't say anything, just watched me with those pale-blue eyes. "Don't. If you're nice to me, I won't be able to hold it together," I said. "You should go inside."

"Okay, well, if you want to talk, I'm around."

I snorted. *Very attractive.* He was never around.

"Today I'm around, and I'm always at the end of a phone."

My stomach tilted. He was being so kind. No one ever saw me like this. No one except Ash and Luke. Since my parents died, I hadn't let anyone else in. Harry had seen a side of me that was reserved for those I allowed close to me.

"Thanks. I'm fine," I said as I swiped my eyes with the sleeves of my sweater and took a deep breath.

"If you're interested, a little gallery is showing some of my photographs on Wednesday, you could come along with a friend or two if you wanted. It might cheer you up." He pulled out his wallet and handed me a card.

"Okay, so this is why you keep disappearing." I smiled at him.

"No, well, I suppose a little, but I don't need to be here all the time. I'm just helping out. This isn't my full-time job. Don't bust my balls about it."

I shrugged. He was being so nice, I shouldn't be giving him a hard time. I wanted things to go back to normal between us, to before he'd seen me so open and upset. "Sorry," I mumbled.

"Well, you know what happens when you roll your eyes. I'm only giving you a pass this time because of the tears. You do it again and I'll kiss you again." He grinned and his eyes did that crinkling thing.

Warmth radiated from my stomach and spread everywhere. I couldn't look at him. The thought of him kissing me again made me want to touch him. I reached out and tugged on his jacket sleeve. "Thank you for being so nice to me."

He moved closer and his hand found the back of my neck. He planted a kiss on the top my head. "Are you okay now?"

My heart racing, I managed to reply, "Yes, you go. I'm going to splash some water on my face. I'll be a minute."

"Come find me later if you want to talk."

I nodded and he headed on up the stairs.

I slumped against the wall. I peered at the card he'd given to me. It was nice of him to invite me, although it was probably just because he felt sorry for me. But maybe I'd go if Ash or Luke wanted to come with me. I'd like to see how Harry spent his time outside the office.

Jake

The exhibition of my photography had definitely not been my idea, neither had the party to mark the new stuff I'd produced. I felt like a fraud standing amongst the artsy crowd. What was I doing? I should never have agreed to it. I took photographs because I enjoyed it, not because I wanted people to buy them. I had no interest in making money from them, and I would never consider myself an artist. I was just a cop's kid. Back in Chicago, my school friends would have kicked the shit out of me if I'd had any interests outside of baseball and beating the crap out of nerdy, artistic kids. Gay Dave, the gallery owner and my friend from college had formed a dual pronged attack with Beth. Eventually I'd given in and agreed to the showing just to get some peace.

"This is amazing," Beth whispered, scanning the gallery space.

"It's ridiculous," I said. "I have no idea how I let you talk me into it."

"Enjoy it, big brother. You can go back to telling me it's ridiculous later, but for now, just bask."

"I don't bask," I said, irritated.

"Don't we all know it?"

"What's that supposed to mean?"

"It means that you should learn to smell the roses a little more."

Beth was always nagging me to kick back and relax. But kicking back wasn't what got me up in the morning. It wasn't how I was wired.

"Just because you're doing it in your head doesn't mean I can't hear you growling at me."

"Yes, that's exactly what it means."

"I've known you too long, you can't hide that from me. Stop it. Is Robert coming?"

"I invited him." Well, technically he'd invited himself.

"Good. And other friends?"

"I don't have other friends." I'd asked Haven to come before I'd thought through the consequences, and now I was kind of embarrassed I had. Still, part of me was hoping she would come. I wanted to get to know her better.

"You know half of London, New York and Chicago. Stop being such a grump."

"Just because I know them doesn't mean they're my friends."

"How are you going to sell your work if you're not going to be your own best publicist? Tell me you invited people."

"Haven't you been listening? I'm not interested in selling my photographs."

"You're impossible."

"No, I just like my day job. This is something I do for fun. I agreed to the exhibition to get you and Dave off my back."

"Well, it just means we'll have to arrange another one for the summer. By then I'll have hacked into your computer and stolen your contacts list and emailed all of them about my supremely talented brother."

I couldn't help but grin. It was so nice to see her like this—happy and proud.

"If it makes you feel better, I did invite a couple of people from Rallegra. I don't know if they'll show, but just so you know, I'm not a total grump." Haven hadn't mentioned my invitation so I had no idea if she'd actually come.

Beth reached up and mussed my hair, so I did the same in return, which led to her backing off and yelping as intended. I started to laugh and she punched me. Dave came to my rescue.

"Darlings, no fighting. We've not drunk enough yet. What do you think of your show?"

"He's being a spoiled brat about the whole thing," Beth said.

A voice came from over my shoulder. "Well there's a shock." I spun around and found Haven grinning.

"Hey, you made it," I said to her.

"Very astute." She rolled her eyes. God, it was infuriating and cute in equal measure.

Beth poked me in the ribs. "Beth, Dave, this is Haven, Haven, this is my very annoying sister Beth and my friend Dave." She looked beautiful. Her hair was down again. I wondered for a second whether she'd worn it down specifically for me. And she was wearing red. *Wow*. She seemed softer and more relaxed than I normally saw her. I couldn't help but grin.

"This is Luke and Ash. You've met Ash before." Her cheeks

colored slightly and I grinned at the memory of her drunk in her pajamas in the street.

"Mr. Aston Martin, nice to meet you," Ash said.

"You see." I turned to Beth. "The DB9, basking."

She ignored me and introduced herself to Luke and Ash and I shook Luke's hand. I couldn't work out how he fit in to the picture. Ash was the best friend, that I understood. Was Luke the gay in their relationship, or her boyfriend? If she was involved with someone, she wouldn't have kissed me back, and she surely wouldn't have brought him here. Right?

"Sorry to be a drag, but I need to introduce you to some people, Harry," Dave interrupted our introductions.

"No. I warned you about this."

"Don't be a brat," Haven said.

"You took the words right out of my mouth," Beth agreed.

"So who's the blonde?" Dave asked as he dragged me through the crowd.

"A girl I work with. The one on the Sandy story."

"Really? Sandy didn't mention her. Probably because she's gorgeous and you're so obviously interested. It must be sending Sandy into a tailspin not having your full attention."

"I'm not interested, stop trying to make trouble."

Dave raised his eyebrows at me.

"What do you think of the guy? Does he play for your team?" I asked.

"Luke?" he clarified.

I nodded.

"Unfortunately not. Although I might try and turn him, he's very handsome."

I scowled at Dave. So Luke wasn't gay. And I wasn't a believer in the theory that men and women could be friends. He was either in Ash or Haven's underwear—or wanted to be.

"Let me introduce you to Daniel Armitage and his lovely wife Leah. Daniel, Leah, this is Jake Harrison, star of our show tonight."

"You're very talented," Leah said.

"Thanks. This isn't really my thing. I just do it for fun," I said.

"Oh, you're one of those are you?" Leah asked.

"One of what?"

"I've got one here," she said, squeezing her husband's arm. "Super talented and successful, but too modest to see it. Well, we love your work."

I nodded, hating the attention but trying not to be rude and excused myself. I scanned the room, trying to spot Haven. She wasn't where I'd left her. I wanted to get to the bottom of who Luke was to her.

chapter SEVEN

Haven

When we had arrived at the gallery, I'd wondered if we were in the right place. The exhibition was for a Jake Harrison. It was only when I saw Harry that I was convinced we hadn't got lost.

"These photographs are beautiful, Haven," Ash said, turning her head from right to left.

I nodded. "Yes, they're better than I expected." She was right, they were beautiful. I could see some portraits across the space from where we were, but we were surrounded by landscapes. They were huge and some of them were exposed in a way that gave them an abstract quality. But overwhelmingly, they were very romantic.

"Don't be a bitch," Luke said.

"I'm not, it's just, he works at Rallegra. I didn't expect him to be a serious, proper photographer. You know what Robert's like, he's always getting his friends jobs that they're not qualified for."

"I think Robert asked Jake, not the other way around. Jake's got so much on with raising the money for Elemental Energy that I don't think he would have done it for anyone else," Beth said.

I hadn't realized his sister was still around, I'd been too distracted by Harry's unexpected talent.

"Sorry, I wasn't trying to—"

"It's fine," she said as she rested her hand on my shoulder. "Really, I know Robert and he has loads of friends who dabble in things but aren't really interested in doing anything with their lives. You should know by now that Jake doesn't fall into that category."

I nodded politely. I supposed there was no specific example of him being another of Robert's posh-boy friends—apart from his confidence and that he disappeared every now and then. Harry did seem to be a little different.

"To be honest, I don't know a whole lot about him. Apparently, not even his name."

Beth threw her head back and laughed. "Jake Harrison. Harry is a nickname. But it's stuck and it suits him."

I had thought that Harry and I had become close, so it was a shock to realise I didn't even know his name. My cheeks heated. I felt ridiculous. And embarrassed that I'd assumed we had an intimacy that we clearly didn't. He'd kissed me. I'd kissed him back and it seemed I knew nothing about him. Something about that stung. I wanted to know more. I wanted to know everything.

"And what were you saying about energy something?" I asked.

"Oh, don't ask me about that! Jake always teases me that I can't keep anything in my head for longer than two seconds. I'd better go and find out where he's gone and stop him from snarling at whoever he's talking to. It was so good to meet you."

"So licky is licky even when I'm sober apparently," Ash said as Beth disappeared into the crowd.

"Stop calling him that." Harry was more than just handsome and I didn't like that Ash made him sound like something to ogle after.

"What? Is this the guy that you said was 'fine'?" Luke asked.

Ash nodded. I tried to distract them by wandering over to one of the many photographs on the wall. The one I faced was of a bridge in the Scottish highlands. The print was huge, it must have been six by three. There was a very wistful, romantic air about it. You could see the ends of the sunrise and the morning fog still clinging to the moss that had gathered on the rocks of the bridge. It was beautiful.

"Three thousand pounds!" I gasped when I saw the price.

"How much?" Ash asked. "Well, that explains the Aston Martin."

"No, it does not explain the Aston Martin," Ash said. "You really don't have a clue do you? He's not driving what he's driving by selling these photos. That comes from somewhere else."

"He can't help it if his father has money," Luke said. "Some people have easier starts in life. You can't resent them for it just because we struggled. We should be happy that others didn't have to." Luke had a way of shaming me like no one else could. I wanted to be a sister he could be proud of, but sometimes if felt like a hopeless quest.

I nodded and moved on to the next shot.

Over the next hour or so I caught glimpses of Harry chatting to various people throughout the evening, the ever-attentive Dave at his side. I was at the bar, refreshing our drinks when he appeared next to me.

"You still here? Thought you'd have given up with this boring old stuff before now."

"You think I can't appreciate art?" I asked.

"I didn't say that. Don't get shitty. I just meant these are a bunch of pictures I've taken, I'm not sure why anyone has stuck around."

"Free booze," I said, grinning. He must have known he was talented, but I liked the fact he was playing it down, that he was understated about what he did.

Jake nodded.

"Do you really not think they're any good or is it the attention you don't like?" I asked.

He looked at me, his eyes wandering to my lips and then back up, "I think they're okay. I think if I didn't know Dave, I wouldn't have an exhibition, and I definitely don't like the attention."

"So you *can* answer a straight question with a straight answer."

"Tell me when I haven't, other than when you've been deflecting a question from me."

It was true. He had always answered truthfully when I'd asked him a question. We smiled at each other and something in his eyes made me feel uncomfortable. It was as if he could see into me, to parts I worked hard to keep hidden and I felt exposed. My stomach tilted.

"So which one is your favorite?" I asked, trying to pull myself back into reality.

"It's not here. It's at home."

"The glamazon's minding it for you, is she?"

"What?" He seemed confused.

"Millie, I think her name was."

"Oh. Right. No. I don't think she ever saw it."

I smiled. "I'd better get back with these drinks."

He nodded. "I'm still meeting you at the studios tomorrow?"

"Yes, eight sharp. See you then if I don't see you later."

As we made our way home in a cab, my phone buzzed in my bag.

Harry: You looked beautiful tonight.

My stomach flipped. *How do I respond to that?*

"Who is it?" Ash asked. She was so nosy.

"Just from Harry, thanking us for coming."

"That's sweet," she said.

Ash and Luke exchanged another glance.

Haven: Thanks for the free booze. I liked your pictures.

It buzzed again.

Harry: Because of the alcohol? Nice.

Haven: Are you fishing for compliments?

Despite checking my phone every nine seconds for the rest of the evening I went to bed without a reply.

The next day I drove into Pinewood Studios at ten minutes before eight and found Harry already waiting for me in what had become his usual spot. Last time we'd been here, he'd kissed me. Part of me hoped it would happen again.

"You're early," I said as he opened his door.

"So I could nap," he said.

I smiled. "You're funny."

"I know. It's a natural talent I have."

"Did you have a good time last night?" I asked.

"Hmmm. In parts."

"I was sorry not to see Millie again." How come she hadn't been there? I wanted to see her properly, and I wanted to understand the dynamic between her and Harry. Maybe it was wishful thinking, but I found it difficult for me to picture him with a high-maintenance glamazon.

Harry stopped and looked at me, then continued with our walk toward the stage.

"So your hair's up again," he said.

"Very observant."

"Why did you wear it down last night?"

Why are we talking about my hair? "I normally have it down when I'm not at work or running."

"I like it down."

My heart skipped. I wasn't sure of the appropriate response. Did he just go around saying that to all the women he came across? Was I wrong to like it when he said things like that to me?

Jake

I'd decided that I wanted Haven and there wasn't much I didn't get when I set my mind to something. She was movie-star beautiful and didn't seem to realise it, and she was sharp and challenging and soft and vulnerable. I wanted to know her and I had to have her.

I needed to understand if Luke was going to be an issue, then I would convince her that she wanted me like I wanted her.

I'd had mixed signals from her so far. She'd kissed me back but then seemed unaffected in the post-kiss aftermath. She'd come to the gallery opening, but potentially brought her boyfriend. And now she was not so subtly asking about Millie. Next week we were in Paris, and if I couldn't seduce a woman in Paris then I'd chop my dick off.

Sandy came running up to us as we arrived. Things hadn't kicked off yet. The atmosphere on set was much more relaxed than last time.

"Harry, Harry, so sorry to have missed your exhibition. Dave said it was wonderful. You're so talented!"

I caught Haven rolling her eyes and grinned at her. I didn't know if it was Sandy or Sandy's flirting she didn't like.

"No worries. I'm sure you had better things to do."

"You look beautiful, Sandy," Haven said, using my words about her.

"Thanks. We're getting to know each other more and more. Can I introduce you to the director?"

"See what happens when you're nice to people?" I whispered to her as Sandy led her off toward the throng of people.

I took out my camera and started taking shots of Sandy from across the stage. She seemed to be constantly on show, as if she was aware there were people watching her at all times. It must have been exhausting. I pulled out the zoom a little so my shots included Haven. Her cheekbones sliced through the light. She was completely oblivious to the fact that anyone saw her.

She was clearly a little shy meeting the director, but Sandy did most of the talking for them. Eventually, the director stood up and Haven took her cue to come back to our seat. I continued to capture her as she came toward me.

"What are you doing?" she whispered. "You're meant to be photographing Sandy, not me."

"I've got plenty of her, don't worry." I grinned, and I could tell by the twitch at the corners of her lips that she was trying not to smile.

She fired up her laptop, as was her usual routine, and began tapping away.

"Have you got your angle now?"

"I'm not sure I need one. I'm just going to write what I see and not make a big deal of it. As Emily said, I'm not working for the—" she lifted her fingers in the air and made imaginary quotation marks "—New York fucking Times."

"Well, she's probably right, but come on, Paris might give you inspiration. Aren't you looking forward to it?"

She half-nodded.

I was looking forward to Paris. It was a great city. All about sex and romance.

"What flight are you on?" I asked her.

"I'm going by train. I'm not crazy about flying."

"I love flying. What are you scared of?"

"I'm always astounded when people ask me that. I don't know . . . what could it possibly be? Perhaps the falling out of the sky and dying thing?"

I chuckled. "Fair enough. I'll get the train with you. It'll be easier with my equipment anyway."

"You don't have to travel with me."

"I know." I wanted to spend every minute I could with her.

"Hey, sleepyhead." She had drifted off about twenty minutes ago and her head had fallen on my shoulder as the train sped through the French countryside. The announcement that we were pulling into Gare du Nord had disturbed her. I'd managed to take a few shots of her sleeping, which I was sure she'd give me hell for. I couldn't resist. She looked so peaceful, so beautiful.

"I wasn't asleep. I was just resting my eyes."

"You sound like my grandma," I said.

"You're full of compliments. Let a girl wake up before you overwhelm her with your charm." Her voice was croaky, sexy.

"I thought you weren't sleeping?"

That earned me the back of her hand in my stomach. "Careful, if you resort to physical violence I might have to kiss you again."

"Well, we wouldn't want that, would we?" she replied.

"Speak for yourself." I grinned at her.

The redness in her cheeks widened my grin.

I grabbed her bag and headed to the door. We were staying at the W in Opéra, so not far from the station.

"I think we should get the Metro," she said as I led her toward the taxi line. "We won't be able to claim back cab fare."

"Don't worry, I've got it covered."

"Of course you do. Or should I say, thank you Harry's trust fund."

"I can assure you that I don't have a trust fund." Jesus, I was trying to be nice. How could she turn me paying for a cab into something that undermined my entire character? "You have no idea, Haven, so zip it before I do more than kiss you."

That shut her up, and we drove silently to the hotel.

Once we were checked in, we were shown up to our rooms by a porter. We were next door to each other and I couldn't help but grin at the coincidence. I liked the thought of her naked in the shower with just a wall between us.

"I thought Sandy would have arranged for you to have a room next to hers," Haven said.

I glanced at her and shook my head. There was no point responding. She clearly hadn't managed to sleep off her bad mood.

"They said they would start filming at ten this morning. Shall I see you in the lobby in ten minutes?" I asked.

"Sure, but I can probably hear the television through the wall, so no porn," she said. She was definitely getting kissed for that. Later.

At the agreed time, I made my way to the lobby. Haven was waiting for me. Of course she was. Most of the filming in Paris was taking place outside. Although there were apparently a few scenes in cafes, that meant being in the cold for most of the day and Haven was prepared to the point it was almost comical. She really didn't seem to care that she looked a little insane.

"You look warm." If I didn't know her better, I'd say she was smuggling duvets under her coat and she had at least two scarves on and a hat. She could barely move her arms.

"I'm a little too warm, actually. Let's get outside."

"You know this isn't Antarctica don't you?"

"I'm not good in the cold. You'll be laughing on the other side of your face when you're frozen to the bone later on."

I couldn't not laugh at her. She made it too easy. "Come on." I put my hand on her lower back and guided her out.

When we arrived at the set we found people running about in different directions, shouting and waving. It all seemed very chaotic. We were ushered to our pre-assigned chairs, which Haven struggled to get into because of all her extra layers. There was no sign of Sandy, Phil or the director. Haven would be pleased not to have missed anything.

The sun was out and Haven stripped off her hat, taking with it her ever-present, neatly arranged bun. "Can you hold this for me?" she said passing me her hat, and pulling out the pins that held the last of her hair. As it all tumbled down, it winded me. I picked up my camera and began taking shots of her. At first she was so focused on getting her hair under control that she didn't notice me.

"What are you doing?" she said more softly than I expected when she eventually realized what I was up to.

"Taking beautiful pictures."

"Harry, no."

I put my camera down. "Call me Jake." The only people who called me Jake were my family and a few old buddies back in Chicago, but I wanted Haven to use my real name. My friends used my nickname and I didn't want to be a friend to her.

"What?"

"I don't want to be Harry to you. Call me Jake."

She watched me studiously, her mouth half open as if she was about to ask me a question. She didn't, though, and her lips curled into a breath-taking smile.

"Okay, J—"

"He's here!" Sandy's voice cut across our connection and swiftly Haven finished securing her hair, took a seat and opened her laptop.

"Hey, Sandy." I greeted her with a kiss on the cheek.

"Harry, we're in Paris, there's going to be lots of French kissing. Get ready!" she said as Phil directed her toward the front of the crew.

"Holy hell," I muttered to myself.

"Like I said, a sure thing," Haven said. I didn't reply. She surely couldn't think I was interested, even if Sandy *was* a sure thing.

The scene that they were shooting was an argument between Sandy and her male co-star, Bobby. As usual, we couldn't hear anything and so we sat watching, trying to seem interested.

We'd never gotten to see the script, so from time to time we guessed what was going on. Sandy was waving her hands in the air and Bobby seemed exasperated. "I think he left his pants on the bedroom floor," I said.

"No, she's really mad. I think he asked her to try anal."

I spat out my coffee. "Jesus. You sound like you're talking from experience."

Haven laughed. "Yeah, I waved my arms about just like that."

I joined in her laughter.

"I imagine your girlfriend Millie doesn't take such offense," she said.

Did I hear her right? "Wow. There are so many things wrong with that statement I don't know where to go with it. The fact that you might have imagined Millie and me discussing anal sex is just plain disturbing, and then there's you insinuating that's what I'm into. I think that constitutes a record for you in terms of how many insults you can pack into a single statement. Anyone would think you're asking to get kissed by me."

"I was trying to be funny."

"And, another thing. She's my ex-girlfriend."

chapter EIGHT

Haven

Shit, did I piss him off? I couldn't tell sometimes. I thought we were having fun with the anal joke. I had difficulty navigating boundaries with new people. Somewhere Harry, or Jake, or whoever he was, had stopped being a new person in my head. I'd forgotten myself. I certainly wasn't asking to get kissed. Well, that wasn't quite true, but I didn't want it to happen because I'd offended him. And *ex*-girlfriend? That was new information.

"Sorry—"

The crowd started mumbling. I pulled my eyes from Jake and focused on the crew. People were breaking for lunch. That meant my time to speak to Sandy was up. Phil came over and I hopped off my chair.

"Haven, sweetie, I think Sandy might be coming down with something. She's not going to be able to do lunch. Mucho apologies."

"He knows that was Italian not French right?" Jake said as Phil disappeared.

"Do you think she's really sick?" I asked.

Jake shrugged. "Let's go and get some lunch."

When we came back to set an hour later, there were a few people milling about, but it was very quiet. "I wonder what's going on," I said to Jake. "Something seems off."

"Let me go investigate."

He strode toward one of the people I'd seen operating the camera. They chatted as if they were old friends. I watched as Jake charmed the pants off him. God, he was dangerous. My heart quickened as I thought about our kiss and how easily I'd given in to him, like he had some unseen power over me. It was frightening. I liked to be in control, to be able to predict what was going to happen next. My pants needed to stay firmly on. As he made his way back to me, Jake stopped and chatted to a number of other people, laughing and making them laugh. It seemed he was old friends with all of them.

"Sandy and the director are fighting apparently," Jake said as he returned.

Phil came over to us, more red faced than usual. "I'm sorry guys. I don't think there will be anything else happening today. I suggest you go and enjoy Paris."

"Really?" I said. "What's happened? Is Sandy upset? I thought she was having a hard time this morning."

Phil pursed his lips. "I can't say anything. There's been a few creative differences." He threw his hands up in the air. "I've said too much already. Please assure me I'm not on the record."

I shook my head. "Your secret is safe with me."

When Phil left, I turned to Jake. "Poor guy. Who'd have his job?"

"I think it sounds like fantastic news. Let's do what he says and go and enjoy Paris." Jake grinned.

"I can't, this is a working day. I should go back to the hotel and catch up with some of the work I'm missing."

"Over my dead body. You're in this amazing city, Haven. Let your hair down. Literally and figuratively."

I grinned at him. What was his obsession with my hair?

"I can't. I have a million emails to send," I said.

"No one will ever know. They think you're on set. For me?" he asked.

I started to chew the inside of my cheek. I wanted to go with him but I really should be working.

"I'm going to take you to my favorite place in Paris," he said, and I knew I had to go with him.

"So basically, you could have brought us anywhere in Paris, and you chose *The Gates of Hell*?" I asked, glancing up at him. We had arrived at the Rodin Museum and we were staring up at one of his most famous works.

Jake threw his head back and belly laughed. "I suppose."

I followed the sinewy bodies up and down, trying to make sense of the shapes as they merged into each other. "Is it a metaphor?" I asked.

"The door?" he asked.

"No, our trip here."

"A metaphor for what?"

"For what's next," I replied. Were we at the start of something between us? Did he think it was going to be difficult? Was this a warning?

"I hope not," he said and he clasped and released the top of my arm, making my skin tingle underneath my layers.

I tried to concentrate on Rodin's door. I'd seen stuff of his before but this was so . . . disturbing.

We made our way through the museum. "See, this is beautiful," I said, pointing to a small plaster sculpture of a couple kissing. "Eternal Springtime," I read from the plaque.

"It's not so different to the Gates," Jake said.

I watched him. How could he think they were at all similar? Love and hell were the same thing? Was that what he was saying?

"See, the desperation is the same. The frustration. It's in these figures as much as the ones trying to escape hell."

"How depressing," I replied.

"I don't think it's depressing at all." He smiled at me and his eyes did that crinkly thing at the corner and my stomach tilted. I felt as if we were on dangerous territory.

"Okay, what about this one, Mr. Art Critic?" I pointed to a small bronze of a man whose arms and legs were everywhere.

"Yeah, that's just a guy getting hammered. There's no meaning there."

I laughed. "*Bacchus in the Vat,*" I read from the sign. "You're right."

"I'm always right."

I rolled my eyes and followed him across the room.

"This is my favorite," he said as he stilled in front of "*The Kiss*."

Of course, it was just a representation, but it was such an intimate sculpture. "It's like we're peeping Toms," I said.

He nodded. "It's intense."

"And beautiful," I said as I stared up at the tangle of limbs.

"You can tell he thinks she's totally worth it," he said softly.

"I think he's cast a spell on her. She looks . . ." I couldn't finish what I was saying. I was aware of Jake's eyes on me and I daren't meet them or I might be cast under the same spell as the woman in front of me.

After the Rodin Museum we wandered across to *Ile de la Cité*.

"Tell me about Luke," Jake said as he gestured for me to sit at a table outside one of the cafes. He looked at me as he ordered some wine from our waiter. He didn't even try to speak French.

"What do you want to know?" I asked as the waiter scurried away.

"Anything. Pick something." Jake moved his chair closer to mine and his thighs brushed my knees.

Where was he going with this? "He's a lawyer, although I think he'd prefer to have done something creative. He'd never tell me that, but I think he probably regrets that he didn't do something else. When he was younger, he wanted to be a chef."

"What else?" He looked at me as if he could pull out all my secrets with a blink of his eyes.

I unwrapped my scarf from my neck and opened the top buttons of my coat. "We're close. We always were and then after our parents—and Ash has been in love with him for the longest time."

He grinned. “Ash is in love with your brother?”

“What’s so funny?”

“It’s just, until about a minute ago, I thought Luke might be your boyfriend.”

“Ewww, that’s gross.”

“I thought so too. Any other men in your life I need to know about?”

My heart jumped in my chest. *What was he asking me?* “Jake.”

He reached across and cupped my neck, pushing his fingers into the bottom of my bun. “Take your hair down, Haven.”

I paused, not knowing how to respond. My fingers fumbled over his as I pulled out a pin, and then another. There were five altogether. After the third my hair started to sag. I took a deep breath and took out the final two.

“I like it like this,” he whispered and leaned into me and placed a small kiss on my neck.

I closed my eyes. “What are you doing?”

“What you’ve been thinking about me doing all day,” he replied as he lowered his lips to my neck again.

My skin heated as if I were being branded by him. What was happening? I didn’t fall for men like him, but every part of my mind and body was being pulled toward him. I turned slightly as he shifted his head so our foreheads met.

Here we were, at the gate to somewhere. I just hoped it wasn’t hell.

“I want to go back to the hotel with you,” he whispered.

I started to chew the inside of my cheek. I wanted to go back to the hotel with him too.

I reached up and quickly pecked him on the lips and pulled away, creating a newly formed gap between our bodies.

"Jake, stop," I said. I needed space before I lost all control.

He raised his eyebrows. "I bet you are so sweet on my tongue."

"I'm serious," I whispered. "I can't go back to the hotel with you. We're colleagues and you're . . . "

Jake

I put my fingers to her lips. I wanted her to stop giving herself an explanation as to why she wasn't going to sleep with me. I'd have her in Paris and she knew it. We were being drawn to each other.

"Let's go," I said, indicating to our waiter that I wanted our bill.

"I'll get this," Haven said, reaching for the ticket.

"No you won't. Don't try and argue with me."

We flagged down a cab back to the hotel.

"I can't sleep with you Jake," she said. Her eyes were on her lap as she twisted her hands. She wasn't very convincing.

"Maybe not today," I replied.

Although we didn't speak, the silence between us wasn't heavy, it was just the buzz of something to come and I was impatient.

We took the elevator to our rooms.

"I'll see you tomorrow," she said.

"We should eat, we've not had dinner," I said.

"I'm tired. I want to get into my pajamas and lie brainless in front of the television. I think I'll order room service."

"Great idea. Give me ten minutes, you can change, I can shower, and I'll be back and we can have room service." I grinned. If we weren't going to sleep together, then just being with her was the next best thing.

She rolled her eyes. "Room service isn't a euphemism you know," she said.

I laughed. "I know. If you try and jump me, I'll be offended."

She shook her head. "Okay. Don't be long because I'm hungry."

I unlocked the door to my room. I dumped my bags and went into the bathroom to splash my face with cold water.

Shit. I liked her. *Shit.* I really liked her.

I kicked off my shoes and grabbed my phone, finding my sister's number in my recently dialed history.

"How's Paris? Been to see Rodin's naked bodies yet?" she asked.

"Am I so predictable? But yeah, this afternoon."

"Did you take Haven?"

"Why do you ask?"

"I think you like her. I think you'd want her to see your favorite place in Paris."

I smiled into the phone. "I think I like her too."

"Does she like you?"

"I think she's holding herself back, stopping herself. I need to find out why. You people with the vaginas are so complicated."

"Don't blame it on the vaginas, brother, or I'm going to start to talk to you about penises, then you're going to heave and it's all going to go very badly."

"Point taken."

"Listen, if I know you at all, I know you always get exactly what you set out for. If you want her bad enough, you'll make it happen."

She was right. I needed to encourage Haven to let go and take a risk with me.

Haven opened her door with a hairbrush in her hand. I took in her hair spread across her shoulders, semi covering a lace camisole. Jesus, her tits were amazing. How had I not noticed them before? She'd taken off her make-up and she seemed more beautiful, if that was possible.

My gaze travelled down her body. She was wearing pajamas similar to the ones she had on when I bumped into her in the street. They clung tight like leggings across her body.

Room service might have been a mistake. I wasn't sure I would be in control of what I was doing if I stepped across the threshold.

"Haven."

"Don't look at me like that," she said. She released the door and headed back into her bedroom. It was as much of an invitation as I was going to get. I took it, and strode in after her. I followed her across the room. As she realized I was heading toward her she spun around to face me and backed away. I kept walking and she moved back until she couldn't go any farther. My body was just inches from hers.

"Give me the hairbrush," I said.

"What? Why? I'm not going to hit you with it," she replied.

"Hairbrush," I repeated, in a low, controlled tone.

She reluctantly gave it to me. I took her hand and led her back over to the bed. I took a seat and pulled her between my knees. "Turn round."

"You're not going to hit me with it either, right?" she asked, her eyes wide.

"Jesus Haven, I'm going to brush your hair. Why do you think I might hit you with the hairbrush?"

She shrugged. "I don't know what you're into. I've read *Fifty Shades of Grey*."

"What, and he hits her with a hairbrush?"

She laughed. "No, but . . ."

She turned around and I started to brush her hair. "I'm not going to hit you—I would never do that. When we sleep together, I'll be in charge, make no mistake, but I'm never going to hit you."

"*When* we sleep together?"

"Yes, when. It won't be tonight, but it will happen, Haven."

She turned back around to face me. "I'm not a possession to have and then throw away, Jake," she said.

"I know." I cupped her face in my hand.

"And I'm not going to have sex with you."

"Soon," I said. I was even surer of that now. Every moment I spent with her, my feelings for her grew. I wanted to spend time with her, share things with her.

"No, Jake."

"Shhhh." I turned her back around and set to work freeing the knots from her hair.

"How long have you and Ash known each other?"

"Since we were two. Our mothers were best friends. I know what she's thinking before she does."

"And Luke's not interested in her?"

She glanced over her shoulder at me. "Why? Are you?" Was she jealous at the mention of another woman? That I could work with.

I fell back onto the bed, pulling her down next to me. "I think you know that the only person I'm interested in is you."

I propped myself up on my elbow as she lay on her back, watching me as I looked at her.

"I think you're used to getting what you want," she said, giving me a small amount of insight into why she was holding herself back. I couldn't argue, she was right.

"And I think I've become a challenge," she continued.

"Maybe that's true." I liked that she was challenging, that she hadn't just given in to me, but that wasn't it for me. Haven was a total package and I liked the whole thing.

"I think that when you've conquered that challenge, you'll be on to the next."

I couldn't blame her for assuming that, but I knew myself well enough to know that wasn't it. "I can understand why you would think that," I said as I trailed my fingers across her full, red lips and down her neck.

"You're not going to try and convince me that that's not what will happen?"

I shook my head as my hand continued its journey between her breasts.

"How come?" she asked, her words uneven as she tried to keep her breath steady. I smiled at her reaction and bent to kiss her.

chapter NINE

Haven

What was I thinking, letting him in my room? I must be crazy. I was in my pig pajamas for god's sake.

As he dragged his lips across mine in a half kiss, my body bowed to his and I pushed up my chin. *What is he doing? What am I doing?* I put my hand to his chest in the hopes of pushing him away, but as my palm met the hard, hot surface of him, I wanted to feel more.

I reached up to his shoulders, which were straining the material of his shirt. I wanted him closer. His hand trailed from my neck to my waist, pulling me deeper under his spell. I knew I shouldn't give in to him, but it was as if I had no choice.

He moved his leg between mine, the denim of his jeans scraping against the cotton of my pajamas. His hot breath was sweet on my skin just before his tongue pushed between my lips and gently traced the underside of sensitive flesh. *Holy crap*.

My breaths came short in my throat and my mouth widened, my tongue desperate to meet his again. He crashed against me like he couldn't wait a moment longer, my groans meeting his.

He shifted so he was on top of me, the weight of him all consuming. His erection pushed against my thigh and I wondered how long it would be until he was inside me. My fingers pressed into the hard muscles of his back. He felt so good, so right—as if he were mine.

"Jake," I whispered as his lips moved to explore my neck. My hands found his hair. "Jake." He went lower, not stopping at my cotton-covered breasts, down to my stomach and the exposed skin between my camisole and the waistband of my pajamas.

"Do you want me to stop?" he asked as he paused and watched me looking at him.

Stop? Why would I want him to stop kissing me? I shook my head and he smiled. His kisses travelled to one hip and then to the other, his teeth skimming my skin in the most delicious dance. Air breezed over my stomach as my camisole rode up and Jake started to pull at my pajamas. I twisted my body to discourage him, but it did anything but.

"Jake," I said, sitting up on my elbows. What was he doing?

"Do you trust me?" he asked.

Did I? I knew I shouldn't, he was way too handsome, too charming, too . . . "I don't know."

"Trust me, baby. I'm going to make you feel so good."

He brought my pajamas down, revealing my nakedness and I rolled onto my stomach in embarrassment.

"Haven, no." He pulled at my hips, turning me back toward him. "Don't turn away from me. Not ever."

I stopped resisting him. I couldn't say no to him, didn't want to.

He hooked my leg over his shoulder and slid his hands under my ass as he began kissing my inner thigh, higher and higher.

"Jake, what are you doing?"

"Shhhh." He quietened me like his kisses were opium. His lips were soft and gentle with an undercurrent of passion, hiding, waiting.

His mouth went straight to my clitoris, circling the nub of nerves and it started pulsing, coming to life. He slid lower and the torture of his tongue leaving one place was replaced with the ecstasy of it reaching another. I began to give in to him, then I remembered where I was and who I was with.

"No," I said sharply, and scrambled from underneath him.

He caught my wrist. "What is it?"

"I just . . . "

"Did you come and I didn't notice?" He grinned at me.

"No, I just . . . I won't." I was starting to panic at the thought of what was happening.

"What?" he asked, dragging me back to him.

"I won't. I won't be able to. Come. Not with you."

I'd had one serious boyfriend and he was the only one to ever make me come, and it had taken him months of trying. In the end I think my clitoris took pity on him. I'd given up hoping that I'd have something more with a lover.

He looked at me quizzically for a second, then growled. "Oh yes you will." He pulled my legs open and pushed his tongue against me. Just as it got to be too much he slid his fingers into me. I hadn't any strength left and collapsed back onto the bed.

"Shit, Jake."

He didn't say anything, he just kept his rhythm pushing and pulling, licking and sucking, circling and pressing. My breath was being chased out of my lungs as he drove me higher and higher. I fisted the sheets below me.

The sensation of his touch and his tongue and his breath coursed through my body, reaching the tips of my fingers.

At some point I lost control. In that moment, my body belonged to him. I belonged to him.

From somewhere far away my orgasm came barreling toward me, quickly surging, pushing. What. Was. Happening? It was loud, like thunder. A huge wave crashed over me, wiping me out. My eyes clamped shut and my lids burned red.

I came back down to earth, panting and barely conscious. Jake was pulling up my pajamas and I managed to lift my ass to help him.

"You look beautiful," he said softly and disappeared into the bathroom. I was sure I looked like I'd been in the very thunderstorm that had just passed through my body.

When he returned less than a minute later with two glasses of water, I hadn't moved.

"Hey," I said.

"Hey," he replied as he set the glasses on the cabinet by the bed and crawled up the mattress and sat against the pillows. "Come here." He held out his arm, gesturing me toward him. I was unsure of this bit. Did he expect me to take the lead? I moved nearer to him and he pulled me closer, my head on his chest. "You okay?"

I nodded. "I don't normally . . ."

"So you said." He chuckled.

"Don't be an asshole about it." I was so embarrassed by my confession, which was compounded by the fact that he'd proven me wrong.

"I love that I made you come, Haven. It will be the first of many times. Relax and get used to it."

My belly flipped over and then over again. I couldn't wait.

I smoothed my hand across his chest, feeling his heartbeat thumping through the fabric of his T-shirt. As I moved my hand lower he caught it.

"Stop," he said. "I won't be able to control myself."

"That's okay," I whispered. I was more than ready for him. I wanted to see how far that small scar on his upper arm spread. I wanted to check his body for others.

"No, it's not okay. I don't want you to be rushed into this, I should have resisted you back there. It's too important to fuck up so early."

"You don't want to, you know . . . ?"

He chuckled and pulled my chin up, forcing my eyes to his. "I think you can see I've got a hard-on the size of Africa—"

"Show off," I said. But he wasn't wrong. There was nothing he needed to be shy about in the locker room.

He laughed. "I just meant that's how it feels. I wasn't trying to tell you what a huge penis I had."

"Okay, if you say so."

"And in any event, you'll find out soon enough."

I prodded him in his abs and he feigned injury, then squeezed me toward him, kissing the top of my head.

We lay in comfortable silence, his heartbeat calming the anxiety building in my stomach. The regular rhythm drowned out my thoughts of consequences and what would happen next.

"I don't want you to go," I said. It was the truth, but saying it made me feel so vulnerable.

"There's no place I have to be."

Jake

With the images of her coming so hard I thought she might pass out and the remembered feel of her in my arms, it took about four hours and copious thoughts of my grandma to get my hard-on under control.

I'd wanted her for a while now, but she had surpassed all my incredibly high expectations. Her milky-white skin was soft like feathers and she was responsive and passionate despite her vulnerabilities. She had assured me I wouldn't be able to make her come, but all she needed was to open up and let someone take control.

For a moment she had let me in and it was like she'd let me see a part of her soul. I felt a sense of responsibility, a sense of ownership. I had to get this right.

Her breathing became even and deep—she'd fallen asleep in my arms, in Paris. It was perfect.

I woke to water running in the bathroom.

"Hey, did my snoring wake you?" I asked her as she appeared at the door.

She shook her head. "I think I was cold."

We were still on top of the covers. "Let's get under," I said, pulling back the sheets. She was tentative as she got in. "Scoot closer. We can share body heat."

She grinned at me and wrapped her arm around my waist as she got into bed.

"What are we doing?" she asked, laughing. "How did we end up here, with me in my pig pajamas?"

"I'll tell you what we're not going to do." She looked up at me. "We're not going to dissect and analyze this. We're just going to go with it. Deal?" Haven could get so negative and she was able to talk herself out of any sense of pleasure. I wasn't going to let that happen.

"Another deal? Does that mean the first one is null and void?"

"Nah uh. You still have to tell me the truth, the whole truth and nothing but the truth."

She leaned forward and kissed me on my chest. Within seconds she was asleep again. I smiled to myself.

I woke before her the next morning. "I'm going to grab a shower. We have to be at the set in forty-five minutes."

"What the what?" she said, suddenly wide awake. "Shit."

"Wow, you wake up fast. This is good to know," I said, wiggling my eyebrows at her.

"Don't be a pervert." She flung a pillow at me, and I leaned forward to kiss her quickly on the lips.

"Morning."

Her blush spread across her throat.

"Morning," she replied coyly.

"You look beautiful when you sleep."

“Was I snoring?” she asked, seemingly horrified.

“No, you were perfect.” I kissed her again, this time the kiss was deeper, and she pulled me closer to her. She wanted me. I groaned against her mouth and it brought her back to the present. She jerked away. My stomach dropped.

“Shit, I have to get in the shower.” She grinned at me and pecked me once on the lips and disappeared into the bathroom.

Part of me had been worried that Haven would have closed down on me completely overnight, but the opposite seemed to be true. I had the shit-eating grin and just-kissed lips to prove it.

“I’ll see you downstairs in twenty minutes,” I shouted through the bathroom door.

“Yeah, in your dreams. Make it thirty.”

When we arrived on location, it was pretty much deserted, despite the fact we were late. Haven looked confused.

I went to find someone who could fill us in.

“Didn’t someone call you?” one of the grips asked. “Sandy hasn’t come out of her hotel. We don’t know if we’ll get anything done today.”

“I thought it was the last day of filming?”

“It was meant to be, but who knows what will happen now. Phil’s in there trying to talk her off a cliff.”

I went back over to Haven. “Sandy is still mid-tantrum, apparently. Phil’s trying to calm her down.”

“Why don’t you call her or text her? I think she’d do anything for you.”

I watched her, trying to make out whether or not she was being snide, but she didn’t seem to be. “You think?”

She nodded.

"I might make it worse," I said.

"I'm not sure how that's possible. And make it good. Flirt. You're talented at that."

"I don't flirt with her."

"I wasn't talking about her." She grinned, and it was infectious.

I typed out a text.

Harry: We're missing you down here, beautiful girl. Paris isn't the same without you.

"Oh, you're good," Haven said when I showed her what I'd written.

"You know I don't mean it, though."

"Get a grip and press send."

I wasn't sure if it was my text, but eventually Sandy made an appearance after lunch as if nothing had happened.

"Harry," she squealed at me and ran over, throwing her arms around my neck. "It's nice to know you missed me."

"We all did," I said, trying not to encourage her attentions any more than I already had.

"And you're coming to the party tonight?"

"Sure, we both are. Right Haven?"

Haven nodded.

"I can't wait. I've got something very short and very sexy to show you." She winked at me, spun around and headed off.

"Now look what you've got me into," I said to Haven.

"I think you can handle it. Anyway, I'm sure that not even you get movie stars offering themselves up to you every day of the week. Perhaps you should take her up on it."

"I'm going to fuck *you* in Paris. I'm not interested in her," I replied, enjoying the blush that spread across her throat as I did.

"Maybe I got off and that's it for me. Had my fun."

I reached across and stroked that beautiful face of hers. "You know that's not even close to being true. There's plenty of fun left to be had."

The end of filming party was being held at Buddha Bar. Haven refused to let me in her room while she was getting ready, saying I was a distraction so I had a restless forty-five minute wait for her in the hotel bar.

When she walked in, I had to work hard to keep my cool. She looked incredible. Her hair was tumbling across her shoulders in waves and her eyes were sparkling. I couldn't stop staring at her.

"You're amazing. Sandy won't be happy."

"What?"

"You know how she likes the spotlight. Everyone is going to be looking at you tonight, you're so beautiful."

I tilted her chin toward me and kissed her lightly on the lips.

"What do you want to drink?"

"Shouldn't we get going?"

"I think we have time for a drink. I need to have you to myself for a little while." If it had been up to me we wouldn't be going to the party. I didn't want to share her.

She grinned and took a seat. A waiter came and got our drinks order.

"Harry?" I heard a familiar voice behind me.

I turned around. "Hal," I said surprised. I stood up and shook his hand. "Good to see you."

"I would ask what you're doing here, but given your company, I don't need to." He was staring at Haven and my temperature began to rise. He needed to keep his eyes off my girl.

"Hal, this is my friend Haven. Haven, this is Hal."

"A pleasure to meet you." Hal leaned over, took Haven's hand and kissed her knuckles. "I'm Harry's soon-to-be business partner."

"Soon to be?" I asked.

"I was just talking about you with my corporate finance guy. He said your numbers were solid. I think you're going to make me a rich man. Again."

"Well, that's great news. We should talk. I'd like to get my guy from Palo Alto signed up like, yesterday. And if you and I can finalize things, I'll need to stand down the other potential investors."

"Yeah, about that. If you didn't want to put the whole fifteen mil in, I'm sure we could come to some arrangement and I could take a bigger slice of the equity."

I laughed. His corporate finance guy must have really liked my numbers. "I'm comfortable with the fifteen mil, but thanks for the offer."

"It was worth a try. Let's talk on Monday. I'll leave you to your beautiful girl. Have a good night."

"What was that?" Haven asked as I sat down.

"That was the beginning of Elemental Energy. Fuck, this is brilliant. Now we've got even more to celebrate."

"Elemental Energy?"

"The business I've been working to get funding for," I replied. This trip to Paris had exceeded my expectations in so many ways.

"Oh, exciting. What was the fifteen million about?"

"My investment. I think he wants a bigger slice of the pie." I was a little distracted, my mind ticking over next steps with Hal.

"And you're putting in fifteen million?"

I nodded. We needed things on paper before I turned down the other investors. Hal didn't do anything on a handshake.

"Fifteen million?" Haven asked.

I nodded again and tried to push everything but her out of my head.

"What, your father is putting in fifteen million pounds?"

"Jesus, Haven. My dad is a cop in Chicago. I'm not sure he has a spare fifteen million anything. Where do these assumptions about me come from?" I'd never denied I had money, I had the car to prove it, but I didn't understand why she thought I couldn't have made it myself. She was so ready to think the worst of me.

"So your father isn't rich?" she asked.

"No. He lives on a cop's salary. Won't take a dime from me."

"But what about the Aston Martin?" Did she think I robbed banks? Was it so difficult to believe that I might have made it myself?

"It's my money, Haven. I started up an energy trading business. Hal put in most of the cash. It did very well. We sold it to Shell."

"It did fifteen million well?" She asked.

"It did a hundred and eighty million well." I wasn't trying to show off. I wanted this discussion finished for once and for all.

"Holy crap."

"Yeah, it did better than we expected."

I watched her process the information, and it cooled my irritation. "You have a hundred and eighty million? You're like rich with your own money rich," she said.

"No, we sold the company for a hundred and eighty million. I only got about seventy."

I relaxed and grinned at her. I'd never talked specifics before. Only with Beth. Which was probably why Beth moaned about still being in my old student flat.

"Only? You poor thing. How are you managing to get by with just seventy?"

I liked that nothing stopped her from giving me shit. Having money had changed the way people were around me. Somehow my opinions seemed to count for a bit more. It had affected even some of my longest friendships and made me question people's motives a lot more. I hated it.

"When did you sell?" she asked.

"Almost two years ago now. I need to get moving with Elemental Energy. It's taken so long to get it to this stage."

"So you're setting up another business? Why aren't you on some Caribbean island somewhere bathing in asses' milk, eating truffles with diamond encrusted cutlery."

I laughed. "It's not really me, is it? And anyway, you said I was a walking cliché having an Aston Martin. How come you're encouraging me to be more extravagant?"

"I'm not encouraging you. I just . . . It's a shock."

"And you don't hate me for it?" I wondered if it would change how she saw me.

"Why would I hate you?" she asked.

"You don't like people with money."

"I don't like lazy, spoiled, entitled people that live off other people's money. You've proven you're not any of those things."

I found her knowing about my situation was a relief, and it pulled me closer toward her.

"That almost sounded like a compliment. Careful, I might get complacent."

"Don't worry, I'll keep you on your toes."

I stood up and held out my hand. "I have no doubt. Let's go. I want to dance with you."

chapter TEN

Haven

As we entered Buddha Bar, it was like stepping into a womb. The dim lighting made everything that wasn't red, glow and the loud bass of the music sounded like an unrelenting heartbeat. It was sexual and provocative, as if we'd stepped into a different world where new rules applied. We started up the stairs to an area that was cordoned off as private. Jake held out his hand as I reached for the balustrade. I willingly accepted it. Ash had talked me into these shoes and they were fine for standing or sitting. But they were not made for walking.

"These shoes are ridiculous," I said.

"They're perfect. I'm going to fuck you in them."

My stomach lilted and I had to pause for a second. I took a deep breath and continued the climb.

How long would we have to stay? An hour?

We rounded the corner, went through some red velvet curtains into a seating area where there were various faces I recognized. We found ourselves a seat with some of the cast who Jake seemed to know. Jake pulled my knees toward him, resting his hand on my outer thigh, inching me closer. Any doubt that we were together had just been erased. It felt good. I couldn't hear their conversation and I didn't try to join in. I let myself soak in the atmosphere. I didn't know if it was the beat of the music that seemed to thrum against my heart, or Jake's fingers stroking the stocking-covered skin of my thighs, or just the anticipation of what was next with him, but I felt like I was going to explode. I wanted to be alone with him. I wanted to be touching him. I wanted his warmth pressed against me.

Breaking into my thoughts, Sandy arrived with the director. They seemed to have got over their creative differences and were smiling and laughing. I wasn't sure if Sandy had realized Jake and I were together, but either way as soon as she saw him she ran over and put herself on his lap, her arms round his neck.

"I'm going to miss not having you around, Harry. Say you'll take me out when we get back to London," she said, pouting.

"I'm sure we'll arrange something. I told Dave I'd take him to dinner to thank him for the showing, so we should all get together."

"Don't you miss our one-on-one time, Harry?"

I didn't like her so close to him. His touch felt like a finite resource that I didn't want him using up on her. His hand didn't move from my leg and I swept my fingers across his, wanting to deepen our connection. He glanced at me and stood, sliding her off his knee, excusing himself and heading to the loo.

"I really appreciate the time you've spent with me," I said to Sandy as she scowled in Jake's direction. "I really hope you'll like the article when it's finished."

As she turned toward me her smile reappeared. "It's been my pleasure, Haven. If you need anything else, let me know." She wandered back into a crowd of people, leaving me to my cocktail.

With the distraction of Sandy gone, I sank back into the dark, heavy beat of the music, the dim lighting, and my memories of the previous evening. The way Jake had made me feel under his tongue had been shocking and renewing.

Jake appeared next to me and he bent and whispered in my ear, "Come with me. I want to show you something." He held his hand out and I slid my palm against his.

He led me through some velvet curtains at the other end of the room. On the other side was a dark, empty corridor. It was open to the restaurant below on one side, as if it was a large balcony. Jake kept walking.

"Where are we going?" I asked him.

He just cocked his head and continued our journey across the balcony corridor. At the other end was another curtain, black this time, and Jake led me inside another dark room and through to another corridor. Where was he taking me?

"Here," he said.

We went up some steps and found ourselves in a small, unlit room with a small Juliet balcony overlooking the whole restaurant from front to back. The chatter of the diners was drowned out by the sexual hum of the music. We were on our own, but surrounded by people.

Jake slid his hands around my waist and I turned to meet his eyes.

"I've been wanting to get you alone all night," he whispered.

"We're not alone, Jake." My nipples tightened against the lace of my bra and my resolve to wait wavered.

He bent forward and scraped his lips against mine, then dropped small kisses at the corner of my lips. My skin started vibrating from the warmth of him so close, combined with the bass of the music pumping through the speakers.

"Hey, what are you doing?" I asked.

"I'm kissing you," he replied as he worked his way up to the back of my ear and down my neck. My arms went to his oh-so-big shoulders and I sighed. He felt too good, hard and tight. I tipped my head back, allowing him easier access.

"You found a place for us to make out?" I asked.

"I couldn't wait," he replied against my skin.

My hands pushed into his hair and he groaned as I pulled him gently back to my mouth. His tongue pressed against mine. I could kiss him for hours, days even.

He was hard, ready for me, pressing into my stomach. Tonight, we would be together. When the spell of Paris was broken who knew what would happen, but tonight would be perfect. I was ready to let go and see where Jake could take me.

"Turn around," he whispered, moving my shoulders so I was facing the restaurant. The Juliet balcony was only wide enough for one person and Jake stayed hidden in the shadows behind me. If the diners looked up, I wasn't sure whether they could see me. Maybe an outline, or just my face.

"Put your hands on the balustrade," he said. He wasn't asking. He was telling me, and I liked it. I did as he asked, wanting to be led, wanting to unravel and have him catch me.

His palms were flat against my stomach, pressing me closer to him.

"Feel that?" he asked, pushing his erection against me.

I nodded.

"You can feel how ready I am, can't you?"

"Yes," I stuttered.

His left hand trailed down from my belly and gathered up the skirt of my dress. The music seemed to get louder, the bass deeper, twisting round and through us, providing a cocoon against prying eyes.

"Jake? What are you doing?"

"I'm going to feel how ready you are."

Jesus, what was he saying? What was he thinking? His fingers travelled up my inner thigh and he paused and he took a short sharp breath as he found my bare flesh at the top of my stockings.

My hands gripped the balustrade as my legs weakened.

"Jake, someone will see." I couldn't bring myself to feel panicked by the thought, the cocktail of music and Jake had me floating away from anxiety, away from a version of me I wasn't sure I'd ever see again.

"Shhhh," he whispered, sliding his fingers beneath my underwear and pushing against my clit, circling once then twice, then driving lower.

"Oh yes, baby, you're so wet. So ready."

"Jake, no. We can't," I said, no real resistance in my tone.

"Oh, but we can and you *will* come for me."

He reached down and plunged two fingers inside me. I fell forward at the sensation, but he pulled me back against him with his free hand.

His thumb began circling my clit while his fingers pushed in and out. Jesus.

I tried to control my breathing, but every time I thought I'd steadied myself he pushed harder and faster.

"Do you like that, baby? Does it make you feel good?" His words vibrated on my neck.

I nodded and my head fell back against his chest. His lips dipped to my skin. His hardness moved behind me. God, I wanted him inside me.

"I want you, Jake."

"I know. And you'll have me. You have to be patient. I'm not fucking you here."

"Please," I groaned.

His fingers quickened at my plea, blood throbbed in my ears and my skin set alight.

"See all those people down here? Do you think they know how good you feel right now?"

"No. No one could," I sputtered as my orgasm grasped me and pounded through me like thunder, every bone in my body vibrating with pleasure and desire.

I would have collapsed if it weren't for Jake holding me. He'd weakened me, physically and emotionally. He kept me clenched to him as I caught my breath and some of my strength returned.

"Hey," he said, kissing my neck.

I brought my hands to his forearms that surrounded me. "Hey."

"I love making you come," he said.

"I love you making me come."

"Let's get out of here. I want to see you in nothing but those shoes. Can you stand?"

"I think so."

He held his hand out for me and I took it. I was still unsteady.

In the cab Jake kept his hand clamped to my knee, like he wanted to make sure I wasn't going anywhere.

"I'm going to need you to do what I say," Jake whispered.

"When?" I asked, my head still fuzzy from my orgasm.

"When we go upstairs."

"What do you mean?"

"I mean, I need you to do exactly what I say when we get upstairs."

What was he saying? I wasn't sure it mattered I thought I'd do anything he ever asked of me. I didn't get a chance to ask him again as the cab drew up to the hotel and Jake paid the driver.

As we got into the lift, my hand firmly clasped in his, he pulled at his tie with his free hand.

"Have you ever been restrained, Haven?"

Did I hear him right? I looked at him but his eyes were fixed on the elevator doors in front of us.

"Restrained. Tied up," he said in a very business-like way.

"Um. No," I replied.

"Have you thought about it?"

I shifted my weight from foot to foot. I had thought about it, even fantasized about it occasionally. "Umm . . ."

"Speak honestly."

"I've thought about it a little."

"Does the thought scare you? Be honest."

"Not in the abstract," I said.

"What about the idea of me restraining you when we get inside? Does the reality scare you?"

"A little," I said. I trusted Jake, I knew he wouldn't hurt me and it wasn't what scared me. I supposed it was that he could if he wanted to, that I wouldn't be able to stop him if I needed to. I'd become good at protecting myself and giving that up was a scary thought, but I wanted to do it.

"Does it turn you on?"

"With you, a little," I admitted.

His chest rose and fell, and he squeezed my hand as he led me out of the lift.

"My room or yours?" he asked.

"Mine please."

He nodded and took my key and opened the door.

"I want you to undress for me and lie on the bed. Leave those shoes on," he said as we closed the door. His tone was serious and my stomach flipped in anticipation. He was showing me a different side to him.

Jake leaned on the dressing table, his tie in his hand, his eyes never leaving me. I fiddled with my side zip, yanking it open. I stepped out of my dress and threw it on the chair. I hesitated and he raised his eyebrows.

I reached behind my back and released the clasp on my bra. I heard his intake of breath as I slipped the straps over my shoulders, releasing my breasts. Finally, I dragged down my underwear and let it fall to the floor. I stood before him naked apart from my stockings and my shoes. Any embarrassment or self-consciousness was cloaked in desire for the man in front of me. He said nothing, but his eyes burned a slightly different blue to normal, they were deeper, more intense.

I stepped away and the backs of my legs found the bed. I lowered myself and then lay back as he had instructed.

"You are such a beautiful girl, Haven."

My stomach contracted and the wetness between my thighs that had been there all night was fresh on my skin.

Jake circled the bed, walking to the edge by my head.

"I'm going to tie your hands," he said. "Put them above your head."

I hesitated, but brought my hands up.

"I won't hurt you," he said.

"I know," I replied.

He took my hands and used his tie to bind them together. Then he shifted my body round and tied the other end to the bedpost. It felt illicit and erotic, but I was nervous—scared of how far I would fall when I let go.

"You're going to feel so good."

Another rush of liquid slid between my thighs.

"Jesus, the things I'm going to do to you," he said and I couldn't help but moan at the thought. He seemed to know how my body worked in a way no other man ever had.

Still fully clothed, he crawled onto the bed and swept my hair from my forehead. He trailed his fingers down my face and across my throat. As he moved down, he palmed my breasts, then circled a nipple, once then twice, and then flicked his finger off his thumb across the puckered flesh.

"Shit," I cried as sharp pain gave way to a peak of pleasure followed by a new wave of desire.

"Good?" he asked.

"So good," I whispered, pushing my thighs together.

He flicked again and I cried out. He moved to the other breast, repeating the same movements, then he replaced his fingers with his tongue and his teeth, alternating again between pleasure and pain, the sensations mixing until I didn't know one from the other.

I whimpered and pulled against his tie as he moved his attention from my breasts down to my stomach.

"You can't escape, Haven. You can't control this. How does it feel?"

"Jake," I cried.

"This is what you need. You need someone to take it all away from you and give you something more. You don't get to choose. I'm going to use your body how I wish."

My back arched off the bed at his words. *What is he doing to me?* He continued to nip and suck at my skin, setting each part of me alight, working his way down my body tantalizingly slow.

My eyes opened as the mattress dipped and his touch disappeared from me. He pulled off his shirt one handed, revealing his hard, sculpted torso and he turned to the dressing table, picking up his wallet and bringing out a condom. My hips twisted in anticipation. I couldn't wait for him to be inside me.

He turned back to face me, standing at my feet and pulled off his jeans and briefs in one quick movement. I gasped as I saw him hard and flat against his stomach. Suddenly I was nervous. He was big.

"Don't worry. We're going to take it slow," he said as he reached down and stroked himself. "You look so good. I can see your wetness, you're more than ready for me, aren't you?"

I hoped I was. I took the sides of my cheek between my teeth.

"Bring your knees up. Let me see you."

I slid my feet up the bed.

"Now open them wide."

"Jake." I was embarrassed to be so exposed to him.

"Do as I say, Haven."

Slowly I parted my legs and saw his eyes glaze over as he took me in.

"So beautiful," he said. He moved closer to the bed and with both hands, swept down my inner thighs, pressing them farther apart. "Jesus, your pussy's beautiful."

My hips lifted off the bed, desperate to feel him.

"Oh yes, baby, you're greedy for me. That's what I like to see."

He rolled on a condom and lowered himself over me. He rubbed his tip against my entrance and then ran it up to my clitoris and down again, each movement driving me closer and closer to the edge.

"I have to be inside you."

He pushed into me, just slightly and blood began to thunder in my ears. I pulled my legs farther apart, wanting to make room for him.

"More?" he asked.

I nodded. Slowly he moved in deeper and checked for my reaction.

"More," I whispered.

He groaned and pushed in farther and farther, pushing all the air out of my lungs, pulling the most intense orgasm from me that I'd ever had. The pleasure rattled through every muscle and bone and exploded in my head, across my skin and deep within me.

"Oh baby," he said. "Watching you come is my new favorite thing to do in Paris."

He stayed still inside me as I came down from my climax. I'd never felt so full. Full of him, of desire, of life. It was like I'd been shown something that couldn't be unseen and it had shifted my world, just a little, but forever.

He reached above me and quickly untied my hands. I clamored for his back and traced his muscles under my fingers. His skin was so soft and tight and perfect.

"Are you ready?" he asked, his eyes burning as he waited for my reply.

I was more than ready. I nodded and he started to move, gently pulling out and pushing back in. I lifted my knees farther and he held them in place. He was deeper than before, if that was possible.

"Let's never leave this bed," I said.

"Sounds good to me," he replied, pushing into me again and then reaching under me and pulling me and my legs around him so we were sitting face to face, nose to nose. He clamped his hands around my hips and started to rock in and out of me. I put my forehead against his and concentrated on his breathing, trying to keep my next orgasm at bay as long as possible. It was futile. It began again, deep in my belly and I pulsed around him.

"Oh baby, again?"

"Yes," I breathed against him. "You're making me come again." I thrust my head back. "Faster," I cried and I started to increase the rhythm of my hips against his.

"Oh fuck," he shouted.

We both exploded at the same time, our bodies juddering and shaking, grasping at each other.

chapter ELEVEN

Jake

"Hey," I said as I got back into bed next to Haven, kissing her lightly on the lips. It was morning, but there was no incentive to move. "What do you think about extending our stay by a day? We could go back on Sunday."

She grinned at me, then frowned. "I have to be back. It's Ash's birthday. We're having a girls' night out."

It didn't sound like an excuse. I could live with that. I just wanted to spend as much time with her as possible. Last night had been incredible. She seemed to get off on the restraints and I'd come like a teenager.

"Okay. When can I next see you?"

"Sunday? Although I'll be grouchy and hung over. I'll let you rub my feet and make me toast."

I smiled. "Sounds tempting. I have to work in the day, but the evening?" My lack of time was one of the reasons I fucked girls like Millie. They wanted to be wined and dined. They didn't really care about what I was doing with my time as long as the dates were impressive enough. And I didn't *need* to see them. Then, three months in, when they started to want a little more, I ended it.

With Haven it was going to be different. I'd wanted more from the moment I first met her. I couldn't seem to get enough. But Elemental Energy was just kicking off. It needed my time and attention as well. The timing sucked, but I would make this work. She'd crashed into my world and I wouldn't let her go.

She grimaced. "Sunday night I cook for Luke and sometimes Ash. I'd invite you but—"

"Let's leave dinner with the family to next weekend, okay?"

She nodded in agreement.

"Monday?" she asked

"Monday? At the morning meeting?" That seemed so far away. I wanted to keep her naked and with me between now and then.

"Well, yes and after work? You could come over and I could cook." She yawned.

"Let's order in. That gives us more time."

"I like that idea." She smiled at me.

Her defenses were low and I wanted to keep her like this, to see every layer of her, but I could tell she was sleepy. "You're tired," I said as her heavy eyes drifted shut.

"You've worn me out," she said.

"Sleep, baby."

By Sunday morning I was aching to see her again. She'd clearly had a good time with Ash on Saturday night. I'd enjoyed the evidence through a series of drunken texts telling me all things she wanted to do to me, and then the Sunday morning messages apologizing.

At two o'clock my phone vibrated.

"How's the hangover?" I asked, answering her call.

"A little better. Sorry about those messages."

"Don't be sorry. And we're going to try the thing with the whipped cream."

She laughed. "Okay, but not in my bed. It'll ruin my sheets."

"Practical to the end."

"How is your work going? Am I interrupting?" she asked.

"No, it's good to have a break. I've been working since five."

"Tell me. What have you been doing?"

I grinned into the phone. I liked that she was asking me about work. "Hal is transferring the first tranche of investment tomorrow so I need Eric, our computer whizz, on board as soon as possible. To speed things up I think I'll have to fly out to see him face to face."

"That's sounds great. When do you go?"

"Tuesday," I said carefully. I wasn't sure how she was going to react or what I wanted her reaction to be. I needed her to be cool about it, but I'd also like her to miss me a little. "I should be back Saturday morning. I'll know more when I get there."

"Okay, so we'll have to make the most of tomorrow night then." That was the answer I'd been hoping for

"Do you want more coffee?" Beth shouted from the kitchen.

"No, I'm good, thanks. On the phone," I replied.

"Sorry, are you not alone?" Haven asked.

"It's just Beth," I said. "She's been keeping me hydrated all morning."

"Oh, she's come round to look after you?"

"She lives here. You knew that didn't you?"

"Oh, I don't think I did. Say hi to her from me," she said. It was a reminder of how much we had to learn about each other. The pull I had toward her made me believe that she knew everything about me that she needed to, but that couldn't be true after knowing each other such a short time.

"I will. She wants us to go to dinner, the three of us. When I'm back?" There was nothing I wanted to hide, I wanted to show her everything, offer myself up to her. I wondered if she could do the same in return.

"Sure. Anyway, I should go and start on dinner."

"Okay, I can't wait to see you tomorrow."

"You too."

I got into work early on Monday to grab a few minutes with Haven before the meeting. But she wasn't at her desk.

I wandered across the office to say hello to Robert

"Morning, Harry," Robert said as I walked in.

"Hey. I need to talk to you about timing. Things have started to ramp up with Elemental Energy."

"Okay, let me catch up with Human Resources on where we are with the new guy. How was Paris?"

"It was good. Really good." I couldn't help the shit-eating grin stamped across my face.

"And the Haven and Sandy dynamic worked?" he asked.

I nodded. "It did, I think because they are so different, completely opposite really."

Robert laughed and I lent him a tight smile. "I knew it. You were right, we needed someone challenged in the looks department. Sandy could never have seen Haven as any kind of rival or threat."

Robert was a good friend but at the moment I couldn't think of him as anything other than a total douche. I ignored my instinct to defend Haven. She and I hadn't discussed how public she wanted to be with what was going on between us, and I knew she was fiercely private at work. Hell, we hadn't discussed anything. My heart started to speed up. If I defended Haven, I was sure to give away my feelings for her, and I didn't want her to be mad for telling her boss about an intra-office relationship so I just rolled my eyes and tried to ignore his comments about the woman I saw my future with.

chapter TWELVE

Haven

I stumbled from outside Robert's office into the nearest meeting room and collapsed onto the chair. My heart was beating so quickly I thought I was going to throw up. My vision blurred so I closed my eyes and placed my head in my hands. What had I just heard? I had wanted to catch Robert before our meeting, but when I got to his office, Jake was already in there, the door ajar. I hesitated, not knowing whether I should interrupt, and overheard them talking about Sandy and me. Replaying it in my head created a fresh wave of nausea and I clasped my stomach, willing myself not to throw up. I'd had about all the humiliation I could take for one day.

I'd opened myself up to Jake completely. Had it all been a game to him? Was I just a conquest? And apparently, not a particularly attractive one. Had he wanted Sandy all along? None of it made sense. A sharp pain twisted through the center of me. I wanted to run and hide. I needed my people, I needed Luke and Ash.

One thing was clear—I should have never let him so close.

chapter THIRTEEN

Jake

The cab pulled up in front of Haven's apartment. I leapt out and pushed some cash through the window to the driver. I kept my eyes fixed firmly on the door to Haven's building in case she went in or out. I had to convince her that the conversation she'd overheard between Robert and I wasn't what she thought it was. My heart had turned itself inside out when I'd received her text saying that she never wanted to see me again, that she'd heard Robert and I discussing her. I didn't know exactly what she thought she'd heard—or what she was thinking. All I knew was it felt as though she was slipping through my fingers. She hadn't answered my calls, or responded to my texts.

I climbed the stairs to the door, then stopped. Now that I was here, I wasn't sure what to do. I didn't even know if she was home. Was I supposed to force my way in and pin her down until she listened to me? My mind whirled. I liked order and logic. Normally I could read people and predict how they would react in a million different scenarios. Haven tore right through any theories I had about her and people in general, changing direction every time I thought I had her figured out. It was exhausting and invigorating at the same time. But this felt dark. Like her trail had gone dry. I should have set Robert straight when he'd talked about picking Haven for the Sandy interview because she wouldn't rival Sandy's movie-star glamor. I shouldn't have stayed quiet, but I'd been trying to do what I thought Haven would want me to do—keep our relationship private.

I pressed the buzzer and held my breath, waiting for a response. Relief and shock made my stomach flip when I heard the intercom pick up.

"Haven, it's Jake. We need to talk."

The intercom went dead but it wasn't followed by a buzz of the door being released. I pressed again. No response.

I tried to recall exactly what Robert had said to me and precisely how I'd replied. But the memories seemed muddied from pulling them out and trying to rerun them. I could understand why she'd be upset with Robert; he'd been a prick. And I got that she might be angry with me for not defending her, but did it justify her not wanting anything to do with me? Why wouldn't she at least talk to me?

I was pacing outside her building when I saw her brother Luke approach. His eyes bore into me and he wore an expression that said he wanted to rip my face from my body.

"Has she spoken to you?" I asked.

"Don't speak to me, mate, or I might have to punch you," Luke replied.

"I need to understand why she's so upset, what she heard. I need to talk to her." I'd lost my normally balanced, cool exterior as panic started to rise. If her brother was over here in the middle of the day, Haven must be really upset. I hated to think of her in pain and the idea I'd caused it, directly or indirectly, made me feel as if my gut was rotting. It was the last thing I wanted. I couldn't lose her.

Luke entered a code into the panel next to the intercom and pulled the building door open. "Save it. I'm not interested. I've been encouraging her to open up and have some fun for the longest time, and then some wanker like you comes along and fucks her up. I don't know what you did and I don't care. The only thing that I could make out through her tears were the words 'pity fuck' and if you think you're too good for Haven, then you don't know her at all."

He let the door slam in my face. For a second I was catatonic as what he'd said sank in. Shit. *Pity fuck?* My gut twisted and I felt as though I might vomit. She thought I agreed with Robert? Surely she knew better than that after Paris.

Questions flew through my head like boulders. How was I going to get her to speak to me? Would she believe me? How was I ever going to get her to trust me? I was due to go to Palo Alto tomorrow, should I cancel? But then I would probably lose the key to the future of Elemental Energy. Maybe it would be good to give Haven some space. Would I ever see her again if she refused to speak to me? I was no longer needed at *Rallegra* so it wasn't as if I'd bump into her at work.

The rot in my gut started to spread.

I dialed her number again and it went straight to voicemail, so I typed out another text.

Jake: I'm sorry. Please let me explain.

My head should be buried in Elemental Energy, but instead I was trying to figure out a way to postpone my trip. This was why I'd always dated girls like Millie. Women who required financial, rather than emotional investment. They were easy to predict, easy to keep happy and easy to keep at arm's length. Haven was oil to their water.

I tried her phone again. Straight to voicemail. There was a sense of relief at the thought that Luke was with her. Hopefully, he would be able to provide some comfort to her.

After a sleepless night, I decided to go to Palo Alto. Haven wasn't responding to me and I being away would give her some space. I couldn't exactly set up camp outside her apartment building and I could call her from wherever I was. And I would email her. Try and explain when I could think more clearly. I just didn't know how to make this right. I'd never cared enough about anyone but my family to have to deal with a situation like this. Hurting Haven had hurt me. Her pain had become mine.

Haven

"If you're not going to help chop those vegetables, then get out of my kitchen or pour me a glass of wine," I told Ash as I prepared Sunday dinner. It was a ritual Luke and I'd had forever, and Ash was frequently a part of. Rituals and traditions between us had become more important since our parents had died. And Sunday dinner was the most important of all because it felt as though it was what we'd be doing—congregating, sharing, spending time with each other—if our family were still whole.

Ash went to the fridge and pulled out a bottle of wine.

"A normal girl would go dressed to kill if she thought she were going to see her ex for the first time," Ash said.

"What can I say? I don't want him to think that what he's done has affected me in any way." But Jake had affected me in every way.

I had cried non-stop for twenty-four hours after I'd overheard Robert and Jake's conversation. I wasn't sure which stung more, that Robert thought my best qualification was my unattractiveness, or that Jake had agreed with him. On the rare occasions something got under my skin and created a chink in my armor, my floodgates opened and I temporarily drowned. I wept for everything that had ever gone wrong. I wept for my carefree teens and twenties that had been ripped from me. I wept for my parents who never got to have the lives they dreamed of. I wept for Luke, who had given up his dreams to get a reliable, well-paid job so he could take care of me. And then I wept for the poor, the dying and the hungry. On the rare instances I mourned, everyone's grief and sorrow became my own.

Luke and Ash were the people who could pull me to safety. Order me into the shower. Make me laugh. Show me the absurdity in my reactions and overreactions. And just as suddenly as it started, it would stop. The chink would heal over. Life would go on.

I was fine.

The knots in my stomach had disappeared as I read Jake's email, explaining Robert's view, how he had decided who would take the article before Jake and I met, and how Jake had never shared Robert's viewpoint. I believed him. But at the same time, that didn't alter the fact that the whole situation had metaphorically thrown a bucket of ice water over me. Whatever we had, or might have had, had been tarnished. The heartbreak reminded me why I didn't really date. I had enough people in my life that I loved and cared for, and I needed to hold on tight to them. The thought of falling for someone, properly letting someone in and then having it disintegrate—having them leave—was too painful. It was much better to clutch onto the people that would never willingly go anywhere.

Luke and Ash had been constants in my life since before my parents' deaths. There was no possibility they would leave me, and that's what I needed. That was enough.

"So you're going to go dressed like a puritan?" Ash asked.

"I'm going to wear what I always do. Nothing has changed."

"His email though, Haven. It made my insides melt."

"Yes and I replied. I told him it was fine, that I believed him and there were no hard feelings. But you get that things are different, don't you? I can't see him in the same way. Hearing that conversation changed things for me."

"I'm not sure I do get it. He likes you—really cares about you. And you like him. Just because you had a road bump doesn't mean you give up."

It isn't a road bump, it's a wake-up call. I was grateful that I hadn't fallen deeper before I'd come to my senses. If I'd lost Jake once he'd become really important to me, it might just have finished me. I couldn't lose anyone else.

"I need you to drop it. It's done," I said. "I don't want to talk about it anymore."

I had to put a stop to the conversation. Part of me couldn't wait to see him at our Monday morning meeting—I was desperate to hear how his trip to the US had gone but I couldn't think like that now. We weren't anything to each other anymore. Talking about him, thinking about him, made it worse—made the feelings about him bigger when all I wanted to do was have them disappear as if he'd never existed.

"Can you get that?" I asked her when the door buzzer went. "It's likely Luke."

"As long as I can leave Emma on the doorstep."

I rolled my eyes. She wasn't a big fan of Luke's girlfriend, Emma, mostly because she was jealous. But also because Sunday nights with Emma were different. The three of us were a unit and Emma's presence altered the dynamic. "I'll get it, you freak."

When I opened the door, Luke leaned forward and kissed me on the cheek, handing me a bottle of wine and a bag, which I hoped had stock cubes and broccoli in it. "Hey," he said.

"Where's Emma?" I asked.

"She's not coming."

I pursed my lips at him and he gave me a gentle shake of the head. His heavy eyes told me he didn't want to talk about it.

"All the more for us."

"How are you feeling about work tomorrow?" he asked.

"Fine. Why shouldn't I?" I replied.

"You know, you'll see Jake. I'm just asking."

The truth was I didn't feel fine but I desperately wished to. I wanted to be over him. I hated myself for looking forward to seeing him. I needed that part of me under control and back to normal so I could prove to myself I was back to Haven pre-Jake, that he hadn't got under my skin. It was done. We were over before we began.

I took a deep breath and opened the door to the conference room, relieved to find I was the first one to arrive.

I set my pad, pen and Diet Coke down as I took my usual spot and then smoothed the stray wisps of hair back into my tight bun. *I can do this.*

Within a few minutes, people started filing into the room and filling chairs. I kept my eyes on my to-do list, waiting for the seat opposite to become occupied with too-long legs and a wicked smile. I waited. And waited. But the chair remained free.

Robert arrived and called everyone to order. Had Jake deliberately avoided what had become his usual seat? I glanced down the table and then across. He wasn't here.

He'd been due back from the US on Saturday. Where was he? His calls had slowed from all day, to three times a day, to a single call since my reply to his email. I had told him that I accepted his apology and that I understood that it wasn't him that had picked me over Emily. And that was all true. I had added that it was also the case that I didn't want to continue things between us, but I hoped that we would still be friends.

I had to protect myself, and that meant I couldn't have Jake in my life. Jake had the ability to pierce my armor and he had to be kept at a distance.

Maybe he was just late. Or perhaps he had told Robert he didn't want to work at *Rallegra* anymore.

"First piece of news is that we've managed to replace Brad. We made an offer to a great *Marie Claire* photographer yesterday, so we're hoping he's on board within a month."

I held my breath, waiting for Robert to say that Jake would continue to fill in until the new guy started, but there was no discussion of any interim help. No mention of Jake. I suppose I was meant to feel relieved. This should have felt like a reprieve, I was getting what I wanted, but instead my heart shrank in my chest.

"Haven?" Robert asked.

I looked up and found everyone staring at me. I hadn't been listening.

"How's the Sandy Fox piece coming along?" he asked.

"Good. I'll let you have something later on in the day. I just need to pick the photographs. I was hoping to get them from J—Harry today."

"Good. And your dating feature?"

"Yes, elite dating. There are a number of high-end agencies that have established themselves recently and I'm working on a piece centering around them. I want to interview them and their clients. The idea is to work out what rich men look for in women. Are these men searching for love, or just a quick shag and then it's back to the day job because their career is really the only thing they can focus on? Do they want a housekeeper that puts out or a soul mate?" As I was explaining the concept to the meeting, I couldn't stop images of Millie, Jake's ex, from floating across my brain. Was she who he would end up with?

My idea would involve actually having a couple of dates with these men. I wouldn't be undercover, because I needed the dating agencies' cooperation. I was, after all, single. I'd write about the disastrous dates, the wealth, or the lack of spark. I suspected that these agencies were little more than high-end escort services for men who didn't want to think of themselves as guys who needed to pay for it. It could be fun. I wouldn't need to feel anything real. It would be easy to keep my distance. It would keep my heart safe and create a distraction.

Back at my desk, I scanned my in box and found an email from Jake. It said nothing other than he was attaching photos of the Sandy article.

My stomach cramped and I steadied myself against the table. The lack of covering message assured me that he understood there was no future for us. It was what the sensible part of my brain wanted. The bit of my body I was trying to ignore, the part that wanted him to never give up on me, slumped in defeat. But it was always for the best when my head ruled my heart.

I clicked on the photos. There were over a hundred. They were beautiful and seemed to capture the very essence of Sandy. Her almost-black hair was glossy and glamorous, her smile wide and generous. She came across as warm and sensuous. Jake had captured what she looked like, but more, he'd brought out her very best. Was this how he saw her?

When I clicked on the last picture my stomach jolted again. It was of me, on my own, staring directly into the camera. I barely recognized myself. My cheekbones were highlighted and some stray hairs had escaped my bun. I looked relaxed, my eyes seemed to dance and there was a small, secretive smile on my face. The picture captured how I felt when I forgot myself. When I was with Ash and Luke and we were just . . . us. Was this how he saw me? Did he know me like that?

Did I want him to?

chapter FOURTEEN

Jake

"So you're still sulking?" Beth asked me. I was sick of sitting at my desk in our guest bedroom all day and had decided to change my surroundings. It may have been a bad idea because now I had my papers spread across the dining table, and Beth had more access to me to give me a hard time. She rarely needed an excuse to bust my balls but since Haven and I had stopped seeing each other—assuming we had ever really started—that was where her attention was centered. She thought I'd given up too easily. She thought I should fight harder. I was trying not to think. I had Elemental Energy to concentrate on.

"I'm not sulking. I'm working. There's a difference. I have a million things to do if I want Elemental Energy to achieve what it's capable of."

"I thought you had a month before the Palo Alto guy started?"

Could she not stop pushing? She'd been like this since I got back from California. Couldn't she just leave things alone? Haven had made this decision, not me. I ignored her.

"So you have some time. I thought the new photographer at *Rallegra* didn't start for a while? I'm sure Robert could still do with the help," she continued.

"I have a lot to do. Robert will call me if he needs me. I've finished the Sandy piece. I wasn't assigned to anything else." I was pretty sure that the last place I should be was *Rallegra*. Haven wanted us to be "friends" but that was not something I could comprehend. If I couldn't be with her, then I couldn't see her.

"Keep telling yourself that, Jake. You should go in there, scoop her up in your arms and tell her how you feel."

She had gone way past irritating. Haven had decided, it hadn't been my choice. There was no point in revisiting all this stuff. Maybe I needed to go for a run. "Will you back off? Haven and I were . . . it was . . . It's over. I've had far longer relationships. You didn't seem to have a problem when Millie and I split up."

"This is different and you know it. You like Haven. Millie . . . wasn't worth it. I think you're punishing her for pushing you away."

There was no point in talking about this. Haven had been clear. She didn't want anything from me. At least she'd responded to my email. When I saw she'd replied, I'd thought she'd finally come around and we would be able to move past this misunderstanding. After reading her very cool, calm response about how she accepted my apology and wanted us to be friends, I knew she was gone.

The shutters had come down.

Haven was no longer mine.

"How am I punishing her by giving her what she wants?" It was true I was angry at Haven. She'd not trusted me, or how she felt. She'd just shut down and pushed me out. I could cope with her crying in my arms or being mad with me, but just to walk away as if we'd been nothing? Maybe I was punishing her.

"Perhaps you're determined not to allow yourself to be happy."

"Thank you, Dr. Daniels. I've allowed myself to be happy with a lot of women. It's not like I don't date."

"No you haven't. You've fucked a lot of girls, but you've always been the one in control. You've never lost yourself; found a great love. More than that, you *choose* women that you are never going to fall in love with deliberately."

"I'm going for a run," I said, standing up and staring at my papers strewn across the table. Worse than having Beth bust my balls, was Beth making sense while she did it. I didn't want to think Haven might have been special, or right for me, when such thoughts were entirely futile. She wasn't mine anymore.

Losing Haven hurt in the pit of my belly. I'd never felt like that after a break up before, but I figured it would pass. Our paths weren't likely to cross again after I finally finished up at *Rallegra*. We would be just memories for each other, or at least she would be for me. I didn't know if I'd ever been anything to her.

My phone vibrated against the table. Beth glanced at the screen and grinned. "That, my dear brother, is what you call fate. I don't want to hear any excuses about how you're too busy."

"Robert," I answered.

"Harry. How was the US? Make another ten million while you were out there? Bang a supermodel?"

"You have a twisted view of what my life really is." I would have normally found Robert's assumptions about my life amusing, but today it just seemed a little sad. The life he was jealous of wasn't a life I recognized or wanted. "You remember I live with my sister, right?"

Robert chuckled. "We've got a couple of new pieces for you to work on. The first is on celebrity lookalikes. It's going to be great. Emily is working on it with Jenny. They've found some proper crazy people who dress to look like their idols. Some have even had surgery."

I rolled my eyes. How utterly pointless. Sometimes it surprised me that Haven liked her job. It seemed to jar against the rest of her—it was so superficial. Haven was the opposite. You couldn't look at the surface of Haven and know anything about her. *It doesn't matter anymore*, I reminded myself.

"I thought we could do that as a studio shoot; it'll take less than a day. Are you good with that? We're thinking Thursday next week," Robert said.

"Yeah, that will be fine," I said, as Beth stood over me. She gave me the thumbs up and I gave her the finger.

"The second one will be a bit more time consuming. It's a piece about dating agencies that only accept millionaires or something. Haven has the details. You'll need to go along to the meetings and a couple of dates."

My throat tightened and I tried to push down a swallow. Robert seemed oblivious to anything that might have happened between Haven and I, and there was no need to tell him. "Right. Well, you know it will depend on Elemental Energy," I said. Beth glared at me. I ignored her.

"We'll work around you on this. If it runs long, I can just get our new guy to take over. Really appreciate it, mate." He wasn't giving me much of a choice and I wasn't sure I wanted him to.

"And Haven's happy with me doing it?"

"Yeah, she told me she thought you were very talented when she saw the Sandy Fox photographs. Coming from her, that's huge. You know what a ball buster she is."

I had no idea whether or not Haven knew Robert had asked me to be involved in this piece specifically. Did she want to see me?

"Okay, let me know when you need me in the office," I said.

"I'll get Haven to call you."

"Happy now?" I turned to Beth as I hung up.

"Not happy, but I don't want to kill you, so that's a start."

Beth would get used to the idea that Haven and I weren't together. I just wasn't sure I would.

Predictably, Haven arranged the details of our meeting. Jenny called the day before the shoot to say when and where I needed to go. I knew Haven would be early, so I planned to arrive fifteen minutes before our appointment. Glass Introductions was a high-end-dating agency. I didn't really understand why we were going, or what Haven's article was about. All I knew was I had to turn up and take some shots.

I had done everything that morning to distract myself from coming face to face with Haven. Nothing had worked. As much as I was trying my best to get over her, the thought of seeing her again was like a punch to my stomach. How could she have just walked away so easily? I couldn't stop the images of her that were running through my head like a slideshow. Was she still angry with me? Would we get the opportunity to talk about what had happened, or to talk about anything at all? Hell, I'd settle for hearing about Luke and Ash. The more I thought about it, the more I realized I was looking forward to seeing her despite myself. And more than that, something in me wanted to know she was still the same. She might have called time on anything between us, but I couldn't bear it if she'd cut her hair or started wearing red to work. In the short time we'd been apart, I needed her not to have changed. I didn't want to see evidence that she'd taken what she needed from me and moved on. I wanted to believe a part of her was still mine.

I checked my watch when I arrived. Glass Introductions was on one of the beautiful Mayfair Squares that surrounded a small garden. The sun was shining, the birds were chirping—it was enough to induce a good mood . . . almost. I was early, so I crossed the road and wandered into the greenery, hoping to find a seat where I could try to calm the pulse thrumming through my body. I passed between two bushes at either side of the entrance, and found Haven sitting opposite me on a bench. I saw her a split second before she looked up. From the moment our eyes met, she was all I saw. I wasn't sure if I was still walking, breathing, or whether all my energy was used to look at her. She was so beautiful. I couldn't help but grin at her.

"Hey," I said.

"Hey, Harry."

Her voice was clipped and I couldn't help but wince. She hadn't called me Jake. Harry was the name my friends used. Haven would never, could never, be just a friend. She glanced away from me as I sat next to her on the bench. At least she was wearing her severe bun and funereal clothes. Maybe my Haven was still in there somewhere.

chapter FIFTEEN

Haven

Men like Jake should be illegal. I thought I'd successfully built a shield to render me immune to him when I saw him again. Not so much. He grinned as he greeted me as if nothing was wrong—for a moment I wanted it to be true. I wanted him to kiss me as though we had nowhere to be for days. I wanted to grab him and pull his hard body against mine.

But I didn't. Instead, I gave him a terse nod and I said hello.

Perhaps I was seeing what I wanted to, but I thought the corner of his eye twitched and his nose crinkled when I called him Harry.

I tried to make conversation as if things between us were normal. "I don't think you'll have to stay long. Just to get a couple of shots of Paula and some of the building. As you're early, you could take the outside pictures now."

His chest rose as he inhaled, then hung suspended mid breath, as if he were about to say something. But he didn't and he exhaled. He nodded and turned to the exit. What had he been about to say? Could whatever it was take away the ache in my heart?

Being on another assignment with him was a bad idea. I checked my watch to give me something to do. Was he affected by me at all? He probably had so many women that there was always another waiting in the wings, ready to step in at moment's notice. My throat constricted and I gripped the bench as I tried to catch a breath. I needed to be logical. I couldn't let him see how just a look from him tore me apart inside. There was no time to be affected by mistakes or history. He had been with Millie before me, and no doubt he'd been with someone since. Perhaps he'd met someone on his trip to the US. I had to find a way to be okay with that.

I stood, smoothed my hair, took a deep breath and headed toward Glass Introductions. Jake appeared at my side as I rang the doorbell and almost instantly we were greeted by a very petite older lady and were shown through to Paula's office.

"Good to meet you, Haven," Paula said. She grinned at me, placing her hand over mine as we shook. She kept eye contact with me as though she really was pleased to see me. Some of the tension around having Jake so close began to leave my shoulders. I was so preoccupied with Jake, I'd lost focus on what we were here to do. I needed to get my head in the game.

"Thank you so much for seeing us. I really appreciate you making the time," I replied, smiling at her. She was in her late thirties or early forties and was one of those tall and naturally elegant women who made me feel short and frumpy. "This is Harry, who is going to take some photographs, if that's okay?"

"I never say no to a handsome man who wants to take my photograph," Paula said, smiling at Jake.

Hearing Jake referred to as handsome grated on me. Jake was a good-looking man, no one could dispute that, but he wasn't just a pretty face. It had been his insides that had made his outsides all the more appealing to me. His easy manner, his warmth. The way he called me out on my bad behavior. The way he said my name when we were in bed, as if it were a prayer.

I closed my eyes. *Head in the game.* Paula rounded her desk, which was set back into the huge bay window overlooking the square, retrieved some papers and headed toward two sofas opposite each other at the other end of the room. She gestured for Jake and me to sit. "You founded this business, is that right?" I asked. Paula nodded. "Did you start off working for a competitor and then decide to set up on your own?" I took a seat in front of Paula. Jake sat beside me. The sofa was wide enough that we weren't too close. It wasn't that he made me uncomfortable, more that, with him sitting next to me, it was an insight into how things might have been if we were together. And although we were there as colleagues, for a moment, I could let myself imagine that we were more. I sat forward and reached for the water on the coffee table.

"No, I was a dancer," she said. Something in my face must have given me away. "No, not that kind of dancer." She threw her head back and laughed as I smiled uncomfortably. "I went to ballet school and when I was just past my twenty-first birthday I took a fall and had to stop dancing completely. I had to rethink all my plans at that point. I had no idea what I was going to do until I spoke to an accomplished family friend who told me I should make a business out of what I enjoyed doing." She sat forward and began to pour the tea into the cups set out in front of us. "Everyone assumed I'd end up a dance teacher, but what I really loved was helping people find love. Even as a teen, I liked to set up my friends on dates and play Cupid. And really, that's what I do here. I get to know people, and then I put two together who I think have chemistry." Paula smiled at me. "Milk?" she asked.

"Yes please. That's so inspiring and great advice," I said as I scanned my notes. "Perhaps you could take me through what would be an initial interview with a new applicant? Or is it a form that you fill in?"

"We call them members, but of course, whatever you need." She set my tea in front of me and poured a second cup for Jake. "The normal process is split into two parts. First, we discuss you and how you spend your time—your job, how many hours that takes up, and whether or not it involves any traveling and also any family commitments or hobbies you have. Then we get deeper into your character—your values and pertinent background. In the second part of the interview, we get into your previous relationship history and what you are looking for in a partner. I would never set it out like that to a member. Normally we would have a relaxed conversation. I try to ensure we pick up all the relevant information. Perhaps I could profile Jake and you can take notes? Then, of course, if you're going to date our members I'll need to hear from you as well."

My face started to heat as Jake's presence in the room became bigger and bigger as I considered Paula's suggestion.

Did I want to hear what he was going to say about what he wanted in a woman? He was all I was aware of as I faced the prospect of giving this stranger lots of personal information about myself.

"I'm just here as the photographer," Jake said.

"Have you already found love?" Paula asked.

He held up his left hand, showing her his ring finger. "I'm still single," he replied, and smiled tightly. "I'm very busy at work. I'm establishing a new alternative energy company. I don't have much time for dating."

Paula looked at me, as if I could elaborate for him, and then focused back on Jake. My heartbeat was so loud I wondered if they could hear it. He hadn't answered her question. Had he found love?

"So you're not looking for love?" Paula asked.

"Harry," I managed to say. "So we don't take up any more of your valuable time than we need to, why don't you take some shots of Paula and then we can let you go and Paula can take me through the interview process?" I stared at his oh-so-broad chest. I couldn't bring myself to glance up to meet his eyes.

He nodded and stood. Paula didn't push the point. I watched as he expertly moved around the room, directing Paula and taking shots with various backgrounds and in different poses. I buried myself in my notes, pretending to be doing anything but absorbing every detail of Jake's movements.

Twenty minutes later Jake seemed to have what he needed.

"You were great, Paula, so natural. I think I have everything I need, so I'm going to head out," Jake said.

"You can come back anytime. Let me give you a card."

"Thanks," he replied. "I don't seem to get it right on my own; so you never know, I might give you a call." My gut twisted. I'd thought about Jake with another Millie, but the thought of Jake finding *love* was a whole different ball game. It was as if I couldn't think about that and breathe. Somehow the two things weren't compatible. Thank goodness he had resisted Paula giving him the full interview. I didn't think I could take much more of him being so close, let alone hear about his potential future without me.

"Well, I have a couple of beautiful and successful women who I would love you to spend some time with, so keep in touch."

"Thank you." Jake smiled. "I'll let you get down to the real interview now."

"It was a pleasure to meet you, Harry."

"The pleasure was all mine," he replied.

His smile receded when he turned to me. "Haven, I hope you find what you're looking for," he said, and then he was gone.

I watched as the door closed behind him. If I hadn't been sitting down I would have fallen. I reached for my tea, trying to stop myself from rewinding and replaying the last words he had spoken. My hands shook as I brought the glass to my lips. What did he mean when he said that? Was he angry with me? Hurt?

"How long have you been single?" Paula asked, pulling me out of my head.

This was going to be a bit more difficult than I expected. I wasn't great at opening up to strangers at the best of times. "A while."

"Okay, so, talk to me about what you want when you're dating," Paula interrupted my thoughts of Jake.

"I'm not sure," I replied. I wasn't aware that I looked for anything in particular. The fact that they had asked me out seemed to be the common factor among the men I'd dated.

"We have to narrow down the pool. Let's start physically. What are your turn ons and turn offs."

"Well, obviously, if he looks like David Gandy, that would be a bonus."

"Or Harry? He's very handsome. Are you sure he's single?"

"I don't know. He always has women on the go," I replied. I couldn't imagine he would stay single for long.

"I'm sure he has plenty of options, but that doesn't mean he's making the right choices. Is he wealthy?"

I shrugged. I wanted to get off the subject. Why was she still talking about him?

"Sorry, so yes, David Gandy. You like them tall and dark."

"I guess." I shifted in my seat.

"And successful, obviously."

I stared across the room at a painting, trying to think about whether a man's wealth made a difference to me. Before Jake I would have said categorically that I preferred a man who wasn't wealthy, but now . . .

"I'm not sure money and success matters so much to me. More that they love what they do. I don't like men who are too . . . cocky? Not unless they've got something to back it up with. And that can't be just wealth. There has to be more to them than that."

"That's interesting," said Paula. "And what else? Describe what sort of person he is."

I paused and then said, "Confident." She nodded, encouraging me to continue. "Kind and funny. Strong and hardworking—and family should be important to him."

"Anything else?" she asked.

"I like the idea of being better because of the man I'm with, you know?"

"Tell me," Paula said.

"Someone who sees the best version of me and nurtures that part of me so that's the side that grows."

I took a deep breath and my mind wandered to the picture of me that Jake had sent along with the Sandy interviews. That was the woman I wanted to be.

I was describing Jake.

"And are you sure you haven't found him?" Paula asked, pulling me from my thoughts.

I smiled and shook my head, though I wasn't so sure.

"Okay. I have some ideas of who you might be a good fit with. I'll need to make sure they're fine with the article, though."

"No identifying information will be put in the piece."

Paula nodded. "That's important and I'm trusting you. We guard our member's anonymity as fiercely as they guard their wealth."

"Of course. You don't need to worry," I said.

"So, I'll arrange three dates for you. Can I make a personal suggestion?"

"Um . . . okay." What was she going to say?

"You're a gorgeous girl who's not making the most of herself."

My cheeks began to heat. I was used to Ash saying stuff like that to me, but I wasn't prepared for the oh-so-charming Paula, a woman I had only met an hour ago, to say it.

"You need to loosen up a bit. The hair needs to be less . . . rigid. And perhaps show a little cleavage or leg, or both."

"Um." I tried to formulate a response that wasn't defensive. "Should we be judging people on their looks?" I asked.

"I don't work with 'shoulds.' All I know is that in reality, people will and do judge others on their appearance. And it's such an easy win for you—you're a beautiful girl."

I raised my eyebrows at her. I didn't know how to respond, I just felt awkward being assessed by a stranger. I had armor for a reason—I didn't want people to have access to the fleshy truth of me.

"Don't get me wrong, I advise strongly against having sex until couples properly know each other and have committed to an exclusive relationship. This isn't about being slutty. Just, brighten things up a bit. Just be you, but the best version of yourself."

She really sounded like Ash. It smarted, because I knew she was right, they both were. I was deliberately hiding and had been ever since I could remember. The clothes were a form of protection. If people didn't see the real me, they couldn't hate the real me, they couldn't hurt the real me. I just didn't know how to do anything else.

"You know that this is for a magazine article, though? I'm not actually searching for a boyfriend. And shouldn't love be based on more than looks anyway?" I asked.

"Are you telling me that you don't look at a cute guy over an ugly one? Looks are important but they're only a part of the package. A beautiful diamond is always a gem, but it doesn't hurt to put it in a velvet box and tie a satin bow around it. You're single. You never know, love might just find you. Be open."

chapter SIXTEEN

Jake

A few days later, I was due to meet Haven again. It was the first of her dates with the so-called eligible men from Glass Introductions. Jenny, of course, called me to make the arrangements.

"I'll give you the details of the three dates, then the idea is that you'll photograph Haven before she leaves, then do a couple of shots at the beginning of the evening. But you have to make sure you don't include her date's face. It's all totally anonymous," Jenny said, explaining the set up for the rest of this feature. "Haven will pick one who she'll have an additional date with and you'll do the same with that one."

"And what's this article about? How to land a rich man?"

Jenny laughed. "I suppose. I think it's an insight into the lives of the wealthy, what the moneyed look for in a woman, that's all. But she might meet her Prince Charming. You never know."

It was part torture, part insanity, making me watch her date other men . . . even if it was for the magazine. The thought was bad enough, but actually having to witness it? It was as if the gods were laughing at me.

"So tonight I have to go to Haven's apartment to shoot her pre-date prep before going with her to the Holly Club?"

"Yeah. We thought you could photograph her in a couple of different outfits. I'm going to come along as well to make sure she wears something appropriate."

"Okay, I'll see you later." I zoned out. I was trying to think of something that would take the edge off what wasn't going to be my favorite way to spend my Saturday night.

I cancelled the call and started scrolling through my contacts. I found a name and pressed the green button. "Hey, Nicola." One of my exes, Nicola and I had dated for three months, and despite it not working out, we still went out for dinner every now and then.

"Long time, no speak, handsome. What have you been up to?" Nicola answered.

"Work. I've been in the US recently. What about you?" We both knew that was code for asking her whether or not she was dating.

"Same, I've just come back from Milan." Her response told me she was single.

Nicola was a model and was abroad a lot. She was a cool, drama-free girl who cared less about where she was seen than Millie and wasn't as selfish. I hoped seeing her would distract me from having to work with Haven.

"Are you exhausted or can I take you to dinner tonight?"

"I'm never too tired to spend an evening with you, Harry."

"Sounds perfect. I'll pick you up," I said.

"Let me meet you there. Where did you have in mind?"

I hadn't expected Nicola to be free so I'd not thought of where to go. "The Holly Club?" I suggested. I was a member and I was going to be there anyway, and it meant I could see how Haven got on with her date.

"Great. See you there at eight. Got to go, darling. *Ciao*."

I slumped back in my chair. Nicola would be good. She was easy to be with and fun. She'd be the perfect antidote to Haven.

Later that evening, I pulled up outside the familiar railings in front of Haven's apartment block. A rush of guilt passed through me as I looked up at the door to her building. I wondered what would have happened if I had set Robert straight that day and told him I thought he was crazy for thinking Haven wouldn't outshine Sandy. Haven still may have run from me at some point—there was always that risk with her. She was naturally distrustful and didn't open up easily, but if I'd had more time with her I could have at least shown her what she'd be missing.

It was pretty twisted—being at Haven's to photograph her before she went on a date with someone else. The last time I was here, she wouldn't let me in. As much as I'd accepted our situation, when I was forced to think about it, her decision frustrated the shit out of me. Being here, working with her, meant I could think of little else.

I pressed the intercom and was buzzed in without a greeting. When I arrived at her apartment, Jenny flung the door open.

"Who knew? Haven's hot," Jenny said excitedly, her eyes wide. "I'm styling her, it's so much fun. She has color in her wardrobe, Harry! Colors that aren't black and gray. Can you believe it?"

I forced a grin at her. I knew Haven well enough to guess that when she was with people she trusted, like Ash and Luke, she became more colorful in every way. I didn't want Jenny to know that too—it made me just another work colleague.

"I'm going to get you to come and photograph her amongst a mountain of discarded clothing options. Sound good?"

"Sure," I replied.

"You're not very talkative. Are you okay?" she asked, leading me down a corridor.

"I'm fine. Just want to get this right. I didn't bring any lighting or anything, so I'm not sure how it's going to look." We passed a huge mirror taking up most of one wall that had sticky notes and postcards plastered all over it. I wanted to stop to take it in, but Jenny was excited to get started and I was moved on quickly.

"Don't worry, it'll be fine. We want them to look like they've just been snapped by a girlfriend."

Haven had her back to us as we walked into the dimly lit room. "Can you zip me up, Jenny?" she asked as she squirmed, trying to fasten the back of the dress herself. The curve of her neck was revealed as she scooped her hair up, out of the way of the zipper. My blood started to heat. Memories of my lips pressed against that exposed flesh punctuated my breathing. I hovered in the doorway, not wanting to make things worse by being closer to her. It wasn't meant to feel like this. I was supposed to be fine with her decision to end things. I was supposed to be over her.

Jenny hurried over and zipped up the back of the dress. I tried not to look at Haven, but it was impossible. She was beautiful. She always was, but it was the way she was so unaware of it—totally oblivious to the effect she had on me. I couldn't stop trailing my glance up and down her body, taking her in as if she were still mine, pausing on the curve of her hip, then the roundness of her ass. I was pulled out of my thoughts by an awareness that she was wearing this dress for another man. On second thought, it seemed kinda short and very tight.

"Let's get a look at you," Jenny said.

Haven turned and something popped inside me. I had to dip my eyes from her. I couldn't bear to see her excited about the evening. I scanned the rest of the room, looking anywhere but Haven. It was my first time in her bedroom. I hadn't expected it to be under these circumstances. I'd wanted to be in here after Paris. I slid my eyes over the patterned bed quilt that was worn and homemade, and then to the metal-framed bed. We could have had some fun, tying Haven to that. Watching her come as if it were the first time her body had ever felt anything like it.

Jenny poked me in the ribs, pulling me out of my fantasy just before I lost myself in it. "See, what did I tell you? She's hot. Give us the man's perspective. What do you think?"

"You look beautiful, Haven," I said, trying to sound as detached as possible, as I attempted to conceal that all I wanted to do was peel her out of that dress and tie her down. She was stunning. As I met her eyes, she seemed unsure. She was pulling on the inside of her cheek with her teeth. She had no reason to doubt herself. I smiled gently and she caught my eye, then looked away quickly as if she'd remembered herself.

"Do you think it's right for a first date?" Jenny asked, turning her head toward me.

"I have no idea what your objective is, so I can't comment," I said. If she was going out with me, she could dress in a garbage bag for all I cared.

"We're trying to find her a man, silly. She's bound to impress in this."

"I'm not wearing it. It's too short. This guy could be a total pervert. And it's too dressy for dinner," Haven said.

"I'm not going to let you wear black, just be warned, but okay, let's photograph it and then we can put in the article why we didn't choose it. I'm going to pick something else out."

Haven stood awkwardly as I took out my camera. "Why don't you go and stand by the mirror—you can pretend you're trying to decide if it's right."

She nodded and moved across the room.

"What about this? Great color," Jenny shouted from the closet, holding up the red dress Haven had worn in Paris.

I watched for Haven's reaction and she flicked her eyes quickly to mine, and then back to Jenny. "Not that one."

"But it's awesome. It will go beautifully with your hair," Jenny said.

"No, not that one. What about the electric-blue, one-shoulder number? It's Ash's. She makes me wear it sometimes."

Jenny was easily dissuaded.

I took a dozen or so shots, not bothering too much with setting, or direction. I just wanted to get this over with.

"I'll go and wait in the living room while you change," I said.

"Okay," Haven replied without meeting my eyes.

I wandered back down the hall. The sitting room was bright and warm. There was none of the order that I might have expected of Haven. On her sofa, there were a thousand mismatched throw pillows. On a dresser in the corner, there was a collection of frames. I drew closer and saw pictures of Ash, Haven and Luke through the years. At the very back was a picture of what looked like her mother and father on their wedding day. Then another of what I could only assume were her parents, her and Luke. What all the shots had in common was that they showed a carefree, happy Haven. The Haven that, for a brief moment, I'd known.

"Harry, get in here," Jenny called.

"This is totally the date dress, isn't it, Harry?" Jenny asked, her attention focused on Haven. "It's not too tight–it just hugs in all the right places."

"I don't know," Haven said, sounding unsure.

Haven looked incredible. The dress came to well below her knees and her perfect tits were well covered, but the fact was, any guy was going to be imagining every inch of her body underneath that dress. It clung to her like a second skin. The room seemed to close in on me as her vulnerability and uncertainty hit me, mixing with images of her writhing on her quilt under my tongue.

I started taking shots in the hope that the camera would hide my desire, which I was sure showed all over my face.

"I think it's too informal. It's just jersey," Haven said to Jenny as if I wasn't there.

"No, if we add on some jewelry, it will be perfect. You don't want to seem as if you're trying too hard."

"Jenny, I'm not going there to impress anyone, remember? This is work."

"For crying out loud. First rule of dating, Haven—just because you don't like them doesn't mean you don't want them to worship you."

"That's a stupid rule," Haven replied.

"Says the single girl," Jenny said. "Anyway, I thought we were doing three outfits. There might be something better in there."

"No, I'm done. I don't care enough about this shit."

Warmth spread inside me. I'd missed her feisty mouth and the way she had no time for things that would have kept women like Millie occupied for hours. She was special and I'd not fought for her.

chapter SEVENTEEN

Haven

"Perfect. Now, perfume, shoes and a bag and you'll be done. Harry, can you order a cab?" Jenny asked as we finished up the date preparation.

"I've got the car. I'll drive us. Are you coming, Jenny?"

"No, I'll just get the tube."

I needed some air, some space. Having Jake in my bedroom, taking my photograph was too much. It was as if I were faking it—trussed up like a prized cow, trying to present my best side, the side that wasn't me. I couldn't breathe. I was suffocating. I wanted to scream at them both to get out. I wanted to get a cab on my own, but now Jake was driving. This was too overwhelming, too confusing. Why was he here? Why were his kind smiles and his long fingers picking at the edge of my resolve?

"Okay, guys, I'm going this way," Jenny said, pointing left as we got outside. "Good luck tonight, Haven. Let me know how it goes."

"I don't need luck. It's not a date. It's work," I replied, being more scratchy than I'd intended.

"It doesn't mean you can't enjoy yourself," she said as she headed off down the street.

"Thanks for your help," I called after her.

Jake opened the car door for me as if it were our date. "You've brought the fuckmobile?" I asked, then immediately wished I hadn't. I navigated my way gingerly into the car. I felt stupid dressed up like this for what was essentially a work meeting.

"It's the weekend, give me a break," he said, then closed the door as I got in. He rounded the hood and slid in the other side.

His proximity was more than distracting. I'd never been so aware of him physically. His denim-covered thighs tensed as he braked before a traffic light and I couldn't pull my eyes away. He turned up the air and all I could think about was stroking his hand. The smell of him—that clean, warm, masculine smell—was all around me, making my skin buzz wherever it was exposed. I had to work to control my breathing, to stop myself reaching for him, to hold myself back from asking him to kiss me.

I needed out of the car.

"This feels weird," I said, breaking our silence as we drove along Edgware Road, stopping at more traffic lights.

He nodded but didn't say anything. Maybe it didn't feel odd to him.

My phone buzzed. It was my date, Gerald, texting to say he'd arrived and was looking forward to seeing me. It was nice.

"That him?" Jake asked.

"Yeah. It's just work," I said, for some reason, needing to explain getting a text from another man while I was with him.

"It is what it is," he replied.

What did that mean? We drove the rest of the way in silence.

The nearest parking space was a block away from The Holly Club. Jake offered to drop me off, but I didn't want to go inside and meet this guy on my own.

"Aren't you going to struggle to walk in those?" Jake asked.

My cheeks heated as Jake glanced at my feet. The last time he'd noticed my shoes was in Paris. He'd told me he was going to fuck me in my heels. He'd made good on his promise. Jake's eyes met mine and I quickly looked away.

"I'll be fine. They're not that high," I muttered.

"The club is fine with me taking some shots?"

"Yes, Jenny checked."

He held the door open for me and I stepped inside an oak-paneled hallway. A hostess stood behind a dark wooden table toward the rear of the space.

"Good evening, Mr. Harrison. Nice to see you," she said, looking directly at Jake and ignoring me. Anger seared through me. Of course they would know him. I wondered how many women he'd brought to dinner here. "Are you planning to have a drink in the bar before going upstairs?" the hostess asked.

"Mr. Harrison is here to take some photographs. I'm here with *Rallegra*. My assistant should have arranged something?"

The hostess seemed confused.

"I'll be having dinner afterward, Belinda. Please let me know if my guest arrives early," Jake said.

Belinda smiled warmly. "Oh, I see. That's fine. Let me take you through. So you're Ms. Daniels?" she asked, looking at me. I nodded curtly.

"You're eating? Here?" I whispered. "With Millie?" Was he trying to sabotage things, or make me jealous? The pieces weren't fitting together properly.

"Yes to the dinner part and no, not with Millie. We broke up, I told you that. This is my Saturday night, Haven. There's no reason I should waste it because I have to spend ten minutes taking some photos of you on your date." He sounded exasperated and I hated myself for creating that in him. I wanted to be the cool, sexy girl he wished he hadn't let get away.

Belinda led us down a dark corridor, where old satirical cartoons were displayed on the walls on either side of us. I turned back to Jake. "Why do you have to bring her here?" I said it before I realized that doing so gave away that it bothered me. I didn't want to see Jake dating other women.

"What's the problem? I'm a member here," he replied.

I didn't respond. I didn't want to reveal anything else and Belinda was showing us into the bar.

"Hi, Gerald," I said as I extended my hand to my date. I recognized him from the picture I'd seen at Glass Introductions. He was quite a bit older than me, but still attractive. Though, his photograph hadn't told me how short he was.

"Haven? Hi, it's a pleasure to meet you. You look beautiful."

My cheeks heated. I felt anything but. I felt fake and overly made up but he was hardly going to say anything else, was he?

"Thank you. I thought we could just get the photographs out of the way and then enjoy our evening, if that's all right with you?" I tried to sound enthusiastic about our evening. I didn't want Jake to think my mind would be on anything but Gerald. I wanted Jake to think that I was looking forward to spending time with someone else.

"Sure thing," Gerald said.

"Why don't you guys just have a drink and get to know each other. Pretend I'm not here," Jake said, his normal collected self. I wished I hadn't mentioned him bringing his date to the club. If he was unaffected by this situation then I was going to do my best to match his indifference.

Gerald may not have been my type, but I wasn't going to give Jake the satisfaction of giving any of that away in my interaction with him. This was a job and I was good at it.

I was laughing overly hard at something Gerald had said when Jake approached the table.

"I think I have what I need, so I'm going to leave you to it. Have a wonderful evening. Good to meet you, Gerald," he said. He shook Gerald's hand and gave me a nod before leaving.

"Where do you live?" Gerald asked me.

"Little Venice. What about you?"

"I have a place by Hyde Park. And then a place in Surrey. And a small pad in New York."

I laughed to myself. I didn't think he was really interested in where I lived. Was his question simply an opportunity for him to tell me all about how wealthy he was? Perhaps that was what women expected and wanted when they joined Glass Introductions. Or perhaps he just wanted me to like him.

“Do you travel much?” he asked.

“I love Paris,” I said before I’d thought about it. It was true; I just didn’t like to think about why.

“You do?” he said.

I smiled. “It’s a beautiful city. I was there recently for work.” I shouldn’t have brought up Paris. I needed to change this subject. “What do you like to do in your spare time?” I spotted Jake moving toward the door of the bar. I followed his line of sight and came to possibly the best-looking woman I’d ever seen. She was tall and very slender with a chest small enough to be natural but big enough for men to notice. She had long, silky black hair and eyes that screamed wild. She wasn’t dressed up like Millie had been. She wore skinny jeans, a silk vest and killer heels. Of course that was Jake’s date. It couldn’t possibly be anyone else.

“Do you like to ski?” Gerald asked.

I hadn’t been listening. I turned my attention back to him. “Not really. I never learned as a child and I think it’s hard to start as an adult. I’ve only been a couple of times.”

Jake had never struck me as a boob man in particular. He’d seemed to like every part of my body equally.

“Skiing in the US is better than Europe. There’s just more space,” Gerald said.

“Do you go a lot?” I asked.

Jake took a table at the other end of the bar, so once he was seated I couldn’t see him or his date. *Good, I should be focusing on Gerald.*

“As much as I can. Aspen mainly, but other resorts in Colorado and sometimes Whistler. I like to mix it up. I have a lot of friends who ski and a couple of them have places, so if I'm visiting them I get to go to different areas."

"Sounds fun." I smiled.

"It is. My job can be stressful, so it's good to blow off steam. And the après-ski always helps."

"That's the bit I'm better at."

He laughed as Belinda approached our table. "Would you like to go through to the restaurant?" she asked.

I nodded and we stood up. I took the opportunity to steal a glance at Jake and Queen of the Glamazons. They were hunched toward each other over the table, much closer than Gerald and I had been. I wondered how long he'd known her.

It was good to go into the restaurant for dinner. A bit of distance between Jake and I was what I needed.

"Can I ask why you joined the agency?"

Gerald nodded. "I have a small circle of friends who I've known for years. Some are married. I don't really meet anyone apart from at work and I don't like mixing business with pleasure. I'd like to find someone, and the agency seemed like the way to do it."

It was a logical answer. He seemed like a genuine guy. "That makes sense," I said.

"And you're single?" he asked.

"Yeah but . . . "

"I get it. I know this is for an article."

I squeezed a smile from my lips.

"I just thought you seemed interesting. When I saw your headshot and your profile, I thought, hey, she's not seeing anyone. I might just win her over, even if she is working." He smiled and I thought how nice it would be if it were possible for Gerald to win me over. For life to be that simple.

Thankfully, we were seated at the other end of the dining room to Jake and his date. But I could still see them. Effortlessly beautiful, she sat facing me. At least I couldn't hear what was being said. Not that I was interested. I needed to concentrate on my date, on the article.

"Have you ever been married?" I asked Gerald.

"I've come close a couple of times, but no. No kids either." He looked a bit sad and I wondered why he'd not found a wife. Wasn't he the type of guy that Millie would have had her claws in in a minute?

"You're a rich, handsome man. How come it hasn't worked out for you?"

"Well, I'd like to think I've not lost hope," he said, his eyes twinkling at me. I could feel the heat in my cheeks.

"Sorry. I just meant—"

"It's a fair question. I spent my twenties and early thirties working really hard and didn't have much time for anything else. When I came up for air, the music had stopped and there were no seats left. That's how it felt anyway."

Wow, the idea that the time to find our soul mate had run out was depressing . . . but not unrealistic. There was an age by which people tended to have paired off.

"All your friends were married off?"

"Most of them by the time I noticed."

"There's definitely a window for women," I said.

"A window?" he asked.

"Yeah, I mean, with the girls at work? I feel like they're on a countdown to get a ring before the clock gets to zero. I'm not sure it matters who the guy is."

He chuckled. "Yeah, now that you say that I think women can be a bit like that. My first proper girlfriend really wanted to get married before she hit thirty. She had a complete obsession about it."

"You didn't want to marry her?"

He took a beat, clearly thinking before he replied. "I think I did for a while there, but . . . "

"Sorry, you don't have to tell me."

"I'm just trying to remember what it was, but I think it was that she didn't want to marry me, she just wanted to get married. It soured it for me."

"I get that. I'm not sure I believe in 'the one.' I just know I don't want to settle for someone who isn't right for me," I said.

"I could tell you were a romantic."

His comment caught me off guard. Deep down I considered myself a romantic but I didn't expect anyone, not even Ash or Luke to see that in me. "I'm not sure I'd describe myself like that," I said, grinning at him. He was nice, and kind and subtly flirtatious. He was good company. I rarely talked to people about how I saw the world, but it felt easy to talk to him.

"Of course you are. It's one of the reasons I know we'll get along," he said. I smiled at him. "What wine would you like?" he asked, indicating the list.

"Surprise me," I said.

"I intend to," he replied.

For about twenty minutes, I forgot about Jake and his impossibly beautiful date. I felt good.

chapter EIGHTEEN

Jake

I didn't like Gerald. I certainly didn't like the thought of him having dinner with Haven. And after dinner what would happen between them? Was he driving her home? Would she invite him in? I messed about with the food on my plate, then dropped my fork, my appetite having disappeared. I glanced across at Nicola and she was staring back at me.

"Are you okay, Harry? You seem a bit . . . off."

"I'm sorry. This new business is taking a lot of energy."

She raised an eyebrow at me. "Really?"

I grinned. "No pun intended. There's a great deal at stake. I just want it to go well. Anyway, tell me about Milan."

"I will when I've been to the ladies'. I'll be right back," she said as she left the table.

I took the opportunity to glance at Haven's table. I had deliberately sat with my back to her so I didn't get distracted. It hadn't worked. She didn't notice me look. She was smiling, as if she was enjoying herself. *Perhaps I should offer her a ride home?* Then she wouldn't have to go home with a total stranger. I pulled out my cell and texted her, offering to take her home at the end of the evening. She must have had it switched to silent or ignored it because she didn't check to see who was texting her. She was having a good time with Gerald and I was just making myself miserable. It was ridiculous. Haven had made her choice, and I needed to leave her to it. It didn't matter how I felt. Beth was wrong about that.

I resolved to make more of an effort when Nicola came back to the table. She was a nice girl and I was a dick for bringing her here.

"So, Milan?" I asked when she got back. "How was it?"

"Oh, you know. Full of Italians. It doesn't seem to matter which city I'm in these days, it's the same old, same old. You know?"

I nodded. "You're a smart woman. Do you not want to do something with all that brain power of yours?" I'd always liked how sharp she was—she'd made some really good decisions during her career.

"I've been thinking the same thing. I'm considering doing some talent management at the moment."

"That sounds great. Managing other models?"

"God no, they would drive me crazy. More like actors and musicians, maybe? I'm just talking to a few people at the moment. I want to set up on my own. And I can still model here and there for the time being."

"Well, if you want some help on your business plan, let me know," I offered.

"You'd do that?" She smiled. Right there was why she'd been so successful as a model. She was gorgeous.

"Of course," I said as I grinned back at her.

"So, dessert?" she asked.

"You know that you'll just have one mouthful and then leave the rest. It's such a waste."

"Well, it's better to have a taste than to miss out altogether."

Was that true or would it be easier to have never known Haven, never had the promise of something so sweet?

We pulled up in front of Nicola's building just before midnight and I cut the engine.

"Are you sure you don't want to come in? I could do with a little company," she said.

Part of me wanted to spend the night with her. To lose myself for a couple of hours, to get a break from having a head full of Haven, but I couldn't do that to Nicola. I'd had a really nice evening and genuinely enjoyed myself, but before I started something new I needed to clear some space in my head.

"Another time? You're great but—"

"Your head's somewhere else?" she suggested.

I nodded. Had she guessed I was distracted by another woman? I couldn't imagine it happened to her very often. She was beautiful, clever, funny. She just wasn't Haven. "I had a really great time," I said.

She leaned across and kissed me on the cheek. I watched as she made her way into her building. When the door closed behind her, I pulled out my phone. Still no response from Haven. She and Gerald had left the restaurant before us. *Should I call her?* Just to check she was okay? I dialed.

"Jake, what is it?" I hadn't expected her to pick up. It was the first time she had since the weekend after Paris.

"I just wanted to make sure you were okay, and to offer you a ride home." Jesus, I sounded like a douche.

"Thanks. Of course I'm fine, I don't need a lift." Her voice was softer with me than it had been when we'd first arrived at the restaurant. Was that the alcohol? Was she drunk? Was Gerald still there?

"Are you sure? It would be no trouble." I wanted her to tell me she was at home already, or in a cab on her own.

"I'm sure—and you don't want to be rude to your date," she said.

"I just dropped Nicola at home," I said. "So, you're not in a ditch?"

"I'm not in a ditch," she replied, giving me nothing.

"Are you at home?" I asked.

"Where else would I be?" She hung up the phone.

I grinned as I slung my cell onto the dash. Had she deliberately used my proper name? Something in my gut fluttered. I'd missed our jousting.

"How was it?" Beth asked as I joined her on the sofa. "I wasn't sure if you would be back."

"Yeah, good. Nicola's great but my head is spinning at the moment. I need to work some stuff out," I said. "How was your date with Saturday night TV? Have you ever thought you should go out, like with a real-life person?" I asked her. "I mean, things have been good for a while now. Do you want me to set you up?" Beth had been sober for over two years and she seemed happy, but I was worried that she had shut down after what had happened with her ex-boyfriend.

Beth scowled at me. "No, you weird brother slash pimp."

I tapped her foot with my knee. "I'm not expecting you to have sex with my friends for money." I rolled my eyes at her. "I just know some good guys who periodically tell me you're hot. I punch them in their face when they say it, obviously, but, you should think about maybe going on a date or something."

She took a breath. "I'm not ready," she said softly, concentrating on the television.

"What does your sponsor say? She must have mentioned it. It's been nearly three years."

"Can you drop it? I said I'm not in that place yet. And anyway, you're hardly a glowing recommendation for dating. Have you ever made it past three months?"

"I'm a guy. What can I say?" I said, trying to brush over her point.

"You can say that you're a commitment phobe with bad taste in women." Beth was always needling me about not being able to get past the three-month mark. Wasn't I just living most guys' fantasies?

"So what's the problem—my taste in women, or my inability to commit?"

"Both."

I threw a pillow at her.

"I like Haven," she said. "I know I've only met her briefly, but she seemed different from those other girls you date. And I like how tied up she's got you."

I wasn't sure how to respond. Haven was different, that was for sure. "I'm not sure she's got me tied up."

Beth raised her eyebrows. "And before you tell me she doesn't like you and that she's moved on or whatever excuse you're formulating, she does like you. I could tell at the gallery and it doesn't matter what shit's happened. If she's the right girl for you, then fight for her. Stop making excuses."

"It's not that simple."

"Well, you see, I think it is. You can make it that simple. You're good at that, Jake. You're good at getting things you want."

"Things yes, but not people. If I was, we'd still be a family." A wave of regret swept over me when I thought about what we didn't have back in Chicago. At one time, we'd been the archetypal American family.

"How did you work that out? You can't control people. You weren't responsible for Mom getting shot any more than I was, and you're not in control of the fact Dad finds it all too difficult to handle and doesn't know how to be with us. We are a family, Jake. It might be just you and me, but we're still a family and you made that happen."

"Beth," I warned. She knew I didn't want to get into this. I never did. It was too painful.

"What, you can start pushing me on dating, but I can't call you on your shit? I mean it. I think you deliberately pick women you know it's not going to work out with so you don't have to feel responsible for anyone else."

I let Beth's words sink in. Was she right? I knew I picked women who didn't require much emotional investment from me but I'd never really thought about why. "Jesus, I need a drink. Why the fuck don't we have a single bit of booze in this apartment?" I asked, grinning at her.

"Because I'm an alcoholic, dickhead."

"Oh yeah. That must be it." We both laughed. "Wow, we can joke about it. Who'd have thought?"

I stood, ruffled her hair and headed to bed. I'd never connected my short-term relationships with anything other than being a guy. Was Beth onto something? Perhaps I held off on anything I couldn't control.

Maybe I'd given up on Haven too easily.

chapter NINETEEN

Haven

"Morning, Haven," Jake said as he sat down opposite me for our usual Monday morning meeting.

"Hi Ja—Harry." I'd lost track of what I should be calling him and why. He was Jake to me, but somehow that felt too intimate to say.

"Have a good evening on Saturday?" he asked.

"Yes, thank you. Did you?" *Did you kiss her, touch her, take her to bed?*

"Yes, very enjoyable," he replied.

"I'm sure," I mumbled. Jake grinned and I couldn't bear to think about what had caused his smile. I tried to catch my breath, to push down the panic in my chest. He wasn't hers . . .

"When's your next date?"

"Tomorrow night, if you're free, and the final one on Thursday." I tried to sound breezy. I wanted to get this over with. Dating with Jake hovering just made my feelings for him refresh. I needed distance from him.

"You're packing them in."

"It's work, Harry." For some reason I wanted to reassure him these weren't proper dates—even if he seemed relaxed, as if we had never been anything, part of me wanted him to understand that I could never be so casual, I could never move on so quickly.

"And when's the super date?" he asked.

"Saturday. I need to write it up on Sunday. Our big celeb feature for next week has pulled out and Robert asked me to move this up." Finishing off this article so quickly would be a challenge, but I was excited that Robert had trusted me. I wanted to be the one he could rely on to get him out of a hole. The more he felt that, the better my chances of promotion. "I might just see if Gerald is free, then if he can't make it, choose one of the others."

"You liked Gerald then?"

I shrugged, trying to keep my eyes on my to-do list. How did he switch into friends mode so easily with me? Asking about my dates as if we were nothing to each other. As though we had never had anything.

Robert took his seat between Jake and me.

"Great job on the Sandy Fox piece, you two. Did Haven tell you the first part is running next week?"

"No, she didn't. I'm glad you're pleased with it, but Haven did all the hard work," Jake replied.

"I wouldn't have got the story if you hadn't been there, Harry, we both know it," I said.

"Well, it's an excellent job. If you ever want to give up making millions to come and be a full-time staff photographer, consider yourself hired."

Jake laughed. "Thanks, I'll bear it in mind, but no promises. In fact, I'm out from the end of next week, I'm afraid. I've got to fly to Palo Alto again, and then all my attention has to be focused on Elemental Energy."

I swallowed at Jake's announcement. I'd known it was coming. The new guy was about to start. But now the time had arrived and I didn't feel prepared. There would be no reason for me to see Jake once he left *Rallegra*. My heart was thundering through my chest. Confronted with the reality of Jake being gone, I realized that it was the last thing I wanted. My mind started racing, trying to find reasons to make him stay, for excuses to see him. Perhaps he would have another exhibition I could go to? My breath became shorter as my panic increased. This was all my fault. I'd pushed him away, blamed him for things that he wasn't responsible for. I needed to find a solution, to convince him to be in my life in some way. I'd never experienced anything like I had with Jake and I'd just ended things assuming I would be okay and life would move on. But I couldn't imagine anyone ever knowing me like he seemed to.

I dared a glance up at him to find him looking at me. I tried to blank my thoughts, concerned he could read my anxiety. I couldn't seem to look away, scared that if I did, he would disappear. The corners of his mouth turned up and I remembered what his lips could do to my body, how his tongue elicited sounds from me I didn't know I could make, how he seemed to free a part of me with his touch. I squirmed in my seat and his grin deepened. It was as if he could see what I was thinking. A familiar warmth spread across my cheeks. I dug my fingers into my hair, pulling strands out of the pins. I needed to think, to breathe.

I stumbled out of the meeting, desperate for air and needing a plan.

"Jake, I mean Harry," I called as he passed my cubicle, wanting time with him before he left for good.

"I want you to call me Jake," he replied as he leaned against the entrance of my work area. I wondered why he wore his shirts like that, without a tie, open, and hinting at the hard body beneath the fabric. A body I'd seen in all its glory in Paris. A body that made my body sing.

"That was before, you know . . . "

"No, it's forever. Call me Jake." *Forever.*

I had no answer to that. "I just wondered if you wanted to see the Sandy article mocked up?"

"Sure." He came toward me and put a hand on the back of my seat. He leaned over me, placing his other hand on my desk. He was just inches from me and I was hyperaware of every last molecule of him. He smelled delicious—a mixture of clean laundry and an unmistakable scent of warmth and passion. I tried to concentrate and brought up the Sandy article for him.

He leaned farther forward and his arm brushed against my shoulder. I froze, desperate to feel more of him, terrified he'd see what I was thinking. *Was he doing this on purpose?* Tiny flickers of energy buzzed in my stomach. I inched away so there was a little more room between us. The man would swallow me whole if I wasn't careful.

I looked up at him. He was scanning the screen, obviously interested in what he was reading. It reminded me of the way he'd examined the sculptures in the Rodin Museum. My heart ached. Was there any way back for us?

"I like the way you write," he said. "It's funny and quirky—irreverent even. It's the Haven I know. Not the *Rallegra* Haven."

I closed my eyes. What he said hurt—it showed me again how wrong I'd been to push him away. He saw me. His observation was something Ash had said to me before. I twisted my mouth to hide the smile pushing through my pain. I liked that he saw the difference, that he knew that side of me. I hated that I'd messed things up between us so badly.

"Your photographs are excellent, Jake. Thank you for giving up your time."

"It was my pleasure," he said. He stood up, removing his hands and his body from almost touching me. A physical loss gripped me in my stomach. "So, tomorrow is the next date. Do you want me to come over first and do the pre-date photos like last time?"

"Actually, no, I don't think we need to this time." I couldn't live through that again. It was just too difficult to have him in my apartment when we weren't together. Too intimate. It had me mentally running through what could have been. "I'll text you to let you know where we're going to meet."

"Okay. Well, you know where I am," he said.

"Thanks," I said.

Don't leave me.

Tuesday's date was with Louis Romano. I had left it to Paula to pick out my dates, but from his application, he didn't seem anything close to my type. He was older and shorter than what I typically found attractive. But it didn't matter. This was work. Gerald wasn't available this Saturday and I was on a deadline, so I was hoping that Louis or my date on Thursday would be bearable enough to have a second date with.

Louis had wanted to pick me up, but I had insisted I meet him at our venue. He had mysteriously said that he would see me at the bottom of the London Eye.

As my cab pulled up at the drop-off point for the huge Ferris wheel at the edge of the Thames, Jake was waiting. He took photographs of me stepping out of the cab.

"Hey, how did you know I'd be here? Or are you meeting your date for the evening?"

"This is the drop-off point, so call me a genius but I guessed this was where you'd be dropped off. You look beautiful as ever," he said.

I'd let my hair down and decided on a dress that Ash convinced me to buy three months ago. I'd never worn it because it had an abstract print on it that seemed a bit too much, but I'd thought Jake would like the color.

"So, have you arranged for your date to meet you here again?" I asked.

"Nope." Jake grinned at me as if he had a secret he wasn't sharing.

What was he thinking? I pulled my eyes from him and headed toward the Eye, a towering white spider's web that looked as if it had captured the London skyline as its next meal. There was a chill in the spring air as the sun started to go down. I shivered.

As we neared the Eye, I could see Louis. He was even shorter than I'd expected and the photograph I'd seen was clearly taken a few years ago.

"Louis Romano is your date?" Jake asked.

"Yes." I snapped my head around to look at him. "Why, do you know him?"

"The guy is a gold-plated asshole." Jake was obviously tense, something I'd never seen before. His jaw was clenched and his eyes narrowed in my date's direction.

"I'm sure he's fine," I said, trying to say something that would calm him.

"Seriously, I don't think you should do this . . . "

Before Jake could elaborate, we arrived.

"Haven Daniels, I presume. You look even more beautiful than in your photograph." Louis grasped my hand and leaned forward to kiss my knuckles as if we had time-warped back a hundred years. It was uncomfortable and I took my hand back as soon as I was able.

"Pleased to meet you, Louis. Let me introduce our photographer, Harry."

"Ahhh, but we need no introduction. Mr. Harrison and I are old friends."

"We're not friends, Romano. I had no idea Haven's date was with you, or I would never have allowed it."

"Jake! You don't get a say. Please don't be rude or I'll have to ask you to leave." This was a Jake that I'd never seen before.

Where was it coming from? It wasn't like him. Even if he were jealous, which seemed highly unlikely, there was no need for his reaction.

"Can I have a word?" Jake asked me.

I looked to Louis, who put his hands up in defeat.

"I'm sorry," I said. "I will just be a second." I marched away from Louis and heard Jake follow. I stopped and then I turned to him.

"Jake, *you're* behaving like the gold-plated arsehole at the moment. This is work, as I keep telling you. What is your problem?" I was furious. I couldn't risk Louis giving up and leaving. I was on a deadline and Paula had confirmed he was available on Saturday if I wanted a follow-up date with him. Was he deliberately trying to hurt me? Trying to pay me back for not forgiving him?

"I know this guy. He's bad news. He's mixed up in all sorts of things that I don't want you to be a part of. I don't trust him."

"What sort of things?" I asked. What had Jake so concerned? And how could they affect me?

"I . . . I can't tell you. I just—" Stuttering replaced Jake's confidence. It felt so unlike him.

"It's one evening," I said.

"But if you knew—"

"Stop. Please don't bring your personal issues into this. What is your problem? Anyone would think you were jealous or something?" I desperately wanted him to be.

"No, that's not it. Well, maybe I am, but that's not the reason I want you away from Romano. I wouldn't want anyone

I cared about going anywhere near this guy. He's bad news. He's hurt people close to me."

I shouldn't have been concentrating on the bit where he said he cared about me, but those were the words that were chasing each other round my head. How did he care about me? As a friend? As something more? I glanced over at Romano. I didn't want to upset Jake, but I wasn't going to walk away from this article.

"I don't know what to say, Jake." I had no real reason to believe Jake would overreact unnecessarily, but Romano and I weren't getting involved, we were just spending an evening together. There was nothing to be upset about. "I can't just ditch him and this article because you don't like him." With that, I turned and walked back to my date.

"I'm sorry about that," I said to Louis.

"It is no problem, princess. I'm delighted to see Mr. Harrison. It's a shame he doesn't feel the same way."

I stepped into my capsule and watched him as he poured her champagne. She was smiling, unaware of the poison so close to her.

As the wheel turned slowly, they were out of sight of my pod for over ten minutes. I spent the time pacing from one end of my capsule to the other. Each step brought clarity to my feelings for Haven. I was undeniably jealous and if I thought about it rationally, I knew Haven would eventually see through Romano. He wasn't the real problem. Any guy she could be serious about was who I was concerned about.

When they came back in to view, Romano stood behind Haven, too close, pointing out the window.

Nausea washed over me and I had to stop myself from banging on the glass.

When I stepped out into the fresh air at the end of the journey, I couldn't see Haven immediately. I scanned the heads of tourists and finally saw her, her hand in Louis' as they headed back to where the cab had dropped her off.

I ran toward them. "Hey, wait up," I shouted.

Haven stopped and turned. "Sorry, we were talking. I didn't realize we'd walked so far."

Romano grinned at me. He had been trying to lose me, no doubt. I couldn't believe he had the nerve to look at me, let alone try to hit on a woman in front of me, when I knew everything about him.

"I have dinner waiting at my hotel. I'm not sure Mr. Harrison needs to join us," Romano said.

Haven glanced at me and I had to hold myself back. My heart was beating out of my chest and my eyes flicked between Haven and Romano.

"I'd love to capture some photographs in the hotel, if that's okay with you. Just at the beginning, and then we can let Jake go on and enjoy the rest of his evening," Haven said, and my chest sank with relief.

"As you wish," Romano replied. "I'm afraid I didn't take into account more than one passenger, Mr. Harrison. You'll have to find your own way to the Dorchester."

A canary-yellow Ferrari pulled up and the driver got out and handed Louis a set of keys. Surely Haven would see straight through him as soon as she saw his car. If she thought my car was a fuckmobile, what would she think of his?

"Your carriage awaits, my princess," Romano said, holding the passenger door open for her.

Before Louis had rounded the hood to get into the driver's seat, I'd flagged down a taxi.

"We need to go to the Dorchester, but if we could take the same route as that banana on wheels, I would appreciate it," I said to the cab driver.

"The Dorchester's not a problem, mate," he said. "But I can't guarantee we'll be able to keep up with that thing. It might be ugly, but it's worth a few bob. If it were mine, I'd get my mate, Gary, to re-spray it," he said as he pulled out after them.

Predictably, Romano sped off and did everything he could to outdrive us.

It worked. We lost them within minutes.

When we arrived at the Dorchester, I leapt out of the cab and ran into the lobby, looking left and right.

"Jake." I spun around to find Haven behind me.

"There you are. Thank God."

"You need to calm down. Louis might be a bit over the top, but he seems harmless."

I shook my head. "He's anything but. The sooner you're out of here, the better. Where is he, anyway?" I asked.

"Trying to arrange a dinner reservation. He'd planned to have it served in his suite but I said I didn't think that was such a good idea."

"Presumptive prick," I said.

"Seriously, Jake, calm down. He's a typical Italian. He's a bit flash and is used to getting his own way."

"Yes, things I would have thought you'd hate."

"Jesus, I'm not marrying the guy. I'm having dinner with him. For work. Will you stop already?"

Romano returned. "I've arranged the perfect table. Will you be joining us, Mr. Harrison?" he asked, his eyebrow raised in my direction.

"Do you want to do some photographs at the table?" Haven asked.

I shook my head. "I'll take some as you walk in."

After I'd taken a few shots, they went into the restaurant and I started pacing up and down the lobby. I didn't know whether I should stay and wait for them to finish their dinner, or leave them to it. I couldn't bear the thought of him or anyone anywhere near Haven. I decided to wait.

I counted every minute that they were gone. I passed the restaurant several times, but couldn't see them from the door. I took a seat in the lobby and kept my eye on the entrance. Various staff members eyed me suspiciously, and a couple asked if they could assist me, but I shooed them away and kept waiting.

Finally, I saw them emerge. Romano had his arm clasped around her waist, pulling her toward him, and kissing her knuckles again. Haven looked unusually relaxed. Jesus, didn't she see what a penis this guy was?

"I'm sorry, I have an early start tomorrow, but thank you for the offer," Haven said as they walked toward me.

I stood up and Haven's eyes met mine. She didn't look angry or pleased that I was still there. At that moment, neutral would do.

"I'd love you to see this new Renoir that I bought. Are you sure I can't tempt you?" Jesus, he wasn't subtle, was he?

"Another time, perhaps," Haven replied.

"You'll have to show her your etchings another evening, Romano. I'm here to see Haven gets home safely," I said. There was no way Haven was going up to his room.

Romano turned to me. "Is this what you're reduced to now, Harrison? Loitering in hotel lobbies?"

I ignored him.

"My driver will see you home, my princess," Romano said.

"Haven and I will be fine in a cab," I said. I pulled her elbow, trying to put some distance between her and Romano.

"Thank you for a wonderful evening, Louis," Haven said.

"I look forward to Saturday," he replied as I led Haven toward the exit.

Blood thundered through my veins and I had to be careful not to tighten my already forceful grip around Haven's elbow.

"Saturday? Are you serious?" I asked her as we got into the fresh air.

"Let go of me, Jake." Haven twisted away from me and I dropped my hand.

"What about Saturday, Haven?" I asked again.

"He wants to take me out again." She indicated to the doorman that she needed a cab.

"And you said yes?" What was she thinking? Did she like him?

"Yes, I said yes. What is your problem with him?" she asked. She sounded confused and I couldn't blame her. I couldn't tell her what Romano was really like—I needed her to trust me.

She started to climb into the cab and I quickly followed her.

"What are you doing? Get out!"

"I'm making sure you get home okay." I was pissed that another guy, and Romano at that, had gotten to spend his evening with her. It should have been me, so I wanted to be the one to see her home. I could at least have that.

"Jake, you're not my dad. Get out."

I gave the cab driver Haven's address and we started moving. She sat as far away from me as possible, looking out the window. I could deal with that. As long as I knew she was safe and with me. Even if she was angry, I could live with that.

We drove along in silence until I couldn't bear it any longer.

"The guy is a joke," I said snappily.

"You're the joke," she replied. She sounded resigned to the fact.

"Haven."

She turned to me. "I mean it. You've acted like a complete jerk this evening. Louis was fine—a little sleazy but tolerable. You, on the other hand . . . you should trust me. I'm a grown woman. I don't need rescuing."

"Haven."

"What? Stop saying my name like you have some kind of hold over me."

"I think you have that the wrong way around." Haven's hold on me seemed to be increasing. She was right. I had been a prick and I hadn't trusted her. There was a foundation for my concern, but most of my actions tonight had been about my feelings for Haven. I was angry at Romano and what he had done to my sister, but I was angrier at myself. I'd let Haven go so easily. Beth had been right, I'd not fought hard enough for her and now I didn't know how to get back in the game.

chapter TWENTY-ONE

Haven

In the back of the cab with Jake, on the way back from my date with Romano, I couldn't figure out why Jake was behaving so out of character. It was confusing but at the same time, I loved that he was so determined to protect me.

"I'm sorry," he said softly.

I continued to stare out the window, acutely aware of the space, or lack of, between us. He'd seemed to grow physically bigger during his interactions with Romano. "It's okay," I said eventually. "I do trust you." Jake had been so spooked by Romano it was difficult to ignore his concerns, even if I didn't know exactly what they were. I wanted him to tell me; I wanted to know everything about Romano . . . but also about Jake. I was hungry for information, hungry for him. "But I need to get this article written. Robert is relying on me."

"Haven," he whispered. I turned to him, watching his full lips try to say something.

The cab jolted to a halt and the driver sounded his horn.

I clambered out and turned back to Jake. "I'm sorry, too,"

I said. Did he know I wasn't just talking about today? Did he realize that I regretted pushing him away?

His eyes widened and he drew a breath. I closed the door, my eyes still fixed to his and the taxi sped off.

As the cab drove into the distance, I watched, a thousand things I wanted to say and no one to listen.

The next morning I was on speakerphone with Ash while I got dressed for work. I was bored with my work wardrobe and I couldn't decide what to wear.

"You still like him," she said.

"And you've been dreaming about Channing Tatum. It doesn't mean you're going to do anything about it."

"If I knew Channing Tatum and he wasn't married, I would totally do something about it."

"This conversation is ridiculous. Can we change the subject?"

"It's early. That's what's ridiculous. So how was the millionaire Italian?"

"Short. A little over the top. But I have to have the Saturday date with him because the other two aren't available and we need to get this story in."

"You'll have licky Jake there though, won't you?" Ash asked.

"Yeah, but Louis is pretty pushy. I think he'll try and get me on his own, away from Jake. I can handle him, though. And Jake won't let anything happen to me."

"That's so shady. Do you think he was going to try to shag you?"

I shrugged as I held up two skirts that looked almost identical. "I don't know. I guess. It doesn't matter—I wouldn't fall for all his over-used charm. It's weird that Jake would think I would."

"Be careful and make sure you're always in a public place with him. Who's tonight's victim?"

"Mark from Brentwood in Essex is my *date* tonight."

Ash started laughing. "Are you kidding me? You're going to have to hoist those boobies past your ears to keep up with the girls he's used to."

I giggled. Girls from Essex had a reputation for making the most of their assets. "I think I might have to have a boob job before this evening."

I was being careful about what I was wearing today. I was going straight from work, which was a bit of an issue as my work outfits were, well, drab. I was also aware that I would be seeing Jake again today. Other than saying he would meet me at the office at six this evening, I'd not seen him since he dropped me off after my date with Romano. I was looking forward to seeing him, despite knowing that was against my better judgment. I wanted him to forgive me for pushing him away. It was too much to hope for anything else.

"What about my black shift with the chiffon sleeves?" I asked Ash. I wasn't dressing for Mark from Brentwood—I wanted to look good for Jake.

"That's stepping it up for work, much more like it."

"Only because I have this date afterward. Everything will be back to normal tomorrow." I pulled the dress from my closet. It was still wrapped in the plastic cover from the dry cleaners.

"You're wearing your hair down?"

"I'll take it down for the date." Of course I would, Jake liked it down.

"Live a little," Ash said as she sighed in exasperation.

"I have to go. Love you."

"Love you, bye." I canceled the call, threw the phone on my bed and ripped open the plastic.

I zipped up the side of my black dress. It worked. Jake would like it.

"Have you canceled Saturday with Romano?" Jake asked as he walked up to me in the office lobby. We were both early.

"And hello to you, Jake."

"I mean it, Haven. You need to cancel."

"You know full well I can't move Louis. I'm up against a deadline. I'm having to write this up on Sunday as it is." I was pretty sure Louis was harmless, but Jake was so dead set against me going near him, it unnerved me. "But I won't go anywhere without you. I promise. And he said I should bring a passport, so I guess you should too."

"He said what? Fucking hell, Haven, are you kidding me? Can't *I* take you for your Saturday night date?"

"Please calm down. What do you think he's going to do? Sell me into slavery? And no, I can't date you for this article. Unless you've been keeping things from me, you're not a member of Glass Introductions and I don't manipulate the facts. End of story. Please try to work with me on this?"

"You are impossible," he said, rolling his eyes.

I swiped him across his abs. My hand hit granite. Our eyes met as I touched him and his face softened.

"If he's bought you a ticket somewhere, and not me, you aren't going."

I was prepared for the ultimatum, and I was okay with it. I did trust him, and if he felt this strongly then I needed to listen to him. "You have yourself a deal."

"We have a deal?" Jake seemed surprised. "Okay then."

We headed outside and Jake flagged down a cab. I gave the driver the address of the restaurant where Mark said he'd meet me.

"So who's the chump tonight?" Jake asked.

"We don't say chump in the UK, you'll have to translate."

"I don't know, someone gullible, a general douche?"

"And Mark is a chump because he's agreed to go on a date with me?"

"No. He's a chump because it's an entirely futile evening for him. You're mine."

What? Had I heard him correctly? For once in my life, I was left with nothing to say. I had run out of snark. I didn't want to contradict him. I wanted to turn over the possibility of belonging to him in my head and look at it from different angles. Could it be true? Would it be true?

The rest of the journey continued in silence. I wanted to ask him what he'd meant, but every time I tried to form a sentence, it came out wrong. I stole glimpses of him a couple of times, studying the contours of his jaw, my gaze sliding over lips that could do things to me that I'd never known before him.

Part of me would be his forever.

Mark was good looking, tall and a little rough around the edges. I liked that about him instantly. He was clearly a bit awkward about having Jake taking shots of us. He asked several times about anonymity.

"Okay, I'm going to leave you two to it," Jake said as he packed away his camera. "I'll see you Saturday," he said as he turned to me. I searched his face for something that would help me believe I hadn't made up what he'd said about being his in the cab but his eyes were blank, all business. He shook Mark's hand and headed out.

"Portraits are the normal start to a date for me," Mark said, a bit dazed.

I laughed. "Sorry about that. And honestly, we won't identify you in the photographs. You have my promise."

"And you seem very trustworthy. A nice, normal girl as my granny would say," Mark said, smiling at me.

"I'm going to take that as a compliment." I laughed.

"You should. My granny didn't say it to a lot of people. She was a cantankerous old biddy. Even I was scared of her. I should say you look beautiful." Mark's rambling was rather endearing. He was nervous and that made me more confident, as though it was my responsibility to put him at ease.

"It's not obligatory," I replied, smiling at him. He was as bad at this dating thing as I was but the compliment felt genuine and I accepted it as such.

"I'm really not good at this, am I?"

I laughed again. "You're doing fine. I feel great after all these compliments, so you're doing better than you think."

“Yes, it’s all part of my master plan to win you over,” he said, a gleam in his eye.

I relaxed and sat back in my chair. Mark was going to be good company.

chapter TWENTY-TWO

Jake

Beth was curled up on the sofa when I got in from dropping off Haven. "I need to tell you something," I said to her. I had hoped that I wouldn't have to bring this up, but I was going to meet Romano for a second time on Saturday. If Beth ever found out that I'd knowingly met with him, and I hadn't told her, she'd never forgive me.

"Did you elope?" Beth asked.

God, I really didn't want to destroy her good mood. "Nope."

"Kiss her again?"

"Nope. I left her on a date with another man and came home as my penis shriveled up and fell off."

"That's a delightful image."

"Well, you asked." My phone rang and I glanced at the screen. Millie. Why was my ex calling? I pressed cancel and turned back to Beth. "I've only got Saturday and then there will be no reason for me to see her again. I'm in California next week and unless I think of something by then, I guess we'll go our separate ways." I slumped on the sofa, grabbing the tub of ice cream from her and digging out a spoonful for myself.

"Hey, you're interrupting my threesome with Ben and Jerry."

"You're gross," I said, shoving the tub back at her.

"So, have you decided to fight for her?" Beth asked.

"I have. I'm just not sure I'll win. I'm not quite sure what to do." My stomach churned at the thought of not seeing Haven again. I was running out of time and I didn't have a plan.

"So what did you have to tell me, my penis-less brother?" Beth pulled me back into the moment.

"I don't want you to get upset," I said and then instantly felt like an idiot.

"Well, problem solved, because if you tell me you don't want to get me upset then that's that—I won't," Beth said around a mouthful of ice cream.

"Sarcasm isn't your thing," I said as I grinned at her.

"Oh yes it is. It's exactly my thing. Come on, get it off your chest."

I took a deep breath. "Well, you know Haven's been dating these guys."

"Yes, I kinda gathered from your hideously bad moods and the fact that you've told me so like a million times. What about it?"

"Well, the second guy was someone we both know."

Beth paled instantly and put the ice cream on the coffee table.

"Romano," I said.

She looked at me. "Shit."

"Fuck. I'm sorry. I never wanted to hear his name again. I just didn't want to keep it from you." If I could have scooped out her pain and taken it on myself, I would have. I hated seeing her upset; it reminded me about how bad things had been for her and how I could do nothing about it. Romano and losing the baby had been a tipping point for Beth. She'd spiraled so far down I wondered if she'd ever be my sister again.

"I think I should call my sponsor," was all she said.

I handed her the phone. "Do you want to talk about it?"

"I never want to go back to that place again," she said quietly.

"I know. You're stronger now. What can I do?" I asked her.

"You're right. I am, and you can't do anything. You've done so much for me already. Thank you for telling me. Does Haven know?"

"No, she knows we have a history and that I hate him. I've begged her to stay away from him, but I haven't told her any details. She's having her follow-up date with him."

Her eyes widened. "She is? You can't convince her not to?"

"I've tried. The other two guys can't do Saturday apparently and she's on some deadline for Robert. He's told her to bring a passport." I pushed my hands through my hair.

"Wow."

"She's agreed that if I can't go with her—I bet the sleazeball will try and pull some stunt to get her away from me—that she won't go."

"Okay, well that's good. He's not going to physically hurt her. And if Saturday's the last time they see each other, then that will be the end of it," Beth said. She seemed very composed.

"If it were up to me, he wouldn't be breathing."

Beth rested her palm over my clenched fist. "He didn't turn me into an alcoholic, Jake. It wasn't all him."

"I know but . . . but I want to kill him," I said.

"Yeah, well, you in prison is the last thing I need, so calm down. And I need to know you're not going to lose it on Saturday." Beth looked at me, waiting for my reply.

I nodded. "I promise you."

"I'm going to call my sponsor," she said as she got up.

"I love you, Beth."

"I know, and I couldn't love you more. I'm okay. Honestly. It's a preventative measure."

Haven had agreed that I could meet her at her place as Romano was picking her up at nine in the morning and he hadn't told her where he was taking her.

"A stretch limo? Really?" I said as we stood at the top of the steps to her building, under the awning, avoiding the rain as the car pulled up.

Haven laughed. "It's ridiculous. It's like we're going on a hen party."

"A hen party?" I asked.

"Translation alert: a bachelorette party," she explained.

I nodded. She was right; it was tacky. "That would be far more preferable."

"For you, I'm sure. Loads of drunk women who aren't wearing much," she teased and poked me in the ribs. A jolt of energy ran through me.

I smiled at her and she smiled back. I wanted to reach out for her. "I'm not going anywhere without you," she said.

Her reassurance relaxed me and I followed her down the steps to the car. She'd worn her hair up today. It placated me slightly and made me think that she was keeping a part of herself back. A part of her that I'd seen.

Romano stepped out of the car to greet us. "Haven, my princess. You look so beautiful." He kissed the back of her hand. I could do nothing but stand there and watch.

"Mr. Harrison, or should I call you our third wheel?" He laughed heartily at his own joke. Haven smiled tightly and I glared at him in between capturing photographs of our ridiculous transportation.

We got into the car and Romano made sure he was sitting next to Haven on the back seat while I was to her side. He arranged himself far too close to her.

"Are you ready for the time of your life, Haven? I've got something very special planned for you."

"Are you going to tell me what it is?" Haven asked.

"I'm taking you to Paris," Romano replied.

My heart stopped dead. Paris? Paris was our city. Going back there might just kill me. It had been the place I'd cracked through Haven's hard shell, the place where she'd given herself to me. I glanced over at her but she looked away as soon as our eyes met.

"I don't think I can," Haven said. "I have to be back. I've got house guests, I—"

"Nonsense, we'll be back this evening. Unless of course, by the end of the day, you'd like to stay over. I can arrange that too," Romano said.

My fists were clenched by my sides.

"Louis—"

"Shhhh." He placed a hand on Haven's knee, silencing her.

"You have a ticket for Jake, right?" she asked.

"Mr. Harrison can come too if you'd like, or perhaps it would be better just the two of us. More intimate."

Haven looked at me as she chewed the inside of her cheek, clearly uncomfortable. Her hands swept her hair back and then twisted in her lap. I wanted to reach across and pull her to me, assuring her that everything would be okay but I resisted, just. If she said the word, we'd be out of there. I willed her to give me the slightest indication that she wanted to leave. I knew this article being ready on time was important to her, but was it worth spending time with him?

She turned to Romano. "Wherever I go, Jake goes," she said firmly. Relief swept through me. I wasn't sure if it was because of what she said or if it was because we felt like a team; we were on the same side and she was going to let me look after her.

Louis sat back in his seat and shrugged. "Okay. For now."

Nausea rumbled in my stomach. I'd imagined going back to Paris with Haven, but never under circumstances like these.

Romano had the bladder of a camel. He didn't leave Haven and me alone once on our journey. I wanted to check how she was feeling. She continued to look nervous, although she hid it well with an affected smile.

Conveniently, I was booked into a train car behind theirs, but I managed to negotiate a seat change, so I was two rows up and across from them.

As we pulled in to *Gard du Nord*, I glanced across the aisle at Haven. I wanted to be the one that brought her back here. As if she could tell I was watching, she turned to me. I saw something in her eyes I hadn't before. It wasn't about Romano. It was sadness, regret, longing. My breath hitched. Did she want me? Each memory of our time here played through my head in slow motion—her head on my shoulder, the last time we pulled into *Gard du Nord*, her flushed face when we stood in front of Rodin's *The Kiss*, the feel of her at Buddha Bar. Was she thinking what I was?

"Have you ever been to Paris, princess?" Romano asked her, breaking our connection.

Haven flickered her eyes to me. "Yes."

"Of course you have. But today you get to see it through my eyes."

Haven was silent.

There was a car waiting for us outside the station. My muscles were jumping, my body on full alert. I wasn't sure if that was because Romano was here or because Haven was. I could have run to Paris with all the energy I had.

chapter TWENTY-THREE

Haven

Jake's reaction to Louis was starting to have an effect on me and I couldn't wait for the day to be over. Jake was normally so laid back about things. Nothing seemed to faze him, but now I couldn't ignore the tension radiating off him. It was as if he were about to explode at any moment. I hated seeing him like that. It upset me that my actions might be causing him pain, again. A huge part of me wished I hadn't agreed to this second date. I should have found a way round it.

We made our way out of *Gard du Nord* to a car waiting for us. If Jake had his way, he would have piled in the back, but Louis was quite insistent that he sit in the front.

Being in Paris was confusing. When Jake and I had been, I'd had a wonderful time. It'd felt like the beginning of something. Now it was a gigantic reminder of what never was. Of how stupid I'd been.

The weather matched my mood. It was gray and cloudy, as if Paris wasn't quite in focus, wasn't quite as beautiful and vibrant as when I'd been here last.

"You're quiet, my princess," Louis said. I simply smiled at him.

I'd never been called someone's princess before and I didn't like it. It made me sound as if I were untouchable and removed from life. Jake had never seen me like that. He had seen through to my core as soon as we'd met—and I'd just let him go.

"We need some color in those cheeks," he went on. "That calls for fresh air."

It was starting to drizzle, so an outdoor activity didn't sound particularly enticing, but I didn't say anything.

"Here we are," said Louis as the car pulled up to the curb.

I got out of the car and realized we were at the Eiffel Tower. Of course we were.

"I thought it would make a nice shot if we walked hand in hand toward the tower. Jake could shoot us from the back," Louis said as if he were directing Jake.

Jake didn't say a word. I was concerned that the slightest thing would tip him over the edge, so I tried to defuse the situation.

"Let's head toward the tower; Jake won't be too far behind."

Jake nodded and I started toward the tower.

Louis was soon beside me and grabbed my hand. His palm was clammy. I suppressed a shudder. How long would it be until we were on the train back?

"Paris is romantic, no?" Louis asked me.

I glanced back at Jake. "Sure."

"Not as romantic as Rome, I think. Next time, we'll go there."

I smiled and he squeezed my hand.

"So, we'll go to the top now," he said in his exaggerated Italian accent. "And we will see the beautiful views of the city."

The cloudy sky would probably get in the way of the panorama. It was impossible to see Paris properly in this weather. But at least we were going to be in public.

"So, what do you like to do in your spare time, Louis?" I asked as we made our way to the top.

"I like spending my time with beautiful women of course, like you," he replied, smiling at me, trying to look into my eyes as he spoke. I did everything to avoid his stare.

I thought it was meant to be a compliment, but it sounded wrong. It was fake and forced and I wondered who fell for men like this?

Jake was quiet, resigned, and I fought an urge to take his hand, to feel his soft, smooth, warm skin against mine.

"Of course, my company keeps me very busy. I'm always flying from country to country, trying to ensure people are doing things the Louis way. I have very few people I trust in business." He scowled for a second and then remembered to be charming. "And here we are. We need champagne," he announced.

We wandered around the top of the tower. It was cold and windy and as I had imagined, there wasn't much to see because of the clouds. Louis seemed oblivious. He ordered two glasses of champagne.

"Mr. Harrison, why don't you get some pictures of us facing the beautiful views?" he said. He seemed to like the fact he was being followed around and photographed. Was that because it was Jake? Or was it because he liked the attention?

The only thing I could think about was how long we'd be up here and whether or not we'd head straight back to London afterward.

"Have you ever been married?" I asked. Jake snapped away behind us, getting closer and closer. My skin warmed when he was near and I fought the urge to reach for him.

"No, I haven't been lucky enough." He bowed and kissed the back of my hand again.

"Children?" I asked.

He smiled wistfully at me. "Regrettably, no. It is something I've always wanted. To be a father, that is."

"You're a total prick," Jake said from behind us. I froze. Whatever had happened between him and Romano seemed so personal. I could feel Jake's pain through his anger. I wanted to reach for him, to reassure him that Louis wasn't going to hurt him.

Louis' smile disappeared and he glared at Jake for a few seconds, as if contemplating how to respond.

Louis looked down and when his eyes met mine, it was with his smile back in place. "I get the impression Mr. Harrison is not my biggest fan." He raised an eyebrow and I tried to keep my face as neutral as possible.

"I want to take you to my favorite place in Paris," he said abruptly.

Memories of the Rodin Museum flooded my head and I glanced at Jake. He wasn't looking at me. He was fixated on his camera, and wore a frustrated expression.

"Okay, let's go," I said. I was ready to get out of there.

I recognized *Place de la Concorde* and various images started pulling together in my head. I leaned forward in my seat, removing my hand from Louis', and tapped Jake on the shoulder. "Are we near Buddha Bar?" I asked him.

"It's right around the block," he replied.

"Oh." That evening all came flooding back, sluicing through my brain. I'd wanted him so badly. And the way he had looked at me as we'd entered Buddha Bar, as though he wasn't going to be able to hold himself back for much longer—I'd never felt so desired. The way he'd told me he would have me. How he'd tied me up and made me come and turned my most hidden vulnerabilities into pleasures. Jake was all around my body and mind. I couldn't breathe.

The last place I wanted to be was in the back of a car with a man who wasn't Jake. I wanted to go home. I wanted to go home with Jake.

"This is a beautiful hotel, my princess. It's my favorite place in Paris. Hôtel de Crillon."

"We're going to a hotel?" I asked.

"Yes, for lunch, and of course, longer if you wish."

My stomach churned. I hoped he didn't think he was going to be holding anything but my hand.

As we walked into the lobby, Jake trailing behind, I tried to push images of Jake and me in Paris back into the corners of my memories where they'd been hiding. The hotel was beautiful, somewhere you could imagine Louis XV hanging out, but I wondered why of all places, this was Louis' favorite.

Memories of Rodin's *The Gates of Hell* crashed over me. I smiled to myself.

"I knew you'd like it here, princess," Louis said as we sat at a table for lunch, mistaking my smile. I could see Jake in the lobby, looking agitated. Today was the last time we'd have any reason to spend time together. My heart sped up and I started to think of more excuses to see him again. Maybe the wrap party for the Sandy Fox film? She said we'd get an invitation.

Louis followed my line of vision. "Excuse me. I'll be back in a second," he said as he got up to leave the table.

He went to Jake. They hadn't said much to each other all day. I wondered what it was all about. Jake started to gesticulate with his hands. I couldn't make out what was being said, but the volume of their conversation increased and I stood, wondering whether or not I should go over and interrupt. Louis leaned forward as if to whisper something into Jake's ear. Whatever it was it didn't go over well. Jake punched him square on the jaw and Louis landed on the floor.

What the hell?

I raced over. When Jake saw me coming, he lunged toward me, took my arm and dragged me toward the exit.

"Jake, what's going on? Are you okay? What happened?"

"Let's get out of here," Jake said. "Please don't fight me on this, Haven." His gaze was flitting around the lobby.

"I'm not fighting you, Jake. I told you that I trust you," I said, and he looked at me, as if he were trying to confirm what I was saying.

He exhaled and grabbed my hand in his. I had to half skip to keep up with him. We crashed out of the hotel and into the

Parisian rain. Jake looked left and right, then pointed toward a rank of cabs. We ran toward them just as the last one sped off.

Shit.

"Will he call the police?" I asked.

"I don't know," he said. The rain came heavier and Jake's hair darkened as it clung to his face. The wet had felt dark and foreboding with Romano, but with Jake it became intimate, romantic.

"We're getting soaked," Jake said.

"I don't mind," I replied.

"You're going to get cold and you don't have your nine hundred scarves and twelve coats to keep you warm." Jake smiled, then scanned the road. "Let's head up here and try to get a cab."

Finally, we came across another rank with a taxi waiting. I was wet to the bone, and so was Jake. When we climbed in, Jake met my eyes. Where to? "We need to dry off," I said. I wasn't ready to leave Paris now that it was just us. Jake nodded and I could see his mind start to whirl. Before he said anything, I leaned forward. "The W, Opéra," I said.

chapter TWENTY-FOUR

Jake

Jesus, it had felt good to punch that sleazebag. The adrenaline was racing through my veins. I should have done that a long time ago. I looked at my hand and stretched out my fingers. The skin hadn't broken and everything was moving. There didn't seem to be any physical damage. Not to me anyway.

I glanced over at Haven. I owed her an explanation, but where did I start? I didn't want her to think I was acting like a jealous idiot. That hadn't been it. Well it hadn't been all of it.

And now we were on the way to the hotel under her direction. The place where I'd first got to know her body. What was she thinking? I wanted answers from her.

We pulled up outside the W and got out. Everything was enticingly familiar as we made our way across the lobby. She'd suggested a hotel and I'd not really had time to think about the implications. "I'd like a shower. I need to cool off and warm up," I said. "Shall we get a room?"

Haven laughed. "That you do, Mr. Harrison."

"Ugh, don't call me that. That's what that creep called me all day."

She put a reassuring hand on my arm. "Sorry, come on. Let's get a room."

"I can get two," I offered. Last time, we'd been here together despite our different rooms and now?

"That's just a waste. It's no big deal. Just get one room. We don't need two if we're not staying. We can shower, dry off, order room service and decompress." I didn't have to convince her. I was surprised, relieved and full of anticipation.

"Sounds like a plan," I tried to keep my voice even as we approached the reception desk. I stopped myself from putting my arms around her.

"Do you want the first shower?" I asked as I closed the bedroom door behind me. Haven was standing awkwardly by the window. We were in the same layout of room we'd had when last we'd been here. The atmosphere felt thick with memories, with possibility and anticipation.

"No, you go first. I'll check out the room service menu. Just hand me a robe and I can change out of these wet clothes," she said.

I stepped under the water and cleansed off the stench of Romano. I hoped I hadn't fucked it up for Haven. He might withdraw his consent to the article she was writing. I was grateful that she had come with me and abandoned him back at the Crillon. She trusted me. That had to mean something. And now here we were—it was as if we were being given a second chance.

I wrapped a towel around my waist, rubbed my hair dry with another and headed into the bedroom.

I locked eyes with Haven as soon as I opened the door. Her hair had started to break out of its bun. She looked less than her normal perfect self—she looked totally amazing.

"Feel better?" she asked, fiddling with the pins in her hair and laying them on the table.

"Yeah, much."

Being wrapped up, most of her hair had avoided the rain. She ran her fingers through the strands and spread it across her shoulders. There she was. My Haven—soft, open, unraveling. She knew what that did to me. Was it an invitation?

She caught me looking at her. "What?" she asked in an almost whisper.

"I've been thinking," I said. I watched as she scanned up and down my body, giving herself away in a look. My skin tightened under her inspection and her breath hitched. I stopped half a step away from her and brushed my knuckles down her cheek. She turned her face into my hand and I closed my eyes, overwhelmed at the feel of her and the small movement that suggested she might want me.

We stood, the gray skies of Paris as our backdrop, watching each other, waiting for what was next.

"I'm sorry," she said softly.

My chest tightened at her vulnerability. "I should be saying that to you."

"It's difficult for me," she said, turning toward the window. "Letting someone new see me. I used what I heard when you spoke to Robert as an excuse."

"But I knew that and I should have fought harder," I replied, cupping her face.

Her chest rose, as she shook her head. "You didn't do anything wrong."

I pulled her toward me and wrapped my arms around her as she slid her hands around my waist. She felt so good, so right and I became lighter, better just from touching her. I rested my cheek on her head as we stood there, holding each other, the past weeks apart just melting away.

My clothes were piled on the chair behind her and I reached to take the belt out of my jeans. She watched me, her mouth slightly parted.

"Do you remember last time in Paris?" I asked as I looped one end of the belt through the buckle and pulled, creating a small noose.

"Jake . . . "

I shook my head. "I won't let you keep me out anymore. I'm fighting for you and I'm going to win."

"Jake," she said again as if it were a final plea before she gave in and stood tentatively. The inches of air between us seemed charged with energy. They were pulling us closer together.

"You know you only tell me what you want me to do to you, and you do as I say. Did you forget?"

She looked up at me as she chewed the inside of her cheek. I brought my thumb up to her face and stroked the puckered flesh.

"Tell me you don't want this."

She took a deep breath, closed her eyes and presented her wrists.

Jesus, that got me hard as steel. The way she struggled,

then submitted like that. As if I had real power over her, when in reality she totally owned me.

I looped the belt over her hands and she opened her eyes as I pulled the leather tight.

"I won't hurt you," I reassured her.

"I know," she said. "That's not what I'm frightened of."

"Tell me what scares you?" I wanted her to feel completely protected.

"Myself. Wanting you. Needing you."

My knees buckled slightly at her admission. I placed a small kiss on the corner of her lips. "I want to take that feeling away." Using the belt, I led her over to the bed. "Lie down."

She didn't hesitate. She lay back and put her hands overhead. I tied the other end of the belt to the bedpost.

"Jesus, you are beautiful," I said as I walked to her feet and drank her in from the tips of her toes to her incredible hair fanned out behind her. I luxuriated in her laid out like that. All for me.

Where should I start? I untied her robe and crawled up the bed and lay on my side, my head propped up my hand. I watched her as she waited for me to touch her.

"Jake," she said.

"Yes, baby?" She twisted her body toward me. "Patience," I said as I rolled her hips back to the bed.

chapter TWENTY-FIVE

Haven

I was feeling anything but patient. Somewhere along the line, I'd let Jake in, but it hadn't been today. Maybe it had been the last time we were in Paris. And now I needed him.

He swept his hands over my partially revealed body. I closed my eyes and groaned.

"Baby, you're desperate aren't you?"

It was embarrassing. I *was* desperate and I couldn't hide it from him. Was it just me?

He answered my question by pulling his towel open and revealing his hardness.

"Is this what you're desperate for?" he asked, circling his cock with his hand, dragging his fist upward.

Relief crawled up my body. He wanted me. I couldn't take my eyes from him, and I was sure I'd suffer further embarrassment when he discovered the wetness between my legs.

"You want it?"

He didn't need to ask. I wore the answer all over my body. I strained against the belt, but that just pushed another jolt of desire through me as the leather scuffed against my skin. Did he need me restrained? Did I need to be restrained?

He brushed my hair from my face, leaned down and ran his tongue underneath my top lip.

"You want it?" he repeated.

I nodded. "Yes," I whispered.

"I need you to understand a couple of things first. So I'm going to explain how it's going to be."

I drew my eyebrows together, my breaths becoming shorter, tighter. Why was he prolonging this? I needed to feel him.

"This is not a Paris thing, Haven," he said softly. "You won't run from me when we get back to London."

Initial panic gave way to relief as I realized that I didn't want to go anywhere. I wanted him right then; I needed him, always. He began to sprinkle kisses down my neck.

"There is not, and there will never be, a reason for you to push me away. Do you hear me?"

Right then I'd say anything to get him inside me. "Yes," I breathed. I was tired of building walls.

"I mean it. We're together now and when we get back to London. We're together when I go to Palo Alto, when I come back, and the week after that and the month after that. Do you hear me?"

I nodded as he scooped his fingers into my bra and found my nipple, squeezing it between his thumb and forefinger. I arched off the bed.

"This is the start, not the end, Haven," he said.

I couldn't bear it any longer—my words broke free. "Please, Jake."

"We're crazy for each other, and I'm hard as a rock for

you. This is going to be a night to remember."

He moved off the bed and dragged off my panties.

"Oh, yes, beautiful. You are so completely ready for me aren't you?" he asked as his gaze skimmed my underwear. I couldn't hide my desire from him.

I scrunched my eyes, embarrassed.

"Never be shy about wanting me, Haven," he said. "I enjoy seeing the evidence. Now I want to hear it." He rubbed his hands up my thighs, his eyes flitting from my face to between my legs. "Tell me."

I didn't know what to say. I was half-crazed from his touch, half-mute with shame from needing him as much as I did. If I spoke, I was afraid he'd know everything. He'd see into my soul and although it was what I wanted, I'd fought so hard for so long to keep it hidden, buried from his light.

"Tell me." He sucked hard on the flesh of my inner thigh, first one side, then the other. It felt dangerous and delicious, as if he was cracking me open. Then again, higher and higher. My breaths came shorter. I could breathe in, but not out. I couldn't let anything go.

"Do I need to spank you? Is that what you're waiting for?"

Something in my head snapped and I felt myself let go of whatever I'd been holding. "I want you, Jake. I want you to fuck me, please. I need you inside me," I said on an exhalation.

I heard the rustle of a condom wrapper and he crawled over my body, his hands on either side of my face. "I can't wait a moment longer," he said as his tip hovered at my entrance. I widened my legs and lifted my hips toward him, urging him forward.

"I'll try and be slow, baby," he growled.

I didn't want him to fight his urge to slam into me. I wanted it as he did. My body needed to feel him. "I want it hard," I said.

He groaned and pushed into me, farther and farther. Despite my plea, he was giving me time to adjust to him. I slid my knees up, trying to make room for him, but I gasped as he hit the end of me.

"Fuck," I said, my hands clenching above me.

He brought his mouth to mine and pushed his tongue through my lips. I strained at the belt, wanting to be able to touch him. Last time, he'd released me after he'd made me come with his mouth. I was desperate to run my hands through his hair.

He pulled out and then pushed back in, faster this time, slick from my arousal. Then he stilled.

"I'm not going to last long, baby," he said. "But I want you to come first." I was close. He'd been in me only seconds, but my body responded so quickly to his hands, his mouth, his words, his touch. It was overwhelming. I shivered with need. He rounded his hips, pulled away and then slammed into me. The beginning of my orgasm fizzed across my muscles. The power he had over my body was absolute.

He rammed in again and pushed me up the bed with the force of his movement, loosening the belt. He caught me as I tried to break free, and hooked his hands over my shoulders, his fingers pulling me onto him. The sensation of the leather tightening around my wrists, a few whispers of pain mixed with the pleasure of him plunging deep, turned the fizz of the beginning of my climax into a buzz. I wanted to freeze time.

That way I knew he'd never leave me. We could stay this way, a second away from ecstasy, safe, never quite letting go.

He watched me, our eyes locked as he moved above me, dragging my orgasm from every part of my body.

"Now, Haven. Come for me," he instructed, and my body gave him what he wanted as I tensed and I came, juddering around him.

From somewhere I heard him shouting—indecipherable sounds of desperation and desire that intensified my climax and merged our bodies further into each other.

As his muscles relaxed above me, he reached to loosen the grip of the leather and pulled my hands free. I wrapped them round his neck and he dragged me closer as he rolled to his back, still inside me. Somehow, I needed him nearer to me. I moved my hands from his neck and tried to pull at his chest, his waist, but my hands couldn't grasp him.

"Hey," he said as he grabbed my hands and kissed my wrists.

"Jake," I said, my voice quivering. I needed to know he wasn't going anywhere. I wanted him closer.

"Hey," he repeated and looked at me. I glanced away, not wanting him to see my glassy eyes. "What—?" He pulled out and I whimpered.

"No!" I said.

He sat up, took the condom off and discarded it on the floor. He searched my face, looking for reasons for my outburst. How did I explain that I couldn't have him gone, not even for a second?

"Talk to me, Haven."

"I want you near me," was all I could say. How did I say that now that he'd cracked me open and shone a light into the darkest parts of me, I belonged to him? He might get bored, discard me, find someone who deserved him, but I would always be his.

He pulled me onto his lap, his arms engulfing me. It felt good, better, but not enough. I wrapped myself around his waist and buried my face into the hard muscle of his chest.

"Don't leave me," I mumbled against his skin.

"What? I'm not going anywhere." He was talking about tonight, but I meant forever.

chapter TWENTY-SIX

Jake

Sex had always been a physical activity before Haven. With her, something shifted and it became holistic, elemental. It was as if she reached into my soul when she allowed me inside her. And holding her afterward, so vulnerable in my arms, I wondered if maybe it might be like that for her, too.

My dick twitched underneath her, and I tried to think of anything but how she felt, smelled and tasted. I didn't want her to think I didn't want to talk. She moved slightly and I could tell she'd noticed.

"I'm sorry. You're beautiful and naked and, well, that's biology."

She half smiled and reached between us. I grasped her wrist. "No, Haven. I can't . . . "

"You can't fuck me again?" She looked confused, hurt maybe.

"I can't stop myself getting hard if you touch me. I'll make love to you as long as you'll let me."

"I want you hard," she said as she twisted her hand away from my grip and clasped my erection. I groaned at the thought she might want me as much as I wanted her. I didn't need to hold back.

She shifted and slid her knees to either side of my thighs, my dick still in her fist as she dragged up my length. Having her naked gave me endless ideas about what I was going to do with her. And I wanted to do it all now. I reached forward, cupping her tits in my hands, twisting her nipples.

Her breathing stumbled and I grabbed her hips, pulling her toward me. She knew what I wanted. I was hard and I needed to feel her all around me. She grasped my shoulders and trailed her delicious, wet slit up and down my dick, twisting her body slightly as my crown hit her clitoris. She buried her head in my neck.

"Jake," she whimpered. Her movements got smaller. "I can't. It's too much. It's too good."

"Fuck, baby."

I grabbed a condom from the bedside table and flipped her to her back. She needed me to make her feel good and from now on, that was my job.

"Are you ready?" I asked her, searching her eyes for any hesitation. She pulled at me, trying to get me closer. She was more than ready.

She clung to the bed sheets and held her breath as I pushed in in one movement. My eyes were on hers the entire time, checking, assessing my effect on her.

"Oh Jesus," she said. "It's just, I'm so full."

I started moving above her and she cried out again and again. First, the noises she made were small, muffled and then they grew louder, magnified with each movement.

The sounds I created in her thrilled me, made me harder, brought me closer. Her expression told me whatever this was between us was as new for her as it was for me. She searched my face, looking for an explanation as if she were in pleasurable confusion.

I slid her legs up and over my shoulders. I was so deep; I was lost. Sweat coated my body and I wondered how long I would be able to hold off.

I reached forward and found her clitoris with my thumb.

She grabbed my forearm and cried out again.

"Like that?" I asked her, pushing and rubbing.

"Please Jake, I can't . . . " She arched off the bed, stretching, offering herself to me, the force of her orgasm drawing her toward me.

I concentrated on her beautiful face, trying to ignore my desire to empty myself into her. My thumb didn't relent, and as she recovered from her climax, she realized I was going to make her come again.

"Please, Jake," she cried. Oh, I could get used to her pleas. The uptight, sharp-tongued Haven Daniels begging me not to make her come, again and again. "I can't."

"You can and you will." I replied. I pushed into her sharply and she relaxed against me, succumbing, giving herself what she needed. She wanted to submit to me as much as I needed her to. I knew her body. She would get a reminder every time she forgot.

Her muscles began to pulse around me and her hands flew to her face as if she were trying to hide the effect I had on her body. But there was no hiding. I knew what I did to her. Every inch of her was mine.

"Look at me." I twisted my hips as I drove into her. I changed the direction of my circling thumb.

Her hands slid from her face to the pillow behind her. She fisted the fabric as she started to fall.

She was the most beautiful thing I'd ever seen—fragile, but so strong. Open just for me, a private screening. Her clenching muscles pushed me off the edge, and with a final thrust, I was done for.

It felt as if I lost consciousness for a few seconds. I regained it with the help of Haven's nails running up and down my back. I shuddered.

"Shit, that was . . . " I pushed up on my hands to watch her. She smiled at me. Sated.

"What?" she asked and she pulled her arms around my neck and drew me closer.

"I don't want to squash you."

"I like feeling your weight on me, like I can't escape," she said. Did she want to escape? I'd been clear with her—she wasn't to run, and if necessary I'd tie her to my bed. She was all I wanted, and if I needed to fight to keep her, I was ready to battle for the rest of my life.

I slumped over her again. "You're amazing," I said. "I love to watch you come."

"Jake," she said. Her eyes were haunted as she spoke.

"What?" I moved her legs between mine so I surrounded her, pressing my skin to hers. Offering her reassurance.

"Don't," she said. She sounded sad.

"Don't what?" I asked, propping myself up on my elbows so I could see her.

"Say stuff, you know, like that."

"Like what? That you're amazing and I love watching you come?"

She turned her head away from me and closed her eyes.

"You promised me you weren't going to run," I said. "If you shut yourself off, you're doing the same thing. Tell me what you mean." My heart began to thump against my chest. What was she going to say?

She sighed underneath me. "Stuff like that. Things you've said to other women."

It wasn't the answer I expected. She wanted to be special—she had no idea how incredible she was. I'd failed her if she didn't know. And failing Haven wasn't a possibility.

I pulled out of her, discarded the condom and slumped to her side, my face opposite hers. She opened her eyes. "I don't say anything I don't mean, Haven. I've never enjoyed watching a woman come the way I enjoy watching you. It makes me feel like I crash through you and take you over. I see a part of you that's rare and precious in those moments. You *are* amazing. Don't doubt it."

She stayed silent for a few long moments. I kissed her forehead. "You own me. As much as you let me in and that feels like an honor, you also see every part of me in a way I've never shown anyone, ever." I'd spent so much energy trying to break through Haven's tough shell, I'd not noticed that she'd found a wall in me I hadn't realized was there. She'd taken it down, unexpectedly, brick by brick.

"You do," she whispered.

"I do?" I asked.

"You crash through me and take me over. I don't know myself when I'm with you."

I couldn't get her close enough. I pulled her toward me, molding us together so there was no separation, no space between us.

I must have dozed off. Haven's cell woke me and she turned in my arms to reach it. I tightened my grip around her, not letting her wrestle free.

"Hey, it could be important," she said.

"Then they'll call back," I said but she continued to struggle so I released her.

The phone silenced before she reached it. "It was Ash." She burrowed back into my arms. "It's nearly six. We should get going. I guess we'll have to buy new tickets—you punched our ride. What was that about anyway?"

"Nothing. The guy was being a douche about you and about Beth." The last thing I wanted to do now was talk about Romano.

"What happened between them?"

"It's not my story to tell." There was no way I would repeat what he'd said. Not to Haven and not to Beth. "Will you trust me? I don't want you upset and I don't want to talk about him. Especially when we're naked in bed and I'm recovering from . . . "

"Recovering?" she asked, raising an eyebrow at me.

I didn't answer. I just smiled and pulled her closer and she sank against me.

"But we do need to go. I think the last train is at nine."

"Why don't we stay?" I suggested. "We're here, we have the hotel room. I can have you home to cook for Luke tomorrow."

"Ash is cooking this week," she said. It didn't sound as though I was going to have to try hard to convince her. I fought a smile. It would be easier this time.

"So what time would you have to be back?"

"Hmmm, two?" she suggested.

"We can do that easily." I kissed the top of her head.

She opened her mouth to say something, then stopped herself. I raised my eyebrows expectantly. Her ribcage expanded against me as she took a deep breath. "You could come, too, if you wanted? I mean, you don't have to and you're probably busy but—" I smiled at her as her words came out too fast and my heart swelled. She was going to try and make this work. Maybe the fight was won.

"I'd love to come."

She looked up at me and half grinned. I caught her face in my hands and pressed my lips to hers.

"Holy crap. I'm not good at all this stuff," she said. I got the feeling she wasn't just talking about dinner.

"Stuff?"

"With relationships, men. But I want to do better than I did last time. I don't want to mess this up."

"I won't let you. I got us covered. Follow my lead." I wasn't sure where we'd end up but as long as it was together, I didn't care.

"So, you're good at stuff with men?" she asked, grinning at me, her mood lightening.

"Oh, I'm going to make you pay for that. I like it when you're begging me to stop." I grabbed her wrists and pinned her to the bed, rubbing my growing erection against her thigh. "We're together, and that's all that matters, do you hear me?"

She nodded. "I promise I won't beg you to stop again."

"We'll see about that."

chapter TWENTY-SEVEN

Haven

When I opened my eyes to the sunlight, the first thing I thought was that I'd broken my promise to Jake. I *had* begged him to stop—I had begged him *never* to stop. I had implored him to go harder, faster, deeper. I felt the consequence of every plea across my body as my tight muscles stopped me from sitting up. I felt shadows of him across my skin—bite marks, fingertip bruises, his scent.

"Morning," Jake said.

"Hey," I replied.

"We slept, finally. I didn't think I'd ever want to." His words floated over me like feathers. I'd never felt physically needed by someone before. It was grounding, compelling.

"You passed out on top of me, mid thrust," I said smiling up at him.

"I did not. You fell asleep when I was in the bathroom for like a minute and a half."

I grinned at him. It sounded about right.

"We should go if we're going to get you home for your family thing."

I wanted Ash and Luke to meet Jake properly, but I also wanted to stay. To watch him, still sleepy and caught in the sunlight pushing in through the slits in the curtains. I reached for my phone. It was gone ten. I'd hoped that we'd see a bit more of the city today. I wanted to pretend that we were still in Paris the first time; that I hadn't wasted the time since filming. That I hadn't pushed him away.

"We can come back anytime," he said, reading my thoughts.

"Promise?"

"Of course. Wanna come to Palo Alto with me?"

I scowled at him as I sat up. "I have work. I have to sort out this shit with this article. I hope Louis doesn't make it difficult."

Punctuated by long and short kisses, we showered and dressed so we could be back in London in time for Sunday dinner. Before we left, I pulled out my phone. "I should ring Ash to tell her I'll be a bit late," I said. "Normally I'd go round soon after lunch to help her."

He nodded. "I'll call Beth. Shit! Those real estate viewings."

"You still want to come to dinner? I mean, it's nothing fancy. It's just the three of us."

"I want to come, Haven. Never doubt me."

I reached to stroke his beautiful face. "You don't think this is some kind of spell that is cast on us in Paris?" I asked.

Jake looked at me. "What are you talking about?"

"Oh, you know, we'll get back to London and this," I said, swirling my fingers at us, "Will just . . . you know . . . disappear."

"You're crazy. I'm not disappearing and you're not going anywhere. I've told you this."

I nodded, but something gnawed away in the pit of my stomach. I'd had the same feeling the last time we took this train back to London. There was a reason I wasn't close to many people.

We arrived at Ash's flat a little before three so there would still be time before Luke got there.

"Are you ready?" I asked Jake as my finger hovered over the intercom.

"Ready for what? You're not planning to serve me for dinner, are you?" He reached across and pressed the buzzer, then landed a kiss on the top of my head.

A second later, Ash threw the door open and grinned the widest grin I'd ever seen.

"Knock it off, Ash," I said as I pushed past her into the hallway. "You've met, I believe."

"We have. I'm delighted to see you, together," she said and I rolled my eyes.

"Nice to see you again, Ash," Jake said from behind me.

I headed straight to the fridge to find something to take the edge off. I was either going to be teased mercilessly, or everything was going to be awkward. I wasn't sure which was more nerve wracking—that he would fit into our little group or that he wouldn't.

"You're sure Emma's not coming?" Ash asked me.

"I'm sure. Otherwise we'd be doing this at my house."

"Who's Emma?" Jake asked.

"Luke's girlfriend," I said. "We don't have Sunday dinner at Ash's if Emma is joining us."

The door buzzer went again and Ash headed off to answer it.

"You want some wine?" I asked him.

"Not as much as you do, apparently, but I'll have a glass," he responded. It was nice having him standing in Ash's kitchen as though it was the most normal thing in the world. Good, but weird.

"Hey Luke," Jake said, extending his hand as Luke and Ash piled into the kitchen.

Luke took Jake's hand, but wasn't overly friendly. I watched as the cold rolled off Luke. It wasn't like him. He was everyone's friend. But he was worried for me. He didn't need to be. Jake was a protector, just as Luke was. "I'm glad we're meeting under better circumstances this time," Jake said.

Luke nodded stiffly and pushed his hands through his hair as Ash punched him on the arm.

"Come on, cheer up, you misery. Your little sister's getting laid, you should be delighted!" Ash said.

A mixture of "Jesus", "fucking hell" and "Ash" filled the room, but Ash just grinned.

"You see, the ice is officially broken," she said. "We are an equal-opportunity employer here, Jake, so don't think you're going to be able to watch sports while we cook. Strap on an apron and get chopping."

I hopped up on a stool and fiddled with my wine glass while Jake tied an apron around his waist. I knew better than to start anything without express and detailed instructions from Ash.

"I'm going to do everything I can to make your sister happy," Jake told Luke. "I don't think she'll ever find anyone to deserve her, but I'm going to do my best to be that man."

My heart swelled. I sounded so precious when he spoke about me like that.

Luke nodded. "And if you don't, I'll kill you."

"Sounds fair," Jake said, nodding as Luke smiled.

"So, what car do you drive?" Luke asked Jake. Before he had a chance to answer, Ash interrupted.

"What car do you drive? I'm not going to marry you if you keep this up, dork face. You must have better small talk than that," said Ash.

"I like them, and I like you with them," Jake said as we climbed into a cab after leaving Ash's. "Can we go to Little Venice and then Earls Court?" he said to the driver. Jake's easy confidence meant he fit fine into our group and I wasn't as freaked out by that as I'd expected.

"You can stay at mine if you want," I said.

He pulled me onto his lap and kissed my neck, driving me crazy. My skin heated as soon as he touched me, as if it was waiting for him to come alive. "I want to. I really, really want to. It's driven me insane not being able to touch you for the past few hours."

"I sense a *but*." I pushed my hands through his hair as he continued his exploration of my neck.

"I should get home to Beth. She's . . . it's—"

"You don't need to explain. It's fine."

"I'm going to have to work a few things out," he said. I hoped that the spell of Paris was not beginning to weaken. "I need you to trust me. I'm away next week and she needs me at the moment."

Jake followed me out of the cab when it pulled up outside my building, and for a moment, I thought he'd changed his mind.

He took my face in his hands and brushed his lips against me—brushing then pressing, pressing then pushing my lips open, his tongue crashing against mine. He kissed me as though it was our last moment together. I groaned into his mouth and he pulled away.

"Those sounds you make drive me crazy," he said, our foreheads resting together. "If we don't stop now, I'll never leave."

Stay, I thought, but I didn't say anything. *Stay or the spell will be broken.*

"Can I see you tomorrow? I fly out on Tuesday morning. We could go out to dinner. Or stay in?" he suggested.

I didn't want him to feel obligated. "I understand if you need to prep or—"

"Haven, I want to spend the evening with you. You need to stop doubting."

He'd pinpointed exactly what I was thinking. "I told you I was terrible at relationships." My heartbeat began to quicken.

"I'm going to stay. Let me speak to Beth," he said as he reached into his pocket.

"No!" I put my hand on his. "You can't. That will make it worse. I'll feel selfish and high maintenance and I *am* those things, but I don't need to be reminded of it."

"You're not running from me, Haven, and I won't have you push me away. You have to talk to me and tell me what you need."

I nodded.

"You're my girl and we just need to figure this out. We'll get there."

He walked me up the steps to my building and closed the door behind me. I watched through the glass as he climbed back into the cab.

I exhaled. Maybe he was right.

chapter TWENTY-EIGHT

Jake

I stood outside Haven's building, thinking about our conversation when I dropped her off here the night before. I had been kind of relieved on the way home. I could tell she had been waiting for things to go badly. We'd hit our first road bump and we were safely over the other side.

With previous girlfriends, there'd never been much talking. It hadn't been all fucking—it had been dinner and fucking. The food had been the warm up to the sex. I'd never really known a woman before I'd asked her out. And although you couldn't categorize Haven and I as friends, we'd had something before the physical stuff. I liked that. I wanted to talk to her, to hear what she was thinking and feeling. It didn't matter to me that we might be on a rough road and that she was prickly and pushed people away. I'd known that about her all along, it was part of what attracted me to her. We were all a bit crazy—she just didn't hide hers.

I pulled my phone from my jeans pocket. There was a missed call from Millie but no voicemail. Why did she keep calling? There was no going back for us. Didn't she get that?

I leaned against the railing as I saw Haven round the corner. She was smiling to herself, and I couldn't help but grin. She looked so happy. Her smile widened when she saw me. My heart leapt.

"Hey, gorgeous." I bent and kissed her.

"Hey," she replied, grinning as she pushed me away. "No PDAing in front of my neighbors."

"Then we better get inside because you're going to be naked in less than five minutes."

She rolled her eyes at me as she started to punch in the code to her building. I stood behind her, grappling for the pins that kept her hair in place.

"What are you doing?" she asked as she opened the door.

"Trying to get your hair down."

"What am I going to do with you?" she asked through a grin.

"I can think of a few things that I'm going to do with you." I grabbed her hand as we headed to the elevators.

"You pervert."

As soon as the lift doors closed, she turned to me. "So, we're technically not in public anymore."

"And I'm a pervert? You wanna get felt up in the elevator?"

She reached up around my neck. "Maybe," she replied.

I walked her back so she was against the chrome of the elevator wall. I pressed my crotch against her and slid my hand up the back of her uncovered thigh. I'd been hard since I first laid eyes on her. Each time I saw her again she seemed to be slightly more beautiful than before, if that were possible.

"Well, you'll have to wait. I don't put out in public places,"

I said as the elevator doors opened and I released her from where I had her pinned to the wall.

She rolled her eyes at me again and I swiped her on the bottom. “Are you looking to get spanked?”

“Perhaps,” she said with a gleam in her eye. “So what do you want to order for dinner?” she asked as she unlocked her apartment.

“You,” I said as I stepped in. Last time I’d been here, I’d felt like a stranger to her as we struggled to try and be just colleagues. I glanced around with none of the heavy heart that I’d felt last time. I was excited to get to see her like this.

She laughed.

“I’m serious. I can’t wait any longer.” I followed her, trying to unzip her skirt. I grabbed at her turtleneck and she lifted her arms as I pulled it off.

“Don’t you want to hear about my conversation with Paula from Glass Introductions?” she asked as she walked backward into her bedroom.

“Not really. What? You mean about Romano? What did she say?”

I dipped my head to lick her collarbone. Her skin was so beautiful. Her fingers pressed into my shoulders as she tipped her head back to give me better access.

“What did she say?” I asked again.

“Huh? Oh, right, that he had called to apologize to her, but he hadn’t told her what happened. I didn’t say anything either.”

“So he’s okay with you using him in the article?” I skimmed her skirt down her legs.

"Yeah, she didn't say anything at all."

"Good news," I said as I unbuttoned my jeans and threw off my sweater. "It means we never have to think about that prick again."

God she was perfect, standing in front of me in nothing but her underwear. "Take your panties off," I said as I took a step back to drink her in. She hooked her thumbs into the lace and slid them down.

I took a deep breath. I was going to savor this. "On your back on the bed."

She complied quickly and I reached for her ankles, bringing her ass to the edge of the bed. I picked up her panties from the floor where she'd left them. "Give me your wrists."

She held out her hands.

"Next time we'll do this properly, but this will do for now." I tied the panties around her hands, knotting them securely. "Does it hurt?" I asked.

"Almost," she said.

"Perfect. Now put them above your head and don't move."

I watched as she stretched out, her nipples puckered in anticipation. She watched me watching her. Already she was used to me taking a moment to drink her in. She knew I needed that. I wanted to see her whole body before I decided where to start, how I would make her come for the first time.

I pushed her knees apart and plunged my thumb into her and she gasped as I circled. She was so ready for me. "How long have you been like this, Haven? So wet, so ready?"

"Jake," she whimpered.

I withdrew my thumb and sucked off her wetness. Jesus, she tasted delicious—a mixture of sweetness and sex. I fell to my knees and replaced my thumb with my tongue, delving as deep as I could go. She thrust against me, not holding back for a second.

I pulled away. "Every inch of you is so tempting, I want to do everything to you all at once."

She writhed off the mattress and I placed my palm on her stomach to hold her in place.

"I want you inside me, Jake," she panted.

"Not yet baby, you're not ready." I wanted her boneless by the time I slid into her.

I pushed two fingers into her and licked a trail up to her clitoris, circling, licking, sucking. I used my free hand to pinch her nipple hard between my thumb and forefinger. Her sounds, breaths and whimpers, told me she was on her way. She liked the mixture of pain and pleasure.

I was harder than ever. I'd be toast if I thought about her lips wrapped around my cock. How she might gag and her eyes might water. Shit. I sucked, hard. I needed her to come so I could be inside her. Her clit was swollen and throbbing against my tongue as I pushed harder and deeper.

Her body went rigid, then shuddered. I pulled out my fingers, licking her clit softly as her orgasm rumbled through her like thunder.

"Did that feel good?" I asked, knowing the answer from the sedated look on her face.

"So. Good." She pushed out the words as if they were her last breath.

She brought her hands down from over her head as I lay beside her and pulled the knots free. She had marks, brighter than I'd intended, crisscrossing her wrists.

"Does it hurt?" I asked as I trailed my fingers across them.

"I'm not sure," she answered. "It mixes together with everything and makes it all sharper and more intense." She looked down at the marks, tracing them with her nails. "I like it."

"I like it, too." I bent across her and kissed her, reveling in the feel of her hands in my hair.

I reached across the bed to grab a condom out of my jeans pocket. She snatched it from me. Did she want to put it on?

"Can we do it without?" she asked. It took me a second to realize what she meant. "Are you healthy?"

"I've never had sex without a condom," I said. I'd never thought about it, never considered it. Now, with her, it was what I wanted.

"Me neither. And I'm on the pill. We don't have to, though," she replied as if she was going to have to convince me. "I just want to be closer to you."

I rolled to my back. "Shit, Haven, just when I think you don't hold any more surprises." The fact that she wanted it, that she'd had the courage to ask. I'd never felt so close to her. It was as if we were a unit, a couple. "Other than fuck you all night, there's nothing I want to do more. But I'm going to last two seconds."

"We can take it slow."

"Baby, you don't need to talk me into it." I pulled her face toward mine.

chapter TWENTY-NINE

Haven

It felt as if I disappeared into Jake when he kissed me. He knew when to be soft, when to be rough. When to bite and when to suck. It was as though he knew my body better than I did. As though he'd always known it.

I reached for his shoulders, tracing the line that separated them from his chest. The hardness of his body pressed against mine was just right—perfect, as if it had always been meant to be like this.

He shifted between my legs and I brought my knees up and opened my thighs wide. He nudged at my entrance and I urged my palms into his skin. The anticipation had the blood throbbing in my ears and my hands were shaky, as if I'd had too much sugar. I wanted to feel him inside me with nothing between us. That was how it was meant to be.

His breaths were short and hot on my neck as he tried to hold himself back. I twisted my hips underneath him and he groaned. This was it. I could tell he wasn't going to resist much longer. We locked eyes and he pushed into me, but just an inch. I understood in the moment what connection felt like—mind, body and soul. I could have gone my whole life without feeling it. Without knowing Jake, without experiencing great love.

"Jake, more, please." I couldn't hold back, I needed him deep inside me. It was so good; he was so hard. I was so ready.

He lifted himself, his hands either side of my head. "I want to watch you," he said.

"See me driven crazy by the feel of your dick in me?"

"Fuck, Haven, if you talk like that I'm going to blow."

I grinned. It felt good to surprise him. Then he pushed into me, turning my smile into gasp.

"Baby, it feels so good."

I nodded, unable to form words.

He pushed again and I was full of him. I couldn't speak, couldn't move. I was his entirely. After a few seconds, he started to move above me, rubbing, pulling, twisting. His muscles under my fingers hardened and his mouth set in a straight line as if he were putting everything he had into the moment. His angle shifted slightly and it set off the first signal of my climax—a deep, intense rumbling from the center of me.

"Jake," I said as I found the only word I would ever need. "Jake, Jake, Jake." I was being pulled under, drowning in him. My orgasm flashed across my body and my muscles contracted around him a second before he cried out. He thrust once more, quick and hard, and then collapsed on top of me.

"Stay," I said as he shifted to his elbows. "Don't move. Not yet." He buried his head in my neck and pushed our bodies together.

"So, California, huh?" I asked.

"I'm cancelling and you're going to call in sick for a week so we can do what we just did all day, every day."

I laughed. "Neither of those two things are happening."

"Are you sure? Do I need to remind you of what just went on in here?"

I shook my head and took a mouthful of noodles. When we'd finally come up for air we'd managed to order Chinese food. Jake insisted on ordering a meal for four on the basis we'd need our strength.

"I swear to God, I have no desire to go to Palo Alto anymore. Not when I can stay here and worship your incredible body. Thank goodness I made my money before I met you, otherwise we'd have nothing. I can never concentrate properly on anything else, ever again."

"You're crazy."

"You're crazy beautiful." He leaned over and kissed me.

"What time's your flight?" I asked.

"I told you, I'm not going."

I rolled my eyes. "What time?"

"Tomorrow night. Why don't you come with me?"

I loved that he wanted me to come with him so badly. It made me feel warm and comfortable. "You know I can't, and you're only gone a few days, right?"

He scowled and I laughed at him.

"Think of it as another little road bump. We'll be over it by the end of the week," I said.

How did I get so lucky? I'd thought of him as some spoiled, cocky rich boy when he was anything but. He was kind, hardworking and so good looking it should be illegal. Best of all, he seemed to know me.

Jake

My cell buzzed in my pocket as I hit the fresh air coming out of Haven's building the next day. I checked my watch. I had a lot to do before my flight. Absentmindedly, I glanced at the screen. Millie again. Ignoring her apparently hadn't worked, so I took the call.

"Millie," I answered.

"Finally. I've been trying to reach you for a week now."

"Well, I'm here now. What can I help you with?" I looked up and down the street, working out where I'd parked my car.

"Don't be so cold, Harry. Aren't you pleased to hear from me?"

She definitely wanted something.

"I'm heading to the airport. I haven't got much time and I'm about to start driving, so I can't talk. Can I call you back?"

"I need to speak to you properly. Can you pop round before your flight?"

"What? No. If you've got something to say, you can say it now." She really did think the world revolved around her. I didn't want to see her, and I had no time before leaving for the US.

"This isn't the kind of conversation you have over the phone," she said. What did that mean? I stayed silent. I wasn't giving in to her. "I'm pregnant . . . and it's yours."

My breath caught in my throat. Had I heard her right?

"Harry?"

"What? We always used a condom. There's no way it's mine."

"There hasn't been anyone since you, and condoms aren't always effective. I'm sure I remember that time after that party—you were drunk—you didn't have a condom but you said you'd pull out." She was rambling, her voice breathy and panicked. My head started to spin, trying to break down what she was saying. This couldn't be happening.

"What? That didn't happen, Millie. I don't get drunk and I don't fuck without using something." Not before last night. Haven had been the first. I was sure of that.

I ran through Millie's and my times together. No split condoms, no condoms that came off. Nothing unusual. I was OCD careful about expiration dates. This couldn't be happening.

Millie started to cry. I'd never known her to cry. "I found out last week, Harry, and I'm so alone. I always thought I'd be married. Please come round and talk. We're going to have a baby."

Shit.

That road bump had turned into a sinkhole.

I didn't remember any of my journey home. I had driven, but I'd been on autopilot in the thirty minutes since Millie had called. Pregnant? How did that happen? What should I do?

As I opened my front door, I slung my keys onto the hall table and found my way to the sofa. My brain was fuzzy and

I couldn't think about anything for more than five seconds before some other consequence overtook me. Could I get a paternity test? Would I have to marry her? What did it all mean for me and Haven? How would Beth react, or worse, my father? Fuck. I pushed my hands through my hair.

The only thing I did know was that I couldn't see Millie, not yet. I couldn't tell Haven, not until I could formulate a coherent thought. I didn't want to tell Beth. I just wanted to run away to California and pretend it wasn't happening.

My cell vibrated against my hip.

Haven: I'll miss you. Call me when you're checked in at the airport.

Fear sat on my chest, squeezing and pushing. How could I speak to her? What could I possibly say? She needed me to be strong. She needed me to reassure her, but I had nothing. I was empty.

I dove back into my thoughts, and the next thing I was conscious of was the buzzing of the intercom.

"Hello?" I said, praying it wasn't Haven or Beth or anyone.

"Mr. Harrison, this is your driver. Do you need a hand with your luggage?" Shit, my car to take me to the airport. I looked at my watch. Where had the last hour gone? I'd not even packed a bag.

"No thanks, I'll be down shortly." I looked around the apartment. I needed to pack in a hurry.

Haven

I pressed cancel on my phone and leant forward on the kitchen counter. Rain started to tap against my windows. I pulled the blind down so I didn't have to see it. I hadn't left a voicemail. I didn't really have anything to say, but I'd expected him to be through security by now. Where was he? Anxiety nudged at me. Maybe he'd boarded already and forgotten to call me. If I didn't speak to him before his flight, I wouldn't speak to him until tomorrow, or maybe even a few days from now because of time differences and our schedules.

I had little chance of sleep; I rarely slept through a storm and my mind was too full of things that might go wrong while Jake was in California. Why hadn't he called? That question gave permission for the rest of my doubts to break through. Was I strong enough, good enough, patient enough? I pulled out various liquids and gels, sponges and mops from my cupboard. I needed purpose and distraction. Leading up to my exams at University, I would spend all night cleaning bathrooms, communal kitchens, floors—anything I could find. It gave me a sense of order that controlled my stress levels and gave me space to think. I had crawled half way into my china cupboard to reach the back wall with my cloth when my phone started to ring. I banged my head as I fumbled for the source of the sound in my jeans pocket.

"Shit," I said as I answered.

"Are you okay?" Jake asked.

"Yeah, I hit my head. I'm fine," I said, rubbing what was bound to become a lump overnight. It felt good to hear his voice.

"What on?" he asked.

"Cupboards. I've been cleaning."

"You're cleaning? What?" he asked.

“Kitchen cupboards,” I said, trying to sound if that was the most normal thing in the world to be doing so close to midnight.

There was a silence for just a moment longer than there should have been. I shouldn’t have said anything. I forgot that he saw me so clearly—he would know that I was anxious about his trip.

“I’m sorry I’m not there,” he said as the line crackled. Immediately I felt guilty. I shouldn’t have said anything; I didn’t want him to feel bad.

“Don’t be. You have to work, Jake, and you’ll be back soon.”

“Yeah, about that. I might have to extend my trip,” he said quietly. My heart sank. I missed him already. I wanted to pepper him with questions, to ask him why, try to find a solution so he could do what he needed to remotely and come back to me sooner not later.

“Oh,” was all I managed.

“I don’t know yet. I need to think,” he said.

Think? “Is everything okay?” I asked him.

“Sure. Of course,” he replied and we fell quiet, sounds of the imminent storm growing around me. Something was bothering him. Jake was never silent if he thought I needed him, and he knew I did. “I just might need an extra week or so in the US. I might go and see my father. I’ve not seen him in a while and . . . you know.”

Last night Jake was all for canceling his trip because he didn’t want to be away from me and now he was extending it and going to see his father? It didn’t make sense . . . I could feel a distance unraveling between us that was wider than miles. Was he keeping something from me? Was he pulling back?

"I'm boarding, so I need to go," he said before I got a chance to say anything in reply.

"Okay," I said. "I'm going to miss you. You have my heart, so bring it back safely."

I heard his breath at the other end of the line before he spoke. "You have mine. I've got to go."

The phone went dead and I was left alone with nothing but the rumble of thunder in my head. However loud and dark they got, storms passed, they were temporary, weren't they?

I was just thinking too much. Jake had always been honest with me and if there was something wrong, he would tell me, I trusted him. I just had to get through this next few days without him and then he would be back and everything would be okay. When we were together everything made sense.

chapter THIRTY

Jake

As I approached the luggage carousel, I switched on my cell. The flight from Palo Alto had landed late and I needed to tell Haven I'd been delayed. I'd started my trip thinking I needed space so I could work out what I was going to do about Millie's pregnancy, but I'd changed my ticket to come back early. I'd missed Haven. I hated the thought of her sleeping alone. Her warm, soft, naked body, without me next to it, just wasn't right. Now that I was back in the country, I couldn't put off telling her about Millie. I'd justified not saying anything to her so far because it wasn't the sort of news I wanted to deliver over the phone, especially when I didn't have a clue how she was going to react. There was a real possibility Haven would use it as an opportunity to run, to push me away and do what she did best: protect herself. But I had to take the bull by the horns. What I really wanted to do was get naked with her, bury myself in her, come up for air a couple of hours later, eat Chinese food and make her laugh. All I wanted to do was make Haven happy and my news was sure to do anything but.

I still hadn't decided how I felt about the situation. I was sure that Millie as a mother spelled disaster. But under my worry about Haven's reaction, my concern over Millie's inability to think about anyone but herself and the real possibility that the baby wasn't mine, there were parts of me excited to be a father. I pushed my hands through my hair. There was too much to think about. *One step at a time.*

When Beth and I were young, my mother was always concerned about my father getting hurt on the job. Being a cop anywhere, but particularly in Chicago, wasn't the safest of occupations. She was always trying to convince him to get a position in an office. But he loved it and didn't see the danger; he'd focused on the opportunity to make our city better. My father always used to say that we had to deal with what was right in front of us and not worry about things that hadn't happened yet—one step at a time. It had *almost* become a family motto. He'd never said it again after Mom was shot.

My cell buzzed in my hand.

"Hey. I just landed," I said to my sister, Beth.

"I've had a call from Marissa." Neither Beth nor I had a good relationship with my father's second wife, so if she was calling, it wasn't for a casual catch up.

"What's going on?" The carousel started moving and I walked up to where the bags were coming out.

"Dad had a heart-attack," she said.

My feet stuck to the floor and I froze. "Fuck. When? Is he okay?"

"Apparently he's stable and will be fine after a small operation—they've got to put a stent in, Marissa said. It happened yesterday. I'm going to fly out to Chicago." She sounded too calm.

"Do you think that's a good idea? Should I come with you? This has been a shitty week." I could get a flight; I wouldn't even have to leave the airport. Beth was stronger now but something like this could set her back, could trigger her drinking. And Dad? He was always such a force of nature. It didn't seem possible that he was lying in a hospital bed.

"You've got enough to deal with here. I can let you know how things are and whether or not you should come. Besides, if we both go right away, it might be a bit overwhelming for him. From what Marissa said, he's stable and as long as he has this operation, he should be fine."

"Have you spoken to the doctor?" My stomach started to spin. I was standing among strangers. I needed information. I should be with Beth, with Dad, with Haven. "I don't want you going back there on your own. It's too—" What would this do to Beth?

"Listen, I'm a different person now. I'm two and a half years sober. Going back is long overdue. My exams are over. It feels like the right time. A lot has happened and there might be a chance to heal the rift between Dad and us. Let me go and test the waters. I mean, Marissa called. That's got to be a good sign."

When Dad married Marissa, it was as though we stopped being part of his family. It was as if he put a period after us and started a new chapter. Beth had found it harder than I had. She'd felt abandoned, adrift. Since she had joined me in London, we'd formed a unit, a family of two. Reaching out to our father could lead to reconciliation, but it could just as easily bring pain. It was my job to protect Beth from that. Or it had been. Now she was stronger, and perhaps she needed to prove to herself as well as me that she was independent.

The fuzzy gray lines between decisions were so draining, and now I was faced with more of them. I wanted the right thing to be written in neon and flashing over my head. There were too many *ifs* and *buts*—consequences and compromises whatever options I chose. I wanted to be in Chicago with my Dad and Beth. I wanted to be in London with Haven and Elemental Energy. I wanted Millie to take a DNA test without having to ask her and feel like an asshole. I wanted to reach out to Dad with the guarantee he would pull us into a bear hug and not let go until we screamed as he had when we were little. I wanted someone to tell me it was all going to be okay. *One step at a time.*

"Jake?"

"Yeah, sorry. I'm trying to take it all in."

I spotted my suitcase on the carousel and tucked my phone under my chin while I hauled it off the conveyor belt.

"So you think you should go to Chicago on your own?" As much as I might want to keep Beth safe, she was an adult and needed to make her own decisions. And she was right. She was a different person. She'd handled Romano coming back onto the scene, however briefly, well. She'd graduate this summer.

"I do." She sounded resolute and it was comforting. At least one of us knew what the right thing to do was.

"You'll find a meeting in Chicago?" I asked.

"Of course I will. Believe it or not, my sobriety is more important to me than it is to you. Stop fussing."

"I could fly out with you—"

"I'm going to book my ticket for later today, and you have things to do here. You need to talk to Haven."

I filled my lungs and headed toward the exit. "I hope . . ."

"She'll understand. It's not the kind of conversation you can have over the phone."

"It was just shitty timing with me being in California this week, and now this thing with Dad. Can I speak to him?"

"Apparently he can't have calls. You concentrate on Haven. I'll call you from the airport and when I see him. Then, if I think you need to, you can fly over. Let me see how things are."

She was making a lot of sense. I was so proud of her. A couple of years ago she would have been a mess if this had happened. Now she was all over it—practical, thoughtful and caring. All the things that she had always been, but had hidden for so long under the alcohol.

"If you're sure . . ."

"I am. Say hi to Haven for me. Speak later. I love you."

"Aren't you a sight for sore eyes?" I said as Haven opened the door to her apartment. Her hair tumbled across her shoulders. She looked at me totally unguarded, as if I might be about to make all her dreams come true. I loved this Haven. The one she hid away and only showed to a chosen few. I was glad she hadn't disappeared while I was gone. I had been concerned that going away so soon after we were together, would make her withdraw from me.

"Hey," she said, through a wide grin. "I've been waiting for you. Come in. Do you want a shower?"

My dick stirred at the mention of a shower with Haven in front of me, looking so Goddamn beautiful. "I'd love to, but I'll just want to lose myself in you, and we should talk."

"Oh," she replied. "Do you want a coffee?"

"Let's go out, grab some lunch." Talking would be easier if I wasn't kissing her, and not kissing her would be easier if we were in public.

"That sounds ominous for someone so focused on the physical."

She was right. Talking was the last thing I wanted to do. "I want to share some stuff with you."

"Let me get my bag."

Reluctantly, I let her go. "Is there anywhere good near here?" I asked.

"For lunch? Sure. Are you sick?" she asked as she pulled the door closed behind us. "You look tired."

I *felt* tired and I didn't have the energy to keep everything to myself anymore. Now that I was with Haven, I wanted her to know what was going on. "I just found out that my dad had a heart attack."

"Jesus, Jake." She stopped dead outside her apartment. "Are you okay? Is he okay?"

I grabbed her hand and started walking. The sun was shining and the air crisp. I loved weather like this in London. It was good to be home, with Haven. I let my shoulders relax and the muscles in my neck unclenched. Telling her about my dad was reassuring somehow.

"He's going to be fine, I think. Beth's flying out tonight. I might follow her depending on how he is when she gets there. I'm worried about her going out there on her own. She had a few problems when she was last in Chicago. She's not been back since."

"What sort of problems?"

I squeezed her hand as we walked down the road. "I'll tell you about them another time. She's better now. I hope. Chicago wasn't good for her." I didn't want to get into Romano and Beth's alcoholism. It was too much to think about and I'd need to ask Beth before I started telling her story.

"Do you need to go with her?"

"Not today. After that, I don't know. It's complicated. When my mom passed, my father remarried quickly and . . . we grew apart."

"I didn't know your mother died. Jake, why didn't you tell me?"

"She was shot by a guy who my dad put in jail. He came back for revenge and when my dad wasn't there, my mother suffered the consequences." It wasn't a secret, but I didn't have a reason to say the words very often. And although I wanted Haven to know, a familiar hurt welled inside me.

"Jesus, she was murdered?"

"It's been nearly five years. Beth took it really hard. I was older and had made a life for myself here in London. I had my first business, Energy Trade, but Beth was a teenager and lost both her parents. Her whole world fell apart. I think Beth and I reminded Dad of Mom too much and he . . . he has a new family now." I didn't talk about this stuff. I had no reason to, but it was good to tell Haven. I wanted her to know everything about me.

"God, I'm so sorry, Jake." Haven regarded me with glassy eyes. I put my arm around her and she snaked her hand up my back as we walked toward the restaurant. It was so good to be close to her again. I hoped my news about Millie wasn't about to rip us apart. There had been enough revelations for one day. Perhaps I should wait to tell her? Let her absorb one thing at a time?

"Are you sure you shouldn't go to Chicago?" she asked.

"Not today. I'm going to see what Beth says when she gets there and then I'll decide what to do. It's not as straightforward as it should be between my father and I. Anyway, he has to have an operation and then apparently he should be fine, but who knows what the real story is. Marissa has never been particularly open with us."

"If there's anything I can do . . ." she said.

I pressed my lips to the top of her head, taking in the comforting scent of her shampoo. "You being here is enough."

"I'm always here. I had a word with myself while you were way. I was halfway toward meltdown when you left. But I decided I'm not running from you. I'm not going anywhere. And we'll deal with whatever life throws at us together. Okay?" She stopped and gazed up at me. Smiling but solemn, she reached for my face and brushed her fingers against my cheek.

How had I gotten so lucky? I hoped she meant it. We were going to need her steely resolve over the next weeks and months. I had to tell her now. There wasn't ever going to be a good time and she was always going to be a flight risk, no matter what she said. I took a deep breath. "Yes, but there's something else as well."

We'd reached the restaurant Haven had picked. "Do you want to go in?" she asked.

I nodded and we headed inside the canal-side eatery. It was bright and sunny even indoors as the back of the place was all windows to take in the waterfront views. Once we were seated, Haven looked at me expectantly.

"The only reason I've not told you this before is because I wanted to tell you face-to-face. I'm not trying to keep anything from you," I said, my teeth gritted at the prospect that she would see a betrayal in the fact I'd not told her as soon as I'd found out.

"Okay . . . This sounds serious. Talk to me."

I wasn't sure if my voice could be heard over the thundering of my heart.

"Jake?"

"Millie called me just after I left you on Tuesday." *Here we go.*

"On your way to the airport?"

I nodded and closed my eyes.

"What did she want?" she asked.

"She told me she was pregnant. With my baby."

chapter THIRTY-ONE

Haven

A million thoughts rushed to the front of my brain and fought for space. My eyes dropped to the menu I held in my hands and I tried to concentrate on what I should order. I needed to stay calm. I had to keep my crazy from crawling up my spine and taking over my mouth.

"Haven?" Jake asked.

"The sea bass is good, I think," I replied, keeping calm. Millie was pregnant. It was only a big deal if I let it be. I knew Jake wouldn't cheat so I didn't need to ask—I knew this must be from before they split.

Jake sighed, but I couldn't bring myself to meet his eyes. "I don't have many details. I've not spoken to her since. It doesn't need to change anything between us," he said.

Had she waited to tell him until it was too late to have a termination? And how had he let this happen? I didn't look up from the menu as the questions started rolling through my head. "I thought you'd never . . . you know, without a condom." Had that just been a line?

"I never fucked her without a condom. We never had one split or come off. I don't know how this happened. I promise, Haven, I haven't lied to you."

I believed him. I had to. The alternative meant we were done and I knew I wasn't ready to be done, not yet, not if it was up to me. "You think she's lying?" I asked. It was a possibility that would probably be better for us as a couple. But for him? Did he want to be a father? Was he excited? Should I ask him? Was I being selfish seeing all this as an obstacle for us rather than an opportunity for him? Too many questions. I squeezed my eyes shut for a moment, hoping for quiet in my head.

He shrugged. "Beth does. I don't know."

It stung a little that he'd told his sister before he'd told me. But if the shoe had been on the other foot, Luke or Ash would likely have been my first call. *Keep calm.* "Are you going to have a paternity test?"

The waiter arrived and took our order and my question hung in the air like a cliffhanger in a soap opera.

"I guess. I've not had much time to process any of this."

I risked a peek at him under my eyelashes as his voice faltered slightly. He looked gray. I reached across and slid my hand over his. He twisted his palm up so we were holding hands across the table. In the space of the last three minutes, I had found out that this beautiful, strong man, who I had assumed had it all, had no mother, no father to speak of and now was going to become a father under less than the best of circumstances. Could he handle this?

"She wants you back?"

He drew his eyebrows together. "What? No. I don't think so."

"She wants you back." Of course she did. Why wouldn't she? Jake was a great guy and he'd make an incredible father.

"Well, I'm with you. She doesn't get to have me back." He sounded resolute.

I wanted to tell him that I didn't want to be the reason he wasn't with the mother of his child. I wasn't sure I could bear that responsibility. Every second that passed, this road bump in front of us got bigger and bigger.

"Haven?"

"I don't know what to say. Congratulations?"

Jake closed his eyes. I hadn't meant to hurt him, it had just come out wrong.

"I'm sorry," he said.

"No, *I'm* sorry. It wasn't what I was expecting." Despite everything, the only person I wanted right then was Jake. When had he managed to get inside my inner circle? "How are you feeling about it? I guess part of you must be excited?" I needed to be as understanding as I could.

"Honestly, I don't know. At the moment I'm too worried about you."

He was far too good to me. He shouldn't have to be troubled by me. He should be able to count on my support rather than be concerned I was going to run.

The clatter of a dropped glass in the distance broke my concentration. "How about we give ourselves a time out? Talk about other stuff, just for a few minutes. I need to be lighter—*we* need to be lighter."

This was not what I'd planned. I'd thought we'd be naked by now. I'd been looking forward to him taking control, restraining me, owning me. I had wanted that and now? Now everything was more complicated. Now I had to be in control.

Jake swept his hands through his hair and leaned back in his chair. "Sounds good. How did the Sandy Fox article go down?" He stretched his too long legs out in front of him. I couldn't help but enjoy the muscles rearranging themselves under the fabric of his clothes. I wished we were back home. I wanted his arms around me. I stood up abruptly and Jake tensed immediately, watching for my next move. I moved my chair so I was kitty-corner to his, and sat. Our legs touched. I interlinked our fingers, trying to get as much of my skin pressed against his as I could. It felt good.

"I've missed you," he said.

"Good." I smiled at him. "And Robert's happy and it's always good to have the boss in a positive mood. The second part comes out this week."

"Sandy texted me to remind me about the wrap party on Thursday," Jake said.

"I bet she did," I replied, rolling my eyes in an exaggerated way. I wasn't really worried about Sandy, but it felt good to tease him about it. It felt like us. "She wants in your pants. Are you going to go?"

"It depends. Are you? I mean, do you want to go?"

I shrugged. Twenty-four hours ago, heck, even two hours ago, I would have jumped at the chance to go anywhere with Jake. Now I wasn't sure what the next few days held. Could we survive him having a baby with another woman? Could I?

Jake's phone rang and a shiver ran down my spine. Was it Millie? She had a claim on him now. She had a reason to be around him, pull him back to her and her glamazonian world. But he silenced the call at the same time our waiter arrived.

The sea bass smelled good, but I had no appetite. Apparently neither did Jake—his burger remained untouched in front of him as we sat, our hands still interlinked.

"Wanna eat, or hold my hand?" I asked.

"I'll take your hand over food any day." He flashed me his Jake Harrison grin and I couldn't help but smile back. He was still *my* Jake.

"Smooth, Mr. Harrison, *very* smooth."

Eventually, Jake's stomach won out and he stroked the back of my knuckles with his thumb and let my left hand drop. I tried to pull my right hand away, but he tightened his grip. Apparently he was going to eat one-handed.

He swallowed a mouthful of burger and took a deep breath. "Beth is convinced Millie's lying."

"What do you think?" I asked.

"I don't know. It would make life a lot easier, but I feel terrible for wishing I wasn't in this situation, for wishing away a baby. Children should be a blessing—I want to be a good father."

An ache burrowed inside me at the thought it wouldn't be our child that he would be a father to.

"And I know I can't accuse her of lying in case I'm wrong and she tries to punish me by not letting me have a relationship with the kid." Jake shook his head. "It's all such a mess. I have to take it one step at a time. We'll have the test eventually, and in the meantime I'll be there if she needs me."

"What do you mean? Go for scans and stuff?"

"I guess. I need to meet with her and work out what it is she's thinking. What she wants."

"I still think she's wanting you back."

"Well, she's shit out of luck."

There was nothing he could have said that would have made me feel better, but that didn't mean I was okay.

"You shouldn't rule it out. We don't know what's going to happen. You need to think things through. Maybe we need to take some time." I squeezed his hand.

"Think through what? There's nothing to think about," he said. "Millie and I broke up because I realized dating women like her didn't work anymore. I don't even like her. She's spoiled and selfish and I have nothing in common with her."

"All the things I used to think about you." I patted his leg.

"Yeah, but I dated Millie for three months, so I know it's true. You made assumptions about me before you knew me."

"Well she wasn't spoiled and selfish enough for you to not sleep with her . . ."

"I'm sorry," he said. "I have no right to ask you, but I don't want this to come between us. What I had with her doesn't compare to what I have with you." He seemed so sad.

"We've known each other five minutes, Jake. I don't know what our future holds." It might not have been the response he wanted, but it was how I felt. It was reality. It all seemed impossible.

"Holy crap," Ash said "And it's definitely his from when they were together?"

Sunday dinner was at my place this week. I hadn't invited Jake and he hadn't asked why. I wanted to talk to Ash and

Luke and sort through my feelings. I needed someone to tell me what I should be doing, how I should be reacting. I wasn't sure of anything anymore. Ash and I weren't doing much cooking collapsed on the sofa, each clasping a glass of wine.

"Millie is saying it's definitely his," I replied. Ash's question was where I was secretly focusing all my hope. If it wasn't Jake's baby, everything got a lot easier. "He hasn't cheated on me. I'm as sure as sure that's true. I think he's telling me everything. He even asked me to go with him to meet with Millie tonight."

"Are you going to go?" she asked.

I'd scoffed when he suggested it. My initial reaction had been it was the last place I wanted to be, but perhaps I'd not done the right thing. "I said no. It's just too weird, isn't it?"

"I really have no idea. Is there a book called *What To Do When Your Boyfriend Is Having A Baby With Another Woman*?"

I sniggered and took a sip of my wine. "Google it. You never know."

"It was nice that he asked you." Ash always tried to see the best in people.

And it *was* reassuring that he'd asked me. Perhaps I was thinking about this the wrong way. Maybe he wanted me to go to support him and I'd let him down. I reached for my phone to text him. "You think I should have gone?"

Ash shrugged and I scrolled through my messages. *I should be there for him.* I cared about him. I wanted to support him.

Haven: Do you want to come round after you've seen Millie?

I released the clenched muscles in my stomach when he replied straight away.

Jake: Sure. Absolutely.

A bang and a thud echoed out from the hallway and Ash and I said in unison, "Luke."

A minute later, he appeared at the door with a beer in his hand. "Poor fucking guy." Luke ignored me and started speaking as if we were mid-conversation and he'd been here all along. I'd told him about Jake last night and he'd sounded more shocked than I had.

"You stick your dick in someone and it's always a possibility," Ash said.

Luke groaned and grabbed at his chest as if he were in physical pain.

"How would you feel if Emma got pregnant?" I asked him.

"Seriously, can we not talk about it? She's not going to get pregnant."

"What? Ever?" I asked. "You want kids though, right?"

Ash was uncharacteristically quiet. I wondered from time to time how she'd react when Luke got married or became a father. Would she give up on him then? Most of the time she joked about the two of them, but I knew, whatever Luke might say, she really liked him.

"Can we change the subject? This isn't about me, it's about Jake. Are you going to stay with him?"

"Of course she's going to stay with him. They are amazing together—he's *hot* with a capital H and good in bed." That was Ash's M.O. Her dial was set to *deflect with humor*. I wasn't sure if she was deflecting from my situation or the question of Luke fathering Emma's children.

Luke ignored her and looked at me. I shrugged. "I really have no idea. I like him. I've not liked anyone in forever and he's different. He makes me laugh and calls me out on my shit. It's as if he's crawled inside my head and understands how I work. And I trust him, you know? Like, in the same way I trust you guys. I've not felt like that before."

"That sounds like a man you don't give up easily on," Ash said more solemnly than before.

I nodded. I wasn't ready to let him go. "The thing is, it's not only about how I feel, is it? He might think it's best to try and make it work with Millie. I don't want him to stay with me out of obligation or something. I know that at the moment I don't want to lose him. He just gets me. So I guess we'll have to take one step at a time and see how we go."

"I like that plan," Luke said. "Don't overanalyze. Don't try and nail everything down like you normally do. You'll have to take each day as it comes."

"You might have to remind me of that," I said.

"How's *Rallegra*?" Ash asked. That was coping strategy two from Ash, *change the subject*. But she was genuinely trying to be helpful. I was so lucky to be surrounded by people who only wanted the best for me.

"Okay. Rumor is the deputy editor role will be available soon. I heard from Emily that one of the girls met up with Carole, the current deputy editor on maternity leave. She said she didn't think she was coming back."

"That's exciting," Ash said.

"Yeah." I'd been working toward deputy editor since my last promotion. "She might change her mind though."

“Sounds great, babe,” Luke said. I loved that he was so proud of me. He’d worked so hard to take care of me after our parents died that doing well in my career at a successful magazine like *Rallegra* seemed like a way to thank him in some small way for the sacrifices he’d made, to make it worth it and show him that it hadn’t all been for nothing.

“Emily’s in with a good shot. She’s been in her role longer. And she’s popular.”

“Robert knows how dedicated and talented you are. He’s always been supportive, right?”

“Yeah,” I replied. Robert was a great boss. If Carole did leave, I should be in the running for her role. I was trying to sound enthusiastic. I just wasn’t sure if I was feeling it. Perhaps I was distracted by Jake or the pregnancy, but I wasn’t sure that was it entirely.

chapter THIRTY-TWO

Jake

"Hey," I said as Haven opened the door.

"Hey, come in." She lifted up on her toes to receive a kiss, and I bent and brushed my lips against hers. Before I could grab her and turn the kiss deeper, she pivoted and headed down the hall.

Her apartment was full of the sounds of the television but nothing else as I followed her into the kitchen. "Where's Luke and Ash?"

"They left about half an hour ago. I'm just finishing clearing up. Do you want a drink?" She held up a glass she had taken out of the dishwasher.

I shook my head but took the glass, placing it in the cupboard behind me. It was only a few minutes past nine. They must have left to give Haven and me alone time and I was grateful. I'd been dreading meeting Millie and now all I wanted was Haven. I watched as she continued to unload the dishwasher. How did she make the mundane look so graceful?

"So, how was it?" she asked.

I was relieved she was the one to bring it up. I didn't want to hide anything but I didn't want to be the one always introducing the subject. "Weird. Transactional. I thought her sister would be there, but she wasn't." It was true. I hadn't felt anything when I saw Millie again, not even a hint of affection. It was as if Haven had rendered my previous relationship history completely inconsequential. It might be different once there was some physical evidence of my child growing within her, but I'd had no emotional reaction to seeing her at all.

"Did you go to her place?"

"Yeah. I wasn't there long. About thirty minutes, that's all. I guess I was trying to be polite by going to see her face-to-face, but I'm not sure I needed to. We didn't really have anything to say to each other." I wanted to reassure her that there was no connection between Millie and me.

Haven chewed the inside of her cheek. I moved toward her and brushed her face with my thumb. She slid her hands around my waist as I pulled her toward me. "I want to tell you everything, but I don't know what you want to know. I have nothing to hide."

"Is she going to take the test?" she asked, her voice vibrating against my chest.

I liked that she was asking questions. Somehow it felt as though she was invested and that had to be a good sign. "She said she'll talk to the doctor about it. She has her first ultrasound coming up, so she's going to bring it up then."

"Are you going?"

I kissed the top of her head. "No. She's going with her sister. I offered. She said she didn't want me there. She was pretty pissed I asked about the test." Pissed was an understatement. Once she'd realized I wasn't going to back down on getting confirmation of paternity, she'd been furious. I hadn't bothered arguing about going with her to the ultrasound.

"Does she want to get back together?"

It was the question I'd been waiting for. Haven had asked before, and I'd brushed it off. But seeing Millie again made me think differently. My gut said that she wanted more from me than just to be her baby daddy. She liked my money and she was pregnant and alone. But she hadn't done anything specific. "She offered to cook me dinner and she was quite tactile, but I don't think so. She's worried I think." I wasn't exactly lying; I just wasn't telling her my suspicions.

"How tactile?" she asked.

"She didn't grab my junk or anything, but she was a bit touchy."

She grasped her cheek in her teeth again. "I want you to promise me something."

"Anything," I replied.

"Don't say that. Not until you know what I'm asking." She was serious and I wanted to be able to see inside her head. To know what was coming and predict how I was going to react.

"It doesn't matter what it is," I tried to reassure her.

"Well, that's a ridiculous thing to say. If I said, 'promise me you'll stab yourself with a carving knife,' are you going to do that?"

I smiled. "No, but you're not going to ask me to stab myself with a carving knife."

"I might. The night is young." She squeezed her eyes half shut in a mock threat.

I grasped her face in my hands. "You're getting kissed for that," I said and I pressed my lips to hers softly. She didn't resist and smoothed her hands up my back. "What do you want me to promise?" I whispered.

"If you want out—for whatever reason—I want you to tell me straight away. Don't wait until Millie or someone else accidentally falls on your penis, or you hate me or something."

I couldn't stop myself from chuckling. "I promise. No one is having anything to do with my penis except, hopefully, you."

"I mean it. I don't want to be one of those women who are totally oblivious to what's going on under their nose. I don't want to be made a fool of."

She sounded so sad as she spoke and my chest ached for her. By opening up to me, she'd given me so much power. The power to take advantage of her, to hurt her, and there was nothing I wanted less. She'd asked me to be careful with her heart and I don't think I'd ever felt so much responsibility, so much . . . love.

"I promise," I said. "You have my heart, too, you know. We need to keep each other safe."

"I promise you, too." She reached up and brushed her fingers over my cheekbones.

Her touch had its usual effect on me and my dick started to stir. She glanced at my crotch. "Sorry. It's just been like a millennia since I saw you naked."

"It's been a week," she said poking me in my abs, which did nothing to stave off the blood rushing to my cock as a result of my being wrapped round her like this.

"Yeah? It feels like longer."

"For me, too," she said as her hands swept over my ass and she looked up at me from under her eyebrows. "Sounds as though we need an early night."

I groaned as her hands reached the crotch of my jeans. Holy fuck, it almost hurt I was so hard. I was going to have to make her come several times with my mouth so she didn't notice when I erupted after being inside her for a second.

"Actually, I have something for you that I think you might like." She grabbed me by the hand and led me toward her bedroom.

"I only need you."

She reached for my shoulders and guided me to sit on her bed as she went to her dresser drawer and pulled out a brown paper bag. She twisted her mouth and a blush spread across her throat. I had to glance away; she looked so ready to be fucked.

"What is it?" I asked.

She handed me the bag and then covered her face with her hands. I was intrigued. Why was she embarrassed about buying me a gift?

I pulled apart the edges of the paper, my eyes flicking from the bag to her and back. Her mouth was slightly parted, and she was staring at my hands instead of my face. I didn't know what I was seeing at first, then realization trickled into my brain. It was coiled rope, not heavy, more like cord, white, smooth and about half an inch thick. I pulled it out of the bag, fingering the silky fibers twisting together like a never-ending helter-skelter. My pulse banged against my eardrums. She was giving herself to me. After everything I'd told her, she was still mine. My chest tightened with expectation, hope and something more.

Haven took a step toward me. "I didn't know if it was the right—"

"It's perfect." I closed my eyes, trying to steady my breathing. "I like that you like it."

"I do. It's as if I'm giving myself over to you."

I filled my lungs, needing a beat. I didn't want to rush. Whatever we were doing, exchanging, it needed to be savored.

"Undress," I said. I tried to say it as if her gift hadn't brought me to my knees. She wanted me in control and that's what I would give her.

She hesitated as if it took longer than usual for the words to turn to meaning in her head. She pulled her dress over her head in one graceful movement, uncovering black lace underwear.

Watching her, knowing what was next, relaxed me.

She released the clasp of her bra, revealing her beautiful breasts. Her creamy, smooth, white skin might have been marble from the perfection of it. Even one of Rodin's sculptures, but I knew how soft and warm it was. The memory of her heat buzzed over my fingertips.

"Put your hands down," I said, moving her slightly so she was standing between my knees.

She complied quickly and I stood up, pulling the rope through my hands, the fibers bending under my fingers as I searched for the middle section.

"We're going to try something new. I'm going to tie the rope around you so your arms are fixed by your sides. Do you understand?"

She nodded. Her eyes were wide.

"Are you frightened?"

"No. I want it," she whispered.

Jesus. I needed to stay focused. I needed to give her what she wanted.

"You tell me if it hurts or if your hands start to tingle. Do you hear?"

She nodded.

"Haven, tell me you understand." I grazed her peaked nipples with my knuckles.

"I understand."

"You need to be comfortable. I don't want to hurt you."

I pressed the rope against the skin of her belly, trying to distract myself from the way her flesh yielded around the fibers. It was the perfect density to leave that delicious red mark without causing pain. Slowly, using both hands, I began to wrap the rope round her, working my way up and down her torso, wrapping her up, readying her for me. "How does it feel?" I asked as she watched me.

"Good," she replied. Her eyes were slightly glazed and her mouth parted as she drifted under my control.

"How good?" I trailed my fingers down her stomach to her slit. I knew before I touched her what I would find. I could smell her arousal. It surrounded her like a cloud. "Slippery already?"

She groaned and her head fell back. I worked faster, coiling the rope around and down past her elbows, taking care that there was room between the rope and her skin. It was the perfect length. I secured the ends and took a step back to see what I'd created.

There she stood. Her amazing tits jutted out over the top of the rope and were framed on either side by her hair. You couldn't see her flesh through the rope, but I could imagine it compressed, the blood pushed out of the way. When my eyes met hers, I could see desperation.

"Can you move your arms?" I asked.

"No." She made a small attempt to struggle, but she was tightly bound. "Jake?"

"Yes, baby?"

"I need you to fuck me."

I groaned at her request. I wasn't sure I needed to touch her. She looked on the brink of climax where she stood, without any additional help from me. "I want you to bend over the bed. Turn your face to the side so I can still see you."

She did as I asked and thrust her ass into the air as she dropped to the bed.

"Open your legs."

I stripped off my clothes and fell to my knees behind her. Her wetness glistened, inviting me in, but I was going to make her wait until I tasted it. Just a little. I bent forward and licked the back of her knee. She buckled and I steadied her. Her body was so responsive, so perfectly attuned. I dragged my tongue up the back of her thigh in a heated trail; her skin was soft and tight. As I reached her ass, I bit down and thrust two fingers into her at the same time.

She lifted her head from the mattress. "Please," she cried.

I soothed the just-bitten area with my tongue, then sucked and sucked. I wanted her marked. By me. By the ropes, my teeth, my cock. I wanted to own her.

My fingers found a rhythm and quickly became coated in her as I rubbed her clit with my other hand. Breathlessly, she began her climb toward her climax. "No. Jake. Please. God. Yes."

Her words got quieter as she got closer, and I pulled away from her, needing to hold myself back if I wasn't going to fall over the edge with her.

She whimpered. "More," she cried. "Please, don't stop."

I pushed my fingers back inside her, unable not to give her what she wanted when she asked. "Don't stop?"

"Don't *ever* stop."

"Oh, baby, you're going to be begging for me to stop."

I thrust my fingers and my tongue against her, and in seconds she was pulsing around my fingers, crying, "Yes, yes, yes."

I replaced my fingers with my tongue, pushing into her, her muscles clenching around me, my hands prizing her open wider. I alternated between licking and sucking until she started to shake. I pushed deep, deeper, and then my thumb found her clit. When she came again, it was as if in surrender. There were no words, simply her private sounds of pleasure, reserved just for me. Panting, moaning, and juddering.

My cock was thick against my stomach. I had to be inside her. I stood and positioned her now weak legs.

"Can you last a little longer in this position, baby? I have to have you like this."

"Yes, fuck me, Jake. Please."

I groaned and after a single stroke to my cock, I pushed into her slowly but without stopping, so deep I was drowning in her.

chapter THIRTY-THREE

Haven

It was as if he filled every part of me when he was inside me. He made me come as if I was a generator on which he just needed to flick the switch, as if he had some secret code. He could make me climax with his fingers, his tongue, but it was only when he was inside me that I felt completely his, bound to him, my soul stripped bare. The intensity was magnified by the pressure of the rope, as if it squeezed more out of me when I thought I had nothing left to give him. It tied me to him. He owned me.

He pulled out and slammed back into me. He was usually more gentle with me at first, allowing me to get used to his size, but now it was as though he couldn't hold back, as if I had the kind of power over him that he had over me. Relief pulsed across my body with the realization that he needed to be inside me as much I wanted him there.

His fingers fiddled with the ropes, adjusting them slightly. I hoped he wouldn't release me yet, I was sure I would fall apart without the silky fibers twisted around me. The rope tied me to the moment, so I didn't have to worry about what was next, whether what was between us was constant. I felt certain of everything in that moment.

I was still bound as he hooked his hands under my shoulders and pulled me back onto him, pushing into me as deeply as he could go. I cried out, not knowing if any sound left my body. All I could hear was the rush of blood in my ears and Jake's grunts behind me as he took what he needed.

He withdrew unexpectedly and I tried to look over my shoulder to see why.

"I'm going to turn you over," he said, his voice deep and gravelly like disturbed bedrock. "I need to see your face."

He rearranged me on the bed so that I was face up and my thighs were parted, ready for him. My body limp and helpless, he had complete control. I wanted to give him what he needed and this was all that was left—complete submission. He didn't need to ask me, I offered it willingly. "God, you look so good like that, Haven." He pushed back inside me, grabbing my hips, pulling me onto him.

He was concentrating. On what, I wasn't sure. His breathing, his rhythm, my face. My muscles clenched involuntarily around him and he closed his eyes.

"Shit," he whispered and he twisted, making me clench again.

He could do anything to me while I was laid out in front of him, bound. I was completely vulnerable and under his total control. It wasn't frightening; it was freeing. His pace increased and our sounds intermingled. I couldn't distinguish his cries of pleasure from my own, and staring into his eyes tipped me over the edge as my orgasm thundered across my body. It was like nothing else that had come before it. It ripped through me, crushing me and renewing me.

Jake called my name and I felt his grip on my shoulders grow tighter before he shuddered, emptying himself inside me.

At that moment, I needed to touch him, to have his skin against mine and he knew. His fingers plucked at the rope, and within seconds, I was in his arms and my hands were pressed against his heartbeat.

"You're amazing," he whispered to me.

"I've never . . ." It had been as though our previous times together had been leading up to that moment.

"I know," he said. Had he felt it too? "You're mine baby." His fingers traced the indentations across my skin left by the rope. "Are you sore? Do you have cream? It will help soothe it."

"I'm fine. It's good. Like I'm floating, still." What he did to my body made me feel he knew me like no one else. Or perhaps he understood me so fundamentally that he was able to elicit the things he did from my body. Either way, I belonged to him.

He pulled me closer as I lay limply across him.

"You're beautiful. Those marks against your skin . . . They're proof you're mine."

He kissed the top of my head and our breaths synchronized.

"I think we should take a bath or you're going to be sore tomorrow," he said.

Jake left me to regain my strength and went into the

bathroom. The sound of rushing water filtered through the walls as I lay there, not quite believing what had just happened.

"Come on, let's go soak," he said, returning to the bedroom. He lifted me to my feet and guided me through the door.

"Hair?" he asked and I glanced around the bathroom, trying to spot one of the various hair ties littered across my flat. I reached out to one I saw by the sink but Jake got to it before I did, positioned me facing away from him and started to fiddle with my hair.

"What are you doing?"

"Braiding your hair and putting it up."

"Should it worry me that you can do women's hair?"

"I don't think so. I like rope. It braids nicely," he said in response.

It was an admission that I wasn't the first girl he had restrained. It needled me, lifted some of the afterglow. It felt too intimate for it to have happened before. Had he shared this connection with others? I wanted to be special to him, in every way, as he was to me. Maybe it hadn't been as intense for him. I felt silly for assuming that I was the only woman to have experienced this with Jake but I hated the thought of others seeing that part of him.

"Did you restrain Millie?" I asked.

"No. It wasn't like that between us," he replied.

What did that mean? I wanted to know *how* it was different. How I was different. Was I special at all?

He held my hand to steady me as I stepped into the deliciously warm water. He got in behind me and sat down, arranging me between his thighs, my back to his front. I relaxed against his chest.

"There's only been one other girl that I've used rope with," he said without my prompting. "A girl at college. My only relationship that's lasted over three months, as Beth likes to remind me."

"Were you in love with her?"

"Not like I'm in love with you."

"Jake." My breath caught in my lungs. *I'm in love with you.* The words echoed around my head. He'd known what I'd needed before I had. It was as if he could read every thought of mine before it was formed. It was what I craved from him and what I felt for him.

He pulled his cupped hand up my body and let the gathered water trickle over my breasts. Then he stroked my newly warmed skin, following the flow. "I know it's soon, but it's how I feel," he said as if we were simply describing a *fait accompli*.

Jake's phone buzzed, shattering the near-perfect moment. Instead of ignoring it, as I assumed he would, he scrambled out from behind me and leapt across the bathroom to retrieve his phone from the washstand.

"Hi, Millie," he answered and my gut wrenched. "I'm at Haven's. Yes. I'm sure that's normal. Isn't your sister there?" He sighed and gazed at me. "Okay," he said and hung up. "She had blood on some toilet tissue and her sister's out of town. She wants me to go over."

"Oh," I said, hugging my knees to my chest. He was going to leave me.

He took a deep breath. "I'm sorry. Can I call you when I get there?"

"Sure. Go. Do what you've gotta do," I said, trying to sound as though him leaving me in the bath at nearly midnight to go and see his pregnant ex-girlfriend was the most normal thing in the world. I wanted him to be a good man, but I wanted him to be *my* good man. He was the man I loved and I hadn't told him and he hadn't seemed to notice.

"I'm sorry," he said.

"Hey, it's not your fault. Is it better to speak tomorrow?" On top of everything, I didn't want him to feel as though he had to babysit me.

"I guess you need to sleep. I'll call you first thing." He pulled on his jeans and sweater, then grabbed his keys and wallet. Within moments he was gone, leaving a huge space that should have been filled by his declaration, by *him*. I had never felt so physically, emotionally and sexually connected to anyone as I had with Jake. And now? Him abandoning me to go see Millie seemed somehow prophetic.

I stepped out of the bath and wrapped myself in a towel, patting my skin dry. The red marks of Jake's ownership were already beginning to fade from my skin. The doubt that had been held at bay by the ropes, his words, his touch, began to seep back into my head. Jake had told me he loved me and I believed him. I just wasn't sure that was going to be enough to get us through.

Jake

The last thing I wanted to do was leave Haven after the night we'd shared. But Millie had sounded upset and I didn't know how to say no to her. By the time I arrived at Millie's apartment, it was way past midnight.

"Hey," she said as she opened the door.

"Are you okay?" I asked.

"Yeah, come in. Can I get you a drink?" She seemed to have brightened. "I have some amazing vodka that my father brought back from Moscow." I followed her into the living room and she started clinking glasses over at the bar. She and her sister lived in one of the most expensive areas of London, courtesy of Daddy dearest. She and Haven really had nothing in common.

She placed two shot glasses on the counter before I had a chance to answer. "No, and you're not drinking, are you?"

She glanced at me and then back at the shot glasses. "No, of course not." She flashed a wide smile at me. "Habit, I guess."

"How are you feeling? Do you want to go to the hospital?" She was acting as though I'd come over to hang out. She didn't seem upset at all.

"Slightly better," she said as she turned down the corners of her mouth in a pronounced frown. "It's so scary being on my own."

"I think you should rest. Why don't you try and get some sleep, and you can call me if you need me?"

"You're not going, are you?"

"Millie, I don't know what I can do here if you're better and you don't want me to take you to the hospital." I stood in the doorway as she came toward me, her frown giving way to a pout.

"You could keep me company," she suggested, tilting her head to one side.

My eye twitched. "You didn't call me in the middle of the

night and get me to come over because you were bored, did you?" I asked.

She wore a pained expression. "Of course not. I was bleeding, Jake. I was worried. I'm carrying your baby. I would have thought you'd have slightly more sympathy."

Guilt lapped at the edges of my thoughts. "Why don't you go to bed and I'll stay here on the couch?"

Millie nodded. "I'd appreciate that, thanks. Come and get some pillows and a blanket."

I followed her through to her bedroom. I hadn't been there since I'd met Haven. It felt like a lifetime ago.

"You can take those pillows," she said, pointing to the chair in the corner. "And have this quilt." She bent forward to pull the cover from the bed but stiffened as if in pain. She clutched her stomach.

"Jesus. Are you okay?" I rushed over and guided her to sit on the bed. "Are you hurting?" Her eyes were closed and she ignored my question. "Here, put your feet up. I think you need to rest."

"Please stay with me," she whimpered.

"Of course. I've said I will." I covered her with the quilt she'd offered me. "Lie back," I said, and she tentatively lay against the pillows. "I'll be here," I said as I headed toward the chair in the corner. Shit, what was I doing? I wanted to be lying with Haven in my arms, not propped up in a chair in my ex-girlfriend's bedroom. I grabbed my phone from my pocket and started to text Haven. She'd be asleep, but she'd have it for when she woke up.

Jake: Millie seems fine. Just a little spooked. I'm going to stay here. I wish I were there with you.

Being back here was a huge reminder to me of how different Millie and Haven were and how I felt so much more myself with Haven. If Haven had told me she was pregnant, I'd be bursting with pride. She would make an incredible mother. My thoughts wouldn't be of paternity and complexity. Of being tied to someone I didn't want to be with. The situation was so twisted, as if the universe were trying to send me a message. If I'd known Haven had been in my future, I wouldn't have wasted time on anyone else. I would have waited for her. I had been impatient. I'd settled for okay for now and I was paying the price.

I must have fallen asleep because when I came to, my arm had gone dead from me leaning against it.

"Jake, I feel terrible that you're stuck in that uncomfortable chair. You can come and lie next to me; I won't bite," Millie said in the darkness.

I stood up. She was right. The chair was very uncomfortable. "I'll be in the living room if you need something. Get some sleep." I closed her bedroom door, trying to create some space, a barrier between us.

The next morning I woke to the smell of coffee.

"Hey, sleepyhead," Millie said from behind the counter as I sat up on the sofa. "What can I get you for breakfast?"

I checked my watch. It was almost eight. I climbed off the couch. She'd never offered me breakfast before.

"I could cook something, or we could go out." she said. She was showered and ready for the day.

"I need to get going. Are you feeling okay? Are you going to go to the doctor today?" I asked.

"Yeah, I think so. I'm sure they'll say it's normal. Are you sure you can't stay?"

"I'm sure. Do you want me to come with you?" I checked my cell. I'd missed a call from Haven and I badly wanted to hear her voice.

Millie was pouting, probably annoyed that I hadn't taken her up on breakfast. She had to understand that we weren't together. This was about the baby, not her and me. "I'll be fine."

I glanced around to see if I'd left anything but I hadn't really brought anything. "I'm going to go. Call me when you've spoken to the doctor."

chapter THIRTY-FOUR

Haven

I wanted to look good for Jake. Tonight was the wrap party for Sandy Fox's first feature film, and it would be fun to dress up a little. I zipped up the red dress that I'd worn in Paris, checked myself out in the mirror and then changed my mind. I needed something a little more . . . I knew just the thing. I quickly removed the Paris dress and changed my bra for what I called my magic-boob bra. I'd only worn it twice and one of those times had been in the changing room when Ash and I were shopping. When she'd seen me, her eyes had gone wide as saucers and she'd told me she thought she'd turned gay. I needed a little bit of magic tonight. The bra and my black, scoop-necked dress would keep his attention. I hoped.

Jake and I had spent too much time figuratively surrounded by Millie this week, and I wanted us to spend an evening where it didn't feel as if she was invited. It wasn't that it had been strained between us; it was just that there was an elephant in the room, overshadowing every one of our exchanges. We were being careful with each other. I was always trying to say the right thing, which was almost impossible for me.

Millie had called every day since her scare on Sunday night. It seemed as though she was making excuses to speak to him, but Jake didn't seem to think she was being overly demanding and I hadn't said anything. The doctor had said that the spotting was normal and nothing to worry about, apparently, so there didn't seem to be a real reason to keep calling.

I could tell Jake was relieved by the doctor's reassurance and of course, he should be. I just wasn't sure *I* was and I hated myself for it. What I didn't want to do was end up pushing Jake away. I wanted to feel as if we had a shot. It was supposed to be easy this early on in a relationship. Weren't we still meant to be in the phase where one look between us would lead to me being, quite literally, tied to the bed?

I needed to try to not overthink things. I had no right to be demanding. I certainly couldn't stake a claim over and above Jake's baby-mama. We hadn't made any promises to each other. It wasn't as if we were moving in together and getting married, so there was no reason for me to be overly concerned with someone who Jake was clear he'd never been serious about. It was just . . . I was serious about him.

"You look amazing," Jake said as his eyes dropped to my chest when I opened the door. I mentally thanked the magic-boob bra.

"It's black. Ash would kill me. She's always trying to make me wear color."

"It's a very sexy dress," he said.

"Yeah?"

"And the shoes . . . you know what happens to you when you wear heels like that."

I couldn't stop the corners of my mouth from twitching. I was hoping he'd notice the shoes. They had been a deliberate choice.

"You like the idea of me being hard for you all night, watching you walking around in those things?" He moved toward me and cupped the back of my neck with his hand, pulling me closer to him.

"I wonder how long it will take before Sandy makes a pass at you."

"Don't talk to me about her when I'm ready against your stomach like this," he said. "I don't want to think about another woman. You're all I need."

I slid my hands up his back and smiled. "That's good to hear, Mr. Harrison, because these heels can be sharp as well as sexy."

He dropped a kiss on my lips.

"Are we getting a cab there?" I asked, pulling away from him slightly.

"I've brought the fuckmobile as you like to call it."

"Well, I can predict it will get you laid tonight," I said.

"Can we stay in? My balls are already blue."

I laughed and grabbed his shoulder. "Come on. It will be good to go out. You need to blow off some steam."

"I was thinking we could stay in to do that," he said, pausing as we hit the fresh air.

"We don't have to be out long. We should raise a glass to your father's successful surgery." Beth had called from Chicago to say that their dad was out of the woods and should be home within a week. One thing down.

"Yeah, we should. But can we have one drink and then leave?"

I rolled my eyes.

"Harry!" Sandy screamed as soon as she saw *my* boyfriend. As usual, she wrapped herself around him in a way that made an eye roll from me compulsory. Jake raised his eyebrows as if to say, *I told you we should have stayed at home*. I'd reward him for that later. "I'm so pleased you made it."

"Hi, Sandy," I said.

"Oh, hi," she said, her eyes wide with surprise. She took in his arm around my waist. I saw the exact moment the penny dropped. "Are you two together?" she asked.

"We are and we're grateful to you for playing matchmaker," Jake said, as smooth as ever.

"Well, congratulations. I'm going to take credit and I fully expect to be a bridesmaid. Catch you later, I must mingle," she said as she spun off into the crowd.

I wanted not to react to what she'd said about bridesmaids, but I couldn't stop my muscles from stiffening. Jake and I didn't need more pressure.

Jake rubbed my back. "Don't freak out," he whispered in my ear.

Again, he'd managed to climb inside my head and catch what was worrying me, almost before I knew myself. "You know horse whisperers?" I asked.

"Okay, I'm going to go with this bizarre segue. Yeah, I know what a horse whisperer is."

"You're a Haven whisperer."

"I'm not trying to tame you," he replied.

"I know. You just know what I need."

Jake squeezed me closer to him, and the half of my body pressed to his was at least ten degrees hotter. It was how I liked it. Perhaps we would be okay after all.

"Want to come with me to search for office space tomorrow?" he asked after a few beats of silence.

"I'm working. Are you searching for Elemental Energy?"

He nodded. "Eric will need somewhere to base himself when he gets here next week. He's the type who won't know what time of day or night it is; he'll just work. I can't have him in the apartment, or Beth will go nuts. I'm seeing some places near Bank. Can you meet me for lunch?"

Jake grabbed two glasses of champagne from a passing waiter and handed one to me.

"Maybe. So are you working all weekend?" I asked.

"No, I'm hanging out with you," he replied.

I grinned. "What do you want to do?"

He bent his head to my neck and nipped at my skin. "You know what I want to do."

"You're insatiable," I said pushing him away. "No PDAing."

"That's your fault. I take no responsibility. But actually, I think Beth might be on to something with the moving thing. Do you want to come and apartment hunt with me as well?"

"Wow," I said, taking a sip of my champagne. "You've given in to Beth. I thought you might."

"Well she's right. I want somewhere bigger, and then maybe you can stay, and perhaps at some point move in, and then if things with the baby . . . you know. I need more room."

I kept my eyes steady on his face as he watched me for a reaction.

"Are you freaking out?" he asked when it became obvious that I was finding it difficult to find any words.

I wanted to fling my arms around him. The thought of a future with him sounded good, amazing even. But before I could let myself get excited, reality broke through. I didn't want him to think that he needed to make me feel better when he was dealing with Millie, his father being sick and his concerns about Beth. "I think you have a lot going on at the moment with your dad and the baby and Elemental Energy. We don't need to rush anything."

"It doesn't have to be right away, but I want a place that is about my future and not my past, and I see my future with you."

He insisted on saying exactly the right thing at the right time. Maybe we just needed to focus on us and the rest would fall into place. "What are we doing at this stupid party?" I asked and I pulled his tie toward me and gave him a kiss.

"Hey, no PDAing," he teased.

We hadn't stayed long with the cast and crew before Jake dragged me out and back into the fuckmobile for the journey home. His phone vibrated against the dashboard.

"Can you see who that is?" he asked, his hand on my knee.

I grabbed his phone and my heart sank. "It's Millie." Of course it was.

He frowned but didn't say anything.

"How has she been since the scare?" She was going to be the mother of his child and I wanted to be sympathetic.

"Fine, I think. But you never know with her. The ultrasound will make her feel better, I think. She's going next week."

"And you're really not going?"

"She wants to go with her sister."

Perhaps I was being overly suspicious, but it seemed odd that she called him regularly, getting him to come over in the middle of the night, but she didn't want him at the scan? Wishful thinking perhaps.

"Oh yes, you said. Why do you think she's calling?"

"I don't know. She knows I'm out tonight. I'll call her when we're back."

"Did you tell her you were going to the wrap party?"

"Yeah. I told her this morning when I spoke to her."

Jake seemed distracted for the rest of the journey. The desire to get each other naked faded with every mile.

We pulled up outside my flat and I wondered if he was planning to stay over. We'd been spending every possible moment together, but Millie had the ability to interrupt our time no matter where she was. I was relieved when he parked as usual and got out. We walked up the steps to my flat in silence.

"You should call her back," I said.

"I will. Do you want me to do it out here?" That carefulness between us returned. I wanted this to be easier than it was.

"Not unless you want to."

"I have nothing to hide." He seemed so tense and I didn't know if it was Millie or me who was causing it.

"I know." I tried to sound reassuring.

He stayed in the living room while I went through to my bedroom to change. I kicked off the shoes Jake had promised to fuck me in earlier. What a difference a phone call had made.

He came through not long after. I was still sitting on the bed, and for a moment, I thought perhaps he'd come to make good on his promise.

"I'm sorry, but I'm going to have to go," he said as he came in. His shoulders were rounded and he seemed smaller.

"Is everything okay?"

"She's not feeling well. Her sister's not there again, and she wants some things from the pharmacy."

I nodded. What could I say? He was trying to do the right thing.

"I'll make this up to you. We can spend the whole weekend together."

I stood and walked him to the door. He turned briefly, kissed me and was gone.

Left on my own, I called Luke, but he went to voicemail, so I tried Ash.

"Hey, thought you were at the wrap party?" she answered.

"We were until we decided to come home early to get naked, and then on the way home Millie interrupted . . ."

"Again?"

"Don't say it like that. But yeah, again. Who else is she going to get to run around after her? He knocked her up. I understand it. I just don't like it."

"Just because she's pregnant doesn't mean he's at her beck and call," Ash said.

"Well it kind of does, I guess. And then when the baby's born . . ." My voice started to waiver.

"Are you okay?"

"It's just so unfair. I finally start to see a future with someone. Someone who seems to feel the same way and then Millie comes crashing into the middle of it all."

"You think she's deliberately trying to come between you?"

"I don't know. But whether or not it's deliberate, it's having the same effect. I want to tell him I think she's being unreasonable and overly demanding and that she's clearly trying to win him back, but I can't do that without putting him in an impossible position. So I'm faking it—pretending it doesn't bother me. And that's everything we weren't supposed to be. He saw through to the real me in the way that only you and Luke do. I'm not supposed to be able to hide things from him."

"God, you really like him. I hadn't realized how much. It's not just about his huge dick."

I snorted, half laugh, half cry. I did really like him. That's what was so terrifying.

"I'm sure it will get better. Hasn't Beth set him straight on this?" Ash asked.

"She's in Chicago. And on top of the baby thing and Millie, his father is sick and I know he's worried about Beth. And his business needs his attention. It's too much for one person and there's nothing I can do to help. I think that, even if it's not right now, soon I'll just be another obligation for him. He has enough of those already." Saying it out loud made the impossibility of it all more real. My chest tightened. We were fighting a losing battle, weren't we?

“I think you should worry about one thing at a time. The guy is crazy for you. You’re not an obligation. He’s having a tough time. Things will resolve themselves.”

“I know you’re trying to be nice, but how exactly? When the baby’s born things will only get more complicated. I can’t see how this is going to work out. Shit, I have another call coming in.” I checked the screen. “Do you mind if I take it? It’s Jake.”

“Of course not, as long as you promise me you won’t make any rash decisions.”

“I promise,” I said before I hung up.

“Hey, sorry were you sleeping?” Jake said.

“No, on the phone to Ash.”

“Oh dear, am I on the bad boyfriends list? I’m really sorry about tonight.”

“Don’t worry, it’s fine,” I lied. “Where are you now?”

“I’m at Millie’s. She seems okay. She’s nervous, it being her first baby and everything. I was reading somewhere that’s natural.”

It was such an uncomfortable conversation. Talking to my boyfriend about his ex-girlfriend’s pregnancy. I finally wanted to get close to someone and there was this huge space between us.

“I’m sure that’s right. Are you going to stay like last time?” I hated that he’d slept over there before. I’d believed him when he’d said he was on the sofa, but him being there overnight didn’t seem right.

Maybe he caught something in my voice. Perhaps he saw what I was truly thinking because I couldn’t have been happier about his response. "No. I don't want that to become a pattern. Do you want me to come back over when I'm done here?"

Of course I wanted him to come back to me. "No, you're just round the corner from home." I didn't want to be the person he was with when Millie didn't need him. I wanted to be the person he put first. "You should stay at your place tonight. You have a lot going on."

"Haven?"

"Yes?"

"No running from me, I mean it."

Was I running? I felt the distance, but I was standing still. "I'm exactly where you left me."

"I'm sorry. This will get better."

"Get some sleep," I said. Although it was the last thing I wanted to do, maybe for once in my life, walking away would be the right thing.

chapter THIRTY-FIVE

Jake

It felt weird to wake up on my own. Recently I'd either been with Haven or I'd woken to Beth crashing about outside my room, which at least meant I'd got an early start on my day.

I was going to make it up to Haven this weekend. Millie's sister was back so hopefully I wouldn't get any phone calls interrupting my time with Haven and we could just hang out together. Naked.

"I'll take the Lombard Street one," I said to the realtor. I'd seen three office spaces and was on my fourth. I didn't want to spend any more time on this. I had enough to do. "You're sure we can be in right away?" Eric was arriving from California this weekend.

"As soon as you sign the contract, I can give you the keys. If you get yourself a coffee next door, I'll go and get the paperwork and we can go through it all now."

"Great." It felt as though I was making progress on the future, or the part of it I had any control over. If I started looking at new apartments with Haven, perhaps that would help me feel as though my personal life was on track, too.

My cell buzzed in my pocket. I couldn't wait to tell Haven I'd found somewhere, but it was Millie. Tension pulled at my chest. I was irritated that she was calling and at the same time concerned something might be wrong. I accepted the call.

"Hey, Harry. Your baby kept me up all night."

"I'm right in the middle of something. Is this urgent?" I needed to discourage her constant contact without making her feel abandoned.

"I wanted to see if you could come round to dinner tonight?"

"What do you mean?" Was she throwing a dinner party?

"I'm taking a cooking class and I thought you could be my guinea pig."

"You are?" That didn't sound like the Millie I knew.

"Yeah, I want to become more nurturing."

"I have plans, I'm afraid. With Haven."

"Oh, okay," she said, quietly. I immediately felt bad.

Should I have considered dinner? I knew she was scared to be a single mother. Especially coming from her old-school family. She hadn't said how her parents had reacted, but I guessed it couldn't have been well. She needed my support, but there was only so much of me to go around. She had to understand that as a couple, we didn't have a future. I was with Haven.

"I was trying to be nice, Harry." She hung up.

Had I been too hard on her? Maybe she *was* trying to be nice. Just as I started to feel bad about our conversation, my phone rang again. Would she ever give up?

"What?" I snapped.

"Jesus, stress head. What did I do to you?" Beth asked, her familiar voice jolting me back into reality. I was a mess.

"Thank God it's you. How are you? How's Dad?"

"We're all fine. But it sounds like *you're* about to have a heart attack. What's the matter?"

"Nothing. Tell me about Chicago."

Beth sounded excited as she talked about catching up with old friends and meeting new people at her AA meeting. I was relieved that she seemed okay.

"I'd forgotten how much I like this city. I think I had so many unhappy memories that they overshadowed the good stuff, but now the happy ones are starting to poke through again."

"That's great. And how are things with Marissa?"

"She's a bit weird, and she wears way too much makeup but she loves Dad, which I guess is all that matters."

"I think she always loved him," I said.

"I hope so. I just didn't see it. I wanted her to love me. I was too young to focus on the right stuff. But we had dinner last night after visiting hours. We're both making an effort."

"And Dad is okay with you?"

"Yeah. I think he was pleased to see me. He's been asking me lots of questions about you. He still doesn't understand what you do."

"Well, that makes two of you," I said, grinning. It felt good to know he was asking about me. I missed the feeling that there was a safety net behind me. That's what parents did, they caught you when you fell, no matter how old you were.

And I hadn't had that since Mom died. There was no way any kid of mine wouldn't know I was right there behind them.

"I miss you. How are things with Haven?"

"Okay, I think."

"Excuse me? Okay 'you think'? What's that supposed to mean?"

"It means things are . . . I have a lot going on with Elemental starting up and Eric coming over and Millie—"

"What have you got going on with Millie? There's no baby yet."

"Yeah, but she's needed me the last few days. Her sister's not been around, so I've had to get her stuff and it's kind of interrupted things with Haven. She's not said anything but it's—"

"You don't need to become Millie's manservant to prove you're not going to abandon your child, Jake. You are the most kind-hearted, generous man I know. That kid is going to be begging to live with you. You never need to worry about not being there. It's in your DNA, but you don't need to sign over your happiness to Millie to prove that—to her, to the baby or to yourself."

Beth thought I got all the good genes, but she had it the wrong way around. Somehow, her addiction had given her insight that I would never have. As if alcoholism had concentrated a lifetime's experience into a few years. Or perhaps addiction was the cure for real wisdom, a way to drown out the cruelty of reality. "You think that's what I've been doing?"

"I do. And remember, Millie is going to do everything she can to get you back. And preferably get a ring on her finger,

I imagine. She's fucked up by getting pregnant as far as her life plan is concerned. In fact, if you weren't loaded, I bet she would have had an abortion—"

"Beth!"

"Be shocked all you like, Jake, it's true. I'd put money on it. Don't fuck things up with Haven by playing along with Millie's games. You don't even know if it's your baby yet."

Had I been too indulgent with Millie?

"I feel like I've been spanked," I said.

"I don't want to hear about your pervy sexual preferences. But consider yourself told off," Beth replied.

"When are you coming home?" I missed her.

"Holy C. R. A. P." Haven spelled out the letters as if she were swearing in front of a small child. We had just walked through what Debbie, my realtor, described as the master bedroom suite.

"Holy crap?" I asked her. It wasn't entirely clear whether she liked the place or not.

Haven just nodded, which didn't help my understanding at all.

"Well it's good that there wouldn't be anything to do," I said, still staring at Haven to try to work out whether or not she was impressed.

"Everything is brand new. You'd be buying straight from the developer, so no one has lived with any of the fixtures or fittings," Debbie explained. "And it's already dressed. All the furniture will stay, so you simply move in."

"What's through there?" Haven asked.

"That's the dressing room," Debbie said as Haven wandered over and opened a door.

"Well that's ridiculous. It's as big as my whole bedroom." She was wide eyed and so beautiful. I could see her here. She seemed at home.

"Beth would like it," I said.

"Of course she would. It's incredible." So, she liked it, that was good.

"The heart of the apartment is the living space. Let me show you." Debbie moved back into the corridor and we followed. "Views are southwest," she said, sweeping her arm across the room.

The area was at least as big as my entire apartment, and in this light, Haven came to life. She looked as though she belonged here.

"There's a study through that sliding door, which you can open up into the main room if you wanted more space."

"Holy crap," Haven said again, not bothering to spell out the word this time.

"All the floors are engineered walnut. Have a brochure. The full spec is in there. And then you have access to the wrap-around balcony from the master suite and the living space. It's a great property, but it won't be on the market long."

It was a huge leap from my old place in Earls Court. I had this incredible girl and I was going to be a father in a few months. I was ready to take the next step toward my future.

"But there are two more bedrooms, right?" I asked.

The two smaller bedrooms were still a good size and plenty big enough for a baby. "This would work for a nursery." I said as we entered the room next to the master bedroom.

"You're pregnant?" Debbie said, glancing between us. "Or making plans to be?" Haven pinched her cheek between her teeth.

"Just planning," I said, trying to be as ambiguous as possible. "Thanks for showing us around," I said, wanting to steer the conversation to less uncomfortable ground. I didn't want to explain my paternal complications to a complete stranger.

"I'll give you two a moment and I'll see you outside," Debbie said.

When I heard the front door click, I turned to Haven. "So what do you think?"

"I think it's beautiful. Like, amazing." She sounded more subdued than she had before Debbie's comment.

"You like it?" I wrapped my arms around her waist, pulling her toward me.

"How could I not? It's like those places you see *other* people living in. It's the kind of place I'd imagine Millie living in."

That was the last thing I'd expected Haven to say.

"Forget about Millie. Can you see yourself here?"

"It's not for me. It's for you."

Was it too early for me to formally ask her to move in with me? Although she wouldn't just be moving in with me—it would be with me and Beth and the baby. "Yeah, but you're going to spend time here, I hope, and maybe, you know—"

"What do you think?" Haven interrupted as if she didn't like where I was going. When I'd mentioned our future at the wrap party, she'd dragged me home, determined to get me naked. Had she changed her mind?

"I don't know," I replied, and that was the truth. Every certainty I surrounded myself with seemed to be disintegrating.

Haven

"How did the dating piece go down with the readers?" Jake asked. After a day house hunting, we'd decided to go to dinner at my favorite local tapas place. I loved it. No one dressed up no matter the day of the week, you could always get a table and the food was incredible. They'd given us a spot in the corner of the dimly lit dining area, away from the bar and we sat kitty-corner to each other.

The lighting was the other reason I loved the place; candlelight was always a woman's best friend. Jake's, too, apparently. His jaw was completely kissable, covered in a day's worth of scruff, the light emphasizing every contour. I made myself blink. The final apartment we'd seen had been incredible and it suited Jake somehow. He seemed at ease, comfortable in the space. But it reminded me of all the complications that the future held. It was good to get back onto neutral ground.

"It doesn't go out until next week. I think it will be okay, though," I replied. "This squid is good, right?"

"You don't sound excited," Jake said, nodding and taking another piece of squid.

I shrugged. I wasn't excited. Normally when a big article of mine was being featured, I couldn't wait to get feedback from readers. But dating rich men seemed like kind of a silly feature. Was I encouraging women to go after sleazeballs like Louis Romano for their money?

"What are you working on now?"

"I asked Robert if I could do a piece about women in technology. You know that report that came out recently saying how it's one of the worst sectors for women?"

Jake nodded. "Yeah, I saw that."

"Well, I thought it would be good to cover it and investigate sexism in the workplace."

"Robert wasn't keen?"

"No. Thinks it's too heavy." I sighed. "And he's right. We're not the *Economist*. Articles like that don't increase readers, and Robert's all about improving circulation."

"As editor, that's his job, isn't it?"

"I guess." I knew what I was getting working for *Rallegra*. And it had always been what I'd wanted.

"So are you going to apply to the *Economist*?"

I took in a breath and narrowed my eyes as if I was seriously considering his question. "Not tonight." I grinned at him.

"I'm serious, you should think about it. Work should make you happy and I've never seen you happy at *Rallegra*."

I'd never really considered leaving *Rallegra*. I'd been focused on getting a promotion since I'd started there. "Okay, Mr. Fix It, I'll take that under advisement. Talk to me about you. What about the flats today? Are you going to buy one?"

Jake grinned. It was the kind of grin that made me want to jump him right there, in front of everyone.

"What are you smiling about?" I asked.

"Nothing. It was just nice today. Doing that with you."

I reached for some more food, trying to hide the fact that I'd loved that he'd brought me along to see the flats with him.

It hadn't been without incident though. Millie's shadow had even followed us there. Planning space for a nursery pulled me away from the fantasy of penthouses. How often was he going to have the baby stay with him? Because he worked for himself, the custody arrangements might not be limited to every other weekend. Millie's pregnancy was going to have a huge impact on my life if Jake and I stayed together. I'd end up being a part-time . . . caregiver for someone else's child.

"Did you like any of them enough to buy one?" I asked.

"I'm not sure. It's an adjustment," he said. "You liked the places we saw today?"

"Of course. They were amazing."

"You'd live in all of them?"

My stomach flipped. I shouldn't get excited when he said stuff like that. A baby would change everything for him, for us.

"It should be about whether you would live in them, not me."

"I was serious when I talked about our future, Haven."

"You have a lot happening right now. Let's just deal with the here and now. We're together, and I love that we are. We don't have to make long-term decisions about us."

"But if I buy a place you don't like . . ."

"Then we'll move when we get married. Satisfied?"

I said it to shock him and I half expected him to choke on his beer. Instead, Jake's grin transformed from sexy to scorching.

"I think we need to get the check," he said.

"You're amazing," I said, my breathing returning to normal.

"You're only saying that because I made you come three times," Jake said as he pulled me onto his chest.

"You're right, I am."

"You're using me for my sexual skills?" he asked.

"Yup."

"You know you're getting kissed for that."

I giggled and he rolled me to my back and pressed his lips against mine. I pretended I wanted to resist him but of course, there was nothing better than kissing Jake.

I heard a phone vibrate somewhere but Jake ignored it and kept kissing me. He started to harden again against me and I relaxed.

The buzzing stopped and then started again. "Jake, that could be about your dad," I said as I reluctantly pushed him away from me.

He reached across me and then collapsed onto his back with a groan. "It's Millie."

Well, at least she had the decency to let me have an orgasm before she called this time.

"I'm ignoring it," he said.

I got up to go to the bathroom.

"I'm ignoring it," he said again.

"I don't want you to ignore it for me. If you need to answer the phone, answer it." I tried to sound patient. I wasn't angry with him, or Millie. I didn't want to be the reason he wasn't answering his child's mother.

The phone started to buzz again and I pulled on a t-shirt. From the bathroom, I heard him answer. His voice was low and I couldn't make out what he was saying, just that he was talking.

I brushed my teeth and waited until I couldn't hear his voice. I didn't want to listen in to his conversation.

As I opened the door, he was facing me, his head propped up on his elbow.

"Hey," he said.

"Hey, how's Millie?"

"Feeling sick, apparently. She asked me to come over again." He rolled his eyes. I forced out a smile.

I got back into bed and he grabbed my ass. "So, are you going?" I asked.

"No, what can I do if she feels sick?"

"I don't want you not to go because you're worried you'll upset me."

"Are you saying you think I should go?"

"I'm not saying anything. Just that I shouldn't be a factor in your decision." I didn't want to be the demanding girlfriend but at the same time, I wasn't sure how I would have reacted if he'd left again. Millie wasn't going to be a problem that simply went away. She would be hanging over us for as long as we were together. And once his baby came along, I would never come first. Was I strong enough to handle that? Since the flat viewings, something heavy and sticky had settled in my gut and wasn't shifting.

Jake looked at me, his eyebrows knitted together. I reached up and smoothed his forehead with my thumb. He caught my wrist. "Do I need to hold on tight to you?" he asked.

"Always," I replied.

chapter THIRTY-SIX

Jake

"If you find that paper on lignocellulosic biomass that I gave you earlier, that should give you some context," I said to Greg, the programmer Eric had brought on board. We were at the new offices on Lombard Street, which were working really well. Eric and Greg were as dedicated as I was to making Elemental Energy a success. Finally, we had some traction and were making incredible progress.

"I need those results from the lab," Eric shouted at no one in particular.

Now that we were set up in an office, with computers and people, it felt as though we were real. And that seemed more and more important. Instead of the baby splitting my focus away from my business, it had propelled me forward. Now a legacy was not just important for me, but also for my kid. I was going to be a father, and I wanted that kid to grow up in a cleaner world and I wanted him or her to be proud of me. When I was small, my father had been like a god to me. I mean, what was more impressive than having your own real-life superhero father? He caught villains and bad guys, just like Batman. I wanted to be just like him. I might not have a badge or a gun, but I wanted to be my child's hero.

Millie had been due to get her ultrasound today and part of me was excited to hear about it. I wished she'd been okay with me going with her. I wanted to say hello and introduce myself properly. A business, a baby, buying a place to live that didn't look like a squat. Somewhere along the way, I'd become an adult. How had that happened? And Haven. I hadn't expected her to come into my life and shape it so completely. I felt cheated every moment I couldn't be with her.

Fitting all the pieces of my life together was becoming more and more of a challenge, but I was determined to make my kid, my business and my girl a priority. They were all important.

I checked my watch; it was just before seven. I'd been here twelve hours and I'd promised to meet Haven for dinner tonight. I had so much to do here but I wanted to see her.

My cell vibrated in my pocket.

"Hey, Millie. How did it go?" I'd been waiting for her to call.

"The hospital gave me a CD and some pictures if you want to come round and see?"

I'd planned to see Haven back at her place. I'd not made it to her Sunday night dinner because of Eric's arrival and I was desperate to see her, but this was my baby.

"Okay, I can swing by, but I really don't have long." I jumped in the car and made it to Millie's in record time, then texted Haven.

Jake: I'm going to be a bit late, should be with you by eight thirty. J x

She'd understand.

Millie threw open the door almost as soon as I'd knocked on it. "It's so amazing, Harry. I can't wait for you to see."

She had her laptop ready, and with a click the film of her ultrasound started to play.

"You see, that's its head." She indicated on the screen.

I grinned and nodded. I couldn't exactly see what she'd pointed out, but it was amazing all the same. With every day, fatherhood was becoming more of a reality.

She put her arm around my waist and I pulled her into a hug. "Wow," was all I could manage.

"It's so overwhelming, Harry, isn't it?" Her voice was faltering. Millie and emotion didn't often mix. It must have been the hormones.

"It's incredible. Do you have a due date?"

She nodded and couldn't seem to get her words out. "January."

"Okay. Good. Well, I'll make sure I'm around at Christmas. Just in case."

"Maybe we can spend it together?" she asked. "We're going to be family, after all."

And that was the problem, right there. I would never be with Millie in the way that she might want, but whether or not I liked it, and whether or not Haven could live with it, this baby meant Millie and I would be bound together forever. I wanted that connection with Haven, not Millie. I wanted to be married to the mother of my children. My parents had created a blanket of family, safety and love that I wanted to provide for my kid. I didn't know if it was possible for me to do that on my own. I didn't know how it worked when you weren't in love with the mother of your child. When you had to fight over custody arrangements and schooling. I didn't want to bring up children in a war zone. I was going to have to figure it out, and keeping Millie happy was part of that. I just wasn't sure what that would do to Haven and me.

"Let's see where we are at Christmas. I've got a lot going on," I said. I didn't want to give her false hope, but there was no point in upsetting her unnecessarily.

"We could be happy, the three of us," she said softly.

My stomach churned and the sense of obligation that was never far from the surface agreed with her. I got her pregnant. I owed her, didn't I? "I have to go," I said.

She had tears in her eyes, but she nodded. I kissed her on the top of her head and headed out. To Haven.

"Hey," Haven said as she opened the door. "How was it?"

I leaned forward, meaning to give her a quick peck on the lips, but as soon as I got near, her scent drew me in, the sweet honeysuckle and musk that was who she was. I circled her waist with my hands and turned the kiss deeper, wanting to get closer. Pulling back, I smiled at her.

"It was that good, huh?"

"We got the results we wanted from the testing and Eric's happy, so I'm happy."

"You don't *seem* that happy. Are you just tired?"

"It's good to see you. But yes, I'm tired." I headed into the kitchen for a beer. I was shattered mentally and physically. It was okay as long as I kept going, but being with Haven relaxed me and now I felt the weight of everything I was juggling.

"How's Millie?" she asked as she went to sit on the sofa.

"She had her ultrasound. Everything is how it should be. It looks like an alien from the DVD, but apparently that's normal." I fought back a grin. Was it okay to talk about this stuff with her? I didn't want to keep secrets from her, but at the same time I didn't want to make her feel uncomfortable.

"You saw it?" she asked as I sat down next to her.

"Yeah, I stopped by on my way here. Is that okay?" I patted my lap, wanting to touch her. She lifted her feet and I snuck my hand up her trouser leg to stroke her smooth, soft skin.

"Of course it's okay. It's your baby."

I nodded. It was my child. My responsibility. I was going to be someone's protector, their safety net. I wanted it, but the reality was increasingly daunting.

"I was cooking chicken, but would you prefer to go out?" she asked as she removed her legs from my lap and rearranged herself farther away from me.

"Hey." I pulled her closer and wrapped my arm around her, bringing her head to my shoulder. "No, let's stay in. I want you to myself and I want to hear about your day." I didn't want to talk about the things that took me away from Haven anymore tonight.

Her arms curled around my waist and she hugged me tight. Normally, we would be three steps away from naked, but for now, this was what I needed. Haven close to me, holding me as I was holding her. I wanted to know she was with me on this journey.

The alarm on her phone jolted us from our embrace.

"I need to take the chicken out," she said and I reluctantly let her go.

"Hey, are you okay?" I asked. Her eyes were glassy. She nodded. "Are you upset?"

She smiled and shook her head. "No, not at all. I have a bit of hay fever, that's all."

She was clearly close to tears but I didn't want to push her. The situation was impossible. I was asking a lot of her but I needed to know we were okay, that she was mine.

I stood up and held out my hand. "Come on, dinner can wait." I led her toward the bedroom.

There were no ropes that night. No need to restrain her. She'd never looked so beautiful.

"Turn over," I said. She was on all fours and although she had the most perfect ass, I wanted to see her face. I wanted her eyes on mine as she came.

She turned, kneeling to face me, placing her fingers on my shoulders. I loved her hands there. They were so frail and small against my bulk. I grabbed her ass, lifted her and threw her back on the bed. "I have to be inside you right now."

She reached for her breasts and I pulled her hands away. I wanted an unrestricted view as they moved when I pounded into her.

"Oh, Haven, feel that?" I asked as I felt her warmth.

"Jake," she whispered and tilted her head back. She was close. She was perfect when she was at this point. She'd do anything for me. She'd tell me anything. It felt powerful and intimate. I knew only I'd ever seen her like this. So exposed. So undone.

Her fingernails dug into the skin of my upper arms and I tried to focus on the pain instead of the beautiful look on her face. Her body went rigid and I saw the climax on her face a second before her muscles rippled around me. I thrust harder, deeper, my orgasm taking over and crashing through me. I groaned as I came, collapsing on top of her the way I knew she liked. Her hands snaked round my back and pulled me closer. She was usually limp and exhausted, but tonight she wouldn't let go of me. When I rolled to my side, she clung to me.

"Hey," I said.

She kissed my shoulder again and again. Small, sweet kisses.

I tried to move her so I could see her beautiful face, but she concentrated on pressing her lips to my skin and who was I to argue? Eventually, her grip loosened and she moved off the bed to go to the bathroom.

She came back wearing my t-shirt and I pulled at her waist, bringing her back to my front.

"I may be passing your office later today. I thought I'd come in and say hello." Haven was sitting at her dressing table as I came out of the shower, towel drying my hair.

"That would be great. I could introduce you to Eric."

"And Beth's back tonight?" she asked.

"Yeah, this afternoon. Do you want to come over? I could cook for the three of us." The more I thought about it, the more

I was excited about having a new place, with a big kitchen, where we could cook together and have friends round.

"I think you should catch up with her. I have a deadline so I'll probably be working late anyway."

And when I had the new apartment, I could properly ask Haven to move in. I'd mentioned it but she wanted to wait to see how things went with my Dad and Millie and Elemental Energy. But when I was actually moved in, she'd see how great it could be and she'd know how I saw her as a crucial part of my future.

chapter THIRTY-SEVEN

Haven

Last night had pushed me into a decision. Seeing Jake so conflicted, but trying to act as if nothing was wrong, I knew I had to take action. He was going to break if he didn't let something go. And that something had to be me. I loved him and I wanted what was best for him—less pressure, the chance to be a real father, to be excited about his baby. I wanted that for him.

I knew as soon as he started talking about the scan that last night would be our last night together. He was exuberant but didn't want to show it in front of me and that's not how it should be. It nearly killed me, being with him, and knowing it would never happen again. That I would never feel him under my fingertips, inside me, over me—it was almost too much. Too painful.

I wasn't being entirely selfless. I needed to walk away, too. I had to be sure of the people in my life. Jake was a good man and if the time ever came, he would have to choose Millie and his baby, and that was how it should be. But I couldn't live with that. If I gave my heart and trust to someone, I needed to know that they would never leave me.

Shit, shit, shit, shit.

I'd passed the main entrance to Jake's building for the fourth time. I knew I was doing the right thing, but part of me still wanted to believe it could be different. I had to stop delaying. There was no magic bullet, no strike of lightning that was going to make everything okay. It was now or never. I took a deep breath, releasing the muscles clenched in my belly. I smoothed back my hair, making sure nothing escaped my bun as I walked into the Lombard Street building.

A few minutes after the receptionist announced me, Jake rounded the corner, a huge grin on his face. *Shit, shit shit.* This was going to be even more difficult than I could have imagined.

"Hey, beautiful girl," he said as he grabbed me into his arms. I tensed. "Sorry, I forgot about the PDA rule. Let's get somewhere more private."

He pulled my hand into his and led me down the corridor and through a frosted glass door. Three heads snapped up as we walked in.

"Hey, everyone, this is Haven. Haven, this is Eric, Greg and Dale."

I forced a smile. Luckily they weren't particularly interested in me and quickly went back to their laptops.

"I thought it was going to be bigger." I said as I scanned the small room. I thought there would be a corner where we could talk. There was never going to be a good time for this, but I thought with Beth being back today, now would make the most sense. He would have his sister for support.

"Let me show you." Jake led me toward the back of the office and through a door into another much larger space. "They can take the wall down if we want them to. For now, it's better to be in the smaller room when there are just four of us." He was excited and it was lovely to see.

I nodded. "Do you have some water or—" I needed to stay strong but being with him made me doubt myself. I wanted him. I always wanted him.

"Yeah, let me . . ." He walked across the empty room toward a coffee machine on a bench and pulled open a fridge set beneath the coffee cups. He passed me a bottle of water and kept one for himself. "There's not much of a view because it's on the ground floor, but I don't think that matters."

"It's great and the location is awesome. You should be so proud."

He smiled. I hated to bring him down, but he'd understand eventually that this was right for both of us in the long term. And it *was* right . . . wasn't it?

"You've got a lot going on," I continued. "What with this all happening and buying a new flat, your dad and the baby and Millie—"

He stood right in front of me. "Yeah, but it's all good. I can handle it and I know we don't get loads of time together, but it will get better." He stroked his hands down my arms.

"It's not about the time. I'm not demanding more attention. Please don't think that's what this is about." I didn't want him to think I was a monster.

"What what is about?" His eyebrows drew together and his voice changed pitch.

I took another deep breath.

"Haven?" Jake bent his knees slightly, trying to catch my eye.

"It's just, I think you have a lot going on and that maybe I need to let you concentrate on other things." My voice came out smaller than I'd expected. I didn't feel as confident that I could let him go now that I was in front of him.

"What are you saying? Are you running from me?"

I shook my head. "I'm not running. I promise, I'm not. I just think that you need to be consumed with other things and I shouldn't be a priority for you." I wasn't explaining myself very well. I'd rehearsed this speech in my head a million times in the past twenty-four hours and it had all made so much sense when I was on my own.

Jake gripped my shoulders tenderly. "You are a priority for me—"

I couldn't look at him. "But you should be concentrating on your business and your baby and Millie. I couldn't live with myself if I thought I was the reason that you're not in a relationship with the mother of your child, or that you're not spending more time with your kid. You need some space to figure out what you need."

"Haven, I know Millie has been a pain in the ass recently, but I didn't run over to her the other night. And when I saw her about the ultrasound, I told her there was nothing going to happen between us. She gets that—"

"You don't know what things would be like if you were single—" The black molasses that had been rooted in my gut spread across my body at the thought of him with Millie or anyone else.

"I can tell you categorically that if Millie was the last woman on the planet I wouldn't want to be with her. I don't love her. I love you. I always knew that girls like her weren't right for me. But being with you has woken me up to why—"

"Please don't make this harder. I just don't think this is our time." My throat constricted. I really didn't want to cry. I needed to stay strong, to make sure Jake knew I was serious. "It's less complicated to walk away now, while we've not been together long." I blinked more and more rapidly, trying to stave off the tears. "Better that than—"

"It doesn't matter to me how long we've been together. When you know, you know. Clichés are clichés for a reason. You can't tell me you don't feel the same. You might not have said the words, but I know you. I own you." Jake pulled me toward him. I let myself sink into him one last time.

"You do and you always will, but I need to walk away." I couldn't tell him that part of the reason I needed to leave was so I didn't live in constant fear that he was going to abandon me. I couldn't live like that, waiting for him to leave me. If I told him, he'd say anything to persuade me that it wouldn't happen. And I wanted to hear it all. I wanted to hear it too much, which was why I needed to go. I was in too deep already.

"You can't be serious, Haven. I can see you're upset. You don't want to walk away."

I realized I wasn't going to convince him by telling him it was what was best for him. He had to see this was what I wanted. "I'm sorry. I do." It was all I could manage. My resolve was wavering. His touch and his smell were pulling me toward him. I placed my hands on his chest and gently tried to create some space between us.

"Haven, no. I'll speak to Millie and say she can't call unless it's an emerg—"

That's when I knew I'd made the right decision. "Don't you dare do that for me. You see how conflicted you are? You see how you are being pulled in different directions? I never want to feel that you prioritized me over your pregnant ex-girlfriend, but you're right, part of me needs that from you. And that's not fair. It's not fair to you, Millie or me. I can't live like that."

Jake's hold loosened and I stepped away from him. He let me go and my heart shattered into a million pieces. I'd got what I wanted, just as I feared.

He pushed his hands through his hair and turned to the window. He looked so beautiful, but so upset. I hated that I had been the cause. But it was the right thing to do in the long run. There would be more pain, and it would be deeper for both of us, the longer we waited.

"I'm sorry." I left before I could change my mind.

chapter THIRTY-EIGHT

Jake

I'd always known that she'd run at some point. But this wasn't entirely about her fear of letting me get too close. I was distracted. I had Millie making demands on me that I knew must have been difficult for Haven to stomach. And how could I expect anyone to live through me having a baby with another woman? I had been stupid to think that it could end any other way with Haven. I had hoped the way I felt about her would shelter us from everything else. That we could ride out the storm together. I wanted to look after us both and keep our hearts safe for each other.

"Are you okay?" Beth asked as I walked through the door to our apartment. She knew me too well; there was no hiding anything from her. I'd left the office just after Haven in the hope of finding Beth at home. There was no point being at work.

"Not really."

"What's going on? Is it Haven?"

Why had she assumed that I would be upset about Haven?

Had they spoken? Could she tell that Haven had never been mine at all?

I nodded and collapsed on the sofa. "She ended it. She doesn't want to be an additional pressure although she needs to be my priority. Or something." I couldn't remember everything she'd said. The conversation with Haven seemed to be over before it began. By the time I caught my breath and had finally managed to find some words, she'd already left.

"So, you're going to fight for her, right?" Beth asked.

Despite, or perhaps because of, what was going on with me, it was so good to see Beth. She looked great. Her eyes were bright and she seemed more relaxed at the core of her somehow. I smiled, but shook my head. "What do you think I've been doing? I've been fighting for her every day since I met her. I can't make her feel about me the way I do about her. It's not mandatory. And she's right. I can't expect her to stand by me while another woman has my baby. Like she said, it's not fair to her. I was a fool to think we were going to be okay."

Beth pursed her lips. "I don't believe this is about her lack of feeling. If anything, it's the opposite. She sounds like she doesn't want you to be torn between her and Millie. She's sacrificing herself for you. Of course, if she knew Millie, Haven would realize what a lunatic Millie is and that you were a dick for ever putting *your* dick anywhere near her. Scratch that. If she knew Millie, Haven would think your judgment was so off, she'd walk anyway." She elbowed me, trying to elicit a smile.

"You're not helping. You know that, right?"

"I am too. I'm making you feel bad about yourself and that's important because—and I'd know—you need to hit rock bottom before you can start recovery."

I rolled my eyes and she laughed. It was good to have her back. Haven had asked whether Beth was back today. Had she been waiting for Beth to return to end things? Had she been that careful with my feelings? I didn't know if it would be better or worse if she had. My stomach churned with the loss of her.

"So do you have a plan?" Beth asked.

"A plan?"

"Yeah, to win her back. You always have a plan. That's what you do. You plan, you fix, you make everything better."

I let myself consider her analysis of me. Was that who I was? I suppose it was. But this situation wasn't fixable. Maybe Haven had been right. It wasn't our time.

"Of course, it will help when you get that paternity test back to prove that baby isn't yours," Beth continued. "But what else are you going to do?"

"I've told you. I can't make her do anything, and what makes you so sure that Millie is lying? She's vacuous and a bit cold, but she's not a monster. And she's not stupid. She's not going to tell me it's mine if she's going to get found out eventually. Why would she bother?"

"I'm not saying I understand her, I just think she's got a game plan. But time will tell and then I'll take great delight in saying that I told you so."

Beth getting to gloat would be worth it, but the instant I had the thought I felt guilty. If the kid was mine, I didn't want to be wishing it away.

"I can't think about that. It seems wrong that I'd be hoping that the baby is another man's. And I don't think she'd lie. I really don't. I'm going to concentrate on Elemental Energy. It needs a lot of time and attention from me. We're also going to move."

"We are?" Beth asked.

"We are. There's no room for three of us in this apartment." I put my hand out to silence Beth from saying anything else about paternity. "And I need to move on. This place is a dump, you're right."

"Oh my God, breakthrough! You see? Every cloud has a silver lining. You might have lost the love of your life, and you might never be happy again, but I'll be cooking in a nicer kitchen." She grinned and I threw a cushion at her.

"I saw some places this weekend with Haven." I stood up and headed to my desk in the corner of the living room. "These. I think two were ones you'd picked out."

I handed her brochures from the apartments that we had visited. She grabbed my hand and pulled me down onto the sofa.

"Have you considered sharing your feelings with her about everything you've got going on? Rather than just trying to keep everyone happy, you could explain to her the pressure. If you don't let her see the strain, how can she trust you when you show her the good stuff, when you tell her how important she is to you? You have to reveal all of you, and trust her to love you anyway."

I closed my eyes and let what Beth was saying sink in. "Stop with the making sense thing, just for a little bit." I exhaled. I was exhausted.

"Okay, but if you love her, Jake, you can't just let her go.

I've never seen you give up on something you really wanted. Don't let me think that giving up is an option."

I pulled her into a hug. I didn't know what to say. Haven wanted me to let her go, and I had to give her anything she wanted.

"But I'm great at house hunting," Millie said, trying to convince me to take her to a second viewing that Beth had arranged that afternoon for one of the apartments that I'd seen a few weeks before. With Beth's exams finished, she'd thrown herself into finding us a new place to live now that I'd finally agreed it was time to move.

"I'm going with Beth," I replied. When I'd told Millie that Haven and I had broken up she hadn't tried very hard to hide her glee. She dressed it up in concern, but I could tell she was delighted. I suppose it was better for her. Even though we weren't together, Millie was increasingly demanding, asking me to pick up shopping and medication for her, and now that Haven wasn't in the picture, there seemed to be less of a reason to resist.

"But I could see what would work for the baby. If there are danger zones and things."

I sighed, wondering which was the lesser of two evils: Millie's whining or Beth's temper if I dared to bring Millie along.

Beth won. "No, Millie. Stop." The thought of seeing her in that last apartment that Haven and I had seen together was just wrong. Haven owned that space.

"Okay, I'm sorry."

I must have really snapped at her if she was apologizing. My stomach churned with guilt.

"We're friends, right, Jake?"

"Of course, I didn't mean to snap at you—" I pushed my hands through my hair.

"So friends can have dinner. Let me take you out, as a friend, and maybe I can get a smile out of you," Millie continued.

I sighed. I didn't have the energy to say no. "Okay. We can go around the corner for a quick, early supper."

Millie's face lit up and she smiled widely at me.

"I need to go," I said. "I'll see you here at seven. Be ready."

"I like it," Beth said.

I liked the apartment, too. The first time I'd seen it had been with Haven. I could still see her face as she walked from room to room, open-mouthed. She looked good in this place. It was comforting that she'd seen it and liked it. If I ended up living here, I would feel as if a part of her was always with me.

"By the grin on your face, it seems like you like it, too," Beth said, snapping me out of my thoughts of Haven.

"It's big," I said.

"It is. The views are amazing . . ."

"And you don't think I'd be better off in a house, a bit further out, rather than an apartment?"

"No. I think you've got great outside space here. A house takes maintenance, and if you want that, you can buy a country place. If you're in the city, live with all the conveniences." Beth was right, as usual. And I needed to be close to Millie and the baby.

"And you like your room?" I asked.

Beth's chest rose as she took in a deep breath. "I've been thinking,"

"Careful, you might strain something."

She gave me a hard stare. "I've been thinking," she repeated, "that I might get my own place."

My stomach dropped away from me. It was the last thing I was expecting her to say. We'd lived together for years.

"You want to move out?"

"I think it's time. I dealt with so much stuff when I went back to Chicago. I'm so much stronger. I think I need to try to be independent. A bit."

"You'll still be nearby?"

She nodded, and her eyes danced as if it were Christmas, and we were kids. She was excited and it was so good to see. "I thought maybe I could rent somewhere for a while, close by, and then see."

"I hate to interrupt," my realtor said. "I couldn't help but overhear. I don't know what your budget is, but I have a lovely one-bedroom place in this building. I could show you that now, if you'd like to see it?"

Beth looked at me and smiled. I grinned back. This could be the perfect solution.

"It's twelve hundred square feet, so considerably smaller than the penthouse that we've just seen, but that's reflected in the price," Debbie said as we walked into the open plan living and dining area.

"It's a lot of money," Beth whispered.

"But you have enough, and if you need more then you can have that, too."

"Of course I don't need more. You've been more than generous. I've never felt that the money's really mine, Jake. It's yours."

When I'd sold Energy Trade, I'd given Beth a chunk of money that she wouldn't touch other than to pay her college tuition. My dad had point-blank refused to take anything, so the fact that the money sat in an account with Beth's name on it had felt like a victory at the time. I wanted her to use it.

"Can we not do this again? I want you to have that money. I have plenty. And buying this place would be a smart investment for you. The money's not doing much sitting in the bank. Spend it, or invest it."

"You think?" She looked up at me expectantly.

"I really do."

"Does it suit me? Do I seem like I belong here?" she asked.

"I think that you belong anywhere you want to. We both need to move on and move up. An apartment is just the people that live in it." I wasn't sure if moving in here was moving on, it was more like a way of hanging on to something that had never belonged to me—my future with Haven.

"It wouldn't bother you having your little sister living in the same building?" Beth asked.

"I think it would be perfect. I'll have a built-in babysitter."

She punched me on the arm. "You won't need one. When are you going to realize that I'm always right? But it would be good, wouldn't it?" She grinned.

I was sold. The realtor was about to make a killing from the pair of us.

chapter THIRTY-NINE

Haven

"It's Saturday night. We *have* to go out," Ash whined.

"I'm not stopping you," I replied.

"You totally are. You're my only friend. I can't go out on my own."

I rolled my eyes. Ash only wanted to get me out talking to other men to take my mind off Jake. It had been nearly two weeks since I'd last seen him. All the books I was reading and songs I was listening to were telling me how it would get better in time, but each day seemed more painful than the last. I knew I'd made the right decision. He was free to spend as much time with Millie as he really, truly, in his heart wanted to. He didn't have to think about how jealous it was going to make his girlfriend. He could fly to Chicago and see his father, he could concentrate on his new business. But that didn't mean it didn't feel like a red-hot poker in my stomach all day, every day. Scared of completely falling apart, I did my best to keep my longing for Jake hidden, zipped up inside me. If no one else saw the effect on me without him, then maybe the feelings within me would just disappear.

"Jesus, your fridge is barren apart from ketchup. When was the last time you ate?" Ash called from the kitchen. I didn't respond. Food hadn't exactly been the top of my priority list. "Not even any ice cream. That's it, there's no way we can stay in." I heard the freezer door slam shut and Ash pad back into the living room. "You keep telling me how you made the right decision about Jake, but I don't think even you believe it." She started gathering up empty glasses and mugs from where they were scattered about, carrying them back into the kitchen.

"I do. I didn't say it wasn't going to hurt, though."

"Well, going out, even if it's just for a drink, will help distract you. You might start to function like a normal person again."

The only person more stubborn than me was Ash. She wasn't going to take no for an answer. And she was right. I had to accept Jake was gone, and at least act as if I had started to move on. "Okay, an hour. And as long as you don't want me to do anything to my hair. I'm either putting it up or leaving it like this," I bargained. I knew my hair could do with a wash, but even the simplest of things seemed to take all my energy. My laundry was piling up and I hadn't changed my bed linens since Jake left. At first it had been because I could still smell him on my pillow, but now the thought of the sheer effort that was required to put clean sheets on the bed filled me with horror.

"Two hours and can you put some dry shampoo through it?"

"Not a minute past two hours? And fuck off with your dry shampoo."

"Do a shot of tequila with me before we go out, I will no longer care about your hair. Deal?"

"Deal."

Jake

I arrived at exactly seven o'clock. I expected Millie to be still getting ready, but she answered the door with her coat on.

"You ready?" I asked.

"Don't I look ready?" she asked, tilting her shoulder up slightly, and glancing at me from under her lashes.

"You look lovely." She did. She always looked beautiful. It was just difficult to see it through the rest of her crap.

"Thank you. You look very handsome, too. But you always do, Harry."

I smiled and led her out of her apartment. "I brought the car, but we can walk to the Italian place," I said.

"Actually, I booked us something in Soho."

"Millie . . ."

"What? I'm treating you, remember? I want to take you somewhere nice." She grinned at me.

"Isn't this nice?" Millie asked, scanning the restaurant before her eyes rested on me.

"Sure," I replied. A happy Millie was much easier to handle than a miserable one.

"They do a thing with black cod here which is meant to be amazing. It was in *Tatler* last month."

"*Tatler*?" I asked. I thought *Rallegra* was a vacuous magazine but *Tatler* was elitist *and* vacuous.

"They have the best recommendations. This place is super-hot right now. I can't believe I managed to get a table."

I couldn't tell if Millie was simply ignoring me or just didn't notice my reaction to her reading material.

"I like that Italian place by you."

"Harry, don't be a spoil sport. Anyway, I can't eat pasta. I don't do carbs."

"Jesus. You're not dieting when you're pregnant! You have to think of the baby, for crying out loud." A crash exploded in my head. This situation was ridiculous. She was so selfish and trying to be nice to her in the hopes that she would do the right thing by me and my child was utterly futile.

I wanted to leave. The fact that I was having dinner with Millie and not Haven was unacceptable. Even if I couldn't have Haven, there was no way I was going to go back to Millie or someone like her. If necessary, I'd take Millie to court to get joint custody of our child. I wasn't going to mollycoddle her anymore.

"I'm not dieting. I'm just being careful," she said softly. At least she had the good grace to blush.

"You need to be healthy. Are you even taking folic acid?"

"Um, yes, I'm doing everything the doctor recommended. But sometimes it's hard, especially when I'm on my own." She sounded sad again. Was she trying to make me feel bad for wanting her to take fucking vitamins? There was no need for us to spend time together. I'd been an idiot for indulging her. I looked down at my plate. I couldn't wait to leave here and get home, away from Millie.

"Let's change the subject. Did you find a new flat you like?"

"Yeah, I think so."

"Really? So Beth is moving out? That's amazing. Can I come and see it?"

"Maybe," I replied. There was no way she was going to see my place. I wanted to keep it separate from her. Things needed to switch to a different setting between us.

"Do you need a hand picking furniture? You need to make sure you go classic, rather than modern bachelor. I saw a great mirror in Elle Interiors this month, it would look fabulous—"

"Stop." If I could render her mute until I dropped her off, that would be ideal. I could be working at the moment, rather than wasting time with someone who didn't deserve my attention.

The silence between us only lasted a few minutes.

"Did you show your parents the video of the ultrasound?" Millie asked, bringing the conversation back to the baby.

I shook my head.

"Doesn't your mother want to see?"

Had I told her my mother had died? I couldn't remember. I hadn't told my dad about the pregnancy. It wasn't that I thought Millie was lying, but there was something stopping me from telling people. The only people who knew were Beth and Haven. It felt as if I was living in some kind of limbo and when things started to become more concrete, with Elemental Energy, with the new flat, with my dad and the baby, then I'd be able to put words around my future.

I shrugged. "How's your sister?" I asked, trying to change the subject. If Millie was talking about herself then she couldn't be asking me questions. I just needed to get to the end of this meal and then renegotiate our relationship. It wasn't working for me. I was done indulging her. Done with her trying to engineer something more between us, and done with spending any more time with her than was absolutely necessary.

"She's good. She's been with Matthew a few months now. I think she's hoping for a ring at any moment. When they get engaged, they'll move in together. I'll be on my own apart from you and the baby."

"You won't be on your own. You have your parents and your friends. Your sister isn't moving to a new country. Anyway, she's not engaged yet."

"Oh, she will be by the end of the year, whether or not it's to Matthew."

I drew my eyebrows together. "What do you mean?"

"She was always going to be engaged by twenty-five. And she's twenty-five in December."

"But what if she hasn't found the right guy by December? Or what if Matthew doesn't ask her?"

"She'll give Matthew until the end of the summer and then if he hasn't proposed, she'll dump him and have three months to find someone else," she said.

"But she's in love with Matthew?"

Millie shrugged. "I guess. He has family money. They make a good couple."

Everything she said cemented my feelings, or lack of them, for Millie. Relationships weren't about love to her. She reminded me how what I'd felt for Haven had been so different, so amazing. Now I couldn't imagine my life any other way. I relaxed. I'd been trying to find something in Millie that just didn't exist. I could accept that now. I'd made a decision to take her out of my life as far as possible, and it felt good.

"It's so great to spend time together like this, isn't it?" Millie said, scanning the restaurant again, no doubt searching for famous faces. It was the last time we would ever spend time together like this.

Haven

It was about nine by the time we finally got out. I had given in and washed my hair. Ash was right; I needed to feel as though my life was moving forward.

Ash told the cab to head toward Soho. "Where are we going?"

"To find hot men who want to shower us with attention," Ash replied.

"Really?" I was grinning at her. The night sounded increasingly promising. "We're going out with the gays?"

Ash grinned. "Old Compton Street," she said to the driver. "Everyone needs more gay in their life."

"That's exactly what we need." I was excited for the first time in I couldn't remember how long. Maybe I would enjoy myself. I was beginning to remember what happy felt like, even if I wasn't feeling it at the moment, there was a possibility that I might. Especially when men were off the menu—straight men anyway. I wasn't close to being ready for a straight bar. The thought of trying to find someone new, waiting to be approached by a guy only for it to happen and for him to be too short, too weird, too boring. In Old Compton Street, all the men were fixated on each other and would want nothing from me but a dance partner. Kylie Minogue and gay men—the ultimate heartbreak cure.

As we got out of the cab, noise and heat assaulted me. It felt as if everyone was on holiday. The windows of the bars and restaurants that lined the road were thrown open, and people were spilling out into the street, making their way from one place to another so that you didn't know where one party ended and the next one started. In every direction, groups of friends and couples threw back shots and sang along to whatever music was playing closest. Everyone's joy surrounded me. It slid through me and lifted my mood. It was the first time since I'd left Jake that I thought I might just make it through.

Ash led the way into what used to be a favorite bar of ours and we headed through the crowds to find some shots of our own. "What can I get you two beautiful ladies?" the gorgeous barman asked.

"Can we order you?" Ash asked, fluttering her eyelashes.

He grinned. "If I ever decide to play for the other team, you will be first on my list," he replied. "In the meantime, what cocktail can I make for you?"

"I'll have a screaming orgasm please," Ash said with a wink.

"I bet you have plenty of those in your life," the barman said.

"Yeah, but unfortunately most of them are self-inflicted. This one," she said, tilting her head to me, "will have a cosmo."

We got our drinks and headed to a table by the folded back windows so we could, when we'd had enough to drink, touch the tight t-shirted men walking by.

"Why are gay men so much better looking than straight men?" Ash asked.

"Genetics? And they care more about their appearance than straight men."

"Not more than George," Ash said.

George was Ash's ex-boyfriend. He was very definitely a metrosexual. "No. Not more than George. Unlike you, I refuse to date anyone who puts more effort into how they look than I do. It's not what nature intended."

"That's a low bar. Most men shower," Ash said, beaming at me.

I laughed. "Hey, I shower. And I wear makeup and look at me! No hair where it shouldn't be. I even shaved my legs for you tonight."

"And I'm mighty grateful. But you'd have been fine to leave them, you would have just been mistaken for a tranny."

We laughed and it felt good. I hadn't used my laughing muscles recently.

"You ladies seem like you're having a good time, can we share your table?" A beautiful looking black man said as two almost as beautiful men loitered behind him.

"On one condition," I said.

"Name it," he replied.

"I want your friend's hat for the evening." His blond friend, sporting a bright pink cowboy hat, took it off and placed it on my head.

"It's on loan, mind. I'm seeing Dolly next month and it's part of the uniform," he said.

"Understood, cowboy, I wouldn't want Ms. Parton disappointed in you." I winked at him and they all took their seats.

"Okay, I'm going to get some shots, do you boys want in?" Ash asked as she jumped to her feet.

"No Sambuca, Ash, please—"

"Hey, isn't that—" Ash pointed out of the window at something and then quickly turned back to me.

"What?" I asked, briefly turning in the direction she had indicated.

"Nothing, I just thought I saw something," she said quietly. "No Sambuca, got it."

"What?" I asked, ignoring her efforts to try and change the topic. I turned properly so I could see what had caught her attention.

I wished I hadn't. It was the unmistakable sight of Jake. My heart actually stopped beating and I couldn't breathe. *How I missed him.* My Jake. He had his back to me and I realized he was opening a car door . . . for Millie.

I kept watching as he rounded the hood and settled in on the other side. He was laughing as he drove away.

"Haven," Ash said.

I downed my cosmo. "I want to go home and drink a lot of tequila, in private where it doesn't matter if I vomit." I took off my hat, stood up and walked toward the exit.

chapter FORTY

Jake

"I had such a great time. Thanks so much for taking me out," Millie said as we got to her front door after what I was sure would be our final dinner together.

"I'm glad you had a good time," I said as I hovered in the doorway.

"And we never run out of things to talk about. And now with the baby. It could all be perfect, Harry." She placed the palm of her hand on my chest. "Don't you think? And now you're single and I'm single, and I'm having your child . . ."

She stroked her fingers up my neck.

"It's as if life rearranged itself for us," she said.

I gripped her wrist. "Stop. We're not together. We're never going to be together."

"You don't mean that." She grinned. "Don't you remember that thing I can do with my tongue?"

I jerked away from her.

"I said no. It's not like that between us anymore."

"I'm carrying your baby." Her voice became colder, harder. "You need to support me."

"I am supporting you."

"I want a ring, Harry. You should have bought me a ring already." Her eyes narrowed and she pointed accusingly. "You broke it, you *have* to buy it. Don't you get it? I don't understand what your fucking problem is. You're supposed to be smart."

God, she was nasty. But it was no surprise.

"I'm sorry if you ever got the impression that this was different than it is, but I'm going to be really clear. I am never going to marry you. We might be having a baby together, but that's where it begins and ends. I don't love you, Millie. I won't ever love you. In fact, I don't even like you that much. I will support the baby, but that's as far as this relationship goes." I turned and headed toward the stairs and let Millie's shouting blend together to make noise. I didn't hear what she was saying. I just wanted to get away from her.

As I hit fresh air, I gulped it in desperate for renewal. I needed to be away from Millie. She was everything I didn't want in my life.

Haven

"Another," I said as I slammed the glass on the coffee table, my throat still burning from the shot. I was sitting on the floor so I couldn't fall after all the tequila I intended to drink.

Ash looked at me as if she were deliberating about whether or not to say anything.

"Another," I repeated.

She picked up the bottle of tequila and fiddled with the top. "Just because they were out together doesn't mean they are *together* together."

I shook my head. "Another."

"Haven. Seriously."

I narrowed my eyes at her and she relented and poured another shot. I grabbed it as soon as it was full, put it to my lips and tipped my head back. The warmth spread from my tongue down my throat and across my limbs. I could feel tequila in my fingers.

"They don't look good together," Ash said.

"They look great and he seemed happy, which is what I wanted. She's the mother of his child. They should be together."

"He loves you."

I shook my head. "Don't say that."

"He told you he loves you."

"Shut up, Ash. I mean it. Things are how they should be. We were never going to work out in the long run, even if Millie hadn't gotten pregnant. There were always going to be glamazons wanting his attention. It's easier this way."

"Shouldn't you at least drunk dial him and shout abuse at him?"

"I don't want him to think I care. Because I don't."

"Then why are you downing tequila shots like Mel Gibson?"

"Shut up and drink with me."

I'd expected my hangover to be worse, considering. I could tell by the ache in my lower back that I hadn't even made it to my bed. I pried an eye open and realized I was on the sofa, Ash collapsed below me on cushions, with one hand still on an almost empty tequila bottle.

I made it to the kitchen and poured myself some water into the biggest glass I could find, then changed into my flying pig pajamas and got into bed. It was ten in the morning, but I had no intention of getting out of bed anytime soon. It was a day to wallow. The pajamas said it all. They were all about Jake. The first time he'd seen me with my hair down, I had been wearing them. The first time he'd made me come, he'd peeled them from my legs. I closed my eyes to stop the tears. I couldn't give in. I needed to blank it all out. I missed him so much, more than I thought possible. I'd known I was upset, but seeing him had made me realize how much I felt his loss in every particle of my body.

I hadn't expected ever to run into him again. Maybe if I had been prepared it would have been easier. But it had been much worse than I'd ever imagined. The pain hadn't dimmed; it still felt as if my heart were being dipped in alcohol. It burned. It was physical. It was visceral.

I heard banging about in the living room, the clink of glasses and then Ash appeared in my bedroom door with a glass of water in her hand. I pulled back the quilt and she climbed in next to me. We lay on our backs, staring at the ceiling.

"How are you feeling?" she asked.

"Remarkably okay given my tequila consumption. You?"

"I meant about Jake."

I wasn't sure if my outside had reacted as violently as my inside at the mention of his name. It felt as if my heart and my stomach swapped positions and my skin started to twitch. "I'll be fine. I don't want to talk about it. Can we discuss your lack of love life?"

Ash groaned. "Haven, concentrating on my misery won't heal your own."

"I think you should Internet date or something," I said, ignoring her.

"Well, actually, I've been thinking about this quite a lot."

Ash always fobbed me off when I tried to get her to discuss her dating life, so the fact she was engaging with me was new.

"Go on," I said, desperate for a distraction.

"You know that guy at work I told you about?"

"The one that works in the other hospital?" She'd told me several months ago that she'd been flirting with a hot doctor from another hospital, but I hadn't heard about him since.

"Yeah, well, he's at my hospital now, like every day. And he's funny. He seems like a good guy."

I turned on my side to face Ash and propped my head up on my hand. "Sounds good."

"Well he asked me out. Several times actually. I told him I'd think about it."

"Oh my God, Ash, how have you not told me about this? What is there to think about?" I was genuinely excited for her and I welcomed the sense of positivity that dripped into my brain, pushing away thoughts of Jake.

"I think I like him. And I think I need to move on."

"You know that there's nothing in the world that I want more than you and Luke to be together, but I don't think it's healthy to put your life on hold for someone who's not available."

"I know," she said quietly. "And I know I joke about it, but I think that's exactly what I've been doing. I've felt the way I have about your brother since I was in the womb, so I've given myself an excuse not to look anywhere else for love."

"Oh, Ash. I'm sorry."

"It's fine. At least I realize it now. I don't want you to do the same thing with Jake. You still love him. I know you do. It's different for you; he has feelings for you. He told you he loved you. You have a chance at being with the man you love. Don't waste it. And before you say anything, you don't know what's going on with Millie. He's a good guy. He's probably just trying to keep her happy. If he was in love with her, he wouldn't have broken up with her after three months. Don't waste time like I have. Go after him or try to move on."

The thought of moving on, trying to date someone else, was just too much. It was as if someone had their fist around my heart and was gripping tighter and tighter.

"I know you don't want to talk about it," she continued. "I just needed to say it. So, I think I'm going to say yes to Richard. What have I got to lose?"

"Richard is the hot doctor?"

Ash nodded. "And I think I'm not going to come to Sunday night dinner quite as often."

It was tough to think that our happy routine was going to change, but it was the right thing for Ash and I was really pleased for her.

"I get it."

"I could ask Richard if he has a hot friend and we could double."

"Can I take a few days to think about that? I need some time to adjust." It was going to take something more than time.

Ash squeezed my hand.

Emma was visiting her parents, so Luke was doing Sunday dinner at their place. I wouldn't have peeled myself out of bed for any other reason. No doubt Jake would be spending the day with Millie, and if I stayed at home on my own it would be the only thing I could think about.

"You look terrible," Luke said as he opened the door.

"Wow, and they say you don't have any charm. I don't know where they come up with these ideas." I followed him into the kitchen. "So, you're actually cooking? We're not getting Chinese?" Unless Ash and I were there doing it for him, Sunday dinner at Luke's was normally delivered. Although we'd never talked about it, I assumed it was some kind of reaction to not being able to pursue his dreams of being a chef. That if he couldn't be amazing at it, he didn't want to try at all.

"I thought I'd make an effort," he said. "But it's baked potato and salmon, so don't get too excited."

"Okay, I can live with that."

"So, what's with the hangover face?"

"Ash and I went out last night."

"Is that why Ash bailed? Does she know Emma's not going to be here?"

I nodded. I wasn't technically lying because she did know that Emma wouldn't be around, but I was ignoring the first part of the question. Luke accepted that Ash didn't like Emma. I wasn't sure whether he cared. He never seemed to defend Emma or try to justify why he was with her. I suppose he didn't need to. It was his choice and his life, but she was separate, compartmentalized away from the rest of his life. How did he do that? My feelings for Jake ran through my veins and consumed me. I couldn't put him in a box like that.

"So how come you didn't go with Emma to see her parents?"

"I didn't want to and she didn't ask. So what did you get up to last night?"

"We went to Soho for a few drinks and then came home and hit the tequila." There was no need to tell him about Jake.

"Did you meet any new friends?" he asked.

I rolled my eyes at him. "You sound like such a granddad. Yes, I made new friends."

"Good. And Ash?"

"Yes, we both made new friends."

He raised his eyebrows and turned to me. "Really? Anything serious?"

"What?" We seemed to be having two different conversations.

"Nothing. Have you spoken to Jake?"

"No, and I don't want to talk about him. We're finished. That's it. Move on. I have." Last night was evidence that I hadn't moved on. I was exactly where I'd been the moment I broke up with him. I wasn't sure it was as easy as simply choosing to, as Ash had described this morning. I couldn't imagine not feeling like this, so dark, so raw, so empty without Jake, but I needed to try or bury all that deeper.

Monday morning meetings got less painful as time passed since I'd last seen Jake in the chair opposite me.

After Robert rejected my article about women in the tech industry, I'd fallen back into line and he'd approved my research of the rise of the use of Botox. Perfect. I'd asked Emily to take the lead on it and she was excited. It was nice to have someone at work who wasn't openly hostile to me.

"Haven, can I have five minutes?" Robert asked at the end of the meeting.

I nodded, gathered up my pad, pen and diet Coke and followed him to his office.

"The elite dating article has been really well received, Haven. Well done," he said as he closed his office door behind him. "And on top of the Sandy Fox piece, I think the features we've had over the last six months have been excellent."

"That's great. I'm really pleased." Why did it feel as though I was about to get fired?

"I spoke to Carole at the weekend."

I took a deep breath.

"She's not coming back from maternity leave."

My palms were beginning to sweat. I fiddled with the cap of my diet Coke in an attempt to distract myself from what Robert was about to say.

He smiled. "And I'd like you to be my new deputy editor."

My heart pounded through my chest but I wasn't sure it was with joy and excitement. "I . . . I don't know what . . . I wasn't expecting . . ." What was my problem? Hadn't I been working up to this moment since I joined *Rallegra*?

Robert laughed. "Take a breath. I don't want you passing out on me. Don't say anything to anyone at the moment. I've asked human resources to do the paperwork. It's a significant uplift in salary, and you'll be eligible for a bonus. But then, it's never been about the money with you, has it?"

I shook my head. "Thank you. I'm just a little overwhelmed."

"You're great at your job, Haven. You deserve this. Now get out of here."

I went back to my desk in a bit of a trance. I collected my phone from my bag and headed out to the stairwell, dialing Luke's number before I reached the door.

"Can you talk?" I asked as he answered.

"Of course. What's going on?"

"I just got offered the deputy editorship."

"What? That's incredible. Congratulations. Did it just happen?"

"Yeah, Robert just told me."

"It's what you've been wanting since you got there. I'm so proud of you. We should celebrate. You, me and Ash. Are you free this evening?"

For some reason I didn't want to celebrate. I didn't feel excited or even relieved. I felt uncomfortable. My mind kept drifting to Jake and the person I was with him. The person I was able to be with him. That person wasn't the Haven who existed at *Rallegra*.

"It's Monday. And you haven't seen Emma all weekend. She'll kill you."

"She won't care, and she's working late anyway."

"Okay, but can we stay in and celebrate?" I didn't want to run the risk of seeing Jake again, and however unlikely that was in a city of eight million people, I needed to remove all possibilities. I had to create a world without Jake, because if he didn't exist it might just be possible to live without him. I'd learned to live without my parents because I'd had to. I could do the same with Jake.

chapter FORTY-ONE

Jake

"Who are you calling?" Beth asked.

"Millie," I replied.

"What the hell, why?"

"I've not heard from her for two weeks. What if something's happened with the baby? She's not picking up any of my calls."

"I'm sure you would be the first to know if there was anything serious. She's probably trying to con some other ex into thinking it's his baby. She clearly wanted to get married, and saw getting knocked up as a short cut."

"She's not as bad as you think she is."

"What? She's awful. You know that."

"Listen, my kid has half her genes, so you need to lay off. I might not want to marry her or spend time with her, but that doesn't mean I don't want her to answer. Anything could have happened."

"Have you thought about getting in contact with Haven?" Beth asked, changing the subject.

I tossed my phone on the kitchen counter. "I'm giving her what she wants," I said simply.

"But now your relationship with Millie is different. You're not asking her how high when she tells you to jump—"

"Beth . . ."

"You can't deny that's what you were doing."

"I was trying to do the right thing."

I didn't want to hear anymore. I stalked into my bedroom, and decided to take a shower. I wanted to wash Haven from my mind. It had been over a month since I'd last seen her, and she still interrupted every thought I had. I was constantly mentally tracking what she might be doing, who she might be speaking to, where she might be, whether or not she was at all affected by our breakup. Had she just managed to walk away? Maybe she hadn't told me she loved me because she didn't. But I didn't think that was it. There seemed something impermanent about her absence. Something deep inside me told me I'd find her again.

As I stepped out of the shower, I wrapped a towel around my waist and checked my phone. No response from Millie. It was unsurprising. She was sending me a warning that she controlled access to her, and no doubt that would be the case when the baby arrived, too. I was a fool for ever having anything to do with Millie, let alone sleeping with her. I needed to resolve this and come to an amicable arrangement with her. I didn't want my child to become a pawn in Millie's twisted games.

I dressed quickly in my running gear and grabbed my keys and running shoes.

"I'm going for a run," I said to Beth as I stepped out of my bedroom.

"I thought you just had a shower," she replied.

I pulled the door shut behind me. It was starting to drizzle, despite the heat, so it would get dark quickly. My feet began to hit the pavement in a familiar rhythm as I headed toward Millie's apartment. The traffic was heavy for Sunday night. Everyone was pouring back into London after their weekends away. The rain kept the pavements clear and I was able to focus on my breathing and my steps for a minute before Haven drifted back into my mind. She'd have Sunday dinner with Luke and Ash. I wondered if she'd started dating again. Had someone else kissed her? More? I couldn't stop the roar exploding from the back of my throat. She couldn't be someone else's future when she was mine. I couldn't imagine that being apart from her was forever. Perhaps that was why I hadn't fought for her as Beth had urged me to. When Haven left, I'd assumed we'd find our way back to each other. But it had been too long. Not being with her was slowly killing me. I picked up the pace and my muscles started to burn.

It wasn't far to Millie's, so I took a long route, weaving through gardens and around squares. As I got nearer, the streets filled with restaurants, their windows and doors open to let in some air. People sat outside under awnings despite the rain. My mind drifted to Haven again. Could she be in one of these restaurants, outside at one of these tables? No, it was Sunday. She would be with Ash and Luke. Unless she had a date. I started scanning heads of the strangers I passed, waiting to see a shock of blonde hair. I saw one, but then the hair was too short to be Haven. Then another, but then she turned and it wasn't her. As I rounded the next corner, there was a group of girls sitting outside, but no blondes. As I looked away, something familiar caught my eye. I glanced back. Millie. I stopped suddenly. She hadn't seen me, but I could see her very clearly. Anger crashed through me. She was smoking, in between taking swigs from her wine glass. *What the fuck?*

The street started to spin and I rested my hands on my knees, catching my breath. I took several deep gulps of air and then adrenaline took over. I strode over to her table and slammed my hands down. Glasses tumbled over left and right. "What the fuck are you doing?" I shouted. Horror spread across her face before giving way to fury.

"Fuck off," she screamed at me.

I grabbed her elbow and pulled her out of her seat and up the street, away from the restaurant. She was squirming and twisting her arm, breaking free of my grasp.

"Jesus, I knew you were selfish but this—"

"Let go of me. Fuck off, Harry."

My vision was tinged red and my blood felt hot in my veins. "How fucking *dare* you. You are carrying a child. You are harming our baby."

She struggled against me again. "There is no baby, you idiot!" she screamed.

I dropped her elbow. "What?" I asked softly.

"You heard me. I'm not pregnant." She ran her fingers under her eyelashes and straightened her skirt.

The red mist cleared and my heart felt heavy. "You lost it?" I said. "I don't know what to say . . ."

"Whatever," Millie said as she waved her hand between us.

"What do you mean 'whatever'? This is awful. I should have been there." I scanned her face, trying to think what I could do to make this right.

"Christ, you're naïve." She turned and headed back to the restaurant. I hurried alongside her, finally stepping in front of her so she had to stop.

"Millie. What's going on? What are you talking about? I can understand if you're upset with—"

"Don't you get it? I was never pregnant! I haven't lost the baby. It never existed. Now fuck off. I don't want to see you again." She tried to move around me but I grabbed her upper arms.

I wanted to look her straight in the eyes but she kept turning her face left and right. Anything to avoid my stare. "Are you telling me you lied about being pregnant with my baby?"

"I exaggerated," she said.

"How can a person exaggerate being pregnant? It seems fairly binary to me."

I felt her relax against me. "I was never pregnant. I just thought that I could be quickly if I could get you back for a few weeks and—"

I let her go and shoved my hands through my hair. "Who are you?" My head was spinning. I couldn't quite believe what she was saying.

"I'm practical. We would have been good together. We make a good couple."

"You really have no idea, do you?"

She shrugged.

“And you don’t even have the good grace to be embarrassed about it.” I shook my head.

“Embarrassed about doing something women have done for centuries? It’s life.”

“You are poison,” I said as I turned away from her and started walking.

“Good riddance,” she shouted. “You didn’t know a good thing when you had it.”

She was wrong about that. I’d always known what I had with Haven.

Haven

It had taken longer than expected for human resources to produce the paperwork for my promotion. It had been two weeks, but Robert had handed it to me after our Monday morning meeting. Now I held the thick envelope in my hands, I was frightened to open it. This was where I had to sign up to the next phase of my career, but it felt bigger than that. It felt as if I was choosing my future. This promotion was exactly what I’d been working toward for so long, so shouldn’t it feel better? Shouldn’t I be more excited? Instead it felt like a move backward.

I took the envelope and headed to the back stairs. I waited for the door to shut behind me then sat on a step, opened the sticky seal and pulled out its contents.

I carefully read the letter addressed to me. This was it. My start date was at the beginning of next month. It showed my salary increase and my bonus and new title: Deputy Editor. All I had to do was to sign the letter and send it back to human resources. Easy, right?

My bun was loosening and I swept my fingers across my head, trying to push everything back where it should be. It made it worse. I put the papers on the step next to me and reached behind me, pulling out the pins so I could start the bun again.

I took a deep breath. Maybe I wouldn't put them back. Maybe I was sick of wearing my hair like this. It just didn't feel like me anymore. I had managed to be myself with Jake, and he'd liked me, wanted to be with me, respected me. He'd seen the person I wanted to be, the person he believed I was in my heart. I so desperately wanted to be her all the time and not the uptight imposter who worked at *Rallegra*.

I slipped the pins into my skirt pocket and combed my fingers through my hair. I started to sift through the rest of the paperwork. There were details of bonus plans and healthcare programs. A leaflet for a gym. There was a pressure on my chest, a tightness . . . as if my body was trying to warn me. Everything felt wrong. I wanted to call Jake. I wanted him to explain what I was feeling. He would understand. He knew every inch of me. I wanted him to tell me I was going to make the right decision. It was as if I was being led toward a one-way street and if I took the first step, there would be no going back. Right now was where I got to decide the rest of my life.

But of course I couldn't call Jake. I'd given him up. My throat started to constrict, so I took a deep breath and stood up. I'd spent a lot of energy not crying over Jake. I wasn't about to waste that now. I could only change what was in my power to control.

I gathered the papers together, slid them back into the envelope and headed back inside. I needed to decide who I was going to be—*Rallegra* Haven, or the woman I knew I could be.

"Champagne, as requested," Ash said as she pulled out a bottle from her bag and set it on my kitchen counter.

"You're one in a million. There aren't many girlfriends who would turn up on short notice on a Monday night with a bottle of champagne just because they were asked."

"What can I say? I always do as I'm told. Anyway, what's going on? I take it there is a reason I'm here with posh booze and you've just not told me."

"Let's wait until Luke arrives. He shouldn't be long. Are you okay with him being here?"

She playfully pushed my shoulder. "Of course I am. You know I adore that man. I'm just trying to do stuff that doesn't always involve him. I'm creating a little space for someone else," she said resolutely.

"Talking of someone else. Have you been playing doctors and nurses with your new love interest?"

Before she could answer, we were interrupted by the sound of Luke crashing through my hallway.

"How are my two favorite girls?" he asked as he appeared in the kitchen doorway. "I brought champagne as requested."

"So what are we celebrating?" Ash asked.

"Okay, so someone get one of these bottles open," I said as I reached into the cupboard and pulled out three glasses. "Luke, I want you to keep an open mind about what I'm going to tell you."

"Oh my God, are you a lesbian?" Ash asked and immediately started laughing. Luke poked her and she squealed.

"Seriously, people," I said and they both turned their attention from each other to me. "Okay, so *Rallegra* is a good job and everything. And this promotion is a great opportunity."

Ash nodded as she poured champagne into the three glasses. "Go on," she said.

"And I don't want you to think that I'm ungrateful or anything," I said, looking at Luke. My throat tightened. I really hoped Luke wasn't angry with me.

"What do you mean 'ungrateful'?" he asked.

"You know, for everything that you've done for me. For giving up your dreams of cooking and going to law school instead. I don't want to let you down."

"Haven, what are you talking about? I wanted to be a lawyer. I wanted to be a chef too, but I had to choose. I could earn more money being a lawyer. No dreams were sacrificed."

"You didn't want to be a chef?"

"I thought about it, sure. And of course Mum and Dad dying probably meant I took the more conservative choice but, as much as I'd like to be your hero here, I didn't choose for you. I chose for me."

I had to steady myself against the counter. Was he serious? I'd carried this guilt around for a decade, pushing myself to make my brother proud, to ensure his sacrifice hadn't been for nothing.

"What's going on? You're freaking me out. What's happened?" Luke asked.

My heart sped up and my mouth dried. I wasn't sure I was going to be able to get the words out. I took a deep breath and smoothed back my hair, twisting it as if I were about to put it into a bun, then I dropped it. "I told Robert I didn't want the promotion."

"Oh my God," Ash said.

"And I resigned," I said, staring into my champagne glass, butterflies fluttering in my stomach, some of them excitement about my future and some nervousness about the reactions of those I loved.

"Oh my God," Luke and Ash chorused.

"What happened and why? And are you okay . . ." Ash sounded worried.

"I stopped loving it. I used to be proud to tell people I worked at *Rallegra*. I'm not quite sure if I'm not as proud of it anymore, or if it's just not important what people think. I just don't get the same pleasure from saying where I work. And more importantly, they're not interested in running the kinds of stories that I want to write. I'm not sure they ever were. I kidded myself into thinking I would change things as I got promoted, but that's never going to happen. If I ever got Robert's job, I'd have to turn down articles about sexism in the workplace in favor of botched plastic surgery. That's what the readers want. And I think I've decided that I'm not a *Rallegra* reader."

"I never thought you were," Luke said.

"Are you mad?" I asked.

"Why would you think I'd be mad?"

"Well, you had a successful sister up until about two hours ago. And I could never have done it if it hadn't been for you."

"I couldn't be more proud of you, Haven," Luke said. "You are kind and thoughtful and loyal. I don't give a shit what you do for a living. I want you to be happy. I didn't make any grand sacrifice when I chose law over cooking. I don't know how you've tricked yourself into believing that. I wanted to make sure you were safe and secure but I wanted to make sure *I* was safe and secure, too. If Mum and Dad hadn't died, maybe I would have been a chef, but that's about me, not you. I'm sorry you ever felt any pressure to do anything because of choices I made."

Tears spilled out of my eyes, a mixture of relief and love. Luke pulled me into a hug.

"I had no idea this is how you felt," he said. "I just want you to be happy."

I felt lighter, as if each word he spoke lifted weight from my shoulders and spine.

"We never talk about them," I said into his sweater.

"*You* never talk about them. Sometimes Ash and I do. I like to remember them and wonder what they would think about how we turned out. I like to think we would have Sunday dinner with them like we do now."

"But Dad would cook?" I smiled.

"Dad would definitely cook," he said as he chuckled.

"Do you remember that time your mother served us raw chicken?" Ash asked.

I pulled out of the hug with Luke, but kept my arm around his waist. "How we didn't all end up in hospital after that, I have no idea," I said. "Urgh and that weird thing she did with the egg and the fish?"

"She was a terrible cook," Luke said as he squeezed me.

Ash slid off the counter and raised her glass. "Can I propose a toast? To Mr. and Mrs. Daniels and their two amazing children, who I love more than chocolate. They would be so proud of both of you."

Luke put his free arm around her and pulled her into him as I stood silently pulling memories into my conscious thoughts.

Luke broke the silence first. "As an older brother, I'm delighted you have decided to make a change in your life, but I do have to ask—do you have a plan?"

I started to laugh. "Not really. I thought I would research some of these Internet news websites."

"Do you need money?" he asked.

"Thanks, Dad, but I'm okay for now. I have some savings and I've got to work a month's notice. I'm going to see where the wind blows me."

Ash reached over and placed her hand against my forehead. "Have you got a fever? You always have a plan."

I shrugged. "I'm trying something new, breaking my rules. This way, I get to decide the future I want, the person I want to be and the person I deserve to be with."

chapter FORTY-TWO

Jake

"Feeling better?" Beth shouted from the living room as I slipped off my trainers in the hallway. I'd been out for less than an hour and my whole life had changed. My ears rang and I pushed my palms against them trying to get rid of it.

"I'm going to take a shower," I shouted back and headed to my bedroom.

I turned the water up as hot as it would go. I wanted no trace of Millie in my life. I wanted to burn her from my skin.

As I'd walked home, I'd called Millie's sister, Lauren. Part of me wondered whether Millie was still pregnant, but telling me she wasn't because she wanted me out of her life. But Lauren had confirmed that Millie had never been pregnant and it had simply been an attempt to get us back together.

I opened my eyes under the water, wanting every part of me to be renewed and refreshed. It stung and the sensation brought a hint of relief. Eventually, the water ran cold and I climbed out, pulled on some clothes and went to find Beth.

She muted the television and looked up at me expectantly.

"Millie's not pregnant. Never was. It was all an act to get me to marry her or something."

Beth turned toward me. "What?"

"I saw her outside a restaurant drinking and smoking, and as you can imagine, I wasn't very happy about it."

"Jesus, I knew that girl was up to something, but I just thought she'd got knocked up by a plumber and was trying to make you take responsibility for it."

"Yeah, well, you told me so." I hadn't wanted Millie to be the monster that Beth had seen all along. I didn't want to have dated someone like that.

"God, I'm sorry, Jake. Are you disappointed?"

I collapsed on the sofa and she sat beside me.

"Maybe a little," I said. "Not that I would relish having Millie around for the rest of my life but . . ."

"You thought you were going to be a dad."

My chest tightened.

"I'm not sure I'd completely let myself believe that the child was mine, but yeah, I thought I was going to have a . . ." I'd pictured my future as a father, in a new apartment with Haven. Now what was I left with?

Beth shuffled closer and put her arm around me. I concentrated on my breathing.

"I'm sorry, is this painful for you, talking about this?" I asked. Beth's lost baby had been real. Mine just felt that way.

Beth shook her head. "Not at all. The stuff with Louis happened a long time ago and you can't compare them. Maybe it's a terrible thing to say, but that loss provided me with a different future—one I'm starting to enjoy. Maybe you'll feel the same when you've had time to digest things. Millie really isn't the woman you should have as the mother of your children."

I nodded. That was for sure.

"You think I'd have done okay as a dad?" I asked.

"I think you'll be a wonderful father. Maybe it's time to ask yourself who you *want* to be the mother of your children. You need someone who will be just as good a mother as you will be a father."

I closed my eyes. All I could see was Haven.

"Fucking A," I shouted as the results started to trickle in. Eric had been building and testing the simulation model for weeks now, and although initial testing had been positive and in line with the initial model, this was judgment day. We had been able to plug in much more data now, so it was really going to show us whether we were on the right track. Everything about Elemental Energy was going great.

"It's looking good," Eric said. He never got excited about anything.

"Good? It's fucking fantastic."

Eric grinned and nodded. "We need to start on the sensitivity analysis if this works."

"I know, but fuck. Awesome." I banged my fist on the table. Things were going exactly to plan.

My phone vibrated against my leg. I pulled it from my pocket. It was Beth.

"Hey, we just ran the first full simulation with the new data and it's amazing," I said, excited.

"All I hear when you talk about work is 'blah blah blah science.' Don't waste your breath on me."

I chuckled. "Okay. So tell me why you're bothering me at work?"

"The boxes have arrived and I need to know if you want me to pack anything in the kitchen."

"I thought the movers were packing? I hope they are because I'm not staying up all night to—"

"Keep your panties on. I'm packing some personal stuff myself but the movers will do it all if you want them to."

"Yeah, that's fine. The less I have to do, the better."

"Everything in my room will go into my apartment, so I'm going to start moving some stuff from the living room and kitchen into my room tonight so it doesn't get mixed up when they arrive tomorrow."

"It's going to be so strange not having to put up with your mess anymore."

"As if. I'm not messy. You're the one with the aversion to cleaning."

"Whatever, I want to get back to celebrating our major breakthrough, so I'm hanging up."

"Oh yes, and Gay Dave called. He wants to talk to you about your Paris pictures or something."

Tomorrow I'd move out of the apartment I'd lived in for the last decade. I would miss living with Beth but she would only be downstairs. This was good for her. Part of the reason for the move had been the baby but even now, without that motive, I was looking forward to a future that I'd been resisting for too long. With Elemental Energy gaining momentum every day, the next step was the move. Then I'd be ready for the final piece of the puzzle. I couldn't see myself in the new apartment without Haven, and it was partly why I'd bought it. I knew it wouldn't work without her. I just had to figure out how to convince her of that.

"Pizza," I snapped.

"Chinese," Beth countered.

"It's like tradition that you have pizza after you've moved house. And we can't order Chinese in the afternoon. It's wrong."

"Says who?"

"Says me."

"Okay, as long as I can have garlic bread and ice cream." She sighed as if she'd just given up her right to free speech.

I ordered the pizza and joined Beth on the sofa.

"This place is beautiful. It looks like somewhere a multi-millionaire would live."

"It feels like a place I'll grow into." I felt more at home here than I'd expected to. Perhaps because Beth was with me. Perhaps because I was excited about what the new apartment meant.

"The only thing it's missing is a woman's touch—"

"Don't get any ideas. I'm keeping the pool table."

"I wasn't talking about me, dumbass. I mean you. It's been over two months since you split with Haven."

"Yeah, I get it. You're not subtle."

"I think you should call her."

"I got it covered. Leave it with me. I'm not letting her go."

I hadn't called her and I hadn't decided on what I was going to say to her when I did. All I knew was that now I was here, sitting in the apartment she helped me choose, she had to be with me to share it. This was our future, and I wasn't about to start it without her. My thoughts of her hadn't lessened. Instead, I found myself imagining our future together, thinking about her hair, the way she looked right before she came. The images got clearer; they'd never dulled.

"You were right," I said. "I should have fought harder for her. I knew she would try to push me away and when she did, I was so weakened by wanting what was best for her, so confused about everything going on in my own life, I gave in and let her walk away. I should have fought."

"It's not too late."

"It will never be too late." I smiled. It might be the fight of my life. She could be with someone else, but I didn't care. I wouldn't stop until she was here with me. I knew how she felt about me. She might not have said the words, but she loved me and that was worth a fight. And now was as good a time to start as any.

"Where are you going?" Beth asked as I leapt to my feet and grabbed my keys and my phone.

"Dave wants to see me at the gallery, and I have a stop to make first."

"A stop? What about the pizza?"

"Pizza can wait. Like you said, this place needs a woman's touch."

chapter FORTY-THREE

Haven

Getting lost in London was quickly becoming one of my favorite things to do. It was the beginning of my second week working as a freelance writer. I'd contacted various Internet news outlets and one of them had said they would look at an article about sexism in the workplace. I'd barely slept for the last few days as I dug up as much background as I could on the subject. I was more excited about writing than I had been in years.

To get myself out of my flat, a few times a week I had taken the first bus that came along, and got off at a random stop and found myself a café to work in. I enjoyed the freedom of it. Today I'd ended up in Chelsea.

I found myself a seat outside an uber-cool coffee house, ordered a drink and opened my laptop. I sat back as my computer booted up and I watched the world go by. It was a busy street, and I took in the shoppers paused at windows and delivery drivers unloading their packages. Everyone had a role to play. To the left of me, there was someone busying away on their phones, and to the right a group of three women having a catch up over coffee. I smiled. It felt good that this was my place of work.

Jake was never far from my mind, but I pushed him back into my memories whenever he escaped. It was too painful to think about him for long and I was sure the pain would consume me, pull me under like a riptide. I had to hold that in—I wasn't ready to deal with that yet. I wasn't sure if I ever would be. I hoped he was happy. If I could have done things over, I would have fought harder for him. Millie might be having his baby, but I knew I could make him happy. He loved me, and I should have trusted that.

I pulled my attention back to my laptop and began to type.

Two drained coffee cups and a half-eaten sandwich later, it started to rain lightly. The hours had slipped by. I gathered up my things, left money for my coffee and headed back to the bus stop. As I was about halfway down the street, my phone began to buzz in my bag. I stopped and dug it out.

It was Ash.

"Hey." As I answered, I lifted my head and found myself staring into a familiar art gallery window. It looked like the place Jake'd had his exhibition.

"Hi, what are you doing? Do you want to grab dinner tonight?" Ash asked.

I stood back slightly to see the name of the gallery painted above the awning. I was sure it was the one. I squinted through the glass, past the painting hanging in the window to see if I could spot anything familiar.

"Haven?" Ash said.

"Ash, I'm going to have to call you back." Without waiting for a response, I hung up. Was that Jake's picture of the bridge?

It felt like the riptide was calling to me. I couldn't not go inside. The urge to be near a piece of Jake overwhelmed my need to prevent myself from breaking down.

I pushed the door open. A small bell rang and I stepped through the entrance, going immediately to the picture of the bridge. It was just as beautiful as I'd remembered it. I stood staring at it for long minutes before my attention was drawn to the picture next to it. I hadn't seen it before but the scene seemed familiar. It was of a cobbled street, full of people, cafes and street musicians. You could hear the noises from it, feel the atmosphere. I leaned closer to read the description printed on the information card, next to the photograph. It read "Jake Harrison, Falling in Love in *Ile de la Cité*". The words struck me like a thunderbolt and my legs weakened.

"I could get you a discount if you're interested. I know the photographer," a voice said from behind me. My breath caught as my legs started to collapse from under me.

"Hey."

I felt Jake's hands on me, steadying me.

"Are you okay? Come sit."

I couldn't look up. I couldn't see it was him, confirm what I knew was happening. If I did, I would be sure to crumble into pieces.

"Sorry," I mumbled as I sat down. "Too much coffee." I slid my hands over my face to delay the inevitable sight of him.

He knelt in front of me and wrapped his hands around my wrists, gently uncovering my face. I didn't have the strength to fight him. I dropped my hands, and we locked eyes and my heart actually stopped.

"Are you okay?" he asked again.

I shook my head. I wasn't okay. Seeing him was the worst thing that could have happened. The walls I'd built around my thoughts came crashing down and I allowed myself to properly experience the grief of losing him.

He stood abruptly. He was angry at me, and I couldn't blame him.

"Dave, I'm going. I'll speak to you later." I heard a voice respond and then Jake was back, his hands on my back. "Come on. I'll take you home."

I stood as Jake guided me out of the gallery. His car was just outside and he helped me in and fastened my seatbelt for me. I was helpless, unable to do the most basic things.

As we drove, I was aware of Jake alternating his gaze between me and the road.

"Should I call Ash?" he asked. "Or Luke?"

I shook my head. "I'm so sorry." My throat was tight. Being so close to him made my loss all the more acute. I'd missed his smell, his hands, the way he took care of me.

"Don't be sorry. Tell me what's wrong."

I dropped my head into my hands and I tried to concentrate on not crying. We spent the rest of the journey in silence.

"I thought we were going back home? To my place?" I asked as he parked on an unfamiliar street.

"Yeah," he said. "We are."

I didn't get a chance to ask him why we were making a pit stop as he swiftly exited the car, rounded the hood and opened the passenger door.

"Come on," he said and he held out his hand to help me out of the car.

Where were we? Maybe it did look familiar, but I didn't know why. He led me though large double doors into a lobby with a black slate floor and a security guard behind a shiny chrome desk. I'd been here before.

"I want to show you something," he said as he led me into the elevator. I stared at my toes, trying to keep everything inside and contained. Trying to keep myself from crumbling into small pieces. I didn't have spare energy to ask him where he was taking me.

I followed him out of the elevator. We were in an apartment block. He fiddled with some keys and opened a large door, holding it open wide and ushering me inside a darkened hallway. The walls were dark grey panels of silk surrounded by an edge of light. Where were we?

At the end of the hallway, I saw the view and realized where we were. We'd been to this place before, he and I.

"Sit down and let me get you some water," he said as I stumbled between boxes toward the sofa and the huge window.

I felt so ridiculous; he was trying to make me feel better when he was the cause of my pain.

He handed me a glass of water and came to sit next to me on one of the large gray sofas that faced the view. I sipped at the water and set it on the coffee table in front of me.

Despite the irony of the situation, I was so pleased to see him. I was relieved at how familiar he was still.

"You bought it," I said, looking around. It felt like Jake more now than when we had seen it before. It was still an impressive space, with high ceilings and the windows making it seem huge, but it also felt like home. The warmth of the walnut floors and the comforting fabrics were very welcoming.

He nodded. "Are you better? You have a bit more color. What happened back there?"

I smiled. He had no idea that it was him that had me in a state of near collapse.

"I'm sorry. I'm sure I'll be better soon. I *hope* I'm better soon."

He reached out and clasped the base of my neck, his thumb and forefinger rubbing against my skin. "Talk to me, Haven. We had a deal. You tell me the truth, the whole truth and nothing but the truth. Remember?"

I smiled again, a sad smile this time. That deal felt as if it had been made a lifetime ago.

"I just want to stop having to make such an effort to be okay all the time. I just want to be okay," I finally said.

"Are you sick?" he asked, his voice faltering as he moved closer to me.

I shook my head and felt the words begin to tumble out. "It was the picture and you. I just miss you and I keep telling myself that walking away was the right thing to do, but it still feels so wrong. I just want you and I hate that Millie has you, and I just ruined everything—"

His arms swept round me and suddenly I was in his lap, my head on his chest.

"You're missing me?" he asked.

"I feel like I'm dying from missing you," I replied, no longer able to hold it in.

“I should have fought harder,” he said. “I shouldn’t have given in so easily. It’s been killing me, being apart from you.”

“But you have Millie now,” I said, not quite processing what he had just said.

“Millie was never a part of me. You always will be.”

“But you’re together. I saw you. On a date.”

He sighed. “Beth was right all along. Millie was trying to get us back together. I should have seen it, but because I was so focused on the baby, I ignored her or excused her. I don’t know. She was never pregnant.”

My body tensed and I lifted my head off his chest to look at him. Had I heard that right? “She made the whole thing up?”

He nodded, his eyes soft and sad.

“You should have told me. Are you upset?” I asked.

“I think I was, at first.”

I slumped back against him, wanting his warmth. “Wow.”

“I’ve missed you so much. I don’t think there will ever be a time when I’m not in love with you.” His words reverberated in his chest and against my body. I felt them in every part of me.

“I love you, too,” I whispered. I’d been holding it in for so long; I felt lighter for sharing it.

My body moved with his as he inhaled. “You love me?” His voice croaked.

“I do, and I’m so sorry I gave up on us.”

“You have no apology to make. Do you think you can forgive me for letting you go?” Jake’s hands smoothed around my waist. “I want you back and I will do everything it takes.”

"I would forgive you anything, Jake, but I chose to walk away. You just gave me what I wanted. You can't take the blame for that."

Jake's hands slid up my back, and I placed a kiss on his chest.

"I called your place earlier today, before I went to the gallery. I tried to call you too, but it went straight to voicemail."

"You did?"

"I need you, Haven. Even if you're with someone else, I'll do anything to win you back. I know that we belong together."

"There will never be anyone for me except you. Nothing's changed there."

He pulled me closer to him and his heartbeat boomed against my chest. We sat like that, in each other's arms, just savoring being together, letting it seep in and build us both back up. I drew strength from him and for the first time, I realized that he might do the same from me.

"And then you were there in Chelsea, in the gallery. It was as if you were waiting for me. Were you?"

I thought about it. "I think I would always have been waiting for you," I replied.

"You're not at work. That's where I was heading after the gallery."

"I don't work at *Rallegra* anymore."

"You don't? What happened?"

"I was offered the promotion to deputy editor and I decided it wasn't what I wanted after all. I didn't fit there."

"I never thought you did," Jake said. "So, do you just hang out at art galleries now?"

I grinned at him. "I'm trying the freelance thing. I want to write about things that matter to me. I want to be the woman you see in me."

"God, I'm so proud of you," he said, grinning back at me and he pulled me toward him.

"You matter to me," I whispered.

He brushed his lips against mine. My eyes fell shut and hope exploded in my chest.

chapter FORTY-FOUR

Jake

From the moment I saw her standing in front of the picture I'd taken when we were together in Paris, I knew she'd come back to me. She was my future. She was my everything. I would never let her go again.

Now we were in the apartment I'd bought for her. For us. This was the place where I'd propose, where I'd get her pregnant. This was our future.

My forehead rested against hers and her breath against my skin, her warmth under my hands was too much. "I want you, Haven."

Her hands slipped to my shoulders. "I want you, too," she replied. Her words were like a shot of adrenaline. I stood, gathered her in my arms and headed to the bedroom.

"There's no going back now. It's you and me forever. I can't be without you again."

She looked at me and nodded. "I know."

That moment was the beginning of my future.

"Now that you're freelance, does that mean I can keep you in bed for the next week?" I asked as I set her down on the bed.

She fumbled at my shirt buttons as I stroked her hair.

I bent and kissed her neck and she sighed. I'd missed her sounds so much.

"Jake," she whispered.

I trailed my tongue up her throat and then closed my teeth around her delicate skin.

She groaned and her hand slipped to my crotch. Instinctively I pushed against her palm. I was straining against the denim already.

"You'll have to be slow, Jake. I'm not used to you." Could she have said anything to make me feel more like a man, her man? Fuck, she was perfect.

"I'll be gentle, baby, this time, but I'm going to fuck you every which way in the next twenty-four hours, and I can't pretend that they're all going to be slow."

In answer, she unbuttoned my fly and I scrambled to get my t-shirt over my head. Her hands on me felt so good. I kicked off my jeans and underwear.

"How is it you're still dressed?" I asked.

She smiled and tugged her t-shirt over her head. I undid her jeans, kneeling on the bed as I pulled them off with her underwear.

"I'd forgotten how beautiful you are," I said as my gaze wandered across her skin. "You're perfect." I grasped her thighs and slid up her skin to her stomach. I wanted to feel every inch of her, to sharpen my memory of her.

I found her bra clasp and released it, and pulled the bra from her shoulders, her breasts spilling out. I had to look away; the sight was so breathtaking.

I moved across the bed and stood up.

"Jake, come back to me," Haven said as she held her hand out.

"I'll never leave. I'm going to make you feel good," I said as I kneeled by the side of the bed.

"I know you will," she said. "But I need you inside me. I want you to be close to me." She looked at me pleadingly. As if she would have to convince me.

"Okay, baby," I said, smoothing my hands up her thighs, across her stomach and over her breasts. I pulled at her nipples and she arched against the mattress. I would never let her go again. She was mine from this moment on.

I pushed her thighs apart and trailed my fingers across her. "You're so wet, fuck."

"Please," she cried. She reached for me and I bent over her, trying to give her what she needed. She grasped my shoulders and the press of her fingers sent shockwaves through my body.

"Are you ready, baby? I'll be slow. Tell me if it's too much," I said as I reached for a condom.

She grasped my wrist and she shook her head. "No, Jake. I want to feel you."

I positioned my tip at her entrance and pushed just slightly. Haven wrapped her legs around me, urging me deeper.

"I'm trying to be careful. You're not making it easy for me," I said.

"I want you so much," she said as we locked eyes. Without looking away, I pushed into her, slowly, deep, without stopping. She was tight and hot and wet around me, owning me, claiming me.

I pushed as far as I could go. "Okay?" I asked.

"It's better than okay," she said quietly and she gripped tighter. "Don't ever leave me."

"I'm not going anywhere, ever."

I started to move, dragging myself out of her reluctantly so I could push back in, every time getting faster and deeper and tighter and better. I'd been convinced that she was gone from me and now being here, with her, her wanting me like this. My arms juddered. It was almost too perfect. I shifted so I could see her better. Her mouth was open and I bent forward and trailed my tongue along her bottom lip.

"Jake, it feels too good. I never want you to stop."

I groaned at her words, knowing I wouldn't be long. It would take the first spasm of her orgasm around my cock to tip me over the edge.

I twisted my hips and she gasped and closed her eyes. "Oh God, I'm . . ." Her body stiffened beneath me and clamped around my cock. *Fuck.* My orgasm pushed through the mental barrier that had been holding it at bay and crashed over me and I collapsed over her, sweaty, panting, only partially sated. I wanted her again before I'd come down from my first orgasm.

"I love you," she whispered into my ear as I lay spread eagle over her.

"I love you, too," I said, trying to stop myself from grinning like a five-year-old at her words. Hearing her say that was never going to get old.

I rolled over to my back, and pulled her with me so she was half lying on me.

"I missed you," she said as she rested her chin on my chest and looked up at me.

"Well, you're never going to have to miss me again," I replied.

She bent down, kissed me and rested her cheek over the same spot. I stroked that beautifully soft skin of hers.

"You didn't tie me up," she said after a few minutes.

"Are you disappointed?" I asked. I hadn't had the urge to restrain her. Maybe because I wanted her to be exactly who she was rather than submissive. Maybe because I needed her to be able to run and to choose not to.

"No, you could never disappoint me. But I like it when you do it."

"We have plenty of time." I grabbed her leg and pulled it over my body. She moved with me so she was straddling me and sitting upright. I clasped her ass in my hands and urged her forward. "Move up," I said.

"Up?" she asked.

"Hold on to the headboard. I want to taste you."

I could tell she was reticent, but she moved forward so my head was between her thighs.

Slowly, I traced my tongue along her slit. She was slick from our combined orgasms, and tasted so sweet. I went deeper among her folds and found her clit. I pressed her toward me and heard her first gasp of pleasure sweeping away any embarrassment she might have felt. I rounded her clit, one way then the other, flicking and pushing. I could tell she stayed still as long as she could, but as I started to suck, she let out a moan and her hips began to sway.

The blood rushed to my dick in response to every sense of mine being overwhelmed by this woman. I growled against her. One of her hands pushed into my hair and she started to slip lower against my mouth.

"Oh God, Jake, it feels too good."

I didn't stop to respond. My fingers slipped inside her from behind and her breathing became short and choppy. My tongue rubbed up and down her clit, and her hand tightened in my hair as she began to spasm. Her whole body shook as I continued to gently lap against her sex, pulling every last sensation from her.

I couldn't wait a second longer. I pulled her to her back and in moments, I was inside her again.

Haven

I couldn't tell if it was my mind or my body that was so completely overtaken by Jake in bed. He seemed to have a way of connecting them so what had been a physical act with previous lovers expanded to become mental and spiritual as well. He owned my body and I gave him my mind. I would do whatever he asked me.

He moved above me, the delicious drag of him moving me away from my last orgasm, closer to my next. It had been only hours since we had been reunited, but somehow I felt a connection that was deeper than before. Maybe it was simply the knowledge of what it was like without each other that pulled us so quickly, so deeply together. Maybe it was what happened when you loved someone so truly and they loved you right back.

My skin began to fizz, knocking my pleasure up to the next level.

"You feel so good, Haven, so tight."

I pushed my fingers against his beautiful, taut skin, barely able to cling on against his relentless rhythm.

Sweat coated his face in a sheen as he moved so he was on his knees and brought my legs up over his shoulders. He pushed in and he was so deep that way, it was almost too much. I gasped and he groaned in response and thrust sharply. My breasts moved in time to his rhythm and he reached out and flicked my nipple. I arched my back, the pain exploding into pleasure. Blood rushed to my sex and the beginnings of my orgasm seeped in at my edges.

His hands moved away from my breasts and down to my clit. His thumb found the bundle of nerves and I knew if I didn't stop him, I'd be lost.

"No," I said trying to pull his hand away. "No, it's too much."

"It's never too much, Haven," he replied. "It can't be too good or too much or too often." His thumb rounded my clitoris and I could hold back my orgasm no longer. Jake began to fall and I gave in to it as our orgasms erupted through us at the same time, as if we'd both been hit by a bolt of lightning, binding us together forever.

chapter FORTY-FIVE

Haven

I woke to an empty bed, but was aware of the effects of Jake all over my body. I was sore and bruised and felt perfect. I propped myself up on my elbows to see if I could hear him in the bathroom. I couldn't make out a sound. Would he have gone without waking me?

I scanned the huge bedroom and saw his t-shirt at the end of the bed. I smiled. Grabbing it, I pulled it on and climbed off the mattress.

Jake was on my laptop as I wandered into the sitting room. The morning sun lit the room as if he was on a movie set. He was perfect. "I thought you might have left," I said, pushing my hand through his hair. Looking around, my eyes were drawn to the views of London that surrounded us.

"I'm never leaving, I told you," he said as he reached out and pulled me onto his lap. "What are you doing three weeks from Friday?" he asked, staring at the laptop.

I drew my eyebrows together. "I'm not sure. What date is it?"

"It's the twenty-second."

"Nothing, I don't think. Why?"

"Then you're free to marry me?" he asked.

I rested my hands on his cheeks and moved his face so we were eye to eye. "What are you talking about?"

"Friday the twenty-second. The registry office is free. We can get married."

"In three weeks?" I asked.

He nodded.

"We can't get married in three weeks," I said. "We just got back together."

"Do you not want to marry me?"

"Of course I want to marry you! But, we have things to discuss. Logistics. People. Things to do and more things—" My mind was racing but I couldn't hide my grin.

"What do we need to discuss?" he asked.

I shrugged. "I don't know. Lots of things. I don't even know if you want children."

"I want three," he answered matter-of-factly.

"I can live with three," I said through a smile.

"What else?" he asked.

"How is your dad? I'm sorry, I didn't ask."

"He's fine, better than ever, so he says. I've been speaking to him on the phone."

I wrapped my arms around his neck. "That's great news. I'm so pleased."

"It is. It really is. So, what else?"

"Where do we live? Will Beth mind if I move in?"

"I don't care. I bought this place for you, but we can live here or not—"

"You bought this place for me?"

"Yeah, you looked so at home here and I loved that I had memories of you here. And I knew you liked it. At the back of my mind, I believed that if I bought it, you'd have to come back to me."

I smoothed my hands over his neck and I kissed his jaw. He'd always had such faith in us. Why was I questioning things, why didn't I just agree to get married? There was no reason not to.

"Last night was my first night in the place and you were here with me. So it looks like I was right. And Beth has her own apartment on the floor below. We're not roommates anymore, so she won't mind. It's entirely up to you. What else?"

"I want to live here, with you. You're right, it feels like home." I could imagine myself here. I could imagine myself anywhere Jake was.

"Later we can go to your place and get some of your stuff. I'll get the movers to get the rest later in the week."

I smiled at his eagerness. "What's the rush?"

"What's the point in delaying the inevitable? This is it for me and for you, too. I know you. I don't want to waste another moment not being with you, not being married to you." He was right. Everything he was saying was making sense.

"Three weeks?" I asked again.

"Three weeks. And if you want a big wedding reception, we can do that later," he said.

"I don't want anything big. I just want to love you for the rest of my life." I leaned forward and pushed my lips against his.

Jake squeezed my hand and I realized I'd let my concentration wander, trying to take in every detail of this moment. "Are you ready?" he whispered. Standing next to me, in the oak-paneled registry office, his hand in mine, Jake looked as handsome as I'd ever seen him. The bespoke suit he'd bought after he'd sold his first business clung to his frame in all the right ways. My dress was very plain; there was no lace or beading. It was ivory silk, off the rack and it fit perfectly, thankfully, because we had no time for alterations. I wore my hair down because Jake wouldn't have had it any other way, and I had on dangerously high, strappy bright pink shoes. They were the type of shoes that I knew got Jake's attention.

I glanced around the room. Everyone I loved in the world watched as Jake and I were about to be pronounced husband and wife. And even though a few were missing, I felt them with us. My bouquet was lily of the valley—my mother's favorite flower—and Luke's blue glassy eyes as he placed my hand in Jake's echoed my father's. Unable to travel, Jake's father had wished us well and we had promised to visit him soon.

As if marrying the love of my life wasn't perfect enough, I got to share it with these wonderful people—Luke, Ash and Beth. My people. I nodded. Yes, I was ready.

I took a deep breath, recalling the words the registrar had just recited. "I call upon these persons here present to witness that I, Haven Daniels, do take thee, Jake Harrison, to be my lawful wedded husband." I slipped Jake's ring onto his finger and interlinked our hands, not wanting to lose the feel of his skin against mine. I'd never smiled so widely or seen Jake look so happy.

"You may kiss the bride," the registrar said.

Jake slid one hand around my waist and cupped my jaw with the other. He waited a beat, scanning my face and then pulled us together, crashing his lips to mine. I melted against him as his tongue pressed against mine, exploring as if it were our first kiss. I hoped it would always be like that between us. Sniggering from our family filtered through the moment and Jake's kiss turned into a smile as he loosened his grip. Reluctantly, I pulled my lips from his and grinned up at him.

"So, now that we're married, what happens next?" I whispered.

He leaned into my neck, his nose rubbing against my cheek. "Now we live happily ever after."

For Ash and Luke's story, read Promised Nights.

For Beth's story, read Indigo Nights.

playlist

U and ur Hand
P!nk

Through the Barricades
Spandau Ballet

Anticipation
Carly Simon

Magic
Coldplay

Beauty Has Her Way
Mummy Calls

You'll think of me
Keith Urban

Into the Woods
Taylor Swift

Here comes the Rain Again
Eurythmics

I Miss You So
Diana Krall

I Won't Give Up
Jason Mraz

There You'll Be
Faith Hill

Turn my World Around

Gloriana

acknowledgments

My thank you list is as long as this book itself. The more I'm in this world of writers, readers and bloggers, the more generosity and kindness I see. To each one of you who have helped me in my journey, thank you, thank you, thank you.

other books by

LOUISE BAY

THE NIGHTS SERIES

(each book is stand alone, focusing on a different couple)

Parisian Nights

Promised Nights

Indigo Nights

OTHER BOOKS

The Empire State Series

Hopeful

Faithful

the nights SERIES

promised NIGHTS

I've been in love with Luke Daniels since, well, forever. As his sister's best friend, I've spent over a decade living in the friend zone, watching from the sidelines hoping he would notice me, pick me, love me.

I want the fairy tale and Luke is my Prince Charming. He's tall, with shoulders so broad he blocks out the sun. He's kind with a smile so dazzling he makes me forget everything that's wrong in the world. And he's only man that can make me laugh until my cheeks hurt and my stomach cramps.

But he'll never be mine.

So I've decided to get on with my life and find the next best thing.

Until a Wonder Woman costume, a bottle of tequila and a game of truth or dare happened.

Then Luke's licking salt from my wrist and telling me I'm beautiful.

Then he's peeling off my clothes and pressing his lips against mine.

Then what? Is this the start of my happily ever after or the beginning of a tragedy?

indigo NIGHTS

The only thing better than cake is cake with a side of orgasms.

Dylan James has no expectations when it comes to relationships. He uses women for sex and they use him for his money and power. It's quid pro quo and he's good with that. It works.

Beth Harrison has been burned. She's tired of the lies and the game playing that men bring and has buried herself in her passion—baking which keeps her out of the reach of heartbreak. As she begins her career as a TV baker, a new world opens up to her.

Dylan and Beth both know that casual sex is all about giving what you need to get what you want.

Except that sometimes you give more than you need to and get everything you ever wanted.

The Empire State Series

A series of three novellas
Part One: *A Week in New York*
Part Two: *Autumn in London*
Part Three: *New Year in Manhattan*

Anna Kirby is sick of dating. She's tired of heartbreak. Despite being smart, sexy, and funny, she's a magnet for men who don't deserve her.

A week's vacation in New York is the ultimate distraction from her most recent break-up, as well as a great place to meet a stranger and have some summer fun. But to protect her still-bruised heart, fun comes with rules. There will be no sharing stories, no swapping numbers, and no real names. Just one night of uncomplicated fun.

Super-successful serial seducer Ethan Scott has some rules of his own. He doesn't date, he doesn't stay the night, and he doesn't make any promises.

It should be a match made in heaven. But rules are made to be broken.

HOPEFUL

Guys like Joel Wentworth weren›t supposed to fall in love with girls like me. He could have had his pick of the girls on campus, but somehow the laws of nature were defied and we fell crazy in love.

After graduation, Joel left for New York. And, despite him wanting me to go with him, I'd refused, unwilling to disappoint my parents and risk the judgment of my friends. I hadn't seen him again. Never even spoke to him.

I've spent the last eight years working hard to put my career front and center in my life, dodging any personal complications. I have a strict no-dating policy. I've managed to piece together a reality that works for me.

Until now.

Now, Joel's coming back to London.

And I need to get over him before he gets over here.

Hopeful is a stand-alone novel.

*F*AITHFUL

Leah Thompson's life in London is everything she›s supposed to want: a successful career, the best girlfriends a bottle of sauvignon blanc can buy, and a wealthy boyfriend who has just proposed. But something doesn›t feel right. Is it simply a case of 'be careful what you wish for'?

Uncertain about her future, Leah looks to her past, where she finds her high school crush, Daniel Armitage, online. Daniel is one of London's most eligible bachelors. He knows what and who he wants, and he wants Leah. Leah resists Daniel's advances as she concentrates on being the perfect fiancé.

She soon finds that she should have trusted her instincts when she realises she's been betrayed by the men and women in her life.

Leah's heart has been crushed. Will ever be able to trust again? And will Daniel be there when she is?

Faithful is a stand-alone novel.

let's CONNECT

If you enjoyed Parisian Nights, please leave a review. Good reviews really help indie authors!

I love hearing from readers – get in touch!

Instagram me

@louiseSbay

Tweet me

twitter.com/louisesbay (@louisesbay)

Friend me

www.facebook.com/louisesbay

Like me

www.facebook.com/authorlouisebay

Pin me

www.pinterest.com/LouiseBay

Friend me

www.goodreads.com/author/show/8056592.Louise_Bay

Circle me

https://plus.google.com/u/0/+LouiseBayauthor

Find me at home

www.louisebay.com

16985130R00277

Printed in Poland
by Amazon Fulfillment
Poland Sp. z o.o., Wrocław